'FOR MEANING'

BY
JASON A. HUBAL

Jones Harvest
PUBLISHING

ISBN: 978-1-60388-070-1
1-60388-070-4

ACKNOWLEDGEMENTS

I would first like to thank God for giving me the talent and for providing the helpers necessary to make this project happen. Next, I would like to thank mom and dad for their support. I thank Arlene for gathering information on my church's history plus Dema, Diana, Mildred, Marge, Joyce, Pastor Charles, Pastor Danny, Pastor David, and for everyone's prayers. The following people I also thank and you know what you did: Kathy K., Kathryn G., Ken F., Kim Mc., Cheryl P. and her journalism class, Sarah S., and Sheri W. I also thank Jerry and Nina for inviting me inside their yellow house.

In Memory of…
My late dad Anthony (Tony) Hubal
1952 - 2006

Dedicated to…
Our Lord and First Baptist Church of Deer Park, Washington
My brothers and sisters everywhere

Encouraging Christian teens in their daily walk with Jesus.

Chapter One

"Then spake Jesus again unto them, saying, I am the light of the world: he that followeth me shall not walk in darkness, but shall have the light of life." ~John 8:12

WHAT A great feeling it was walking in Jesus' light and knowing He's there for me. His light was brighter than our sun, brighter than all the stars in the Milky Way Galaxy, and brighter than all the galaxies combined in the universe. It was infinite infinite.

I knew the Lord had been in my life since before I was born. "*There's a reason for everything*," became my motto throughout my life. I believed nothing happened by chance. There's always a particular or multiple reasons why we meet people; each one helps us learn on this journey of life. God provided each meeting with a specific need for our spiritual growth. Whatever it was, whether a problem faced, or a challenge to strengthen our faith, He will place the right person in your path, the outcome He leaves up to us.

The other day I came across some old things of mine. I found all my old daily journals that I wrote from the age of ten. Upon opening one of the journals, I found myself reliving my youth. Some of those times I had forgotten, but others were etched in my heart's memory. After reminiscing for some time, the will of God suddenly inspired my desire to write this book. You see, my life was in those journals. My struggles, achievements, sorrows, and spiritual maturity were included in those pages. I felt my experiences would inspire and help others who face similar situations to overcome their obstacles. I also wanted to share how God touched my life and all those around me.

My name was Jay Asher and here was my story.

Both sides of my family, for the past five generations, lived in the central and eastern part of the state of Washington. My dad's side, the Ashers, stayed mainly in the eastern part known as the Inland Northwest, which covers Eastern Washington, Northern Idaho and Western Montana. My mom's side, the Turners, kept to the central part of the state. The families were likely to be in the railroad, farming, or logging businesses several decades ago. Every now and then one of my relatives would step into a family practice from yesteryear.

In the 1960's, my grandpa, Gus Asher, an auto mechanic, married Naomi who worked at a bank. They lived in northern Spokane in 1975 with their eleven-year-old son, Leonard. Meanwhile Ken and Laura Turner moved in next door with their daughter Rachel, who was the same age as Leonard. They were from Leavenworth, Washington.

The Ashers and Turners became good friends and neighbors. Both couples were born-again Christians, dedicated their lives to Jesus, and were very active in the church. They even attended the same Baptist church in Spokane.

As you can figure Leonard, who liked to be called Leo and Rachel became good friends too. They went to the same schools, hung with a mellow crowd of kids from their church, and were involved in similar activities. It wasn't until they hit their teens when they started dating. They became high school sweethearts and knew they would get married upon graduation. Leo courted Rachel with old fashion morals and values.

Rachel accepted Jesus Christ as her Lord and Savior at the age of sixteen and was baptized. Leo, on the other hand, was not yet ready to give his love to the Lord completely. He faithfully attended every Sunday church service, Sunday school class, and other church events, but as the age of sixteen approached his priorities shifted. He was caught in the whole high school scene, as you can imagine with a girlfriend, homework, and sports. He was the star high school running back and captain of his track team. Rachel prayed he would change once school ended. She loved him so much and never gave up knowing one day he would follow the Light.

When Leo was in the middle of his senior year of high school, Gus and Naomi, along with some members from their church heard about a new church being built in Deer Park. It was 1981. With much prayer, they offered their help to mission planters and soon joined volunteers already on site.

As my grandparents helped with the mission, they became attached to Deer Park and soon moved there a couple of years later. Another opportunity came about during this time. You see, Gus and his dear friend Rich Holland, also an auto mechanic, for years played with the idea of opening their own shop. They waited until Leo was out of the house before going full-speed ahead. It just so happened, two shops were for sale in Deer Park. Both were reasonably priced and would work for them, but Gus and Rich didn't buy right away. They sought God's guidance first. For some time they prayed and a decision was made when one of the shops burned down. Then in 1984, Gus and Rich moved into the other location.

Leonard Asher and Rachel Turner were married the spring following their senior year. This young couple had dreams of where they wanted their life to go. Since Leo was good with his hands and mechanical-minded like his dad, he could work on cars or build a house. He could not see himself under a hood for hours on end so he chose construction building as a more desirable trade. Rachel always dreamed of becoming a pediatric nurse from the time she was a little girl playing doctor and nurse.

The newlyweds lived in an apartment for more than two years, saving money and establishing good credit until they were able to buy their first house in a neighborhood close to both their parents. Rachel continued praying for her husband and occasionally talked him into attending a morning service.

1990 started out, after the usual mild winter, with rainbows and sunshine. My parents lived in their new home for about two years when they began making plans for a family.

First they desired for some more space and a yard. They fell in love with the Victorian two-story house before even opening the door. It was lavender and pink with white trim. Leo, already a fine carpenter, enjoyed fixing it up and was Rachel's ever-present handyman. Rachel kept busy making it a home. She liked painting the house and working in the garden. Leo and Rachel felt blessed when I arrived in this world the middle of June, life was good.

A dark cloud appeared on both the Ashers' and Turners' threshold. First Mom's parents moved back home to Leavenworth, due to their aunts' and uncles' illnesses. Then, sometime after my birth, Mom's health began faltering, feeling numbness in her limbs along with other symptoms. She went to see a family doctor who was uncertain of what was happening, so she was referred to a specialist. After a few weeks and many tests, the doctors finally diagnosed Mom with multiple sclerosis, or MS. She was twenty-six years young.

Multiple sclerosis was an autoimmune disease, affecting nerve fibers throughout the body. In a healthy body, nerve fibers were protected by myelin, a fatty tissue. So, with MS, myelin was missing in multiple areas and over time damages the nerves in those areas. MS affects people differently and the severities of their symptoms vary.

On top of all this, my grandpa Gus Asher, while driving alone down the highway one bright morning, another motorist coming in the opposite direction, lost control, crossed the center divide, and hit Gus head-on, killing him instantly. According to the final police report it was an accident. The other motorist, who survived the crash, had a diabetic seizure and passed out at the wheel. This was later determined to be the cause of the accident.

Dad stayed by Mom's side during her MS as best he could. At times Mom's legs were paralyzed and Dad had to help her around the house. Then suddenly, something happened to Dad and he was not in our life. I remembered asking about him when I was six or seven years young. Mom told me not to worry about where Dad was, he'd be home soon, and he loved us. It came to a point that every time I brought dad up she became very sad. Sometimes, I would hear her crying in her bedroom, so I dropped it all together. The way everyone acted about Dad not being there sure seemed like it was a big secret or something. When I was younger, I imagined him being a spy on a secret mission in a foreign country. He was absent in my life that was all I knew.

With Dad gone, Mom found her life suddenly in a violent hurricane, the calm eye out of her grasp. How was she going to live with MS with a child? Who was going to take care of her and me? Could she take care of me when her MS got worse? Mom knew her family would support her, but she had a lot to figure out. God was the only one she really knew could get her through this, leaning on Him, and placing our future in His hands. Going through these hard times of being diagnosed with MS and dad not there, she never once lost her faith in God. She may not have understood, but she knew God was with her and her family. There was a reason for everything and she trusted God. Mom's prayers were answered as the Holy Spirit led her back to Leavenworth where she could relax and be cared for by her parents.

It was arranged for me to live with my grandma, Naomi Asher who in her mid-forties took me into her home in Deer Park the winter of 1990. This was sometime after Grandpa Gus' death. Gramma found herself now taking care of me and the house, as well as helping out at church. Rarely did she complain.

Gramma, as you know had banking experience and used to help grandpa and Rich with the financial aspect of their business. Grandpa was glad because it freed up more time to do what he loved—work on engines.

Up to this point, Gus and Rich's mechanic shop had flourished into a nice successful and respectable business around town, never cheated a soul. Everyone liked to have his or her cars fixed at "G & R's Friendly Auto Fix It Shop"—where you thought your car was fixed in Heaven. As you can figure the shop was closed on Sundays; my grandparents honored the Sabbath, God's day of rest.

Rich stepped in as much as he could to help my grandmother. That was the way he was; Rich would always go the extra mile to help people out. He was also a Christian and never married. Joan, Rich's sister, visited him and offered her time at no expense to be G & R's bookkeeper. This helped Gramma out. Joan was excellent, very sharp with numbers, and a great addition to the business; Naomi and Rich eventually talked her into accepting a wage.

After a while, Rich felt like family and became the dad I never had. We spent a lot of time together going fishing, camping, and other outdoor activities. He was cool and we became good buddies. He taught me a lot as I watched him work on cars.

Chapter Two

June 2000

THIS WAS the year I began to write in my journal and where I will begin my story. I had just turned ten. It became one of my most memorable summers. Six months before Mom moved in with Gramma and me. It was most wonderful to have her with us in our own home all together.

Mom's multiple sclerosis was in remission, meaning her symptoms temporarily disappeared (other times the symptoms' severity lessened). Her MS had been in remission for six months upon arriving here. This was the third time she experienced it. We prayed that her remission would last for quite a while. The previous two times only lasted about a month then she relapsed. When her MS flared-up, she experienced paralysis and/or numbness in her legs and arms. There was also burning pain and her motor controls become shaky.

Mom had the least severe form of MS, called relapsing/remitting, and was healthy right now, thank the Lord. She did physical therapy three times every week, having to relearn her motor skills that we all took for granted. Mom used a manual wheelchair and electric scooter when she had a hard time getting around. She had a minivan with special accommodations for her wheelchair or scooter.

When Mom finally joined us, I felt our family starting to feel more normal as normal as it could be without Dad. Their wedding picture adorned the hall wall next to the den. My dad was a handsome guy, or still was, I can only imagine. He had dark hair, a square jaw, and broad shoulders. I'm told I look more like my grandfather Gus in the face. The men on the Asher's side all had baby blue eyes.

Gramma, Mom, and I lived on the street corner of Eighth and Vernon in the small city of Deer Park, off Interstate 395. Our yellow house was one of Deer Park's original lumber mill houses, at that time close to over eighty years old. At the turn of the twentieth century, the house was a four-hundred-square-foot dwelling. Many building additions and renovations occurred during its history.

My home was full of love for God and His true Word. For the first part of my life God blessed me with my grandma, who was a most wonderful cook, I may add. Now with Mom living with us there was even more love.

Mom was truly grateful, but at times I could tell she was frustrated because she wanted to take care of me. She wanted so bad to be the mom she was meant to be. I think that was why she kept up with her therapy. She was in therapy relearning how to walk and take care of herself all over again. The two most gracious and bravest people I've ever known were Mom and Gramma.

Every night before bedtime, Gramma read me Proverbs and Psalms from the King James Version of the Bible. Those were the first two books of the Bible I was introduced to as a child. If I had a problem those books would show me the answer.

If it were the first of the month she read the first chapter of Proverbs; there were just enough chapters for every day of the month. Psalms was a different story with 150 chapters. It took about three months to read them all.

David, "The apple of God's eye," authored many Psalms of praise and prayer, give or take seventy-three. I admired David's prayers to God; he always knew his Lord was there for him. I learned from David's mistakes knowing there was a God who loves us for who we were and forgives us.

I memorized and tried to live by many of Solomon's and other writers' wise proverbs. They were good because they reminded me especially of how a young man should live his faith and follow righteousness.

Anyway, I awoke around seven o'clock on a shiny June morning. No matter what time I went to bed, I always woke up at seven o'clock. I'm a creature of habit, getting into a set routine during the homeschool year, which Gramma set up to follow the public schools in town.

Usually on Saturday and a couple other days during the week, I attended karate school. Four to six times a week I trained practicing my karate in the backyard. First I dressed in a loose-fitting sweat suit and a belt. A karate student never wore their colored belt where anybody could see them, only in class.

Depending on if it was a nice day, I would do my training in the backyard. During the winter, I cleared some space in my playroom and laid out a mat. Today the weatherman said it would be the same as it was yesterday—blue skies, in the eighties so I headed downstairs on my way to the backyard. I tiptoed passed Mom's bedroom because she typically slept until around eight o'clock on a good day. If she wasn't rested enough, we might not see her smiling face for a couple more hours.

In the dining room Gramma sat reading the newspaper and drinking coffee. She was about fifty-three, small in stature, well groomed with wavy silver hair, and a cheery face that went along with her faithful attitude. Conservative slacks/blouses and occasional dresses graced her presence. Her only desire was to help make someone else happy.

I gave her a hug and said good morning while sitting beside her.

"Morning Sweetie," she answered back, setting the paper down. "Did you sleep well?"

"Sure," I said.

"Remember to pray to the Lord before you do your exercises," she suggested. "Ask for his guidance and you know."

"Yes, ma'am," I said.

"Before you take off," she began, "I made out your chore list this morning and—."

"Be careful with your roses, I know Gramma," I cut her off, knowing the drill.

I walked onto the covered back deck from the French doors, across the back lawn, passed a huge black maple tree, and entered an arched gate. Beyond this was a separate fenced-in-garden. The main feature was an octagonal gazebo with gingerbread lattice. I sat down on a bench beneath an arbor with a climbing bright pink rose vine creeping throughout. This was where I bowed my head, closed my eyes, and prayed.

Dear Heavenly Father, thank You for today. Give me a clear mind and Your strength and guidance when I do my karate training. In Jesus' name. Amen.

After my prayers, the second thing I did was warm-up before working on my karate training. I jogged around the yard and then found a dry place in the grass to stretch. I did twenty full push-ups, which now I had been doing for about a year and my goal was to be able to do quite a few more. Following sit-ups and some other exercises, I opened an orange skinny spiral notebook. It explained the meaning of karate at that level and also showed techniques and forms for the student to master.

Forty-five minutes later, I finished my workout and went back inside for some breakfast. Gramma made me oatmeal with raisins and cinnamon.

"Good morning my little Jaybird," Mom greeted, as I sat to eat at the kitchen table.

She always greeted everybody with a smile, and if you were feeling down, her presence eased your mind. Slowly, but surely, she walked into the kitchen using her cane.

"Morning Mom, how did you sleep?" I asked, with a huge grin.

"Oh the Lord blessed me with a good night's sleep," she replied happily.

Her face would brighten up when she talked about our Lord, Jesus Christ. She had her King James Version of the Bible near her at all times. Her Bible was at least seventy-years old and belonged to her great-grandmother. It was black leather bound; the gold page ends were faded. Gramma Naomi made Mom a few vests, which fashioned large pockets where she could conveniently carry around her Bible.

She wore slacks and medium to long sleeved shirts most of the time, even during the summer. Our house was air conditioned and felt pretty cool. Mom told me people with MS were sensitive to heat. Her golden hair, always in a ponytail, fell to her shoulders. She rarely wore makeup and the only jewelry she wore was her wedding ring and an angel necklace.

Following breakfast, I went out the kitchen door to do my outside chores. I stepped one step down to a covered porch, turned right a few feet along the sidewalk, and entered the unattached garage. Once inside, I grabbed the gardening sheers and a bucket and headed to the roses.

I made my way back down the sidewalk and through the yard in front of the kitchen. This was the west side, facing Vernon Street. Around the corner was another sidewalk lined with rose bushes, which led to the front door. This was the south side of the house on Eighth Street.

Our house was located on a corner lot and there was not a true backyard or front yard, but one joined yard. The front yard, closest to the street, was bordered with a white wavy picket fence and a variety of summer flowers. Two arched gates, which looked like giant birdhouses, greeted you on Vernon Street. From the arches were narrow granite walkways. One gate led to the front porch on the south side of Eighth Street and the other led up to the kitchen door on the west side. The kitchen-covered porch stretched a few feet to the unattached garage. We rarely used the south entrance, as the kitchen entrance was more convenient due to it being closest to the driveway.

There was one neighbor next to the garage and a couple more on Eighth Street.

So as Gramma's favorite yellow roses happily warmed themselves on that bright sunny morning in June, I went to get the garden hose. Gramma was persnickety, as I came to know her, with her precious yellow roses. She babied them like they were fine China. Just recently she put me in charge of taking care of the roses, so as I placed the hose under the bushes I was extra careful not to damage them.

There I was in the front yard, being bored out of my mind, when I heard a full-sized pickup truck pulling a trailer thundering around the corner. I thought it was just going to drive on by, but it surprised me by parking across the street. A big man in his mid-thirties stepped out and stretched. A boy about my age jumped out of the truck and ran to the front door.

"Dad, we're home!" the boy hollered. "There's no place like home!" He gestured for his dad. "Hurry up, Dad. I can't wait to see my room."

"Oh, give your old man a minute. We just got here," I heard the man utter with a groan.

A dog barked from within the truck. The dad yelled, "Will you get ol' Waldo out, give him some water?" The kid reluctantly complied while starting down the sidewalk and disappeared.

About this time a smaller pickup came behind the larger truck. A man and a woman climbed out. There were boxes stacked in the back of the pickup. The two men talked in the shade. One said to the other, "It sure is hot, wished we got an earlier start. What do you want to do first?"

"Let's unload the trailer, then you can help me with the heavy stuff," the dad answered.

I turned my attention back to the kid who called the dog. The woman opened the tailgate and stretched her back.

"Come here, boy," the boy said. "Come here, Waldo. That's a good boy."

A huge golden retriever raced across the yard waving his flag of a tail. The dog went to a bush and lifted his leg. I had to laugh at the fiasco. Suddenly, I realized my chores were not being done. Deciding against it, I quickly turned off the water and started to wind up the hose. It was taking too long, so I threw the hose down and hurried toward my house.

Excitedly, I ran around to the kitchen door where a dwarf red maple greeted me. A brick façade surrounded the kitchen door and window.

Inside the door there was a foyer where coats hung. This led to a fair sized kitchen. Off the kitchen were the dining room and a hallway, which led to a den, Gramma's room and the master bedroom, being Mom's. On the left side of the hallway was a narrow flight of stairs up to my bedroom. Next to the dining room was a large living room where you would find the front door.

"Mommy, Gramma!" I hollered, as I ran.

"Slow down, child," Gramma said. "What is it, Jaybird?"

I stumbled over my words, gasping for air.

"Jay, catch your breath and tell your Gramma what you're trying to say."

"Remember that house for rent across the street?" I said, pointing through the walls where it would be. "Well, someone's moving in..."

"Is everything alright in here?" Mom asked, entering the kitchen.

"Mom, I think we have new neighbors," I said, turning to her. "I saw a big truck parked in front and there's a kid and a dog—and there was another pickup."

"Maybe there will be some kids your age to play with," Mom suggested, walking with her cane into the kitchen.

"May I please go over to the new neighbors?" I asked, rushing to the window in the living room.

"Not right now Jay, they look busy, wait until later," Mom said, hobbling behind.

Anxiously, I waited to meet the new neighbors. Mom said we all would be going soon to meet them. All I could think about was playing with the new boy and his dog. I never had a dog or cat, just a gold fish and birds.

Gramma was busy at the counter just minutes before taking out the last batch of chocolate chip cookies from the oven. She transferred cookies that had been cooling on the rack to a plate. She placed plastic wrap over them and stepped over to us.

"Oh what a coincidence," Gramma said, "I wondered who I was baking these for."

I followed her smelling the aroma of freshly baked cookies. "Gramma, may I have some please?" I exclaimed.

"After you take these cookies over to the new neighbors then you can have one," Gramma said handing me the warm plate.

"But Gramma," I started to protest when she gave me the look. "Yes, ma'am—let's go, let's go."

"Patience Jay," Mom said. "Wait for Gramma and me."

"I'll go out in the front yard to watch them," I said, walking out of the kitchen.

I sat in the grass watching the two guys take out a bulky mattress from the trailer. The woman and the kid were unloading small boxes from the pickup. The dog was nowhere in sight, barking occasionally. After the trailer was emptied and half of the large truck, the people must have taken a break because I didn't see them after they went into the house. I felt bored and took out the western novel I was reading.

Soon the adults returned and sat down in the shade with drinks. I sprang up when I heard our screen door open and close. Mom came first carefully and I ran up to her ready to assist if needed. She made it onto the sidewalk with ease. Gramma came moments later, handing me the plate of cookies. We then all started across the street.

"Rachel, are you sure you don't need the wheelchair?" Gramma asked, holding a pitcher of lemonade.

"I can manage, thanks," Mom replied, concentrating while approaching the birdhouse gate, which I opened with a sidekick of my foot. It was a juggling act with the plate of cookies.

She was a little awkward with her cane as she stepped onto the street. I was at her side in case she lost her balance, but she managed quite well now on the flat surface. We rounded the corner just enjoying the short walk.

I stared down at the plate of cookies in my hands, a sweet aroma made my senses go wild. My mouth drooled and I licked my lips dreaming of sticking my teeth into them.

The big man saw us approach. "Mornin' folks, nice day, huh?"

I didn't see the kid; the man and the woman sat on the front steps drinking water.

When we came upon the kid's dad, I noticed his huge, bulging biceps the size of my head. He could have been a body builder or biker! I pictured him on a chopper bike moving down the highway looking for adventure as the song says. He even had a goatee and shaved head.

"Couldn't be nicer," Gramma began, pointing to our house. "We're your neighbors across the street. I'm Naomi Asher. This is my grandson, Jay and his mom, Rachel."

The muscle man said, "Nice to meet you. I'm Manny, Manny Sanchez."

He shook Gramma's and Mom's hands. When he shook mine I felt power in his grip; his hand felt rough and callused. I don't know why, but the man's tall frame and broad shoulders mesmerized me. I studied the large veins running like a highway twisting through his muscular arms of hills. He wore a tank top and faded jeans.

The boy came around the trailer. "Dad! I'm having trouble setting up my video game?" he said. He wore a Seattle baseball cap.

"Hold on a minute, I want you to meet our neighbors," Manny said.

I noticed right away there was something wrong with this picture as the boy stood next to his father. It was because he wasn't even a boy, but a girl—yikes! A black ponytail stuck out of her cap. Yikes! I felt embarrassed thinking she was a boy. As she stood by her dad, I was feeling foolish. Anybody could have made the mistake.

"This is my daughter Rosa," Manny said.

Both father and daughter had dark features but Manny was a bit darker. They had a slight Mexican-American accent.

Gramma urged me over to them. I became suddenly shy. Gramma whispered, "Go ahead, Jay." I handed the cookies to Manny.

"Thank you," Manny said.

Mom nudged me. "You're welcome," I said, slowly coming out of my bashfulness.

"Hey Jay, what's up?" Rosa greeted.

Oh no, I have to talk to her! "Nothing much," I replied.

Suddenly, from the corner of the truck a dog came running. The golden retriever I saw earlier knocked me down, vigorously licking my face. Manny began laughing.

"Oh, we can't forget Waldo," Manny said between chuckles. He offered me a hand. "Sorry about that, Jay. Are you alright?"

"Think so," I said, brushing off my pants.

"Let's get out of the street and I'll introduce my sister and her husband," Manny suggested.

We followed him up the lawn.

"This is my sister Juanita and my brother-in-law Peter Dillon," Manny said as they stood. "Here is Naomi, Rachel, and her son Jay."

"Good to meet you," they both said shaking our hands.

"Don't want to keep you, enjoy the cookies," Gramma said.

"I'm sure we will, thank you again Naomi," Manny said.

I sighed as we turned back home, but Gramma's words stopped us. *Here it comes,* I thought holding my breath. "What are you all doing for dinner?"

"I don't know, order a pizza," Manny said.

"Why don't you all come on over and I'll serve you some of my famous pot roast," Gramma offered.

"That sounds good," Manny said. "When do you expect us?"

"Sixish, alright?" Gramma asked.

"Dad!" Rosa said, under her breath. "I thought we were going over to Aunt Juanita's?"

"Shush," Manny said to Rosa, then to us, "we will be there."

"We'll be expecting you," Gramma said. As we started back she commented, "They seem like nice folks."

"What did you think about Rosa, Jay?" Mom asked. "She seemed awfully cute."

And I thought she was a boy, I thought to myself again. "Oh Mom!" I pulled away slightly annoyed. "I don't even like girls."

"Sorry, Jay, I didn't mean to embarrass you," she said, holding my shoulders.

"I'm not embarrassed," I said, running the rest of the way, inside our house and up to my room.

I found my novel, hoping to lose myself on the wagon train that was at the moment crossing a river.

My room was decent size with a single bed, tall dresser, desk, and a shelf unit, which were the main pieces of furniture. Across the hall was my playroom.

"Jay, straighten up your room before company comes," Gramma hollered up the stairs. I heard the clanging of dishes as I ran upstairs.

I tried to read for a while, but couldn't concentrate as the new neighbors were distracting my thoughts for some reason. From my bedroom window, sitting at my desk, I had a good view of their house. I watched Manny talk with Peter and Juanita; Rosa was throwing a baseball in the air. *I guess she's okay for a girl, more like a tomboy though*, I thought.

Soon Peter and Juanita followed Manny's truck. I heard they were making one last run. Rosa and her dad had a disagreement, so he had her stay home. She stormed in her house. That was when I saw my friend Billie and his kid sister, Kaylee, riding up on their bikes. I heard the front door open and my Gramma talking.

"He's in his room, Billie. You kids may visit for a little bit."

"Hey Jay," Billie said in my doorway. He had short, sandy-blond hair and was taller than me. "Whatcha doing?"

"Oh, nothing," I said, "supposed to be cleaning my room."

"Kaylee begged me to take her bike riding, so we're stuck with her," Billie explained. "Do you want to come along?"

"Wish I could Billie," I said. "Gramma invited our new neighbors for dinner."

"Do they have kids our age?" Kaylee asked, her ears perking up.

I shrugged. "I guess. There's a girl named Rosa."

"Maybe she'll go riding with us," Kaylee said.

Kaylee was a petite nine-year old girl who seemed to me to be six or seven. She had curly blonde hair, and a huge crush on me, giving me the creeps!

While Billie and I stood in front of the window looking across the street, Kaylee swiped my favorite piece of quartz from the corner of my eye.

"Hey, gimme that," I said, trying to wrestle it out of her hands.

She had a death grip on it and wouldn't let it go. She turned away from me and examined the purple veins in the rock.

"Wow, pretty," Kaylee said. "May I borrow it? I promise to bring it back."

"No, my mother gave it to me," I said. I grabbed at her and she giggled. Billie was laughing and not helping.

"You really want it back?" Kaylee teased. "Then come and get it."

I chased her around the room, Billie joined in. She tired easily, sitting at the foot of my bed so we quickly pinned her down. Kaylee wouldn't let go.

"May I please have it?" I asked.

"I know how to get it," Billie said mischievously.

He began to tickle her and I joined in on the fun. I finally got it back and then we had a pillow fight. About that time, Gramma came in and ended it all.

"What's all the ruckus?" Gramma asked.

"Oh, nothing!" we all said.

Billie and Kaylee stayed for a couple hours. We played card games—Go Fish, War, Crazy Eights. Kaylee bugged us while we played army men. All the while I heard mom's voice echoing, *Share your things, Jay.* I gave Kaylee the quartz to keep her busy as we won World War II.

Kaylee was busy playing with my stuffed animals. She was playing house I guess, wrapping my bear up in a hankie like it was a diaper. I was having so much fun that I forgot about the new neighbors.

"Time to get going kids," Gramma announced, sticking her head inside. "We're having company."

"Do we have to?" Kaylee whined.

"You can come back again some other time," Gramma said.

"You guys helped make this mess, so help," I said.

"Here's your rock Jay. Thanks for letting me look at it," Kaylee said, handing it to me.

"You may have it," I said. "The only rock I need is Jesus."

Chapter Three

A HALF an hour before dinner, I strolled into the kitchen with the clothes I usually wore to church. Gramma busily worked on dinner; it smelled most excellent as always. There was the banging of pans and the opening and closing of cabinets. Gramma was listening to the Deer Park station, which played songs and standards from the 1940's up to the 1960's. Nat King Cole sang an old ballad while Gramma hummed to him. I heard the disc jockey announce after a song ended, "This is the music of your life…"

Bringing my comic book to the kitchen table, I tried to read it, but Gramma insisted I help Mom set the table. I walked to the dining room while reading.

The wall to the right of the dining room table had a rustic dark panel finish like something out of a mountain cabin décor. In the center was a painting of ducks flying over the marshland; a hunter and a retriever huddled in the cattails. A shotgun, antique duck decoys, and fishing nostalgia completed the picture. My favorite thing was a picture of Grampa Gus and Dad fishing in a stream.

On the opposite side were the French doors leading to the backyard. In one of the corners was Gramma's sewing room.

Mom was busy in the dining room setting down placemats and matching cloth napkins. I stood next to her for a moment, watching her.

"There you are my Jaybird," Mom said. "Could you pass out the plates? I will check on Gramma."

"Sure," I said.

I did so and Mom came back. "Looks good, I think we are almost ready. Did you wash up Jay?"

"Yes ma'am."

"Good. Now please go and wait in the living room and let our guests in."

I dreaded opening the door for the new neighbors. It wasn't that I disliked company, I sometimes felt uncomfortable. Well, it was because of the girl, Rosa. I could hear Gramma and Mom embarrassing me.

Trying not to think about it, I opened my comic book and sat on our green and white plaid couch. A few throw pillows were placed neatly in the corners on the couch, a quilt draped behind me, both made by Gramma. The pillows were cross-stitched with a Christian theme. One had sheep with a shepherd watching over the flock and part of *Psalm 23*: "The Lord is my shepherd..." Another had a fortress and a shield with a rugged cross, being from *Psalm 91*. The main furniture included a recliner, an end table with a lamp, and a small entertainment center (the only TV in the house; some of my friends had multiple TV's). Slightly beyond was an empty space then shelves with trophies, family photos, and books.

On the walls in the living room and in a couple other rooms, Gramma had these similar pastel paintings. The one above the couch had two small kids chasing a butterfly with a net while running through a field of daisies. I also had one in my room with a barefooted boy in coveralls, fishing on a bank.

I suddenly sat up when someone pounded on the screen door. I heard it again and saw a shadow. I tried to call Gramma, but all I heard was the radio. "Anybody home?" came a man's voice. He knocked again. I guess nobody heard it and I hesitated to answer. I finally gave in and put down the comic book on the coffee table.

"Coming!" I hollered so Gramma would hear.

Gramma was always cheery and hospitable around new people. I was always quiet at first, mainly listening to the conversation. As I approached the front door, she came shuffling out of the kitchen and stopped in the entryway.

"Come on in!" she said, with a smile in her voice.

Noisily, Manny came in with Rosa in tow. "Hola neighbors," he greeted in Spanish. "Buenas Noches." He saw my questioning look. "Hola, is Spanish for 'hi'. Buenas Noches means good-night or good-evening."

"Glad you came over Mr. Sanchez," Gramma said, then turned to the girl. "Hi Rosa."

"Hi," Rosa replied and her dad nudged her. "Thanks for inviting us Mrs. Asher."

"You're certainly welcome Rosa," Gramma said, gesturing toward the front room. "Please have a seat. Would you like anything to drink?"

Rosa was off to Manny's side wiggling in her shoes. She tugged on her sleeve looking uncomfortable. I didn't want to make eye contact so I wandered toward my comic book.

"Water would be fine, thanks," Manny replied. Manny wore black jeans and cowboy boots.

"I forgot to mention," Gramma said. "I hope you don't mind, but our friends Rich Holland and his sister, Joan will be joining us for dinner."

"That would be fine," Manny started, with bulging eyes. "Did you say Rich Holland? The one who works at that auto shop? G and R--"

"He's the one," Gramma said. "Do you know him?"

"Sure I do, he's my boss—just hired me on as a mechanic," Manny said. "That's why I moved here."

"And to think we are connected as neighbors," Gramma said laughing. "God sure knows how to bring people together."

"That He does," Manny said continuing. "So, we lived about a year on the north side of Spokane and then I was laid off. My sister Juanita and her husband Peter lived a few blocks from us. They have two daughters, Dora who is about Rosa's age and Miranda a little bit older. Anyway, I saw an ad in the classifieds about an opening for a mechanic in Deer Park. It was just what I wanted, small town living, a job I really wanted and we'd be closer to the great outdoors, how perfect."

After a while of listening to the adults' converse, I prayed the night would end quickly. The girl standing next to me made me feel weird. The conversation sounded garbled in my mind. I wanted to escape to my room and have nothing to do with Rosa.

"Rosa has comics," Manny said. I realized I had the comic in my hands. Rosa stepped up to me and read the other side.

"Aqua Man," Rosa said. "I have some of those." I finally raised my chin to look at her, still feeling weird.

"You can look at it," I offered, not really meaning it. Then I felt Gramma's eyes penetrating me.

She met my eyes, now giving me the to-be-nice-look. I was startled when Gramma said to me, "Jay, why don't you show Rosa your pet bird?"

I stared at the carpet dragging my feet and headed to my room. "Okay." I said, turning and talking to Rosa's feet. "Want to see my budgie?" I made eye contact with Gramma's stare and knew she wanted me to be polite.

"Sure," Rosa said, flipping through Aqua Man as she followed me. "What's a budgie?"

Soon we entered my room where I led her to the hanging birdcage. Her face brightened up when I lifted the cover off the cage revealing the bird happily chirping away and fluttering inside. She watched the bird and laughed.

"Looks like a parakeet to me!" she exclaimed. "How cool, never have seen a white one. What's its name?"

I reached inside and brought the bird out and cupped him in my hand. I petted his little white head and answered, "His name is Albie."

"I used to have a parakeet," Rosa said. "But we had to give him away before we moved."

"Well, we call them parakeets. In Australia, the Aborigines call them budgerigar, which means "good bird" I think," I said. "Budgie just sounds cooler to me."

"Cool, can I hold him?"

"Here," I said, handing him to Rosa. The transfer spooked Albie and he squirted to the floor. "He can't fly; his flight feathers were cut."

Rosa kneeled to pet him. "Doesn't that hurt him?"

"No, because we're not cutting any blood vessels below that," I explained. I saw her tug at her blouse.

"My dad made me wear this," Rosa said. "I don't like these kinds of clothes...your Gramma's nice."

"Yep, that's my Gramma," I said. "I see you like the Seattle baseball team. Who is your favorite player?"

"Booner...he's bad," she replied.

I suddenly felt miles away from the others and itched to get out. "It must be dinner time," I said quickly scooping up Albie and putting him in the cage. We headed into the living room. Manny was talking to Gramma.

"...We came from Yakima, wanting a new start," Manny began but abruptly changed the subject as Rosa looked uneasy. "How long have you guys been here?"

"I've been in this house for a dozen years or so," Gramma said. "Rachel moved in here a few months ago..."

"I have MS," Mom added. Manny raised his eyebrows. "My multiple sclerosis is in remission."

"Oh," Manny said. "I'm not too familiar with that. So you were sick—Was it okay to ask?"

"It's okay, I don't mind sharing," Mom said. "MS is a neurological disease—that affects my nerves along my spine. If you want to know more we can talk later."

"I'll take dinner out of the oven," Gramma said, getting up. The phone rang when she entered the kitchen.

"I wouldn't want to impose," Manny said to Mom.

"I don't mind," Mom said. "Not too many people know that much about MS and I think it's good therapy to talk about it."

When I saw Mom and Manny talking, I suddenly thought about my dad. I wondered what Mom and Dad would talk about—how they would converse.

"You sure have a positive attitude," Manny said.

"It beats the alternative," Mom said, trying to get up from the couch.

Feeling weird with the whole conversation, I stepped over to lend my hand to Mom. I pulled her up and she rested comfortably on her cane. "Thanks, Jay—he always wants to help out his mom."

As we stepped into the dining room, Gramma placed a big plate of hot roast beef on the dinner table. I pulled out a chair for mom and she eased into it.

"I got a phone call from Rich," Gramma said, "Joan has a stomach ache so they won't be coming to dinner."

"That's not good," Mom stated concernedly. "I pray she feels better."

"Do you need any help Mrs. Asher?" Manny offered.

"Yes, help yourselves to something to drink," Gramma replied.

With the mashed potatoes, green salad, and French bread on the table, we settled down to a wonderful dinner. Mom and I sat across from the new neighbors while Gramma fixed herself at the head of the table.

"Shall we say grace?" Gramma said.

"That would be fine," Manny answered, as Gramma bowed her head and reached over holding Mom's hand.

With a little hesitation from Rosa and a nudge from her dad to be polite, Rosa took Gramma's hand. I lowered my head, closed my eyes, and found Mom's hand. When she began, I peeked over at Rosa. She had her eyes open and quickly closed them.

"Dear Heavenly Father," Gramma said, "thank You for the food that You have provided for us. Thanks for Manny and Rosa coming over and sharing this meal. Bless our health and strengthen our spirits. Lord, we are blessed to live in a free country and to be able to worship You freely, in Jesus' name we pray. Amen."

During dinner Gramma and Manny did most of the talking. Rosa and I were making faces at each other. Mom saw us and placed her hand on my arm to put a stop to my shenanigans. Rosa's dad told her to sit up straight.

I finished my dinner and felt bored listening to the adults talk. I noticed Rosa was feeling the same way.

"May I be excused?" I asked.

"You may," Gramma replied.

"May I be excused too?" Rosa asked.

"Yes, since you cleared your plate, you may run along with Jay," Manny said. "Not for too long, we'll be going soon."

Rosa paused at the photos hanging in the hall. "That's your mom and is that your dad?"

"Yep."

"Are they divorced?"

"No," I said.

"Where is he? Is he…" Rosa began.

"No, he's away," was all I said.

As we climbed up to my room she said, "My parents are split up and it sucks. I hope they don't get divorced."

I went over to my desk and pushed a toy car across it.

"Hey, do you like to play ball?" Rosa asked.

"Sometimes Billie and I do—he's my best friend," I said, distracted with the car.

"My cousin Dora is my best friend—I hated to move—hey this is cool," she said, suddenly distracted with my uniform. "Do you take karate? My cousin had a white robe like this."

"Yep, Billie and I do," I answered.

"How far up is orange belt?"

"It's three levels. It goes white, yellow, orange, purple, blue, green, brown, black, first degree black."

She examined my belt. "Why is there a purple stripe?" she asked.

"It means I'm working toward my purple belt."

Billie and Kaylee go to our church on and off. A couple years ago Gramma gave me permission to watch movies at Billie's house. We were inspired by those kid karate movies. Since then, Billie's dad drove us to karate lessons. Gramma thought it was a good idea since karate would teach me discipline and respect.

Rosa stood next to me by my desk. "Cool," she said. "I bet you could kick people's butts." She made karate moves in the air.

"It's only for defense, not offense," I said.

"Hey, I wonder if my dad would let me take lessons. That would be so cool," she said.

"You can come with Billie and me," I said.

"This is neat," Rosa said, picking up my camera from the desk.

"Hey watch it," I said, taking it from her gently. I examined it and looked through the viewfinder. "This belonged to my grandpa. He liked to take pictures—his hobby."

"When did your dad leave?"

"When I was a baby…" I began, not wanting to talk about it. "May I take your picture?"

"I don't know, sure," Rosa said. After a few snaps Rosa's dad called up the stairs.

"Time to go Rosa," Manny said.

"Coming Dad!" she hollered, then said to me, "See ya 'round Jay."

I followed her downstairs to the living room where everyone said good-bye.

A while later we were ready for bed. Lately, I would put on my pajamas, go downstairs to the master bedroom, and lay next to Mom while she read to me.

"Oh, Jay, it's so nice to be here," Mom said. "Manny and Rosa seem nice. What do you think of her?"

"She's okay," I said yawning. "I wish Dad were here with us."

"So do…So do I," she said, stroking my head.

It was the first time, in a long time, that we talked about Dad. I didn't feel weird and Mom didn't get upset.

One of the earliest memories of her was when Gramma and I went on a trip to visit Mom in Leavenworth. We went almost every summer when her condition was better. Gramma told me I talked and asked many questions all the way there, barely stopping to catch my breath.

Arriving, I found Mom in an easy chair with her arms stretched out reaching for me. I was so excited to see her that I just couldn't sit still. When I approached Mom it didn't seem like there was anything wrong. I was somewhat timid and unsure as I stepped closer. Gramma encouraged me from behind to go to her. She was so beautiful; her hair glowed like the sun shining from heaven. I thought she was one of the angels they talked about in the Bible. Mom looked like my dream come true, and I wanted to touch her to see if she was real. Her voice comforted me and she made a space next to her for me to sit. I sat and she hugged me so tight. She pulled me closer, then I rested my head on her chest, and I could hear her heartbeat. I wanted to stay there forever, feeling so safe in her embrace. I was startled seeing her hand shake. I knew something was wrong, but I didn't care, because I was with her. She saw my concern and told me everything would be alright. That afternoon we spent a lot of time together. Mom joyously read from her Bible; I could tell she loved Jesus. We spent the night and visited for a few hours the next day. I didn't want to leave. I couldn't understand why we had to go. Although, I could tell when we left she was in a lot of pain.

Chapter Four

THE NEXT morning, following my karate workout, I went to have breakfast. I found Mom at the kitchen table, with toast in hand, but she didn't see me at first because she was totally engrossed in a Christian magazine spread-wide open.

I hugged her from the side. "Good morning, Mom," I greeted.

"Mornin' my little Jaybird," she returned, kissing my forehead.

I poured myself some fruit rings, grabbed an orange then visited with Mom for a while.

Gramma suddenly flew into the kitchen with her purse hanging over her shoulder like she was in a hurry for an important meeting.

"I'm going to the grocery store," Gramma asked. "Rach, do we need to add anything to the list?"

"Lemon yogurt is the only thing I can think of, Naomi," Mom replied.

"Ice cream!" I exclaimed.

"I don't know, you will have to ask your mom," Gramma said.

"Please Mom?" I pleaded.

"I think it could be arranged since you have been doing a good job with your chores," Mom said.

"How about I make you some homemade ice cream when I get back?" Gramma asked and I nodded.

When I finished my cereal, Mom asked curiously, "What are you going to do today?"

"I don't know," I replied, shaking my shoulders. "Billie is visiting his grandpa, so I guess I will read or something."

"How about your new friend Rosa, don't you have anything in common with her?" Mom asked.

"I don't play with girls!" I busted out, squirming in my pants.

"But you play with Kaylee."

"That's different," I said. "Billie gets stuck with her."

"What's wrong about playing with girls?" Mom asked.

"They play with dolls—it's just weird."

"Rosa is more like a tomboy. She likes to play ball."

Mom had a point, but I said, "It's still weird though."

"Will you do your Mom a favor?" she asked. "Would you ask Manny if you could show Rosa around town; she's new here and does not have any friends. What do you say?"

"I don't know," I said, not crazy about the idea. Mom and Gramma always had a way of convincing me to do things like this. I gave in. "I'll try, but I won't like it."

I studied the Bible with Mom. She then surprised me with a pop quiz on some math exercises that I did once a week during the summer, being it was my weakest subject. Following some chores, I did as Mom suggested and planned to ask Manny if I could show Rosa around. I still felt weird even going over there to ask.

After a little encouragement from Mom and Gramma, I reluctantly started out the door. Gramma prepared Rosa and me a lunch. I skipped to the garage and dragged my bike out. I hopped on it and slowly began to pedal down the driveway on my way to the Sanchez's house around the block. Every second was torture as their house came into view. A few more pushes on the pedals and I would be there. As I turned to go onto their lawn, I started to have my doubts—*what am I doing?* Without another thought, I changed direction, passed their house, and rounded the corner. Guess you could say I was like a "Doubting Thomas" who doubted Jesus had been resurrected.

With their house far behind me, I was suddenly reminded about having faith in God, and even Mom. I hated to admit it, but she's right most of the time. I also remembered this was one of the many chances to witness to someone, so I felt more enthusiastic now circling back toward the Sanchez's house, but suddenly braked to a stop picturing Billie belly laughing and rolling on the ground. What would Billie think of me playing with a girl? I grunted looking over at the Sanchez's house and wondered why I had to do this. I rode around the block thinking about this and decided since Billie wasn't here today it would be alright to show Rosa around. A relieved smile came over my face as I decided I was in-the-safe.

I quickly began to pedal with more confidence and before I knew it I was on the Sanchez's front lawn. I set the kickstand, looking around and then sighed. Climbing the stairs, I approached the front door feeling weird again. Raising my hand to knock, I jerked it back, hearing voices echo inside. I turned around and wanted to get out of there fast, but I was too late. Halfway down, I froze knowing escape was not possible, hearing the door open and my name called. I climbed back up the stairs like I just got there.

"Oh, hi, Jay," Manny said. "We were about to go to the grocery store. Did you come here to play with Rosa?"

"Aah, yes sir, maybe another time," I said.

"No, it's a good time," Manny said. This wasn't what I wanted to hear. "I can go by myself. I see you brought your bike. Deer Park seems like a safe town to ride your bike. Rosa may ride with you."

"It is sir," was all I figured to say.

As Manny went to get Rosa, I looked around hoping nobody I knew saw me. No time to think as Manny instantly came out, followed by Rosa, and her dog.

"You two have a good time. Remember use your hand signals and watch for traffic," he said to both of us then turned to Rosa seriously with, "Pórtate bien chiquito."

"Si, Pappa," Rosa said.

Manny locked the front door deadbolt and then the dog followed him into the truck. The engine started and he waved before leaving. I watched the truck back out of the driveway, turn and drive off. There was total silence; I fidgeted in my pockets rattling my change.

"What did your dad say?"

"Behave short stuff."

"Oh."

"Hey, Jay," she said, when I turned to face her. "What do you want to do?"

"So, where is your bike?" I asked, staring into the grass.

"In the backyard—here catch," Rosa said, throwing a ball.

I didn't expect it. Suddenly, the ball headed toward my face, and like a punch coming at me in karate class, I quickly blocked the ball.

Rosa laughed. "You're supposed to catch it silly."

Oh no, I looked at her. She wore her baseball cap and fashioned a mitt. I still felt weird and didn't think I would have fun. Perhaps playing a little catch and riding down the street wouldn't hurt me one bit.

I picked up the ball and threw it at her. She caught it and we exchanged turns. I had to admit she throws a lot better than some of my friends.

As we played catch, she asked, "Did you see that catch Booner made? He's awesome."

"No, we don't get many games," I said. "Gramma doesn't get cable."

"That would suck!" she said. "I wouldn't want to live without it. Don't you get bored?"

"No, I enjoy reading," I said.

"Let's do something else," she said. "I'll get my bike."

We went down Seventh Street and came to Arnim, which parallels with Vernon and Margaret. Rosa pulled off to the side and looked across a schoolyard. "Hey is this your school?"

"No, Mom and Gramma homeschool me," I said. "This is Deer Park Elementary, but you won't go here. It only goes to the second grade."

"Where is my school?" she asked. "I don't care much for school —I do okay—mainly I like recess."

"You'll be going to Arcadia. Come, I'll show you."

She followed me all the way down Arnim, passing First Street. We saw a car coming and rode through some gravel next to a grassy field.

"This is Perrin's Field. They play soccer here," I explained.

"Oh cool! I see a baseball diamond," Rosa said excitedly, pointing further down the field. "What's that white building down there?"

"Civic Center," I replied. "They have functions and stuff."

We crossed the street and stopped our bikes at the corner of a gas station. People were busy pumping gas and running into the convenience store. Traffic was busy on Crawford Street—Deer Park's main drag that intersects with Main and a couple other streets. Across from the gas station was a little strip mall. A truck stopped and we were cleared to cross the street. There were no traffic lights and Manny was right, it was safe to ride our bikes.

We rode into a small parking lot where the city eventually installed a fenced-in skating park. Beyond this was Swinyard Park, complete with a play-area, some swings, monkey bars, a slide and a sandbox.

"Oh, cool," Rosa said excitedly. "They play basketball here."

She pointed to the courts where two teenage boys were playing one-on-one. The sun was beating on our backs; I wiped the sweat away that ran into my stinging eyes. It was barely noon and already hot. A slight breeze relieved us for a moment.

"Let's find some shade," I said, starting across the lawn. A tree was nearby and a fenced-in swimming pool on this side of the park.

"It doesn't look like it's open—and it's a hot day," Rosa said. "Jay, do you swim here much?"

"Oh, occasionally with Billie and his kid sister, Kaylee," I answered.

"Where do they live?" she asked.

"They live on 'A' Street, the one we just rode passed," I replied. "But they're not home."

We left the park; rode down a few shaded streets, passed Deer Park Middle School, and after a few blocks came into the sun. We stayed in the bike lane and passed the Deer Park Hospital. A large structure came into view and we rode into the empty parking lot.

"Arcadia Elementary," Rosa said, reading the sign. "Is this where I will go to school?"

"Yup," I answered.

"Cool," she said. "*So*, do you still have to get up early?"

"Yup, it's okay though," I said. "I do my karate training in the morning."

"Way cool," she said. "I asked my dad if I can take lessons and he said he would think about it."

"Billie's dad drives us to the karate school, I'm sure he wouldn't mind if you joined us," I suggested.

We continued down the road and came to another intersection, while entering a bike lane. To the left was a road next to a field. Mountains were seen in the distance. Rosa pointed to a building that was up ahead.

"Is that another school?" she asked.

"That's Deer Park High School," I replied.

To the right, this bike lane ran alongside a track and football field. We circled into the high school parking lot and explored a little in front of the school. As we walked our bikes up to the main entrance, we looked down the dark halls inside.

"Oy," Rosa said, holding her stomach. "Maybe we should head back, I'm getting hungry."

"Oh, I almost forgot," I said, reaching for my backpack. "My Gramma made us lunch."

"Alright let's get in the shade," Rosa said. She dumped her bike at the nearest pine tree and did a few cartwheels. I rested my bike against the same tree and sat on the lawn unzipping my backpack. Rosa kneeled next to me as I handed her a bottle of water.

I pulled out two sandwiches. "Would you like a peanut butter-jelly or roast beef that was left over?" I asked.

She chose peanut butter-jelly and I then pulled out a paperback book I was reading.

"What are you reading?" Rosa asked. "Isn't that boring?"

"A Western with cowboys and Indians," I replied. "I enjoy it. A lot of action and I feel like I'm really there."

"My mom is part Indian and white," she shared.

"Where is she?"

"She went to Seattle to become a lawyer," she replied. A while later she asked, "Do you go camping and fishing?"

"Yes, I like to do both," I said. "Uncle Rich takes me every summer. He's not my real uncle, but just feels like he is—he actually was my grandpa's friend. He takes me on his boat, too. He is cool."

We left the high school on our bikes, went back to the park and hung out. We swung on the swings and played on the monkey bars. Suddenly, I realized I didn't care what Billie and my other friends thought of me playing with a girl. Rosa was cool and right then I considered her my friend. We were having so much fun joking, laughing and doing things that I had forgotten to check the time.

"Oh no, it's three-thirty!" I exclaimed. "We should go. I have karate class later. Gramma always makes an early dinner before I go to class." We hurried home.

"I had a good time. Maybe tomorrow you can come over and I will show you my baseball cards," Rosa suggested.

"That would be cool—but shoot," I said. "Uncle Rich is taking me fishing after church."

"Okay, later Jay," she said, speeding off with her black ponytail flopping in the wind.

I saw Rich's car parked the second I wheeled into the driveway. He was probably visiting Gramma while she was preparing an early dinner. I needed to eat and rest my stomach before Billie's dad picked me up for karate class. I entered the kitchen and saw Rich at the counter. He placed the last crescent roll on a baking sheet while Gramma was stirring spaghetti in a large pot.

"There's my favorite kiddo," Rich said. I gave him a hug and he playfully ruffled my hair. "Your grandma says you were out riding with Manny's kid. Did you have a good time?"

"Yes, sir," I said.

"I hear Rosa is somewhat of a tomboy," Rich said.

"Yes, sir, she likes to play baseball," I said.

"Where did you guys go?"

"To the park and up by the high school."

I was ready with my backpack containing my white martial artist's uniform, which was referred to as gi, my orange belt, and the all-important sport's cup. After the one time forgetting it, I sure was sorry.

Waiting at the kitchen table for Billie's dad to pull up in front of our house, I soon saw their van through the window, and rushed out the door. Mr. Knight waved from the driver's seat. The middle door opened and I climbed in sitting next to Billie.

"Hey," Billie greeted.

"*Hi, Jay,*" Kaylee said, from the other side.

She drove me crazy talking that way—in the annoying sense. I just ignored her as the van drove away. Our karate school was forty minutes away, south to the city of Spokane.

"Frank saw you riding your bike today," Billie said. "Was that the new neighbor girl with you?"

Oh no the word is already out, I thought. I could still picture Billie bursting out laughing at me. "That was Rosa. I was showing her around town," I said.

"I bet your Gramma or your Mom put you up to it," Billie said. "It would be like playing with my sister all day."

"They ganged up on me," I said.

"Couldn't you get away," Billie said. "Frank said you were having a good time—I can't imagine having any fun—what do you do with a girl, girly stuff?"

"No, she's not like that!" I said. "Okay, I admit, she's cool! I really don't care what you think. She's different, doesn't do girly stuff—she happens to throw a good fastball."

"So she's a tomboy and you liked hanging out with her?" Billie asked.

"I sure did," I replied.

"Well, as long as she doesn't play with dolls or anything like that, it's cool with me." Billie said in agreement.

Twenty minutes later, Mr. Knight parked the van at Lance's Karate School. We referred to our karate instructor as Sensei Lance; sensei meaning teacher in Japanese. Every karate school was different in the way the instructor set it up. Some were more traditional than others.

As Billie's dad locked the vehicle, Billie and I walked inside. We entered a corridor. To the right, it opened up into the main training room. There was a class already in session so we had to be quiet. Down and to the left we entered the men's dressing rooms. Sometime later we stepped cautiously into the training room. Mr. Knight used to sit back with Kaylee, but just recently they were absent because he takes Kaylee to her dance, piano, or flute lessons.

As usual, Billie and I stood on the perimeter of the mats with the other students in our class. When we first joined there were only eight other new students. From that group only Billie, Todd, Aaron, and I were left. We talked softly as the previous class wound down. It was out of respect not to make a bunch of noise. At this time it was a good idea to observe the class in session.

Across the room was the karate instructor's office. Next to this was another corridor leading to other training rooms, one where the black belts trained on more advanced techniques by themselves, especially when they worked on various martial arts weapons.

The first time I saw a black belt, I was awe struck as he walked out of the dressing room. There was something mysterious and grand about him. I wanted to see an aura of energy shooting from his head. I imagined he was a totally different being with powers I couldn't understand. He walked with invincible confidence. The black belt looked my way and I thought his eyes would stab me in the heart, but nothing out of the ordinary happened. He just smiled at me and introduced himself, knowing I was new. In a moment, I left my imagination, coming back down to reality. Even after my encounter with the black belt, I was still intimidated when I entered my first class.

The first thing I noticed walking into the school was the karate shout "Kiai!" as it echoed off the walls. The kiai, (pronounced key-eye) shout helped us focus our energy on one point for more effective results. The next thing I noticed right away was the smell of sweat hitting my nostrils. It was like crossing the border to another country.

The previous class ended in meditation. As soon as they were through, our karate instructor, Sensei Lance, without warning caught our attention.

"Line up," he said.

Sensei Lance was a senior instructor with a third degree black belt. He stood five feet seven inches and was a skinny fellow. You couldn't imagine him inflicting much damage from a distance, but he was a solid individual. His speech was clear and precise. Sometimes he would raise his voice when a student did not focus in class.

Without hesitation we stepped onto the mat and lined up in our ranks. In the front row were always the black belts going right-to-left; from the right were the highest degree black belt ranks. This concept filtered down to all color belt ranks. Depending on who was in attendance, the lines differed with the color ranking belts.

In the second row there was just one brown belt, two greens, and a blue. There was usually a purple belt, but she wasn't there. This made me the next highest rank; an orange belt with one purple stripe. Billie, Todd, and Aaron stood next to me with just orange belts. Behind us were the beginners, five guys and two girls.

Following warm-ups and exercises, Sensei Lance would break us up into groups. Usually brown or black belts led the groups, but not all the time, depending on who was present.

Sometimes Sensei Lance threw us a surprise test or just selected one of his students. Like he would say, "Jay, I would like you to go through such-and-such routine" or "Jay, I would like you to test for your next belt." This occurred anytime during class.

Just wanted to give you an idea of what goes on in karate class for a student. It's not all fun and games as one would think with martial arts, but a lot of sweat, hard work, and dedication.

Chapter Five

SUNDAY MORNING was God's most wonderful day of worship where we were in communion with Him and His Son, Jesus. It was a day to acknowledge that He was our one and only Lord, to set aside a day of rest, to rejoice in His glorious name, and go to Him with our troubles. We sang praises to Him with all our hearts, minds, and souls.

What a wonderful place church was when you step over the threshold. To be in fellowship with other Christians like me worshipping God and His begotten Son, Jesus. I am filled with so much love, joy, and warmth. The ushers greeted you at the door to the Worship Center always making one feel welcome. They handed you the church menu with humble hands and warm smiles. I called the church bulletin the church menu because we're all hungry for God's Word, His guidance, unconditional love, and His Grace. That's how I felt every time I stepped into the First Baptist Church of Deer Park.

Gramma drove Mom and me onto a dirt parking lot (it was soon paved) with our church in the background. Behind the church was a swing set and a decent sized field that was part of the church property.

Our church was a ranch style L-shaped building with white facing and black trim. A small courtyard and flower garden stood in front of the building. The sidewalk led to a ramp and then a covered walkway up to the front entrance.

We descended the stairs that were immediately to the right, inside the lobby. Downstairs was the Fellowship Hall and Sunday school classes. Upstairs Milt, the music director, taught the senior citizens' class.

One hour later, Lon rang a hand-held bell signifying Sunday school was through for the day. We all gathered in the lobby and Worship Center, visiting before the service began. The organ you heard from within, humming gracious hymns, soothing the soul. Mel, a regular usher, always handed you a church menu while greeting you with a twinkle in his eye. He was an elderly gentleman with a white beard and bright face. His wife, Dema could be heard playing the piano prelude in harmonic tune with the organist, Arlene. Diana

Simple* was the choir director. All three ladies and Milt took turns singing Special Music before the sermon. They sang from their own hearts and souls to our precious Lord.

We usually sat in the last pew of the front section on the right side. The wooden pews had rounded edges and burgundy cushions to match the carpet beneath our feet. A few members of the church greeted us; a couple of them were deacons, Lon Inder* and Bob Summer*.

Some of the regulars who attended our church in 2000 include the golden girls Blossom, Dorothy, Gladys, and Gracie who were in their nineties or nearing. Others were Marilyn Stark*, Janet, Ottie and Marge, Dean and Kay, Jim Simple*, Mathew, plus Bob Lark*, his wife, Julie and their children Bella, Katie, Darryl, and Sam.

I settled in between Mom and Gramma and reached for a blue hymnal. I peered down to my church menu and browsed to see what songs we would be singing.

Lon came over to visit us and rested his hand on the back of the pew. He had on his black leather jacket.

I saw our new pastor, Danny Cheak, walking up front and chatting with a few people. He had light gray hair and a mustache. A few months ago in March, Pastor Don passed away and Pastor Danny filled in for the time being.

"Morning kiddies," Pastor Danny greeted the church.

After he adjusted his lightly tinted glasses, he read the church announcements. Danny sat down then Milt, the music director, told everyone what page number we would be singing in the hymnal. Milt was an older gentleman with curly brown hair and similar tinted glasses. He usually wore Western styled suits.

Following two songs, Andy K., one of the other deacons, walked up to the podium, read selected scripture he chose for the week, and finished with a prayer.

We sang the offertory hymn and when the last verse was nearly done, four youth waited in front of the altar to receive the offering. They were Rory, James, Matt, and Sammy. We bowed our heads as Rory said a prayer then music began to play as they passed around the offering plate.

---

* Names changed

Rory's dad, Rick Clair*, worked the church's sound system in the back. Rory's mom, Desiree, sat with his brothers Sam, Joe, and Luke who was just recently born. The Clairs were a true example of a strong Christian family. They came to church as a family and were pretty involved in many aspects of church life. The children were well behaved and homeschooled.

Rory, a few years older than I, was strong in his faith; I really looked up to him–literally, he was at least six-feet tall. Actually, I admired the young man; he just carried himself well with the Lord. He was also intelligent, worked well with the youth group, and was a real joy to be around.

When tithing was finished, Danny stood up for *Pastor's Pals*, one of my favorite parts of the service.

"Where are my pals?" Danny asked, holding his Bible.

A few kids including me gathered with our Pastor who sat down on the choir steps next to the altar. Toddlers were encouraged to join us, but were unsure about the whole deal. Arlene's seven-year-old daughter Kimarie always sat near Danny. She was full of energy and when Danny said something funny she would always giggle.

In *Pastor's Pals*, Danny talked about things in the Bible and explained it so we would have a better understanding of the scripture, which usually led up to Danny's sermon.

About ten minutes later, I was back in my seat. Special music was next where someone would share his or her favorite Christian songs. Today was Milt's time to sing. It varied every week. He stepped up to the podium and the music prelude halted.

Pastor Danny then began his sermon. He presented the Word with passion and seriousness. At times he was humorous, waking us up with a slick joke or talking in a Scottish accent.

---

* Name changed

Chapter Six

First Baptist Church of Deer Park History

Our church motto: 1John 4:19: “We love because He first loved us”

FIRST LET us talk about Brother Lloyd Garrison who was a church planter for the Southern Baptist Convention (SBC) Home Mission Board.

Lloyd Garrison was born on October 17, 1919 in Channing, Texas. He came to the Lord as a senior in high school while attending a revival meeting at his home church.

He met his future wife Marge while she attended college in Plainview, Texas in 1942; he had already graduated. They wed in 1944 and were married almost sixty years.

Lloyd started his seminary education in the early 1950’s at Southwestern Baptist Theological Seminary in Fort Worth, Texas.

He was outgoing, loved the Lord very much, and loved people. He truly enjoyed ministering, visiting and getting to know his congregation. Never met anyone he didn’t like nor said anything bad about anyone. Lloyd was a “rubber meets the road” kind of pastor.

Lloyd had no other occupations because he believed pastoring was his only calling. After leaving Texas in 1955, he began his ministry in The Dalles, Oregon. They moved to Yakima, Washington about 1960 where he pastored seven years. Then in 1967, they moved to Spokane, Washington.

The Garrisons’ lives then shifted in 1973 when Lloyd began church planting. He helped with building nine churches during a ten-year stretch. The first church was in Post Falls, Idaho where he pastored twenty months and performed sixty-nine baptisms, the most from any of his planted churches.

Following Post Falls, he planted two churches in the state of Washington and two in Idaho before coming back to Washington to plant two more churches in both Suncrest and Deer Park.

The idea for Deer Park First Baptist Church began in 1981 when God moved many of His children’s hearts to build a place of worship in the little town of Deer Park. There were already some families strong in our Lord Jesus who lived there. These residents were helpful in many aspects during the planning and building of our church. Notably Harvey and Maxine Franseen, Milt Heimann (who was added as an electrician) and his wife Marie, Tex and Lena Clark, Mel and Dema Orcutt, the Keys, Helbig and their families (plus many others and you know who you were) sacrificed their lives to build the church.

So, a few residents of Deer Park gathered together with Church Planter Lloyd and his wife, Marge to discuss where to put a new church.

After much prayer, a plot of land was humbly found on the edge of Crawford Street. Lloyd and a core group purchased the land and soon the ground was broken. Mission volunteers from around the area and as far as Kalispell, Montana and Wichita Falls, Texas, helped build the church.

At the same time, Rick and Julie Taylor arrived in Deer Park on July 2, 1982, as the Northwest Builders for Christ began to construct the church building. It was like a bee's hive, with workers going here and there. From the hole to a dried-in building took only one week to complete. Sure was remarkable for all involved, which even caught the attention of the local press.

Rick and Julie recently joined the volunteer mission organization of the SBC Mission Service Corporation. God called them, after much prayer and research, to head from their home in Texas to Deer Park to assist Lloyd and Marge. The Taylors became an essential part of the church's growth and ministry. They enjoyed working with the youth department and having Monday Bible studies at their home.

As the church was being built, the Northgate Baptist Church in Spokane sponsored a Deer Park Mission. The Mission was set up at the South Mall in Deer Park and on March 29, 1981 held its first service. Pastor Lloyd preached to twenty-five people in attendance.

The services at the South Deer Park Mall continued into summer of 1981. By this time the mall had become cumbersome, due to the fact that the chairs, piano, and other furniture had to be moved from storage and set up inside before and after every meeting. Soon the only place to meet was the front entrance where motorcycles and unfinished furniture overflowed the area.

Harvey was the first to mention that we should search out a new location to proclaim the Lord's message of salvation and love. in

September of 1981, an ideal place was found and we moved the services to the Old City Hall building on Crawford Street. From the Old City Hall the church services moved into the Mobile Chapel, which had arrived in June of 1982.

After eleven months from groundbreaking, we were able to move the services to a permanent setting. Instantly, you could feel God's presence echoing throughout the new church.

Now Lloyd was our church pastor from 1981-1982. During his first year, our church had its first Deacon Ordination with Harvey, Ralph, and Andy becoming the first board of deacons.

Satisfied with their work in Deer Park, God called the Garrisons to plant a church in Sandpoint, Idaho in February 1983. Lloyd retired in 1993 after he planted his last two churches, one in Idaho and the final in Otis Orchards, Washington.

Just so happened while Pastor Lloyd and Marge vacationed for two weeks in Texas, they met Charles Hargrove who had just finished his seminary studies and was available to pastor. God sure knew how to make things work out.

So Pastor Charles began preaching from the pulpit in March of 1983. Rick and Julie moved back to Texas after working alongside the new pastor, Charles and his wife, Joyce for seven months. Charles was quoted: "From the first time I met with the church, I felt the Holy Spirit's leadership in directing us to minister to this community..."

Charles Hargrove was born on November 9, 1935 in the city of Fort Worth, Texas. One of his first memories of going to church was falling asleep on the pew at a very early age. He enjoyed the hymn "Onward Christian Soldier" and Vacation Bible School in March.

At the age of nine, he went to a tent revival with his sister. She gave her life to Jesus and was saved, but Charles really didn't understand what was going on at that time. It wasn't until a year later at the revival services that he understood a little bit more. During Sunday school the teacher asked him "If this building that we are sitting in should cave in, where would you spend eternity?" (paraphrased) This made sense to him and thus began his spiritual journey.

When Charles was a junior in high school, he met Joyce a freshman, his future wife-to-be. They wanted to get married right then and would have if given the opportunity to walk down the aisle. Of course, sometime after her graduation they did marry. They would have been married fifty years in 2006.

Charles started his seminary education in 1979 and completed it in 1982 at Southwest Bible College in Fort Worth, Texas. The Lord called him to be a pastor; he was forty-seven years young. He did light preaching in that area. During this time he was a farmer and rancher, owning his own property.

In March of 1983, Charles and his wife Joyce were called to pastor in Deer Park, Washington. They said FBC of Deer Park was the most enjoyable ten years they served as pastor and wife.

Joyce was his faithful helper in so many ways during his ministry. She taught Sunday school, played the piano, and sang.

Charles remembered many highlights of serving Deer Park First Baptist. The free service of Rick and Julie, Round-Up-Day at the start of their Sunday school year, and the great revival times with Butch, Bill, Jim, Mike, and Larry.

Then there was Vacation Bible School, trail horse rides, and many Christmas Cantatas. Dema graciously decorated the church every Christmas and Easter. The Sunrise Services at Andy's farm were quite meaningful.

During those ten years of Pastor Charles' ministry, the church grew in number and spirit. It averaged twenty baptisms per year.

In April of 1993, Charles retired. He and Joyce then moved back home to their farm and ranch in Texas.

Our next Pastor was Don Fortney who came here with his wife, Mildred. Somewhere on the plains of Tulsa, Oklahoma, Don was born and raised. He accepted the Lord as his Savior at the age of sixteen in the Eleventh Street Baptist Church, the same church he married Mildred. He was also ordained deacon and licensed to preach there.

Don graduated in 1971 from the Southwestern Baptist Theological Seminary in Fort Worth, Texas. During seminary he served as pastor of Timberlake Baptist Church in Fort Worth. He next served in June 1973 as Associate Pastor of Riverside Baptist Church of San Antonio, Texas, also functioning as Minister of Music, Youth, and Recreation.

His next call to service was to pastor the Clawson Baptist Church in Lufkin, Texas. This went on from August 1984 through November 1986. Don left the ministry for about seven years to take care of his grandmother until she went to our Lord. He did help out a few churches during this time.

Pastor Don began his ministry at Deer Park FBC on January 8, 1994.

He felt the most exciting thing that happened for Deer Park FBC was paying off the church loan. Mildred's greatest joy was starting up the Women's Ministry called G.A.L.S.—"God's Agape Ladies in Service."

Don retired in March 2000 with his health failing and went home to be with the Lord on October 18, 2000.

A pulpit committee was then elected to search out a new pastor. As many résumés from pastors came in, a retired Reverend Dan Cheak became the interim pastor of our church.

Danny was born on June 8, 1926, on a farm in Brownfield, Texas. His folks had split up when he was five and then he went to live with his mom. At ten, he and his mom moved to San Pedro, California. When he was thirteen he hit the road hitchhiking here and there across the country. Seventy-two working hours a week only earned him fifteen dollars.

Before long, he enlisted in the United States Marine Corps at the age of sixteen. He spent two terms overseas during World War II and was discharged on January 2, 1948. Danny accepted Jesus about the same time.

After attending church for three weeks, he met his sweet Sammie and they were married a year later.

Danny worked as a longshoreman on the waterfront. Also, because of his musical background, he directed music in the church, which he dearly loved. When he sang in church, he had a good tenor voice. In November of 1959, he surrendered to preaching and enrolled at the California Baptist College. During his sophomore year, he started preaching at First Baptist Church of Woodcrest in Riverside, California where he stayed until he graduated in May of 1964.

He served other churches in Southern California, which included thirteen years at Chula Vista First Southern Baptist Church. This large church was rundown. It had about seven hundred members with a lot of room for growth. It grew to twelve hundred when they left. God surely blessed Danny and Sammie there. It was unforgettable, they remembered.

They left their church in Chula Vista in 1981. Danny returned to work as a crane operator, which he enjoyed immensely. It was a great time in his life and making good money didn't hurt. Also, he served as an interim pastor for churches who couldn't afford a full-time position.

Thinking he had retired, he and his family moved to Deer Park in the early 1990's. He was then asked to serve at a small church in Suncrest, which he thought would be his last church. God soon shined his choice of our next church leader on the hearts of the Pastor Search Committee. On August 9, 2000, the committee recommended Brother Danny. Then on the first Sunday of September a secret ballot was held. There was a "yea" for Danny to become pastor. Danny and Sammy accepted the position, praise the Lord!

Around March 1, 2000, Pastor Danny Cheak took to the pulpit.

Chapter Seven

AFTER CHURCH I had lunch before Rich picked me up for our outing at his cabin on the lake. I carried out my backpack, sleeping bag, and pillow to the front porch when I saw Rosa and Waldo cross the street. She flung a baseball into the air while Waldo with his big pink tongue hanging over his jaw anxiously watching her.

Rosa came up to the porch, pointing to my sleeping bag. "I guess you're going camping. Where are you going?" she asked.

"Rich is taking me to his cabin on Deer Lake," I said.

"Cool," she said. "Hey, what's the biggest fish you ever caught?"

"Eight-pound rainbow trout," I replied. "That was last season at Fish Trap—that reminds me, I have to get my tackle box."

"I'll come with," Rosa said.

She followed me to the garage with Waldo at her heels. Rosa threw the ball ahead of me and the dog chased after it, but I quickly grabbed the ball. He went after the ball, knocking me off balance. Waldo kept going after the ball as we tossed it back and forth. While we came around to the lawn by the kitchen, Rosa threw the ball. When I went to catch it, Waldo jumped for the ball, striking my legs and sending me flying into the grass. I was stunned at first lying there and then realized Waldo was licking my face. Rosa tried to get him off of me but he was very persistent. She finally got his attention by waving the ball.

"Come Waldo, get the ball," she said.

I thought she would throw or run with it, but the dog was too quick, as he grabbed it, knocking her down next to me. We laughed so hard. Waldo trotted a few feet off with his prize, treasuring it. Our laughter settled and Rosa wrestled the dog for the ball.

"Give me my lucky ball back," she said, pulling the ball from the dog's tight jaws.

I joined in lending a hand as Rosa had a tough time. Just when we were about to be victorious, Waldo jerked his head one-way and we lost our grip on the ball, both of us falling backwards into the grass again. We erupted into belly laughs. At the same time we both stood up, and without warning we bumped heads—our first contact.

"OW!" I cried.

"OY!" Rosa cried.

"OW! You have a hard head," I told her.

"Talk about hard heads," Rosa said, pointing at me, then spoke Spanish. She went on a tangent and I began to laugh.

"What's so funny?" she asked.

"You talk funny," I replied.

I saw her eyes widen and her nostrils flare. In a flash I saw her fist coming at me, and I blocked it, parrying it away. I shuffled off to the side, exposing just my hip, not knowing if she was mad at me. She saw me in a defense position with my right shoulder facing her, my knees bent, and my arms up.

"I was just kidding," she said laughing.

"You're not mad?" I said still not so sure.

"Nah," she said. "I just wanted to see karate."

"Are you sure?"

"Si, I like my new amigo," she replied, patting me on the shoulder.

"Jay, Rich will be here in about five minutes!" Gramma hollered from the kitchen door.

"I guess you gotta go," Rosa said.

"Yep," I said. "What was I doing? Oh, yeah, tackle."

Rosa followed me into the back of the garage. I found my tackle box and fishing rod.

"Hey Jay, would you go fishing with me sometime?"

"Sure, that would be fun," I replied. "I like to fish at the creek."

"Hey Jay, maybe when you get back I can show you my baseball cards."

"Yeah, sure, I guess I'll see you later," I said.

"Adios," Rosa said, hopping out.

"Adios," I said the best I could. "And you can teach me some Spanish."

When I set my tackle on the porch, Rich drove up in his red pickup truck pulling a trailer and boat. He climbed out and approached me. Rich was about age fifty-two and five foot-six. He had a gray receding hairline and a white handle bar mustache. He wore a green plaid short sleeved shirt and jeans supported by suspenders. A fishing hat completed the picture.

"Are you ready my little buddy?" Rich asked me, taking off his glasses to clean.

"I can't wait," I said. "Just need to get my camera."

"Let's load your stuff," Rich suggested, replacing glasses on his face, "then we'll say good-bye to your Mom and Gramma."

After I grabbed my camera case from my room, I joined everyone in the living room. We stood in a circle and held hands while Mom led us in prayer.

"Dear Heavenly Father, we rejoice in Your most holy name," Mom began. "Lord, watch over Jay and Rich when they're out fishing and staying the night at the cabin. Keep them safe as they travel there and back. We thank You for Your loving light and the grace You have given us. In Jesus' precious name, we pray. Amen."

A couple minutes later, Rich and I were driving on the back roads to Deer Lake. Rich would rather avoid the highways when there was time. He liked to take it slow and easy in which to enjoy the landscapes. Also, we had the road to ourselves. For a few minutes we traveled through the flat countryside, passing farmland and private ranches. Up ahead were green mountains and forests sprouting with pines, firs, cedars, and occasional spruces. On the map it showed the mountain peaks of Deer Lake, Loon Lake, and Blue Grouse, all under four thousand feet.

Rich enjoyed talking. He liked to discuss philosophy and the Holy Bible. Sometimes he recited poetry that rolled off his lips. He liked prose with meaning and rich wisdom; mostly they were about God and His wonderful teaching. Rich also shared some poetry he had written. You could tell he had a love for God.

"Are you minding your Gramma and Mom?" Rich asked.

"Yes, sir," I replied.

"How are your Bible studies going?"

"Alright. I'm reading about Moses."

We entered the main road that surrounded Deer Lake. Taking a few turns the truck slowed, entering onto a wooded lane leading to Rich's property. He parked next to his cabin, a cozy A-frame, shielded by many pines and tamarack. Inside the cabin was one open room with a bathroom in the back. A potbellied wood stove stood in the center of the cabin. The only furniture was a table and chairs plus a bed in the back. I carried my sleeping bag and pillow up a ladder to a quaint loft. After we tidied up inside we ventured about the property. Every summer I helped Rich clean up dry brush and dead wood near the cabin. I liked taking photos of the birds and the critters around about.

In the late afternoon, we launched the boat and began to pilot around the lake. Out there you truly appreciated God's creations. The gray mountains surrounding Deer Lake reflected against the cobalt water, puffy white clouds floating in front of the sun, and the sight of many sorts of waterfowl.

An hour before dusk, we found a quiet cove and brought out our fishing poles. Out on the lake it was our place away from demands of life. It was a place where we could talk or not talk. I felt I could discuss anything with Rich, like issues troubling me at home or what not. Sometimes I asked questions about scripture I didn't understand. When I'm out there my mind was relaxed and clear so much that I could feel the Holy Spirit bring to my mind the questions I didn't know I had.

The two days at Rich's cabin came and went. When I got back and after some chores, I went to visit Rosa. I wasn't as nervous when I first approached their house with the intention of showing Rosa around town. The door was wide open so I knocked on the screen door. I heard some music from within. No one seemed to hear me so I knocked harder. Manny finally came to answer the door.

"Hola, Jay," he said. "How was the lake?"

"Great, sir!"

"Did you catch anything?" he asked, opening the screen door.

"They weren't biting for me, but Rich caught an eleven-incher," I said, stepping inside.

"You here to visit Rosa, I'm sure," Manny said. "Come on in, you're always welcome. Let me get these out of here." He squeezed passed me with a couple of empty boxes.

I trailed him to the back of the house and browsed about. There was a beige couch, coffee table, and a small entertainment center where Rosa's video games were carelessly about. Muffled sounds resembling music came from my left. Must be where the bedrooms were. I went to where Manny was opening a sliding glass door by a small dining room. The kitchen was open on that side with a counter bar.

"There we go," Manny said, entering from the backyard. "Rosa's in her room."

I followed him to where the music was louder. He opened Rosa's door and hollered over the music. She was busy putting stuff on a shelf when she saw us at the door.

"Someone is here to visit you," Manny said, after the music was turned down. "Hey, when are you going to clean up this mess?"

"Hi Jay," she said to me and then turned to her dad. "I'm almost done."

"Sorry about the mess, Jay," Manny said. "Rosa, he can stay for a little while and then you have to finish unpacking."

"What are you listening to?" I asked, when he left.

She named some pop group I never heard of before. I thought it sounded awful but didn't tell her. Mom and Gramma wouldn't let me listen to the new secular music.

"We listen to Christian music," I said. Rosa raised her eyebrows and looked like she was about to laugh. It kinda made me a little uncomfortable. She probably thought I was a dork and boring.

"Like hymns and stuff?" she asked.

"Sometimes we do," I said. "Mom and I listen to contemporary Christian rock." I started to turn the radio station and realized I didn't ask permission. "Sorry, I was going to show you that station."

"Go ahead and show me," she said and after a song or two she seemed to enjoy it. "That's cool. I went to church once, it was boring."

"You would like our church—we have a fun youth group," I commented.

"I don't know, maybe I didn't understand what they were saying in church," she said, changing the subject. "Jay, do you like the Oldies station?" She switched to it. "Dad showed it to me and I kinda like it."

"Sometimes Mom and I do," I replied.

"Cool, I like this song," she said, beginning to sing. "Don't you sing?"

"Sometimes, I'm not very good."

After I helped her clean her room she showed me her baseball cards. For a while I felt like I wore out my welcome. I guess you could say, Gramma taught me good manners. Yes sirs and yes ma'ams.

The next day Rosa and I rode our bikes down to Billie and Kaylee's house. It was a narrow rectangular cream colored house with two stories. The garage was behind the backyard, off an alley.

Their parents, Henry and Gayle, both optometrists, had moved from Spokane to Deer Park about three years ago. Henry was Gramma's optometrist and that was how I met Billie and Kaylee. I guess when they were born their mom took a leave of absence in which to take care of them while their dad worked full-time. Henry and Gayle's roles had switched when they arrived in Deer Park. Henry only worked part-time at the office in Spokane and became Mr. Mom. Gayle worked full-time and wasn't around much during the weekdays.

As we approached their front porch, I heard Billie holler in the backyard. We saw him coming toward us chasing Kaylee with a stick.

"Give it back!" he yelled.

When Kaylee saw me, she ran to hide behind me, thinking I would protect her or something. Billie came toward us and tried to wrestle something out of her hand.

"Jay, save me from the beast," Kaylee said.

"Spaz, gimmie," Billie said.

"What does she have?" Rosa asked.

"My favorite army guy—she dressed it up and put doll clothes on him," Billie replied.

"Okay, you can have it," she began with a wicked grin on her face, "but you have to go get it." She threw it across the yard into a bush while laughing.

"I teach you punk," Billie said, after he retrieved his army guy.

"Now we're even," Kaylee said.

"That's fine this time, but you better stay out of my room," Billie said, turning to us. "You must be Rosa."

We rode our bikes to another park called Mix Park. It was a few blocks away across the railroad tracks. We played in the creek and swung on the swings to see who could jump off the highest. At one point, Billie pushed his sister on the swing all so innocently, and then he started pushing her higher and higher into the air. She began to get scared.

"Stop it!" she cried. "Stop, I want off!"

"What's wrong sissy," Billie asked. "Do you want your mommy?"

"I'll tell."

Billie always teased and picked on her. I wouldn't say I never did, but I didn't keep making fun of her. Actually, she liked it when I teased her because I was giving her attention. I'd admit sticking up for Kaylee, but in a way so that Billie wouldn't know—distract him somehow.

"Billie, leave her alone," I said—oops, perhaps too much sticking up.

"You're mean," Rosa said.

Billie stopped pushing Kaylee. "You take all the fun out of it—let's play ball," he said, grabbing his baseball and mitt.

Kaylee jumped out of the swing and punched her brother in the arm—*Oh no!* I thought. *No escape*—I wasn't fast enough as Kaylee had me by the arm.

"Oh Jay, you saved me," she said, hugging my arm.

There I go, opening my mouth and insert foot, I thought, rolling my eyes. Nicely, I shrugged her off and we joined Billie and some more of our friends.

"Hey Jay, we're putting together a baseball game," Billie said. "Frank and some of the other guys are at the baseball diamond."

"Can I play?" Kaylee asked. "I'll tell Mom if you don't let me play."

Billie turned up his nose and reluctantly agreed.

We rode our bikes down to the playing field. As usual, Kaylee got stuck on my team with Rosa. At least we had De'von on our team. He was fast and could cover the outfield. We decided to put Kaylee out in left field.

The game didn't start off very well for our team and before we knew it, Billie's team was up five to nothing. We couldn't get much offense going and at the end of the game we did manage to get two runs with them winning by ten. One highlight was when Rosa showed off her arm in the outfield throwing out Billie at home plate. Boy was he not too happy; Kaylee jumped up and down. Rosa and I wanted a rematch with the same teams.

That rematch was the next day. An older kid offered to be an umpire and it felt like a real game. Rosa, we all agreed, would be our pitcher. I batted much better with a couple singles, barely reaching the outfield. Kaylee was out there again in her own little world, picking at the grass and playing with her doll.

In the first inning, Rosa couldn't get a strike and gave up a couple runs from Billie's double. He began to laugh and celebrate his victory. It was a closer game as we scratched off one run. Rosa struck out two batters in the second and we felt the momentum swinging our way. I led off the next inning, beating out a throw from third. Kaylee struck out and went to the bench to play with her doll. De'von came up next, hitting the ball way into the gap. I chugged around the bases with De'von at my heels. I tied the game and saw the ball coming from left field and thought De'von was going to stop at third base, but he kept going. There was going to be a play at the plate, but the ball sailed over the catcher and umpire's heads.

Rosa shut out the other team the rest of the way and we won the game even with Kaylee in left field. Our team gathered on the mound after Rosa struck out the last batter. We celebrated our victory—high fives, jumping up and down like we had won the World Series. Billie dragged his bat and moped with his team. His teams almost never lost. Our team was like a bunch of disorganized cats in a dog circus. Both teams lined up and congratulated each other on a good game.

"Good game Jay," Billie said. "You can be on my team anytime Rosa. I don't know how you guys did it, especially with the Spaz." He shoved his sister and she hit him back.

"That was a good hit you got off of me," Rosa said to Billie.

"I just got lucky," Billie said. "Man you can throw some heat. Hey, the three of us should play Kids League this year—we would kick butt."

Rosa agreed, but I wasn't too keen on the idea—I wasn't the greatest ball player, just wasn't me. I really wanted to focus on my karate, even though I could do both.

"Sure," I hesitated to say.

"Cool, I can't wait," Billie said. "I'm going to take you home, Kaylee Spaz. Mom must be home from work by now."

"I don't want to," Kaylee sneered, turning up her nose.

"You have to because I said so—I'm the boss."

Kaylee anchored herself to the bench next to Rosa and me. When Billie tried to pull her away, she screamed.

"No!" she yelled. "I want to stay with Jay and Rosa."

"Suit yourself—good riddens," Billie said, getting on his bike.

"He didn't even ask," Rosa said. "Why do you let him do that to you? He's your best friend."

"I don't know," I said with a shrug.

"Because he likes me," Kaylee said, trying to hug me.

I stood up and asked, "So what do you want to do now?"

"Rosa, do you want to jump rope?" Kaylee asked.

"I dunno," Rosa replied.

"Well, if you do..." Kaylee said, twirling her doll in the air by its hair. "We could play at my house—no Billie's there—can we play at your house, Jay?"

"Maybe tomorrow," I said.

"Hey Jay, you don't like baseball do you?" Rosa asked.

"It's okay," I said. "Never was good at it—that was the first time I got hits."

"I'll show you how to play," Rosa said, as we mounted our bikes. "I could give you some tips."

"Thanks, I could use some help."

"I know everything about baseball," Rosa said.

"I could get you started in karate class," I suggested.

"Oh shoot," Rosa swore (but it wasn't the word she used)—"I was gonna ask my dad."

"Hey Jay," Kaylee said, riding up along side of me. "I'm old enough to be in *your* Sunday school class—Hey Rosa, wanna come to Sunday school with us?"

"I don't know," Rosa said.

"You'll have fun," Kaylee said.

"Okay," Rosa said, probably not meaning it.

After we dropped off Kaylee we hung out in my backyard.

"I went to my cousin, Dora's Sunday school class once, but I don't remember if I had a good time," Rosa said, as she swung on the tire swing.

"We have a good teacher and I think you would enjoy the class," I said.

"I dunno."

"You could come once and listen, see what you think."

"If you're there I'll go," she said, becoming distracted with something across the street. A car parked in front of her house.

"I'll be there, guaranteed," I said.

"Hey, I forgot my cousin Dora was coming over. Do you want to meet her?"

"Sure," I replied and we crossed the street.

A few days later, Manny invited us to dinner. He'd be cooking Mexican food for us. When Mom told me that, I turned my nose up. I pictured my mouth on fire, thinking about spicy and hot sauce. I only went to a fast food Mexican restaurant once and didn't like it. Though, Mom and Gramma liked it. Before we headed over to the Sanchez's house, Mom told me to be nice and try the food.

"Gracious for coming," Manny greeted. "I'll try not to make dinner too spicy—I like it caliente."

"Hola, mi amigo!" I said, liking this Spanish thing.

"Sounds like Rosa's been teaching you," Manny said.

Manny led us into the living room where a baseball game was starting on television. Rosa came in with her baseball attire and wearing her hat backwards. She plopped on the couch. Waldo whimpered at the back door, his tail wagging.

"My dad said I could do karate, but not right now," Rosa said. "I wanted to sign-up for Kids League and karate, but he wouldn't let me do both. He said I could join a team because I can do karate anytime during the year."

"I've been thinking about playing baseball too," I said. "Like you said, I just need some practice and a few tips."

"You won't regret it," she said, as the game continued.

"How do you say you're welcome?" I asked Rosa.

"You're welcome," she said.

"No, I mean in Spanish," I said, playfully shoving her.

"Usted es agradable," she said, then I repeated it the best I could.

I watched baseball with Rosa while Mom and Gramma visited Manny. Seattle gave up four runs in the top of the first. Rosa was upset after our team was behind. She yelled at the umpire for making a bad call. At first she would be watching intensely, then suddenly springing excitedly from her seat after Seattle hit a homerun; the camera zoomed to the top of the dome as fireworks exploded. I never saw a girl so animated and into baseball or any sporting event. Of course, I was never inclined to find out. I started to enjoy myself until Mom stuck her head out from the kitchen.

"Hey Jay, come in here, this is interesting," she said.

"I'm watching the game," I said.

"It will just take a second," Mom said. I knew what a second meant—forever. "Manny is making homemade tortillas."

"I'm not as good as my mom or Grandma Elena was at making tortillas," Manny explained, as I entered the kitchen, "but mine turn out okay. Help yourselves to a sample over there."

While Gramma passed out a couple of pieces of a tortilla, Manny continued, "When I was a kid in Yakima, about your age Jay, I would come home from school and Mom had hot tortillas ready for us. Sometimes she let us put peanut butter and jelly on them—"

"Mmm," Mom said. "It's good, Manny!"

"Really, Manny, they are very good," Gramma commented.

"Thank you—I know, they're getting close to Mom's," Manny said. "She was in the kitchen long before we were up in the morning preparing all our meals for the day. During the week, we kids wouldn't see our pa until we sat down for dinner. Speaking of, I should be finishing it—you guys must be getting hungry."

"Yeah, I'm anxious to sit down and eat," Mom said, "It smells wonderful in here!" She turned and asked me, "Jay, what do you think?"

I just smiled and gave a half nod, then I was somewhat curious. "What are we having anyways?"

"We will be having beef burritos," Manny replied. "Now back to showing everyone the process of making tortillas."

"So, Jay, Manny has combined a special corn meal called masa and warm water," Gramma said.

"Now, Naomi just mix the two ingredients together," Manny went on. "You're doing good. After it is mixed through, we let it sit for about fifteen minutes—that's enough Naomi, let's move onto the next step." He stepped to another bowl. "This dough has been sitting and is ready to be worked. Take a wad of dough the size of your palm and press it with your fingers."

"Do you want to try it, Jay?" Mom asked.

"No, I think I'll watch," I replied, distracted with the game, hearing Rosa holler.

"It's kind of like kneading bread dough," Gramma commented.

"It is—Mexican bread, if you think of tortillas," Manny jested. "If it starts getting dry add more water."

"And if it is too wet, add more masa?" Gramma asked.

"Exactly," Manny replied, concentrating on the dough in his hand. "Form the dough into a large golf ball and then we are ready to flatten them into a tortilla."

"I'm not doing too well with my golf ball," Mom said, laughing.

"Rach, you just need practice," Gramma pointed out.

"Usually you can press the tortilla to the size you want by hand, but that takes a lot of practice. Sometimes I get lazy or in a hurry, so I use a tortilla press instead."

"Mom, you need one of those," I teased.

Manny brought the press, which was a wooden device, to the open counter space. "Take two pieces of plastic wrap. Place one inside the press, then the dough ball, followed by the other plastic wrap." He placed his hand on the handle and pressed it down like a waffle iron. "Press it until the tortilla is about six inches or more." Bringing it up, he announced, "And there you have it, homemade masa tortillas."

"That's neat!" Gramma and Mom replied.

"I'll have to get me one of those tortilla presses," Gramma commented and then asked, "what's next Manny?"

"Well, I cooked the beef all day in a crockpot and then shredded it," Manny said, pointing to it on the counter. "It already has spices: cumin, chile powder, and a smidge of garlic. Next, I want to make us some fresh salsa."

"Sounds wonderful Manny," Gramma said, as she finished kneading her dough and placing it in the tortilla press.

At first I was bored, not wanting to be in there, but after watching for a while, I found it interesting. Rosa distracted me by climbing up on the bar stool behind me and spinning on it.

Manny pulled out the cutting board. "We'll be dicing two tomatoes and half of an onion," he said, slicing a tomato in half, then pausing and pointing to the other ingredients, "also serrano chiles and garlic to taste. Last but not least, add these leafy green things called cilantro, which is related to parsley—a strong scented herb."

He dumped these ingredients into a food processor.

"A few turns," Manny said, switching on the processor, then spoke up over the noise. "Depending on how chunky or fine you want it—I like it somewhere in between." He turned the machine off and showed us the contents. "Just like that, fresh salsa."

"Seattle scored two more runs, but so did the other team. We are still losing," Rosa reported.

"Do you guys still have family in Yakima, Manny?" Mom asked.

"Let's see..." he replied and paused to think while putting the salsa in a bowl. "There's Omar and Irma my parents, eight aunts and uncles." He walked off for a bag of tortilla chips. "My oldest brother Roberto is over there helping out with the family business. Then there's me, my brother Jose who is a chef in San Francisco and Juanita, my sister, who you already met. Peter and Juanita have two daughters, Miranda sixteen and Dora who is ten, Rosa's age."

"Dora's my best friend," Rosa said, coming into the kitchen.

Manny placed the bowl on the counter bar. "Go ahead try and see what you think," he said.

Mom and Gramma didn't hesitate, as they grabbed a chip, dipped it, and took a bite. I instantly heard mmm's from them. Now me on the other hand, stared at the chip in my hand.

"Go ahead Jay, it's not hot," Mom encouraged.

Here goes, down the gullet! I thought, dipping the chip and bringing it to my mouth. Without thinking…chomp, crunch… hmmm—"Wow, it is good!"

"It looks like we're ready to make burritos," Manny announced, picking up a couple of tortillas that were just pressed. "Take one tortilla at a time and gently place it in a hot skillet for thirty seconds on both sides until it is lightly toasted. You will know when they are done when air pockets start to form."

"Seems simple enough," Gramma said.

"It is. Mexican cooking is pretty basic with its main ingredients," Manny explained, taking the tortilla out of the skillet. "Now place the tortilla inside a towel to cool. Once cool, take one," he began while grabbing one and stuffing it, "add some meat, cheese, refried beans, rice, lettuce, tomatoes, avocado, and salsa—any combination you desire."

Soon we sat down to eat the beef burritos. They were wonderful—most wonderful. Following the meal we visited for a while. I learned a lot about the Mexican culture that evening. I also learned more commonly used Spanish phrases. Rosa taught me how to count to twenty and the days and months of the year.

Manny invited us to the Sanchez's family Fourth of July barbeque get-together. Juanita's husband's folks threw a party at the lake. Rosa's grandparents and other family members were there too. We had hot dogs, hamburgers, potato salad, and pink lemonade. Rosa was fascinated with fireworks; her dad bought a few for us to set off that night. We also had watermelon and Gramma's famous brownies.

Sometime later, Rosa helped me with my batting and gave me some good pointers before the kids put together a baseball game. Then it was the kids verses the adults, but the adults could only bat one-handed.

"My mom is here! My mom is here!" Rosa announced, as the game finished. She quickly darted off to a car driving up and parking.

I watched as Rosa ran into her mom's arms. They kissed and hugged and then walked our way with big smiles. Manny, I could tell, had mixed emotions.

"Glad you could make it," Manny said.

"Me too. I wouldn't miss our annual Fourth of July family bash," Rosa's mom said.

"Mom, Mom, come meet my new friend," Rosa said, pulling her mom toward me.

"Rosa, your mom just got here, settle down a minute," Manny said sternly to his daughter, then asked his wife, "How was your trip, Ella?"

"Not too bad," Ella replied.

"Hola, Ella," Rosa's Grandma greeted, hugging her daughter-in-law.

"Hola, hola, Irma," Ella said, returning the hug. "You look good."

Rosa's mom greeted several people before getting to me.

"Mom, this is my friend Jay, the one I've told you about over the phone" Rosa said.

"Nice to finally meet you, Jay. All she talks about is you," Ella said.

Ella had dark, mid-length hair up in a ponytail and deep brown eyes behind thin rimmed glasses. She was a little younger than my mom. She seemed real nice and had a real good sense of humor; her laugh was cackling. I found her to be hip for a grown-up.

Before dusk, I saw Manny and Ella by themselves talking from a distance. At times they acted calm, but a couple of times, I think, they were arguing. Rosa mentioned her parents disagreed where they should live. Her dad didn't want to move to Seattle and her mom was establishing her career there.

The evening ended with shooting fireworks from the dock on the lake. We were all exhausted once we got home. I asked Mom if she thought Manny and Ella were going to get a divorce.

"I don't know," Mom said. "Sometimes, adults distance themselves until they can safely decide what they want their lives to become. This may take a couple of years before things settle down."

I thought about asking if she and Dad got divorced and that was the reason why he wasn't with us, but I didn't. I figured she would tell me when she was ready for whatever reason. She was just protecting me.

The next Sunday Rosa joined my Sunday school class. I was somewhat surprised she even came, but was very glad she did. It was my third time inviting one of my friends to church. The first time was by befriending Billie and Kaylee, who became my first witnesses. Of course, Kaylee liked me the first time she laid eyes on me. As soon as Kaylee heard about me going to Sunday school and church, she didn't hesitate to be there. So it wasn't an invitation of words on my part, but an invitation of leading by example. Kaylee saw a person compassionate about his faith and she wanted to be a part of it. Because of this, Billie, being as curious as he was, would be willing to try almost anything once. So, he joined the Sunday school class a few times too.

Rosa was a little leery at first, but we made her feel welcomed. After a while she seemed comfortable, but didn't talk much, just listened as I suggested. I could tell at times she looked confused and didn't understand the lesson. She sat quietly and watched curiously during the service.

I didn't give myself all of the credit bringing Rosa to church because Gramma planted the first seed by inviting Manny and Rosa to dinner. Then after I became friends with Rosa and mentioning how much fun my church was, Kaylee watered the seedling more.

Witnessing sometimes took just one person, but quite often it took many to accomplish God's purpose. There was a right way for a Christian to witness and that was first, lead by a kind, loving, and friendly example. If I get angry or frustrated with a potential witness, that's not the right time to talk about Jesus.

The following Saturday we had the church picnic at Jim and Diana's house out in the country. They had the picnic there every year that I could remember. We enjoyed their homemade ice cream. Everyone brought something for the potluck. Gramma brought gelatin surprise with the marshmallows trapped inside the mold. The adults talked and visited in the shade while the kids participated in some games.

Monday came along with Rosa, Billie, me, and some of our friends beginning Kids Baseball League. Deer Park at this time didn't have any Kids League so our games were played in the Spokane Kids League. The kids who signed up met on a field awaiting their assigned teams. We all wouldn't be on the same team, as I understood. The way it worked, everyone's name was placed in a huge barrel like the ones they use for bingo balls. Names were drawn in anticipation. In the end, from my friends, only Rosa, De'von, and I were on the same team.

Our coach, Nathan, was a really nice guy and had a love for the game. He wasn't a vocal coach and he didn't put anyone down for mistakes. Coach Nathan evaluated us to determine what position we would play. Because of my quick hands and agile feet from my time in karate, Coach Nathan thought it best to put me at shortstop. I understood Billie's coach also put him there. Rosa, of course was our pitcher; she also played outfield with De'von.

The last few days Rosa and Manny helped me with my hitting. Manny suggested some things for my swing and stance. De'von's dad, the Deer Park High School baseball coach, also helped us with our fielding and fundamentals. Now we felt more confident and ready for our first game.

One particular day, after Sunday school, as Rosa and I were hanging around the doorway we saw a couple of different people that we hadn't seen before. At the time I didn't think much about them, but there was a guy in an electric wheelchair. He wasn't driving it. A woman was slightly off to the side working a joystick. Pastor Danny greeted them outside. He talked to them for a moment and the two started inside. I saw something sticking out of his neck and tried not to stare, so I went to take my seat. The guy in the wheelchair sat in front of the first pew in the back section.

"We have two new guests with us today," Danny said during announcements. "Sitting in the back are Jason and his attendant Heather."

They surprised me the next Sunday by sitting in front. When I saw them, I had a feeling something special was going to occur. Sure enough Pastor Danny's attention did turn toward Jason and Heather, but not right away. The sermon ended as Pastor Danny called an invitation for anybody to accept Jesus publicly, or if someone wanted to join the church. As always Kimarie visited with Pastor Danny during the invitation. He waited to see if someone else would come forward. I saw Danny pause for a moment looking around, then, I guess Jason caught his attention. Danny then leaned down to talk with Jason.

I think it was the next morning service when Pastor Danny said he had visited Jason at his home. He told us Jason, twenty-five years young, lived with his parents and had caregivers who took care of him. Danny discovered he had a sharp mind. The young man had muscular dystrophy (MD) and a machine, a ventilator that helped him breathe.

Mom said MD was similar to MS both being neurological diseases, but that's where similarities end. Jason had Duchenne MD. He was one of Jerry Lewis' kids. You know, you've seen them on the Labor Day Telethon.

"I asked him if he ever felt bitter," Danny said. "You know what he told me? He said he never did because it was a waste of his time and took too much energy. Jason has decided to join our church. He hasn't been baptized, but since he has a tube in his neck we know that it would be impossible for him to be submerged. The deacons and I talked it over and Jason agrees since he already accepted the Lord, his situation doesn't merit a baptism."

One reason I brought up Jason, was to show how God used anyone to fulfill His plans and for the spreading of the Gospel. No matter if you were in a wheelchair, walking on one leg, blind—whatever it may be, God had a purpose for you.

Over the years, Jason read the Sunday scripture and prayer, sometimes reciting a poem he had written. He also read his Christian testimony and sang a couple of songs—even through his ventilator, which seemed difficult.

Summer 2000 went really fast. I was busy every waking moment with Bible studies, baseball, karate, and having fun with my new friend Rosa and my other friends. By the end of the summer, Rosa and I became best friends. Manny took us camping and fishing a couple of times and Rich also took us to his cabin.

Before I started Kids League, I had a purple stripe on my orange belt working on my purple belt. I was doing really well with my purple techniques and forms, which brought me pretty close to being ready for the test. At the end of the summer I earned my purple belt.

Rosa really started to enjoy Sunday school and participated in the lessons. She also paid more attention to the sermons and I knew she liked to sing the hymns at church.

Our baseball team did reasonably well, losing a handful of games and making it to the playoffs. Even though we lost in the first round of the playoffs, we had a great time.

Consistently our main group was made up of Billie, Rosa, De'von, and me. Frank and some other friends moved away. Billie would disagree, but Kaylee was part of our group too. Billie had to anyway because their parents worked a lot. A new girl, Zoey, De'von's next-door neighbor in the countryside, soon joined us too. De'von and Zoey both belonged to the Deer Park Junior Rodeo.

Chapter Eight

September 2000

THE SUMMER always came to a fast close and we were back in the school mode. I expected to be homeschooled, but had been hinting about going to a local public school. I wanted to be with my friends for the most part. Mom picked up on my hints and we sat down to discuss the idea of me going to Arcadia Elementary. She left me to make that choice on my own. We brought the issue to our Lord, asking in prayer for which direction I should take. For some time we prayed on this and one day the Holy Spirit told me to attend Arcadia. He emphasized the opportunity to witness others who I may not have had a chance to meet.

Most kids weren't excited when the first day of school came around. I was excited though, but did miss my summer freedom. It would be different with a teacher who was not Mom or Gramma. Kaylee was right behind us in fourth grade and was very pleased I went to school with her now. Wherever I was she wanted to be near me and at times it felt embarrassing. Yikes!

"Oh, I hate school," Rosa said to me, as we rode our bikes to school. "Have to wake up early every day, do homework, and can't stay up late."

"Well, I can't wait," I said.

"Why?"

"I get to hang out with you and Billie every day."

"I like that part, but doing work is boring."

It was planned we would ride our bikes with Billie and Kaylee the first day of school, so when we turned on 'A' Street, we saw them up ahead. Kaylee was the first to see us and smiled sweetly at me. She slowed down to pull up alongside of me.

"Hi Jay, I'm glad you're going to school with us," Kaylee said.

"Hey Spaz, leave Jay alone," Billie said.

"Why, I like Jay," Kaylee said.

"It's okay," I said, rolling my eyes at Billie.

I had relief from Kaylee when we entered Mr. Sebright's fifth grade class. A nice lady, Mrs. Hubert, was the paraprofessional in our class. Later, I discovered she was Jason's mom. I felt very comfortable at my desk with Billie in front of me and Rosa across from me. On our first day, Mr. Sebright made everyone feel welcomed. So did Mrs. Hubert, who every day was cheerful, making the classroom complete.

By the end of the week, I was used to my new school, but often missed Mom and Gramma teaching me.

Recess came along and I was having fun hanging out with my friends. It was fine when Kaylee bugged me during summer, but for some reason I felt more annoyed with her at school. Billie got rid of her a couple of times and then she would be back again. I started to treat her like Billie did—shoving and calling her names. My tactics didn't work like her brother's did because she knew I wasn't mean.

One day, the following week, Kaylee came over to me during recess all lovey-dovey and began to hang on me. Of course, Trevor, the school bully, saw this and couldn't resist the opportunity for a royal teasing. He stated that she was my girlfriend. His voice echoed in my mind—*Jay and Kaylee sitting in a tree-blah-blah-blah*—

"She's not my girlfriend! I don't even know her!" I blurted without even thinking, jerking away from Kaylee.

"Yeah right," the bully said, laughing as he walked off.

"Just leave me alone!" I sternly said to Kaylee, who ran off with streams of tears.

Instantly I felt bad, realizing what I had just done. I wanted to go after her and apologize, but my feet were stuck on the asphalt. I hurt her feelings, not something I had ever been known to do, being mean and snappy—to anybody. I saw myself like Billie. She expected that kind of treatment from her brother, not from me. I did admit I liked Kaylee and considered her a friend. Rosa was the only one who knew this. So, for the rest of the day I felt really bad.

Proverbs 16:32 sparked my mind: "He that is slow to anger is better than the mighty; and he that ruleth his spirit than he that taketh a city." Both the Bible and karate spoke of self-control, but I didn't have it that day. I asked God to forgive me for my actions. I tossed and turned all night long.

The next day, I was antsy to get going so I could apologize to Kaylee. I didn't even wait for Rosa, making my way early on my bike to 'A' Street. I waited on the Knight's front steps, hoping to talk to Kaylee. Soon Billie came out all ready for school.

"What are you doing here, snoozing?" Billie asked.

"Just waiting for you guys," I said.

"I know what you did and I know why you're here," Billie said. "Way to go, my sister was moodier than normal. Try to do something so she is at least livable, please!"

When she came out, I tried my best to approach her and make things right, but she ignored me.

At school, I found Kaylee inside and tried with all my might to apologize, but she still shunned me and wouldn't talk. Every available moment I tried to talk to her. The hours wound down and I only had a few chances left, not wanting this to go on much longer. As the lunch bell rang, I looked for Kaylee in the cafeteria. I saw her across the way being bugged by Trevor. Other kids nervously walked by them.

"You already took my cookies, now leave me alone," Kaylee said to Trevor, as I walked toward them.

A light bulb flickered in my head and gave me an idea. I stepped behind Trevor, who was hunched over, pleading for more food. Like a buddy, I put my arm around his shoulder and patted.

"Hey Trev," I said. "How about I buy you some chips or something?"

I took care of Trevor, leading him away to the end of the lunch line. After he was satisfied, I went back to Kaylee who finally looked up at me.

"Please Kaylee," I began, "I apologize for what happened the other day. I had Gramma make those cookies you always liked. I'll share them with you. You are my good friend."

"I am, really?"

"As God is my witness."

"Thanks, Jay, I accept your apology," Kaylee said thoughtfully.

I didn't care that Trevor saw me with Kaylee. He tried to antagonize me. When it got to the point I knew he wanted to fight, I decided just to make friends with him instead. Trevor was shocked, not expecting this treatment.

Rosa attended Sunday school and morning services for at least three months. I wondered what she thought about God and the Bible. She hinted a couple of times that she wanted the Lord in her life.

One day she appeared to be touched by Pastor Danny's sermon. He preached on God's unconditional love for all His children. I saw a tear form in Rosa's eye and it wasn't caused by a yawn of boredom. Her eyes never left the pastor, hanging onto every word he said. When the sermon came to an end, it was the first time I saw her emotionally moved. It was just tears and sniffles though. Since I had known her, I never saw her cry, not even when she fell off her bike.

The song of invitation began as Pastor Danny invited people in church to come to Christ. Rosa looked at me, then toward my Gramma and Mom. We knew what was happening, could feel a soul coming to a decision. No dialogue was needed and to my surprise she brought her hands to her face, reaching across me. Gramma handed her a tissue, comforting her hand. I patted her back, giving her encouragement. Rosa quickly regained her composure and like a lost sheep, she slowly found her way, walking down the aisle. Danny received her up front with a small hug.

Summer 2001

My fifth grade year ended with much success hitting the books and growing spiritually. Mr. Sebright was a good teacher and made it worth learning. I made a few new friends, some I planted seeds and a couple I witnessed with.

Soon after the last day of school I turned eleven. Rosa and I became closer friends. We shared similar activities and both picked up rollerblading. I enjoyed camping and hiking with Rosa and her dad. I went to Rich's cabin a few times with just him and sometimes Rosa joined us. Rosa and I decided not to sign up for Kids Baseball League because most of our friends had different interests. Some took up soccer and some skateboarding. Our group only camped out a couple times that year.

I followed what Rosa wanted to do because she was my best friend and I wanted to do things with her. Well, we followed each other. Besides, she and I looked forward to Vacation Bible School and the church camp at Waitt's Lake, which we couldn't do last year because of baseball.

Rosa found herself at her first karate class. I taught her the rules and what to expect from Sensei Lance up until she stepped on the blue mats. She was much more prepared than I was on my first day because I had Rosa already doing a few basic techniques. After a few classes, Rosa told me that she never realized how hard it would be. She almost quit, but I kept encouraging her to keep on going. I achieved my purple belt and continued working really hard on my karate techniques.

I grew a couple inches that summer, but Rosa was still taller than me. Billie was always the tallest, keeping stature with the long legged De'von. Frankie and Jordon were always the shortest.

Chapter Nine

September 2001

TOWARD THE end of fifth grade we went on a field trip down to the junior high. After they showed us around the campus, we had a pretty good idea on what to expect in the fall.

During the summer, many changes took place with me and my friends. Some guys, including myself started to notice the girls and vice versa. For some reason, the girls in my class were more interesting and easier to look at than before. Rosa seemed different to me also. She still had the tomboy appeal and couldn't wait for physical education. We still talked about camping on the weekend and watched baseball in the evenings. But on the other hand, she began to act more like a girl—giggly, blushing, and somewhat silly at times. I saw her playing with her hair one day in the mirror, but she denied it.

Billie and I were nothing alike when it came to girls. He was more flirtatious with the girls and approached them like it was nothing. He sometimes tried to be too suave, looking ridiculous. I was quieter and liked to sit back and observe. I thought I was more scared and unsure with everything about junior high, but I knew the Lord would get me through it.

We left Kaylee at the elementary school while the rest of us moved onto junior high, to sixth grade. Of course she was disappointed, but took it better than I thought she would. I thought Kaylee's crush on me had lost its flame and wasn't as noticeable.

I felt nervous the first day of junior high. Rosa and some of our other friends were a little on edge too. When we left Arcadia Elementary, we were the top turtles in a pond full of little gold fish. We felt respected and sure of ourselves. Now, as we stepped off the bus at Deer Park Junior High, we were the little gold fish looking at the bigger fish.

"Here we are," Rosa said to me, as we stood in front of the building.

"Yep, here we are," I said, after I held my breath.

Well, I survived my first week at school and settled into a regular routine. I liked my teachers especially Mrs. Polley who taught art and Mr. Norton the English teacher. The only class I despised was pre-algebra. Mr. Travis was a nice guy, but I could not stand math. I wouldn't say I was terrible with the subject it just wasn't my strong suit. I handled the basic problems, but when they involved numbers and letters, that's a whole other story. Now, English was my niche. I had a knack for writing and making up stories.

Rosa had a mind for math and loved it. She always had her hand up with the right answer, and liked to help others in the class. I was blessed to have her help me with my math homework. Almost every afternoon, we did our homework together. We became good study partners and helped each other's weaknesses. Rosa had a hard time writing essays and understanding key rules in English.

Tuesday, the following week, probably began for most folks as any ordinary work or school day. No one thought it would be the day that would change America forever. We all remember where we were on September 11, 2001. As usual, I woke to my alarm clock at a quarter to six. I climbed out of bed and pulled on my sweat suit for my morning karate workout. As I tied my shoes, Gramma startled me, thundering into my room like I was in trouble or something.

"There's been an accident!" Gramma said urgently. My first thoughts were Mom was hurt or possibly something happened to Rich. "A plane crashed into the World Trade Center!"

"Really? You're joking," I said.

"Just happened a few minutes ago," Gramma said.

I ran with her out of the room like it was a dream. Coming into the living room, I froze in my tracks, staring at the television screen. The news station showed a rerun of a plane hitting one of the World Trade Center's twin towers.

"For those of you just joining us," the news anchor said, "at 8:50 a.m. Eastern Standard Time, an airliner crashed in the North Tower of the World Trade Center in New York. As you can see, the plane hit roughly the 102nd floor. Oh No! I can't believe it! It can't be ...the South Tower has just been hit!"

Like out of a movie, a jumbo jet hit the building with a huge explosion. Everyone knew it couldn't have been an accident twice. Terrorists had attacked America on its own soil.

We were glued to the television as the two towers burned like smokestacks. Thirty minutes later, I had to get ready for school. Karate training had to wait until later. I showered quickly and grabbed a bowl of cereal while watching the news. As the South Tower collapsed, I was on my way to school. During homeroom the teacher had the broadcast running. Throughout the day, we also learned two other planes were hijacked. One hit the Pentagon and the other crashed in Pennsylvania—its destination unknown. They were saying maybe the White House.

I didn't truly understand what was going on then, but as I grew older and in high school, the events became clearer. I wrote the following poem and dedicated it to the innocent workers of the towers, the Pentagon, individuals on the passenger planes, the police, firefighters, and paramedics who risked their lives.

God Left His Mark ~ Dedicated to 9 / 11

That early September turned,
Into an unlikely tragedy.
Like two colossal chimneys,
The Twin Towers burned.

Smoke choked the New York skies,
And at times, it resembled angel forms.
I imagine them calming people's cries,
Throughout the chaotic terror storms.

Quickly NY Police and Firefighters came,
To desperate alarms from the Trade Center.
White and gray ash made it seem like winter,
But they aided in the rescue all the same.

During the morning on 9/11,
Destruction was not on God's mind,
When the smoke reached heaven,
For He is merciful toward His children.

God gives us choices everyday,
Some choose the crooked way,

Others a straighter path.

The buildings began to fall from the top,
Throwing debris, dust, and ash below,
Where people ran and cars sped away,
From the imploding, shrinking buildings.
It was ground zero,
Resembling nuclear fallout.

At first it seemed like an accident,
Then we knew it was a cowardly act.
Four airplanes were hijacked.
The Pentagon in flames,
One heroically diverted.

Tumbling, tumbling the towers went down.
Crumbling, crumbling soon they were gone.
Sometime later God's mark was found,
Three girders shaped like rugged crosses.

You may wonder after the 9/11 attacks why God didn't stop the tragedy from happening? How could He let a couple thousand innocent people perish? Why did He create evil and let it run wild? Why He let a dozen terrorists take over those planes? Couldn't He have stopped them? Why was there suffering? These were all hard questions to answer, but all I know was, "...God is love." ~1John 4:16, "...Love does not delight in evil but rejoices with the truth." ~1 Cor. 13:6 and "...For God is not a God of disorder but of peace." ~1 Cor. 14:33.

Mom told me there were two forces at work: good, which was God, and evil, which was an after effect of sin. Throughout the Bible, God used both good and evil people to fulfill His purposes. The God of Abraham, Isaac, and Jacob, doesn't need to explain Himself on why He does what He does. His ways were beyond our comprehension, but the Lord has His reasons and I trust Him and that was enough for me. It was summed up, "My thoughts are not your thoughts, neither are my ways your ways." ~Isaiah 55:8

Things moved reasonably well a month and half into the school year until one day, during gym class, this seventh grader started pushing me around when the teacher wasn't looking. I just ignored it and had nothing to do with him. His name was Keith and he was a wild kid. I saw him occasionally at the park with his skateboard and he was always getting into trouble with his friends. He cursed a lot too and liked to ditch class.

During lunch period I went to use the john. Keith and his friends were in a stall; where I saw six feet and heard laughing. I smelled smoke, but it wasn't cigarette fumes. I guessed they were getting high. For some reason, I just went about my business, not paying much attention.

"Keith, I think someone's out there," one of the skateboarders announced.

My first thought was to get out of there quickly, but was surprised when another of Keith's friends entered the bathroom. This guy was huge and blocked my escape. One of his paws grabbed my shoulder.

"Lookie what we have here," he said, as the others ran out of the stall. I tried to move away from his grip, but he was too strong. "Oh no you don't."

"I have to get back to class," I said, knowing they had it in for me.

I quickly thought of options. Keith and the other two would be slow in my reaction, but I couldn't do anything with the big guy.

"Hey, I know you," Keith said to me. "You're that new punk in my gym class, aren't you? Do you think you're gonna tell on us?"

"We don't like squealers," the big boy said, tightening his grip.

"I'm not saying anything," I said and really meant it.

"We know what happens with squealers, don't we Big Tom," Keith said laughing.

"We sure do," Big Tom said, with a booming voice.

"Ray, you're on lookout," Keith said. He turned to me, "It is Jay, right? If you tell on us, then we will be your worse nightmare."

"I promise I won't tell," I said.

"Good, but let's give you a taste of what could happen," Keith said, pushing me against the wall.

Big Tom slugged me in the ribs and said, "I could hurt you more than that."

I prayed, please God help me out of this. I readied myself for another blow from Big Tom.

"Principal Walters is coming!" Ray announced, hurrying back.

"It's your lucky day, Jay," Keith warned. "Watch yourself, I'll be watching—let's get out of here." He gave me one last shove and then they were gone.

I left before the principal checked the bathroom.

I told Billie and Rosa what had happened to me as we walked home. "Man, I wish I was there to help you," Billie said.

"What could you have done?" I asked. "I still would have been outnumbered, not to mention cornered by Big Tom."

"I could talk my way out of it," Billie said.

"What if you couldn't?" I asked. "Then you'd be right back where you started."

"We could have fought our way out," Billie suggested.

"Someone has to know," Rosa said.

"No they don't," I said. "It would just make it worse—Please don't tell anybody."

"We can tell them about our karate skills," Billie said.

"Remember what Sensei Lance said, not to tell everybody about our karate," I said.

"I was just joking," Billie said, smiling.

"That's not funny," Rosa said, slugging him in the shoulder.

"I think they will leave me alone after a while—get bored and pick on somebody else," I said, not believing it.

Every now and then Keith, or one of his friends, would shove me in the hall or trip me during gym.

I prayed about it many nights, always putting my trust in the Lord; I knew He would get me through the bathroom incident. I wasn't afraid of Keith and his bozo friends. After a while, they didn't bully me much any more. When I passed them in the hall, I avoided eye contact or them altogether. After that, Billie, Rosa, me, and our other friends decided not to go anywhere alone on or off campus. The rest of sixth grade came and went uneventfully.

Summer 2002

I turned twelve and the summer didn't start with the same passion as in camping and such. For the most part, Rosa and I were still the best of friends. I can't explain it, but there was a shift of sorts in our friendship. For one, at the end of the school year, Rosa started hanging out more with Zoey. They would go horseback riding and I occasionally joined them because I wanted to do things with Rosa.

Rosa graduated to an orange belt in karate and we spent a lot of time in the park training. Sometimes Billie joined in. We also focused on church camp and Vacation Bible School. It was a great feeling to see Rosa's faith growing in the Lord.

Our core group consisted of Rosa, Billie, Kaylee, Jordan, and De'von. There were three new additions including Zoey and Kaylee's twin friends Lana and Lynn. (We pretty much stuck together through high school.)

Zoey and the twins were Rosa and Kaylee's girlfriend group. They followed in a line everywhere they went. You wouldn't see one without the other. Zoey and Kaylee got to Rosa.

One day, before seventh grade, I thought I would hang out with Rosa like we always did. That's when I discovered the girls really got to Rosa. I knocked on her bedroom door and heard a choir of voices say come in. I walked in and found Rosa, Zoey, and Kaylee hanging out. They had their makeup strung out all over with teen magazines wide open. I felt like I was in the twilight zone. Rosa's walls were stripped of baseball posters and replaced with boy group bands. The radio played their songs.

Over the next few weeks, Rosa's sports t-shirts evolved to a softer look. Where was her baseball cap? The teddy bear wore it, sitting high on the shelf. Once faded worn jeans and overalls—now designer jeans, and sometimes skirts and dresses were now found in her closet.

Chapter Ten

September 2002-Spring 2003

THE SCHOOLWORK began to get harder in the seventh grade, but I liked the challenge. Again, I just sat back and observed my classmates' flirtatious games. It was very distracting and I didn't care to join in on the silliness. Though, I was surprised to see Rosa participate.

In the springtime, as red peonies bloomed along driveways, we all heard about the Sadie Hawkins Dance, where the girls ask the boys. The year before I heard about it, but no one I knew went. This time it was a whole different story. Billie loved the idea, and when Amber asked him to the dance, he didn't hesitate to answer, "Yes"—just glad it wasn't me. I dreaded the week before the dance. Every time a girl passed me, I held my breath.

School let out that Friday and no girl approached me. Well, they would have to catch me first because I sprinted out the door, not even caring about mingling in the hall or at my locker. *I'm in the clear! I'm in the clear!* I thought with the junior high getting smaller behind me. A couple blocks away, I heard someone yell my name. I stopped, looked behind me, and saw Kaylee running toward me.

"Wait up, Jay," she said. I thought, *oh no!* There could be only one reason for this encounter.

"Hi Kaylee, what's up?" I asked, regretting her answer.

"I was wondering," she began and I thought, *here it comes*. She had high hopes in her eyes when she continued. "I was wondering—if you would go to the Sadie Hawkins dance with me?"

Oh, my head started to spin. Time froze. I closed my eyes, hoping she wouldn't be there when I opened them. But sure enough, Kaylee was there, fluttering her eyelids. My hands were already sweating and my heart was about to jump out of my chest.

"So Jay, what do you think?" she asked. I made her nervous I could tell. "Sorry if you don't want to go. I'll..."

"Sure I will," I heard myself say. I was always nice, getting myself into these awkward situations.

Her eyes brightened, "Really! Not just saying that?"

"Ya, I will go to the dance with you," I said.

Her face lit up like it was her birthday. "Cool!" she exclaimed and kissed me on the cheek—yikes—and she ran off.

Sometime later, after I crossed Crawford Street, a horrible doubt hit my stomach. I suddenly realized Kaylee asked me to that dance and I already replied with, "Yes!"—what was I thinking? For a moment, I forgot Billie was her brother. The other thing, Kaylee was a sixth grader and I was in the seventh. Oh, what will my classmates think? I took these doubts all the way home. Throwing my backpack on the couch and plopping down next to it, Mom knew something was troubling me.

"Did you have a bad day at school?" she asked.

"Sort of," I answered, wanting to avoid the conversation all together.

"Do you want to talk about it?"

"No—I guess. It's *really* no big deal."

"What's that frown for?"

"Oh, someone asked me to that dumb Sadie Hawkins Dance!"

"What's wrong with that?"

"It'll be boring and stupid," I said. "I don't know how to dance and don't want to learn."

"How do you know you wouldn't enjoy it?"

"I just do," I replied.

"Who asked you and what was your answer?"

"Kaylee," I said, falling against the couch. "I told her I would—I feel like such a dork."

"Why do you say that?"

"Because she is a sixth grader…" I said.

"There is nothing wrong with Kaylee being one year younger than you," she commented.

"My friends will think I am weird."

"It's not what your friends think, it's what *you* think. Would you run out in the middle of the highway if they did?"

"No, I guess I wouldn't," I said. "I will pretend I'm sick."

"That's lying," Mom said. "Look son, if you don't want to go, no one is pointing a gun to your head. Just call Kaylee up and tell her you have changed your mind—"

"Yeah, you're right. It's a free country and I can change my mind," I said, jumping to the phone.

"But remember, it's not all about you," she said, as I picked up the receiver. "You have a verbal agreement with Kaylee, or don't you think you do?"

"I guess," I said, putting the phone back down.

"Son, you know what's right and wrong, but you have to look at yourself in the mirror every day."

"Yes ma'am," I said.

"Would you back out of a contract knowing that you are not really sick?"

"No ma'am," I said, now standing tall. "I guess, I'm going—I'm not going to like it, but I'll be going anyway."

I felt a little better after talking with Mom, but she was right, I had to admit. I would rather be doing something else besides going to that silly dance. When I went to bed, I prayed for God's guidance.

Following a good night's sleep, I woke up with a whole new attitude. I remembered the first time I hurt Kaylee's feelings and I sure didn't want to go down that road again. Guilt was a heavy thing to bear. No reason for me to be selfish. If I were in Kaylee's shoes, I would truly be disappointed. Who knows what I would have to give her to apologize.

"Morning Mom, morning Gramma," I said, springing into the kitchen.

"Aren't you extra chipper today," Gramma remarked.

"Morning son, looks like you had a good night," Mom said.

"I did," I said, giving her a hug, then took a bowl out of the cupboard. "I decided that the dance wouldn't be too bad after all. You're right Mom. I would feel guilty if I didn't go."

"You will have a good time," Mom said. "Kaylee is a cute girl."

"Oh, Mom!"

Rich joined us for dinner and agreed he would drive Kaylee and me up to the junior high. In the Sadie Hawkins Dance tradition you don't dress up, just wear your every day clothes. Usually kids find farmer or hillbilly attire. I wore a plaid shirt, faded jeans, and suspenders. Mom cornered me before I headed to Rich's car. She picked at my shirt and made sure I brushed my teeth. I decided to take my camera to the dance in case I got bored. People were a good subject.

"My son's first dance," Mom said, straightening my collar.

"Gee, Mom, it's no big deal."

"It means you are growing up."

"Just a silly dance," I said. She left the room for a moment and came back with a couple flowers in her hand.

"Here, you could give these to Kaylee," she suggested. I reluctantly took them.

Rich drove me down the street to Kaylee's house. She flew out of her house before we came to a stop. She wore overalls and a purple shirt.

"Hi Jay," she said, after climbing in.

"Hey Kaylee," I said, handing her the flowers. "These are for you, I guess."

"Oh, Jay, thank you!" Kaylee said, placing the daisies in her hair.

Not long and we pulled into the school parking lot. Kaylee wanted me to take her picture when we got out. Rich also thought it was a good idea to take our picture before we all walked inside to the auditorium. There were more than a dozen kids already there. I saw Billie and a couple of the guys. Kaylee saw Rosa and the twins. She dragged me over there to greet them. Rich left us and visited with the other chaperones by the wall, near the entrance. I felt uncomfortable and made an excuse to go and talk with Billie.

"So, Kaylee conned you into this?" Billie asked with a chuckle. "Out of all the girls in the school, you get stuck with her—why didn't you say no?"

"Like you said, she conned me," I agreed.

"I think she does it to annoy me," Billie said.

"So I guess, Amber asked you?" I wondered.

"Yes, I am the luckiest guy in school to have the prettiest girl ask me," Billie bragged.

Some awful rap music hit my ears and the dance began. The first thing I noticed was a division between the girls and the guys. Some of the guys sweated nervously, not wanting to approach the idea of having to dance with a girl. The girls giggled and probably talked about us. After a while, the eighth graders who were used to this concept ventured onto the dance floor. I thought, *oh to heck with it, I am not going to stress about it.* I just stepped out of my comfort zone and walked over to Kaylee.

"Would you like to dance?" I asked.

"Sure," Kaylee answered, while blushing.

The dance was not the drag I thought it would be. I had somewhat of a good time. I probably was not the best dancer, but at least I tried, even sneaking in a few karate moves. I'd admit, I sort of enjoyed Kaylee's company. No strings attached, just because I danced with a girl doesn't make her my girlfriend.

Chapter Eleven

Summer 2003

NOTHING SIGNIFICANT to note really happened the rest of seventh grade. I became a teenager, the big "one-three" that summer and felt my childhood days slipping before me, more or less.

One July morning, Rosa and I planned on studying the Bible and just hanging out. So after karate workout and some chores, I walked across the street. Manny was working underneath the truck, his boots sticking out. I saw Waldo wag his tail and I petted him.

"How are you doing, old boy?" I asked the dog.

Waldo was up there in dog years—*seventy*, I thought. He had a few gray hairs on his muzzle and throughout his coat. Manny heard me talking to the dog and he scooted out from underneath the pickup.

"Hola Jay," Manny greeted, wiping the grease off his hands with a rag. "Just finishing up here. Rosa's in her room."

I walked in and was about to knock on her door when I heard a soft voice singing. I was drawn to it like a baby listening to a lullaby. Recognizing the amazingly graceful hymn, I found myself daydreaming. The girl's voice trailed off into silence and I was awakened.

"Anybody there?" Rosa asked from beyond the door. "I guess not."

Then she began singing the song from the beginning. That's when I realized Rosa had been singing all along. I heard her sing before, but I didn't remember her voice being so clear and angelic. It was so beautiful as if I could hear God's voice synthesized through her vocal cords. I couldn't believe she had such a lovely voice. Instantly, a strange eagerness overwhelmed me, so wanting to see those sweet, beautiful words come off her lips. I knocked.

"Come in," she said.

I walked in quietly with Rosa singing inside my head. My feet moved in rhythm to her song. Rosa was at her desk, her back to me, writing in a diary, I guessed. Usually, I saw it on her nightstand. I sat down on the edge of her bed where we used to look at our baseball cards and talk about the next camping trip. I played with a fuzzy pink rabbit.

"Almost done, let me finish this sentence," she paused for a moment, drumming her pen against the page. Scribbling something down, she said, "There!"

"Were you singing?" I asked, but it wasn't what I was going to say.

"Uhh," she said, blushing. "What did you hear?"

"That hymn you were singing," I said.

"Oh that—I didn't know anyone was listening."

"Can you sing for me?" I asked. "You were very good."

She blushed again and bashfully turned away. "Nah, you are just saying that."

"No, I'm not," I said.

"Are you serious?"

"Honestly, Rosa, you have a great singing voice," I heard myself say and felt my face warm.

"Oh, you are too kind," she said. "It's just something I do."

"Please sing for me—please!"

"Oh, I couldn't."

"Why not?"

"I'll be embarrassed. I don't think I could in front of you."

"Please, just one little song, then I will leave you alone."

"I don't know."

"Okay then, listen to me sing," I said, singing the first two verses.

"Alright, stop," she said, holding her hand up. "Here goes."

She sang it just the way I remembered when I was behind the door. I intently listened to the sweet melody, her face showing emotions of the song. She finished and I applauded. Instantly, she changed the subject, but in the back of my mind I still heard her voice.

"What were we going to study?" Rosa asked.

I couldn't concentrate on what she said. I watched her turn and open her Bible. Her every movement suddenly intrigued me; I caught myself staring too much, she was *so* pretty. I twiddled my thumbs and looked at the closed door—I began to feel claustrophobic—she sat beside me on the bed—aaah. I felt like running, but I was paralyzed by her closeness.

"Weren't we in James chapter two?" she asked, flipping to it and that's when I realized I didn't pick up my Bible.

I was in a hurry and had clumsy hands, reaching for my Bible. I opened it upside down and quickly turned it around before she looked at me. The bed creaked and dipped as she lay on her stomach, one elbow resting.

"Oh yeah, here it is," she said, running her finger down the page. I studied her hands and saw her feet kick. "Jay, are you with me?"

I was startled. "Yes," I hesitated, finding the place. "Yeah, chapter two, where it talks about faith and good works."

"I'll read," Rosa said. "'What doth it profit, my brethren, though a man say he hath faith, and have not works? Can faith save him?'"

She was too close to me. I couldn't breathe, my hands were sweating. I scooted away slightly and tried to concentrate on the subject. I felt like I was dying and had to get up quickly.

"Where are you going?" she asked.

I had to think of something fast. I looked at her desk. "I need to borrow a pen."

"There's one in your hand silly," Rosa said, giggling.

"Oh, so there is," I said, feeling like such a dork. "Actually, I was looking for a highlighter."

"There's one in the desk drawer," she said.

I rummaged in the drawer and found one, dropping it. Juggling and stumbling over my feet, I looked over at Rosa sitting on the bed and smiled. She amusingly returned with one of her own.

"That's one slippery pen," I said.

I turned around and knocked stuff off her desk. I tried to pick up the papers and the things that dropped with the Bible in my hands. I got down on my knees and picked up the things and set them on her desk. I stumbled around and sat on the desk chair.

"Jay, is there something wrong?"

"I have to use the rest room," I replied, hurrying out without a second thought.

Feeling sick to my stomach, I closed the bathroom door behind me. I splashed water on my face, then looking into the mirror. *What's wrong with you Jay?* I thought. It was the strangest feeling I had. I wanted to escape, but at the same time, staying seemed more satisfying. I prayed, please Lord help me understand these feelings. *Just play it cool.* Taking a deep breath, I met Rosa in the hall. She scared me.

"Aaahhh," I began, but finished, "I feel better."

"I'm thirsty, do you want something?" she asked.

"Sounds good to me," I said, following her like a puppy dog.

"Why don't we study in the kitchen?" Rosa suggested, handing me a bottle of water.

I felt more comfortable after talking with the Lord. I concentrated better on the Bible study, but still felt a little antsy. An hour or so later, I closed the Sanchez's door with a gratifying relief. *What a dream, my Spanish dream!*

Rosa was on my mind the rest of the day. Later, before bed, I analyzed my feelings. *What next…*I had a strange dream that night and Rosa was in it. She sang in front of the whole church and wasn't embarrassed.

Waking up, Rosa was still on my mind. I couldn't shake the thought of her pretty face, brown eyes, and how she smiled at me. Then I thought she probably thought I was a dork.

The morning went slow. I was lost in my thoughts, reading a novel beneath the arbor.

"Thought I'd find you here," Rosa said, scaring the crap out of me. "I brought your Bible back. You left it at my house."

"Thanks," I said, but thought *how's my girl today?*

"Whatcha reading?"

"Poetry. It's my mom's," I said, handing the book to her.

"This is cool," she started reading. "God created love for us all."

"Here's my favorite," I said, reading it to her.

"I didn't know you were interested in poetry," Rosa said.

"I like it."

"Hey Jay," Rosa began. "Kaylee, Zoey, me, and the twins are putting together a poetry group at the park. Do you want to join?"

"Certainly, I'd love that."

"I'm headed that way right now if you want to walk with me," she offered.

"Sure, but let me get my camera," I said.

Of course I want to walk with you, Rosa, I thought to myself as we walked side-by-side down the street. We talked all the way to the park like we used to and I was very comfortable with her. My feeling toward Rosa was still there like yesterday.

We crossed through the park, passed the gazebo, and saw Kaylee with the others. They were gathered under a tall, shaded pine tree and I imagined giggly girl gab.

"Hey everybody," Rosa said. "Jay has joined our group."

"Welcome Jay," Zoey and the twins said.

"Hi Jay," Kaylee said, her eyes bright. "You can sit by me."

I agreed without saying anything. I sat down and caught Kaylee watching my every movement. She smiled bashfully and blushed.

"What do we do now?" I asked.

"Duh, it's a poetry group," Zoey said.

"Jay, why don't you share your book," Rosa suggested.

"May I listen first—I've never read in front of a group," I said.

"Sounds fair," Rosa said.

"Kaylee, why don't you read that poem you were writing the other day?" asked one of the twins.

"Alright, but it's not finished," Kaylee replied. "Here goes..."

I know God is there with me.
As I sit under a tree,
He blesses me everyday,
With birds that sing and play

"That's all," Kaylee said.

"That was good," I said. "Do you all write?"

"Whenever we get a chance," Rosa said.

<u>Jay's Favorite Things</u>

God's Salvation
The whistle and rumble of the train
Waking up the morning camping
Smelling coffee and bacon
The crisp sound of a karate move

<u>Kaylee's Favorite Things</u>

A friend's gentle voice
God's Holy Grace
Song we sing in church
Raindrops hitting the pane

The feeling of my cats purring
The sun making snow glitter
And the peach sunset in winter
And the gift of white daisies

<u>Rosa's Favorite Things</u>

The quilt my grandma made me
Smelling the mint in the breeze
When Waldo greets me after school
Gives me happiness
Dad and I laughing together
A surprise visit from my mom
Out of nowhere the falling of a bird's feather
And knowing God is there

We had our little poetry group every weekend throughout the summer and into the fall. Rosa was the leader of the group and had assignments for all of us. Sometimes she would have us find a poem we liked and share it. She also had this poetry game called poetry round robin where someone begins a poem and passes onto the next person. Other times we would write our own poetry and recite it in front of the group.

It was kind of weird being the only guy in the group. Some may have thought I was a softy writing poetry with a bunch of girls. Once I stepped into high school, guys would perhaps envy me for spending time with a group of pretty girls.

My works of prose, I would say, wasn't as good in the beginning as some of the girls. I used to think poetry was boring and didn't care for the sappy part. Of course now with Rosa…Gramma made me read the classic poets. I wrote a few when I was homeschooled and some in the fifth grade.

The twins, Zoey, and some of the others' poetry were pretty close in maturity; I thought they were better than most. Rosa's poetry was wonderful, but with my feelings for her she could be writing junk and I wouldn't care. Now, Kaylee's poetry was incredible. Rosa was a close first next to Kaylee. Anyway, Kaylee had a special gift, and I could listen to her writing for hours because she wrote mainly about God and Faith. Her descriptions were vibrant and heartfelt. There were rainbows, angels, and cotton candy clouds shining from her mind. Kaylee had been writing since the fourth grade and used to give me cute little poems for my birthday. I thought it was silly, not to mention weird.

Kaylee inspired my writing and I noticed it improved while I was in the group. Actually, they all gave me ideas and I picked up on their different styles. I thought of Rosa and Kaylee in a whole new light—especially Rosa. Not only could she sing, but she could write poetry too. Rosa was on my mind all week and I wanted to hang out with her every chance.

Fall 2003

The summer came to a close faster than I really wanted it. I entered my last year in junior high with my-crush-on-Rosa-river still flowing in my veins. I so wanted to tell her my true feelings, but was unsure. There was something special I felt for her, but I didn't know what it meant. We were very good friends and any thoughts of going beyond that scared me. At times, I daydreamed about her and thought about asking her out on a date, but I didn't know where to begin. What would happen with our friendship if we began dating? *Was it too early for this—then there's Manny!* Sure I enjoyed the company of girls, was comfortable conversing with them at school, during our poetry group, and at other activities, yet a romantic venture scared me. I kept all my feelings to myself regarding Rosa. Since I didn't know what to do about her, I decided to concentrate on my schoolwork and especially on the Lord. At first my strategy worked, but it wasn't long before I was starting the maze all over again. *Ugh! Maybe I'll just tell her my true feelings tomorrow*, I thought one night.

I jumped into a routine with my studies. I hung out with the girls from the poetry group during lunch and sometimes after school. Rosa and I were back doing homework together at her house. I calmed down a little since the day she sang to me. Kaylee joined our little study group and after a while the three of us became a trio.

Chapter Twelve

Summer/Fall 2003 and Summer 2004 Church Report

ONE EVENING in July 2003, our church had a deacon ordination for Terry Galley* Sr., Rick Clair*, and Ed Fleet*. The new deacons each gave their testimonies. Following this, the current deacons read from the Bible 1Tim. 3:10-13 explaining the jobs of the deacons, mainly how to lead by a good example. Then the congregation repeated. Harvey stepped down as Emeritus meaning he retained the title deacon while retired. Also replaced were Lon Inder* who retired and Andy who moved. Tom was an inactive deacon who filled in at times. [*Names changed]

October 2003 (Part of a letter from Pastor Dan Cheak)

My Wonderful Church Family,

About March 1, 2000, I began a pulpit ministry here that has been a pure joy and, I choose to believe, productive. God has been good to us…very good.

When I came aboard, I asked God for four years. I felt that what I wanted to see accomplished would take that much time. March 1, 2004, will be four years…

I'm giving you five months advance notice because I would like for you to elect your search committee and begin the search for a new pastor. The work of a search committee is hard enough, but, generally, the church is without a pastor when the search begins, and oftentimes the congregation gets a little anxious and misunderstandings come which are counter-productive.

I do hope and pray that God will lead you to a pastor who will, first of all, love you, and second, let you love him…

Arlene has been a great help to me. She is a very good secretary and has worked hard at understanding and helping me…

Glenn M. has been both the most committed person and close friend I have ever served with. The church is extremely fortunate to have him and Carolyn…

Lovingly, Pastor Danny

As soon as it was known Pastor Danny would retire, a search committee was assembled. Diana Simple*, Kay Summerlin, Jeff Gull*, Laten, Terry Galley* were elected along with two alternatives Desiree Clair*, and Bob Lark*. Thank you all who worked so diligently finding us a pastor.

The first thing the committee did was pray and then discussed what kind of pastor the church needed. They also passed out a questionnaire to get the congregation's input of what qualities in a pastor were most important. With all that in mind, the committee sent out advertisements for the hiring of a full-time pastor. Dozens of résumés soon poured in. Then once a week, the committee read, discussed, reviewed, and prayed about each prospect.

Every first Sunday, Diana Simple* reported on the pastor search. This went on throughout the summer. Soon the committee narrowed the field down to ten potential pastors, and then it was five and three. Finally, it was down to one and we were asked to pray for him, but it just didn't work out with him.

We had many guests, pastors, and a couple of guys from our congregation fill-in until we found our new pastor. Also, in September 2004, a man named Richard Young came to volunteer as our choir director. Richard had done revivals in the area for the last dozen years or more. At his last revival, Diana Simple* approached him about the position. Soon he became our music director. So that was the news from our church during summer of 2003 to summer 2004.

Spring 2004

ONE DAY, the middle of March, Rosa surprised Kaylee and me while we were doing our homework. Rosa set her pen down, looked up with wide-eyes, and sang for us. For the second time, I was impressed and so was Kaylee being her first. Several times before I tried to get her to sing, but she was too embarrassed. As Rosa finished her song, I wondered what I would say. I couldn't think of anything in a hurry so I just sat there.

"I didn't know you could sing," Kaylee said.

---

* Name changed

"Yeah, I didn't realize it either," Rosa said, turning to me—*Oh, oh,* I thought, my face warming and my hands sweating—"Until now, Jay was the only one who knew."

"I wish I could sing that well," Kaylee said.

I sure didn't want to give any signs of my feelings toward Rosa. They went onto another subject about makeup or something; I thought I was in the clear until Kaylee popped a question to me.

"Doesn't Rosa's hair look cool just the way it is?" Kaylee asked. "Hey Jay, don't you think her hair looks pretty the way it is?"

"Ahh—I don't know," I said, hoping I could get out of this.

"You must have some opinion," Kaylee said.

"I guess," I said.

"So, what do you think?" Kaylee asked.

"Sure," I said, my mind spinning while trying not to look at Rosa, but gave in.

"Sure…what?" Kaylee asked.

"Well, I like it the way it is," I hesitated.

"So Jay, do you think I'm pretty?" Rosa asked. I could have died right there. "How about Kaylee, don't you think she's pretty too?" Both girls just smiled and giggled.

"What can I say, yes you both are," I said, feeling bold.

"Oh, isn't that sweet," Kaylee said.

"Okay, you really want to know my opinion, you're the two prettiest gals in school," I said, looking at Kaylee first and then winking at Rosa, holding the stare a bit longer.

The next Sunday, Kaylee, Rosa, and I sat in the back pews during the service. Kaylee and I anticipated the morning's selected hymns. Our ears burned to hear Rosa sing. Milt announced the first hymn. We turned to the page and the piano began to play. Then Rosa sang the lyrics, making it a song. Her voice, sweet as honey, penetrated my ears. I was disappointed when the hymn ended, but knew another would follow. Later on Milt sang in the "*Special Music*" part of the service. I pictured Rosa singing up there with her voice magnified—what a sight with feelings that would be. Kaylee startled my daydreaming.

"Rosa, you should sing the *Special Music*," Kaylee said. "I bet you would be great."

Smiling, Rosa's face turned red, combing her hand through her shiny dark hair. "Oh no, I couldn't," she said bashfully. "I would be embarrassed in front of all these people."

"Please, just one little song?" Kaylee begged. "Me and Jay will sit in front, won't we Jay?"

"Yeah, we'll be there," I said.

"You guys are too kind *but,*" Rosa said, shaking her shoulders and fluffing her hair. "I might fall on my face."

"How do you know?" Kaylee asked.

"I just do," Rosa said.

"I have faith in you that you will do great," Kaylee said.

"Me too," I said.

"Oh, I don't know," Rosa said.

"At least think about it," I said, as the substitute pastor moved up to the podium for his sermon.

It was different without Pastor Danny there at church during *Pastor's Pals* and preaching from the pulpit. Also, there was a void without Sammy, Danny's wife. By this time, Jeff Gull* began doing *Pastor's Pals.* Jeff was my Sunday school teacher and also taught the teens.

The invitation came and the service ended with "Sweet, Sweet, Spirit" as we all held hands across the aisles. A gentleman behind us held my hand then surprised us when he approached us.

"I overheard you kids talking," he said. "And I agree, Rosa sings real well. I know a great voice when I hear it—of course it's her decision to go up there or not."

"Yeah Rosa, it's your choice," Kaylee said.

"I don't know about this, but I'm not making any promises—I'll think about it," Rosa said.

Sometime during April, while we worked on our homework Rosa brought up the subject. It caught me like the wind does a sail.

"I thought more about singing in front of the church," Rosa announced.

"That's great!" I said, hugging her without thinking. I suddenly realized my arm was around her and found her comforting.

"Now, I didn't say I was going to do it," Rosa said, pulling away from me.

"You know you're going to do it or you wouldn't have brought it up," Kaylee said. "What song are you going to sing?"

"You guys really think I'm that good?" Rosa asked.

"More than good—amazing," I said.

"We have faith in you," Kaylee said.

"Okay, I'll do it," Rosa said finally with a sigh. "You better be right or else—just kidding."

We approached Richard, the music director, after the next service about Rosa singing in front of the church. He thought it was a wonderful idea and a couple days later Rosa knew she would be singing. Rosa was scheduled to sing the second Sunday in May. Kaylee and I watched Rosa practice the song she chose. Diana Simple* helped Rosa a few times with her singing. At first Rosa was uncomfortable when she sang in front of Diana. Her voice was off key because I think she tried too hard. After Diana coached her for a few days, Rosa gained confidence.

The Saturday, before Rosa sang at the church, she gave a little concert at her house in front of her dad, Gramma, Mom, Rich, Kaylee, and me. The next day we all sat in the second pew from the front. I saw Rosa and her dad enter from the lobby briefly as they worked their way through some traffic; I could only make out the top of Manny's head.

It was about the forth time I saw Manny at church. The first time was when Gramma invited him; the second at Rosa's baptismal, and one during the Easter Service. Perhaps Rosa's singing was not the only reason for her dad to be here. As far as I knew, Manny hadn't given himself to the Lord. God does work in mysterious ways and maybe He was working through Rosa to inspire Manny.

My thoughts became distracted when Rosa walked into view. She was beautiful and the light yellow dress made her shine like the fresh morning sun. I was in a giddy dream for a long moment—then I woke up remembering I was in church. Embarrassed by my behavior, I looked away trying to get hold of myself so I found my church menu in my Bible.

I briefly scanned the menu and came halfway down the page: "*Special Music by Rosa Sanchez*." Seeing her name put a smile on

---

* Name changed

my face. I knew she was near me, my heart sped up and I couldn't help but look in her direction. Rosa stood there smiling down at me, her brown eyes sparkling under the lights. It was only a few seconds that I stared into her face, but it felt much longer. Next thing I knew, the seat dipped and she was sitting next to me. Without realizing it, I held her hand—had to say something quickly, but my voice crackled and sounded deep.

"Don't worry you will do well," I said, clearing my throat.

"I hope so," Rosa said nervously.

Manny held her shoulders. "Jay's right, you will do fine sweetie," he said. "I'm very proud of you."

"We're with you Rosa," Kaylee said across me. Then she whispered to me, "I feel something special today—the Lord working."

"That's what I was thinking," I said.

For me, the first part of the service was covered in a low cloud. I didn't remember listening to the announcements or the hymns, but was in a nice little world of Rosa. *Jay stop it*, I thought to myself after a few moments. *Concentrate on the Lord's Word.*

Lon stepped up to the podium and read the scripture reading. He then led us in prayer. I prayed for Rosa who would be singing right after. Suddenly, I realized Rosa was holding my hand—*Oh my*—didn't know how to react. From the other side Kaylee held the other hand and made it better.

"Amen," Lon said and everyone followed. He stepped down and walked to the back of the room.

"Our *Special Music* today will be sung by Rosa Sanchez," Milt announced.

Rosa reluctantly stood and with a little encouragement from her dad, she went up front. She had the song on a piece of paper in her hand as she entered the aisle. Milt waited in front of the altar with a wireless microphone, which he handed Rosa. She turned around toward the whole church and looked startled. I felt her nervousness and prayed to God for her comfort and strength. She had an unsure smile when she met her dad's eyes, then mine, in which case I gave her a comforting nod. She turned to Dema at the piano behind her to the right and there was a signal between the two that they were ready.

Rosa timed the piano and began to sing. Her voice wasn't clear as she struggled over her first line. I felt bad for her and knew her heart jumped to her feet. Redness spread across her face and she was choked up with fear. *Come on Rosa you know you can do it.* For a moment it looked like she was going to quit and run out of the room, but she took a deep breath.

"May I start over?" Rosa asked, with uncertainty in her voice.

Dema started from the beginning and Rosa slightly moved side-to-side, getting insinc with the music. She looked at the piece of paper once more and brought the microphone to her mouth. Like before during practice, her voice was magnified through the speakers. This time Rosa sang different, as though something in her inspired the deeper emotions of the song. I knew God was there orchestrating her. She approached the part of the lyrics where she had trouble, her main concern. I mouthed the words singing along with her, helping her through it. *Here it comes!* She pulled it off, I could now breathe again. Rosa's voice was strong and she hit the high notes with ease. She sounded like an angel gliding on the wind from Heaven. Listening, I forgot to breathe and almost fell out of my seat. Her beautiful voice matched her beautiful face and I wanted the memory to stay in my mind forever. Of course, all good things must come to a close. At that moment, when Rosa finished, I knew I was really in love with her. Everyone applauded and she had a big bright smile that made me feel warm and proud.

Coming back to our pew, Rosa's dad gave her a hug and told her how wonderful she did. I didn't have time to say anything as the guest speaker began his sermon. I wondered what I would say to Rosa afterwards. I had visions of just the right words to say to her. Unexpectedly, I felt scared and unsure about Rosa. The newness of my feeling never sunk in until that day when her sweet song tenderly struck my ears.

The morning service came to its completeness. Gramma, Mom, and Rich congratulated Rosa while Kaylee and I waited for our turn. I realized the time wasn't right to express my true feelings and I was kinda relieved. Rapidly, my heart was beating out of my chest. I hoped no one else noticed my excitement. Rosa approached Kaylee who said, "I knew you could do it—the best that you've ever done."

"Rosa, that was awesome," I said, as we cleared out of the church.

Rosa surprised me as she thanked Kaylee with a hug and a kiss on the cheek. I was frozen with delight, melting, not knowing what to do if she did the same to me.

"I'm so glad you guys talked me into singing," Rosa said, giving me just a little hug, then stepped back from the embrace like it was nothing but friendly. "What good friends I have."

Now, the next moment I thought I would die and jump out of my shoes with excitement. I don't know what Rosa had in mind, but she kissed me right on the lips and then turned quickly to other members of the church.

"You may sing for us anytime," the members said.

"Great job Rosa," Diana said.

I escaped when this was going on, finding sanctuary at Gramma's car, wondering about the kiss. Perhaps she was just overwhelmed with her performance.

Chapter Thirteen

Summer 2004

JUNE CAME around and our eighth grade junior high days faded away. Rosa, Billie, and I all turned fourteen; Kaylee was a year behind us. I was back to my summer activities—poetry club, fishing with Rich, and hanging out with Rosa and Kaylee. We didn't see much of Billie during the previous school year. He was out playing eighth grade football and also joined a junior baseball league. Oh yeah, and we can't forget Billie's time with Amber, his "girlfriend."

Once school let out, I thought of Rosa every day for the first three weeks. One night I had enough and decided to tell her my true feelings. I would have gone crazy if I never did. Doubts streamed in my mind. Playing with my pillow, I pushed my face into it wondering if I would fall smack on my nose in front of Rosa. What would everyone think? I fell asleep feeling lost and woke up feeling the same. I decided to pray to the Lord. I always looked for His comfort. *Dear God, I don't know what to do about Rosa. Whatever Your will is, I will understand. Please guide me as I put my trust in You.*

The prayer made me feel much better and I went onto my usual morning routine the next day. For some reason, I wasn't thinking much about Rosa. I was too busy with my karate training and Bible study. The noon hour came quickly as I rested inside the gazebo. There were signs the weather would be hot, but a blessed cool breeze swept through the trees behind me. I was so in-tuned with God's creation that I could feel the Holy Spirit working in me. I prayed to God again; if it was His will for me to approach Rosa with my feelings, He would make it happen. I knew He had a reason for Rosa, so I left it up to Him.

Finishing with the meditation session, I sensed I was no longer alone in the backyard. I opened my eyes and had to re-orientate myself to the surroundings. The angle of the sun entered the gazebo, so I had to shield my eyes while trying to focus on who was approaching me.

When my vision cleared, I saw Waldo, Rosa's golden retriever wandering toward me. The dog was all alone as I kneeled down to pet him.

"Where's your master, Waldo?" I asked. He whined and wagged his tail. "I should walk you home I guess, hmm, where are you going—did you bury your bone somewhere?"

Without warning, someone from behind covered my eyes. "Guess who?" a girl's voice asked.

"Gramma?" I guessed.

"No," she said.

"Mom?"

"Guess again."

"Billie," I teased, knowing who it was.

"Does this sound like Billie, silly?"

"I guess it couldn't be because he wouldn't be able to sneak up on me," I answered.

"Then, who is it?"

"It could only be Rosa," I finally answered, removing her hands and taking a step away from the gazebo.

"I must be losing my touch," Rosa said, giggling. "Only three guesses."

"Actually, I knew right away it was you," I said, taking a step closer to her.

"How did you know?"

"Well, I couldn't forget your voice," I said.

"Whom were you dreaming about?"

"How do you know I was dreaming about anybody?"

"Just wondered," Rosa said.

"So, what do you want to do?"

"Oh, I don't know, talk," Rosa said, slightly hesitant.

"Sure, what do you want to talk about?" I asked, sitting on the bench inside the gazebo.

"I don't know, stuff," she replied.

"How's your dad?"

"He's fine," she replied, sitting down. "Actually Jay, uumm, I have wanted to know something—maybe you don't remember—too silly for me to say. Never mind."

"You can talk to me," I said. "What's up?"

"Okay, where to start," she began. "You remember what happened after I sang at church?"

"Sure," I said.

"Do you remember me kissing you?"

"I wondered about that," I said.

"You probably thought I was weird," Rosa said, hiding her face in her hands.

"No, it wasn't weird," I said. "Actually, I liked it."

"Really!" she chirped with wide eyes.

Hesitating, I began, searching for something to say. "I couldn't stop thinking about it—Whoops. I mean about you—what am I saying?"

"You have a crush on me!" Rosa giggled.

"Me and my big mouth," I said, looking away. "Uh-huh."

"I wondered if you felt the same way about me," she said.

"That's why I have been acting weird around you," I said. "What? What do you mean?"

"Well," Rosa said, hesitating. "I feel the same way. I don't know what it is, but I think about you all the time. Jay, where are you going?"

I was halfway to my house. My mind was racing and I felt like running. "I thought I heard my Gramma calling me."

"I didn't hear anybody," Rosa said, stepping to one side of me. When she did that, I backed away. "Jay, are you scared of me?"

"I don't know," I replied.

"Hey, you know me, Jay," she said. "What are you scared of?"

"Nothing!" I exclaimed, finally looking at her. "I just don't know how to act around you now."

"Just be you," she said. "Like you have always acted—friendly, like the person I know."

"Okay, now what?"

"I don't know… we can walk to the park."

"Okay," I said. "Cool, let's go."

Halfway there Rosa said, "Jay, you're awful quiet, don't you want to talk to me?"

"Huh?" I said, wondering, *how did I get into this?* "Sure… okay… uh. You start."

"Who would have thought, you and me," she said.

"I still can't believe it myself—kinda like a dream," I said, feeling more comfortable.

"I know what you mean," Rosa said, as we entered Mix Park.

We didn't know what to do, so we just walked and held hands. We joked a bit, went swinging, and talked about our first day in high school. For a while we lounged in the grass figuring out our new feelings. Mainly, we stared at each other smiling and giggling. The more I looked into Rosa's face—well, the prettier she became. She asked me something I was thinking.

"Jay, do you want to kiss me?"

"Of course," I said, with butterflies dancing in my stomach. I scooted closer, unsure of what I was about to do. I came in too fast and bonked her on the forehead. We both cried out with laughter and fell backwards. I felt terrible. "You okay? Sorry."

"Yeah, I think I'll live," she said, rubbing her temple.

"I'll try again, want me to?"

"Yes, go ahead."

This time I held her hand while approaching her more carefully. When I was inches from her lips, I had doubts and quickly opted to kiss her cheek instead. She giggled and bashfully smiled at me.

"That was fast," she said. "Come on…give me a real kiss."

I shrugged my shoulders. "I don't know…you mean on the lips?"

I turned slightly and played with the grass between my fingers. Distracted for a moment, I didn't realize Rosa moved closer to me. When I went back toward her direction, I met her eyes just inches from my face. Before I could think of anything, she kissed me like they did at the end of the old black and white movies Gramma always made me watch—well… almost. At first it was awkward when she started to kiss me as I didn't know how to receive it, but soon I naturally let her finish. During this, I wondered should I kiss her back.

"There, you can't keep a pretty girl waiting," Rosa said, pulling away from my surprised face. "Sorry, maybe I should have warned you." She giggled.

"No, you're right," I said, and then decided to return the kiss. "It doesn't matter, I'm just glad you did."

"Me too," she answered back.

We left the park hand-in-hand. As we neared our street, I realized someone might see us. A lump formed in my throat. I heard Manny's deep voice and saw him talking to one of the neighbors. We stopped in our tracks, our hearts beating fast, not knowing if we wanted anyone to know we were together that way.

"What would your dad think?" I asked.

"I don't know," she said. "We never discuss these kinds of things—wanna keep it a secret?"

"Yep, all this hasn't sunk in yet," I said. "Let's act like nothing happened."

We rounded the corner and saw the neighbor walking back to his house. Manny saw us coming. We swung our hands freely, smiling without a hint of our day.

"Hi guys," Manny said. "Haven't seen you all day, did you have fun?"

"You could say," I replied, then turning to Rosa as we held back a big grin.

"We were at the park," Rosa said.

"Wonderful day, wasn't it?" Manny asked.

"Sure was," we agreed and talked for a few minutes.

"Talk to you guys later," I said, paddling back toward my house. When it was safe enough I whispered to Rosa, "Our secret."

I reflected on the whole day as it played over and over in my head that evening. I daydreamed after supper and studied some recent pictures of Rosa I had taken. Sighing, her image gave me a smile. She inspired me to write her a poem. After working hard on it, I was satisfied with the final results. I would give it to her the next day after our weekly poetry group.

For a couple hours I couldn't sleep, holding her picture close to my heart. I thought of all the nice things I would say to her and prayed for her before I drifted off to sleep.

I awoke the next morning with wonderful images of Rosa. She was the only thing on my mind and I anticipated spending the day with her. I stepped into my gray sweat suit and tied on my green belt. Before leaving the room, I looked over her poem, knowing she would really like it.

Quietly, I went downstairs to find Gramma at the kitchen table drinking coffee and concentrating on the newspaper.

"Morning Jaybird," she said, scanning the paper, then looking up at me. "What are you going to do today?"

"Oh, go to the park for poetry group," I replied. "Probably hang with Rosa and Kaylee."

"That's nice," she said.

I strolled out the kitchen door and headed to the backyard for my karate training. The golden sun warmed the morning air, a few sparrows played in our maple tree.

Walking out to the middle of the lawn, I glanced across the street at Rosa's house. No one was around. I sighed. I turned toward the gazebo and smiled as thoughts of yesterday came to mind. I still couldn't believe I told Rosa my feelings and that she felt the same way.

Halfway through my karate training session, I heard the familiar clang of a door and saw Rosa crossing the street. I couldn't help but smile as she walked into my yard. She wore a sweat suit similar to mine except hers was purple. I had to pinch myself suddenly having memories of her tomboyish days, yet, at the same time, images of her feminineness dancing before me. My mind spun with her there in my reach.

"Hi Jay," Rosa said, her beautiful voice and smile hitting my heart. "I wondered if you would help me with my techniques...if you're not too busy for me. Since yesterday—"

"Of course, I have time for you," I said, giving her a hug. "You're my girl." Without me thinking, the latter words slipped out and I felt embarrassed.

"I am?" she asked, hugging back. "How do you figure that?"

"I don't know," I replied, looking at her. "I just know."

She giggled. "Jay, I will be your girl."

"Cool," I said, then jumping back when I heard a door nearby open and close. "So, what do you need help with?"

We trained for about fifteen minutes and then began our cool down exercises under the maple, on the side so no one could see us. We held hands, laughed, joked and enjoyed our new feelings. I felt more and more comfortable with Rosa near and words became easier. Bravely, as we sat next to each other, I put my arm around her and moved the loose strands of her hair from her face. I felt like one of those private eyes comforting Rosa, a damsel in distress. Becoming lost in her brown eyes, I kissed her.

"I don't remember this in karate class," someone said, startling us. We both bolted up and stared at Billie, his mischievous smirk glaring.

"Billie!" we both hollered.

"What are you doing here? You scared the crap out of me," I said. Billie just laughed.

"I never expected you two, way to go," Billie said and I wasn't in the mood.

"You made your point, Billie, now what do you want?" Rosa asked.

"Just wanted to hang out with Jay, Rosa," he said. "But I don't want to interrupt..."

Rosa stood. "Actually, we have to get ready for our poetry group."

"Yeah, I saw Kaylee and Lana headed that way," Billie said.

"Bye Jay, I'll see you there," Rosa said. "See ya Billie." She started across the lawn toward her house.

"I gotta hand it to you Jay," Billie said, following Rosa with his eyes. "You smoothie...Rosa—I see you're doing well. Jay you surprise me. Where did all this come from?"

"You're not going to tell anybody about this?" I asked.

"What, are you and Rosa doing something you're not—"

"Oh, nothing like that!" I spit out suddenly.

"Easy Jay, you know me, always a kidder," Billie said, holding his hand up. "No games, it's nothing to be ashamed of, just hanging out with your girlfriend and all. At times, I may have a big mouth, but you're my friend. I promise, I won't tell anyone."

"Thanks, Billie," I said. "For now, I don't want anyone to know."

"Especially my sister," Billie said with a straight face. "I know she has had a crush on you for years—maybe you didn't know that—"

"Yeah, I knew that a while back," I said. "So it doesn't surprise me."

"Don't worry about Kaylee, she'll get over it," Billie said. "'Sides, you have Rosa. Tell me about her—she sure has changed a lot." He whistled.

Every time we talked about Rosa, I felt my ears turn red and I began to feel giddy. Now, when I say her name out loud, it always sounds like the most beautiful word ever written.

"Not much to say," I said, shrugging my shoulders. "One day I had this strange encounter with Rosa—I don't know I just saw her differently."

"That's cool," Billie said. "Anyway, gotta meet up with Amber now, bowling or something I guess."

As I showered and changed into something cooler, I thought about the morning with Rosa, followed by Billie's conversation. Keeping the secret that Rosa and me were lovey dovey scared me, yet, exciting nonetheless. I wondered what the Bible said about secrets. Proverbs 27:5 came to mind: "Open rebuke is better than secret love." I read it many times and heard it from Gramma, Mom, Rich, and in my Bible studies; I never knew what it meant until now. Maybe Billie was right; maybe I shouldn't be ashamed that Rosa's my girlfriend—not like we're doing "it" or anything.

The poetry group had likely begun and I became anxious. I grabbed Rosa's poem and hurried out the door. When I approached the park, I composed myself and thought I should act like nothing had happened between Rosa and me. I saw our group gathered at our usual spot on the lawn in the shade. Immediately, I saw my beautiful Rosa sitting near Kaylee and Zoey. I casually glanced at the twins and without much thought, I lowered myself next to them, while being greeted. I carefully scanned the faces of the group and hoped my body language wasn't telling on me. I looked a little longer at Rosa and met her bright brown eyes. She blushed and quickly turned her attention to Zoey who began to read her poem. Every now and then I caught Rosa sweetly smiling at me.

"Let Jay read his next," Kaylee said, waking me from my dream.

Earlier in the week, I wrote two poems, one for the poetry group and one for Rosa, which I stuffed in different pants' pockets. Suddenly, I had doubts where both poems were. I sweated as I stuck my hand in the right-side pocket wondering which poem I had. Unfolding the paper, I had a strange feeling it might belong to Rosa and then what would I do? I held my breath as I peered down to read the first line. I exhaled with relief knowing I had the right one.

"A Black Bumblebee by Jay Asher," I said.

I saw a black bumblebee,
In my Gramma's garden.
He happily danced free,
Around a golden daisy,
Pink pansy,

To name a few,
That nicely grew.
But all of fairest,
Was the rose his favorest.

When I got to the last line, I rested my eyes on Rosa sensing she looked impressed and knowing I made it for her.

"I know, it's corny," I said, folding up the paper.

"No Jay, it was beautiful," Kaylee said. She said that about all my poems. Everyone thought it was good.

"It was very nice Jay," Rosa said. "I like the way you played with the words at the very end—fairest, favorest."

"Last but not least, Rosa," Zoey announced like we're on TV or something.

Since the group's attention was on Rosa, I felt safe watching her read. I hung onto every word and she snuck a glance at me.

When the group ended, I hoped we would be alone so I could give Rosa her poem. But that wasn't the case as Kaylee stuck around. Rosa and I didn't want to hurt her feelings or give anything away that we were together, so we acted the way we always had. The three of us talked for a while and then we started home because it was getting hot. We agreed to cool off at my air-conditioned house. Again, Kaylee was there. Finally, she excused herself for dinner. Gramma came from somewhere and began to prepare dinner, so again we weren't alone.

"Kinda stuffy in here, let's go outside," I suggested.

"I thought Kaylee would never leave," Rosa said, closing the French door behind us.

"I know what you mean," I said, holding her hand. "I couldn't wait to do that."

"That bumblebee poem was more than really good," Rosa said, as we walked to the arbor. "I super liked it…I knew you wrote it for me, I'm the rose." She thanked me with kisses. We then sat under the arbor, talking and holding hands.

"Oh, I wrote you another poem," I said, taking out the piece of paper.

She smiled broadly with anticipation, moving closer to me and resting her head on my shoulder for the moment as I read these words.

If you were a flower to me,
Which one would you be?
I know your petals are pretty
With perfume that is sweet
And butterflies agree,
That you are my dream,
A rose I definitely see.

"Oh Jay, that's the loveliest poem I've heard!" Rosa exclaimed, leaning over to kiss me, which seemed to last forever. Suddenly, we broke away when we heard her dad's truck rumble around the corner. "Have to go, thanks for the poem."

Hesitantly, she was about to leave, and then had mixed ideas as she turned to kiss me one last time. I held her hand until the last possible second. Watching her as she hurried across my lawn, I felt a sense of loss like after opening all the birthday presents and kinda wondering, was this it? I wanted to be with Rosa longer. Those thoughts lingered as I saw her greet her dad and they disappeared into the house. Part of me wanted to run over and drop on by for a visit, but I heard Mom call me from the French doors. I didn't know what she was saying until I shook away my empty thoughts.

"Dinner time Jay!" Mom hollered.

"I'll be right there!" I called back, shifting my gaze at Rosa's house.

I shrugged my shoulders knowing there was no reason to stand there, so I started to walk toward the house dragging my feet. All composed at the backdoor and with a sigh, I ventured inside.

"I haven't seen you all day," Mom said, setting the table. "Did you have fun with your friends?"

"Yep," I said, with the best smile I could give. She was too busy to notice my demeanor.

"How's Rosa?" Mom asked.

"She's doing good," I replied, holding back a big smile.

Chapter Fourteen

FINISHING OUR dinner, Gramma said, "You've been awful quiet this evening. Are you feeling okay?"

"I feel fine," I replied. "Actually, feeling a little tired—must be the heat—or all the turkey I ate. May I be excused?"

I went upstairs to my room and closed the door. I wondered if Gramma knew there was something different about me. Was it that obvious? It had only been two whole days since Rosa and I found out our feelings for each other. Rosa's picture was right where I left it. I picked it up, falling back onto my bed thinking of her—

—Suddenly I woke up and my room was dark—the red digits on my alarm clock showed 2:00 a.m.—I couldn't believe it! Maybe I was actually tired. Still with my shoes on, I untied them and kicked them into the dark void…thump, thump went the shoes landing. I didn't care that I was dressed as I slipped under the covers and tried to go back to sleep.

For some reason, I just could not put my head back to sleep. I laid there tossing and turning for about an hour still wide-awake. After trying everything I could think of that wouldn't disturb anybody, I decided to switch on the desk lamp and began writing in my journal. It was quiet gathering my thoughts, which flowed naturally on the pages. I knew the last couple days were memorable with Rosa, so I wanted to get it down on paper. My two poems went very well and I was pleased with Rosa's approval.

Billie's conversation flashed into my mind. He was a stinker when he found Rosa and me together making-out—that term registered in my mind of what we were doing. It hadn't really occurred to me until then as I sat there writing. It felt good, but at the same time it was scary or different.

I turned away from the desk and rested my face in my hands. Looking up, I saw my Bible over on the nightstand. I felt guilty not really putting much effort into studying the Word. My Bible was open and it wasn't marked where I remember reading. Usually I had it closed after studying. It wasn't like me leaving it open like that, so I bent down with intentions of closing it when something caught my eye. A verse was highlighted. Must have been something Mom wanted to remember because it was her Bible and she used a yellow highlighter verses my neon green. The word "**secrets**" jumped out at me. "Shall not God search this out? for he knoweth the **secrets** of the heart." ~Psalms 44:21

I sat on the bed pondering this. I forgot there were no secrets because God already knew my thoughts. He knew everything about me, my actions, thoughts, and my every step. Lying back, I began to pray.

"Dear God, I know I can't keep anything from You. Please forgive me. I really like Rosa and want to do this right. I'm confused about all of this and I do not know how to act around her or keep things right. Lord, guide me through this and give me Your wisdom, in Jesus' name. Amen."

The prayer made me feel better and relaxed. With my eyes closed, I fell asleep.

I woke a few hours later, close to my normal time. Jumping out of bed, I felt reenergized and ready for the day. Rosa was the first thing on my mind, go figure! *This has to stop right here! Priorities first, Jay,* I thought.

Swinging my legs out of bed, I picked up my Bible and began to pray obediently with a clear mind to God. A Bible study came after and I felt refocused, more in-tuned spiritually. A few chores followed before I met up with Rosa on the way to the park.

"Hey," she greeted and gave me a somber smile.

"Hey," I said, while wondering about her troubled look.

She took my hand as we rounded the corner. "Oh Jay," she said, resting her head on my shoulder.

"What's the matter?" I asked concerned. "You're not your cheerful self today."

"I *so* wanted to talk to my dad about us," she said.

"I've been thinking about that too, telling Mom or Gramma," I said.

"We're getting closer you know—I know it's just been a few days but it feels like forever."

"I know what you mean," I said. "Let's go to the park."

At first we tried to sit in the grass where our poetry group met, but Rosa was antsy, which made me nervous. We ended up talking while we swung on the kids' swings.

"You're not alone my little rosebud," I said. "Let's take it one day at a time."

"Thanks Jay, that makes me feel much better," she said, kissing my cheek. "Maybe you're my little honeybee."

"Someday the whole world will know… when we're ready."

"It's just that…it's just that I'm afraid to tell him you are my boyfriend."

"I know what you mean."

"I never really—really talked to him about this stuff."

"It gives me the willies just thinking about telling anyone."

"Why does this have to be so hard? Maybe we won't have to tell them. But then I would be embarrassed if someone caught us like Billie did—that's what else I want to talk to you about."

"Me too… I didn't really realize, when we were in my backyard, what we were doing," I said. "It felt wrong and right at the same time."

"About what I felt," Rosa said. "I wondered if we were going too far—not like we were…you know."

"Well… that's true," I said, shrugging my shoulders. "I felt okay. The Bible doesn't say anything about kissing, so I'm comfortable. Are you okay with it?"

"Of course, you're my boyfriend," she said with a serious smile, gripping my hand. With our closeness and her brown eyes twinkling at me, I couldn't help but pull her closer for a kiss.

A metallic noise startled us for a moment. We turned and saw a couple of kids playing on the slide. Rosa pulled me off my swing and we ran off to a quieter place in the park.

A few days went by with no one suspecting Rosa and I were together. It was alright with me not telling anyone unless they beat it out of me. We didn't spend much time at my house because either Mom or Gramma were always home. Our backyard was not very secluded and anyone on the street could see us. Mainly, we stuck to one of the two parks or in front of the high school where no soul would bother us. Occasionally, we hung out at Rosa's house when her dad was busy at work. We knew about when he came home and we kept an ear out for his truck, which had a very distinct sound. None of our other friends questioned why we spent so much time together.

"I tried finding you guys yesterday," Kaylee began before poetry group.

Rosa and I exchanged glances wondering if Kaylee was on to us. I held my breath waiting for the rest of her statement.

"Jay's Gramma told me you were out here—must have missed you. Anyway anything exciting going on while I was at my cousins?"

I exhaled.

"Nothing much, trying to find things to do," Rosa replied. "Let's see…it's been kind of hot, so we bowled the other day, which is about the only thing to do here when you're fourteen."

"Can you believe that I bowled a 275?" I said.

"That's cool," Kaylee said. "I think the highest I got to was 120."

"Mainly, we hang at the park," Rosa said.

"Ya, sometimes we just sit around and read," I added.

"This may sound strange," Kaylee began. "Summer is fun for a couple months, then it's boring and I can't wait to get back to school—I bet you guys can't wait for high school—wish I was going with you…oh well."

"It will be interesting," Rosa said. "I thought about trying out for volleyball."

"I think Billie is keeping up with football," I added.

"What are you going to do, Jay?" Kaylee asked.

"I don't know," I replied. "I will probably stick to karate. Football is too dangerous and I'm too short for basketball. Maybe baseball if I work on it."

"Hi Lana, hi Lynn," Rosa greeted the twins cheerfully.

I saw De'von arrive with Zoey just moments later.

"Hey De'von," I greeted him. "Are you joining our group?"

"Yeah, Zoey invited me," De'von replied, "I have an interest in poetry."

"Welcome and now I'm glad I'm not the only guy here!" I commented.

"Now we're about to begin," Rosa announced.

"Does anyone have anything to share?" Kaylee asked.

"I just wrote a new poem," Rosa volunteered.

<u>What A Wonderful Feeling</u>

I have a wonderful feeling,
It snuck up close to my being
My senses a drift

Thump, thump, my heart beating
Curious I am
For a presence very near
Does it notice my fear?
All doubts became clear
When lightning flies appear
They dance around my mind
and I wonder if God sent a sign.

"That's interesting," Zoey said. "Sounds like you are curious about love or something."

"Just something that came to mind," Rosa said.

"The 'it' could mean someone," Lynn said.

"Like she is curious about a guy," Lana said.

"It's just a poem," Rosa kind of spit-out.

"Yeah, it depends on what the readers are thinking," I said, coming to Rosa's rescue. "Sounds like she was overcoming her fear and she was looking for God's guidance."

"Whatever," Lana said. "I think she has a crush on someone."

"Ya, fess up, who is it Rosa?" Lynn asked.

"It is just a poem!" Rosa stated, raising her voice. "Sorry I didn't mean to snap. No, I don't have a crush on anyone—so what if I did, or do—oh, I don't know what I am saying."

I started to swallow wrong and coughed up a violent storm. Zoey patted me on the back. The twins were giving Rosa a hard time. After a while, I felt like they were teasing me about it too. I know the feeling, sticking my foot in my mouth.

"Which is it?" Lana pressed. "You do or you don't."

"Guys, leave her alone," Kaylee said. "She never said she did. She said, if I did, so what."

"Yep, it's none of your guys' business anyways," I said.

"That's right, now drop it," Rosa said.

With that, the group agreed to quit for the day.

"That was a close call," I said, after everyone left.

"Sure was," Rosa said. "I guess we should watch what we're saying. You know what is weird? Part of me wanted to tell them and get it over with. Maybe it's my conscious talking."

"Gramma says, when people say that they hear their conscious, it is the Holy Spirit talking to them," I commented.

"So maybe God was telling me not to keep us a secret," Rosa said. "I guess it really isn't a secret if He knows already."

"Yep, right before creation He knew," I agreed. "I'm not sure about all of this. What if someone finds out and tells our folks? All I want for now is whatever makes you happy, my girl."

The summer was slowly unwinding with September and my first day of high school just days away. It was the last weekend Rosa and I could spend time freely together. We wouldn't have many excuses for running around town with our secret romance. Lounging in the grass at the park, we talked and enjoyed each other's company.

"I hope we're in some of the same classes," Rosa said. "What electives do you think you're going to take? I think I want to take choir for sure."

"Spanish for one, even though you've taught me a lot," I said. "Mí muchacha hermosa."

"Soy?" Rosa asked.

"You sure are," I replied. "La muchacha más angelical de la—I forget what town is in Spanish."

"Cíudad," she translated. "That's so sweet to say and you deserve a kiss from your angelic girl."

In one motion she took my hands and pulled me in the grass, kissing me. I discovered I was hovering above her. Without warning, I saw Rosa's eyes widen in surprise. Instantly, I knew we were caught!

Suddenly, I jerked away from Rosa. We both stared up at Rich like two cows about to go to the slaughter. Quickly, we sat up straight brushing the grass off like it was stinging ants. Of course, we were speechless with horrible embarrassment. There was an eternity of silence for the next few moments. The only thing I felt was my heart racing a mile-a-minute. My voice was paralyzed and I could not speak.

"Jay, Rosa, hi—" Rich began.

"Uncle Rich!" I yelped, able to speak. "What are you doing here?"

"On my lunch break," he answered, trying not to look embarrassed. "I drove over here to eat my lunch, when I noticed you guys."

"Well, now you know about Rosa and me," I said.

"Please don't tell my dad," Rosa begged.

"Or Mom," I added.

"I won't, don't worry. You're embarrassed enough as it is," he mentioned.

"I suppose you're going to lecture us," I questioned.

"No, it isn't really necessary because I feel you are both mature enough to make your own choices. But let me paint you a word picture. Think of all romantic relationships as a car race. You are one pair of cars moving 200 miles an hour, with thirty other cars going out of control toward the finish line so faraway. The faster you go the more chance you might crash and burn. Being patient by conserving fuel and tires while pacing the race, will ensure you get there safely. God is your crew chief as you drive around your racetrack. Ask for His guidance and wisdom. He knows when you should pit and when to stay on the track. Listen to His advice. The pace car is the guardian angel sent by God. Our Lord set the concrete and has the winners' circle planned for you. Don't worry about finishing first because in God's eyes, first is last."

"I think I get it," I announced after Rich let it sink in.

"Me too," Rosa agreed.

"Thanks Rich," I said. "It sure helps to understand."

"Yeah, thank you Rich," Rosa said.

"I'm glad to be of some help," Rich proudly replied. "Let me leave you with this thought. You found each other naturally attractive from the inside out and you want to express those feelings. There's new excitement and a curiosity when around each other and you think about them all the time. You experience a wonderful high, warm, giddy, fuzzy feeling around each other."

"You got that right," I pointed out, feeling a lot more comfortable.

"Yeah," Rosa agreed, smiling widely.

We both giggled.

"Anyway," Rich continued, "you want to express your feelings physically—to hold hands, to kiss, and to hug, but don't make it all about that. Remember, this is a special moment in your lives. Make your passions and affections special and for meaning, not just because it makes you feel good."

"'For meaning,' eh?" I stated with curiosity.

"Cool!" Rosa expressed.

"Yeah, make it count," Rich advised. At this time he was kneeling down in front of us. "Let's join hands in prayer. Dear Heavenly Father, watch over these kids and guide them through a tender time in their lives—especially in these times where morals are tested. Give them wisdom and Christian armor to deflect satan's attacks. You know what's right for them. There's something they can learn from this, which will help them to become stronger in their walk of faith...In Jesus' Glorious Name...Amen."

"So...you're not going to tell my dad or Jay's mom, are you?" Rosa asked.

"No, I'll leave that up to you," Rich replied. "I know the thought of that isn't near to you right now. Remember, your folks went through similar situations like this before too. You guys have a lot to think about right now. If you need to talk about this or anything else you know where I live." With that he walked off.

We watched him cross the grass and head to his car by the curb. He closed the driver's side-door; it echoed through the park. His car circled the road around the gazebo and then we saw the back of his car go by. We sat in the grass in our own thoughts.

"Man, I thought we were in big trouble," Rosa said, breaking the silence.

"Me too," I said, picking at the grass. "I was so embarrassed."

"Yeah, the most embarrassed I've felt," Rosa said. "Sorry Jay, I was just curious. You just needed a kiss and I guess I got carried away."

"No, we both did," I said. "I am so glad it was Rich instead of your dad."

"Yeah, that would be horrible," Rosa agreed somewhat relieved. "Oh Jay, what are we going to do? I don't think I can tell my dad."

"Don't worry mi muchacha hermosa," I said, squeezing her hand and pushing the bangs away from her eyes. "When you think the time is right to tell him, you'll know."

"Jay, you make me feel special," she said, smiling, followed by a kiss. "For meaning."

We sat on the grass, holding each other for a few moments, and listened to the wind as it sailed through the pine trees.

"Can you believe in a few days we'll be in high school—hey, we can be high school sweethearts," Rosa said, with eyes twinkling.

"That would be great—can't wait," I said, relishing the idea. "We'll have our lockers together and maybe have the same classes…"

Suddenly, I felt somber.

"Why the face?" Rosa asked.

"It's just that—it's just that nobody knows about us. We can't act the same way like we do here."

"Yeah, I know what you mean. We have some time anyways."

"You're right. And remember, it's all in the Lord's timing."

"Then we have nothing to worry about."

We learned a lot that afternoon about ourselves. I figured God's will that day was to wake us up from disaster. He selected Rich to help us when we needed an outsider's different perspective.

Rosa and I parted before hitting our street. I stood on the front porch watching Rosa walk up to her house. She turned toward me with a huge smile, knowing I was there, blowing me a kiss. Giggling, she trotted into her house.

I faced my house, composing myself. After a sigh, I stepped into the cool air inside. As I headed passed the living room, a voice startled me.

"Did you have a fun day?" Mom asked, looking up from a novel she had in her hands while sitting comfortably in the recliner.

"Sure, I had a good time," I replied across the room.

I tried to escape, but she wasn't through. Standing there on pins and needles, I tried to give her my full attention. I could just see her interrogating me about Rosa.

"Did you hang out with Rosa today?" she asked.

"Yep," I said.

"What did you guys do—come over here so I can talk to you," Mom said.

I walked over to her, dragging my feet. On my way a bunch of terrible thoughts crossed my mind. Did she know about Rosa and me? Had Rich been over here? I tried not to imagine it. I sat on the arm of the chair and hugged her, trying to distract her.

"Love you mom—haven't told you in a while," I said.

"Love you too, son," Mom said, returning the hug. "Let me look at you…did you grow today? You look different." *Oh no! Is she onto me?* I thought.

"I don't know."

"How is Rosa?"

"She's okay."

"You sure spent a lot of time with her this summer—more than usual."

"I suppose," I said, wondering where this was going. "Well, she is my best friend."

"That is true," Mom said, "but she is a very pretty girl, I'm sure you've noticed."

"Oh Mom!" I stammered as I jerked away from her, my face warming up.

"Sorry, there's nothing to be ashamed of if you think Rosa, or any girl is attractive," Mom began. "Soon, you will be going into high school with new and wonderful things happening. I just want to let you know that you can talk to me about anything."

"Okay," I hesitated. "I have to use the john." *Really I had to go.*

Chapter Fifteen

September 2004

MANNY HAD us over for dinner the following evening before we all headed over to Deer Park High School for freshman orientation where schedules and locker assignments would be issued.

"Before we say grace," Manny began, as we sat down in our seats, "there's something I want to tell you guys—and I've already discussed this with Rosa..."

At that moment my heart jumped to my feet...I held my breath looking at Rosa who knew what I was thinking. She shook her head indicating Manny wasn't told...I started to breathe again.

"These past few weeks I've been thinking about my life," Manny continued. "I've been soul-searching and reading the Bible for some time. I also began praying to God about six months ago. I felt in my heart a deep void, which I know now can't be filled with worldly things. I thought I could do things without God by myself. Man was I wrong." I could tell he spoke from the heart, not even batting an eye.

"My family, especially my sister, has been telling me about the Lord for some time too, but I wasn't ready to listen—hard headedness I guess. It finally hit me deep down there in my soul. I realized I am a sinner and my puny self can't do anything without God. The other day I got down on my knees and I asked for Him to forgive me for my sins. Rosa helped me through the acceptance prayer and I accepted Jesus Christ as my Lord and Savior."

At this point Manny broke down and everyone had tears in their eyes. Here was a big man crying with humility. He brought himself down to a child's understanding, one who, easily without any doubt, followed Jesus.

"Welcome to the kingdom of God, Manny," I said, getting out of my seat to hug him.

"Hallelujah, praise the Lord!" Mom and Gramma said. We all hugged, showing support.

Rosa began singing a hymn and we all joined in, welcoming Manny to the "Family of God." I imagined the angels in Heaven shouting "Hallelujah" and blowing joyful gold trumpets.

From the time we first met Manny, we had planted hundreds of mustard seeds in his path. With some nutrients, plenty of sun, and water, plus patience, it turned a speck into a lively growing beautiful green succulent tree.

"I told myself I wouldn't cry in front of you like this," Manny said with a sniffle.

"It just means the Holy Spirit is in you and all burdens have been lifted to Jesus," Mom said.

"Now the hard part begins," Gramma said.

"Sure does," Manny agreed.

"We will be here for you, Dad," Rosa said.

"Let's pray for this new babe in Christ," Gramma said. "Heavenly Father, guide and protect Manny in his early walk in faith in Your Son. Give him wisdom and knowledge; teach him to stand with the Armor of God. We all know these are vulnerable times for Manny so give him Your shield to deflect satan's fiery arrows. As we sit down to eat and celebrate, we ask You to bless this food, in Jesus' name we pray. Amen."

We had an awesome meal and then we were off to Deer Park High School for orientation.

Rosa and I were a little disappointed that we only shared two classes, English and algebra. But when I got to thinking about it maybe it wasn't too bad—we could have had no classes together.

The following week was the first day of high school. Manny would be driving Rosa and I there. Quietly, we climbed in the backseat of the truck and exchanged our good mornings with Manny who was looking at us through the rearview mirror.

"Are you guys ready?" he asked.

"Yes," we both said, fastening our seatbelts.

"Wait a minute," Manny began. "I forgot the mail—oops and my wallet and my keys—you would think I was going to my first day of high school. Be right back."

We laughed with him and then he left. There was silence. We were finally alone for the time being. It seemed like he was gone forever. We smiled and blushed at each other. We were both nervous about the day, so I just held Rosa's hand, reassuring her.

"Jay, you are so handsome today," she said. I wanted to return the compliment, but Manny opened the door—we broke away, like the truck was on fire.

I had been looking over my shoulder ever since the day Mom seemed a little suspicious about me spending so much time with Rosa. Mom and I were pretty close, but I was afraid to tell her about Rosa. Rosa was also tight-lipped with her dad. Going to high school, none of our friends had any clue that we were a couple.

"There, I think we're ready," Manny said, starting the engine.

Deer Park High School was a mile away on Webber Street, so it came up quickly with the football field on our right.

"Looks like a nice day," Manny said. "Are you going to walk home?"

"Yeah, I think we are," Rosa replied. We had already discussed it the night before. It may be the only time we would be alone.

He dropped us off just as a big yellow, noisy, school bus appeared. We anxiously stood off to the side with the huge gray building looming in front of us. A stag, our new school's mascot's head was painted on one of the facings. For those who do not know, the stag was a male of various deer species.

"Isn't this exciting?" Rosa asked with bright eyes.

"Yeah, it is," I said, taking her hand for a moment, "especially with you, mi muchacha."

"Aww, gracious," she said giggling.

"I wanted to tell you when we were in the truck that you look very lovely this morning," I said.

"Hi guys," De'von said; I almost jumped out of my shoes. "Here we are at the home of the 'Stags'"

"Hey Rosa," Zoey said, standing next to De'von. "I like the way you did your hair." *I did too,* I thought to myself.

"I like your top," Rosa told her.

"And Jay, those jeans are really you," Billie said, bursting in with his girlfriend, Amber who joined the girls.

"Why thanks," I said, rolling my eyes. "Always up on the latest fashions."

"I haven't been in karate class for a while. How's everybody doing?" Billie asked.

"Good. Jeb got a brown stripe," I replied, then talked about a couple of others in the class.

"Jay, how about you?" Billie asked.

"Aren't you pretty close to your black belt yet?" De'von wondered.

"I have a black stripe on my brown belt," I said. "Two more stripes before black belt..."

The first bell rang and we all followed the rush. I found my homeroom without any trouble. We weren't doing much that day. Mainly it was teachers introducing their classes and writing down on a list the textbooks we'd be using.

First period went slow as the day was long. It was world history and we weren't doing much. I sighed when the first hour was over and stepped out into the crowded hall anticipating seeing Rosa. I saw her up ahead and we exchanged a couple of words.

The next class went a little faster since De'von and Billie were in it. I wondered what it would be like to share a class with Rosa. I guess I would find out in the next two classes, being English, and algebra.

RING, went the third period bell and I was out the door before it even finished. Rosa was already there in the class seated in the middle row. The teacher was at the door talking to someone. No other students had filed in yet.

"Is this seat taken?" I asked, nearing Rosa.

She smiled up at me with those big brown eyes and I saw a witty remark in them. "I don't know," she said. "But I hope some cute guy will sit next to me."

"Do you think I will do," I returned.

"Well, you are cute," she said.

Ever since last night, I figured it was time for me to tell Rosa that I love her. All day long, I procrastinated whenever I saw her, knowing it was still not the right time. When the last bell of the day rang, I convinced myself I had to tell her on the way home.

We left the school parking lot and entered the bike lane between the road and the football field. We walked a few blocks to the corner and then turned left toward Arcadia Elementary.

"Jay, you're awfully quiet," Rosa said. "You haven't said a word to me since we left the flagpole."

"Sorry, just have something on my mind," I said. "I was just thinking about you, my girlfriend."

"Ah, so what were you thinking?" she asked.

"I was thinking how blessed I am to be with you," I replied.

"Ah, you think I'm that special?"

"More than... more than any other flower."

"Jay, isn't there something you want to tell me?—I think there is," she said, taking my hand.

"Let's cross the street here," I said. We were on the sidewalk running along side the Deer Park Hospital.

"Are you ignoring me?"

"No, just thinking about you again," I said.

"Will you quit that—you can think about me all night long," she said. "I know what you're going to tell me—no one we know is around."

"So, what am I going to tell you?"

"Well, how much you miss me today and all the romantic things you were thinking you wanted to say to me," she said.

At this point, we turned the corner where the street was more secluded. I stopped, turned, and faced her.

"You're so pretty," I said, moving her bangs from her eyes. "Like a bright glistening spring blossom next to a cascading waterfall."

"So which flower am I?"

"You know," I said and she giggled. "But actually, there's something else I want to tell you…Um—I, I, well… you know."

"What is it?"

"Okay, I'll just tell you," I began searching for courage. "The thing is, I haven't told you that I love you yet—there, I finally said it."

"Oh, I dreamed you would tell me," she said. "I love you too, Jay."

"Wow!" was all I could say and she kissed me on the cheek.

"I wish we could stay here forever," she said. "People would start to wonder where we are."

"Oh, we still have some time."

The weekend came along and Rosa's dad drove us to the Spokane Fair. It was strange that the fair began about the same week many of the schools opened. The fairgrounds were about forty-five minutes away on the south side of Spokane. After purchasing our tickets, we split up and meet later at the entrance. Manny said he would be at the farm implements and then at the stage listening to a band.

Rosa and I browsed the inside vendors, looking at glass figurines and jewelry, where we bought each other friendship bracelets. The farm animals were nearby so we were in there for a few minutes. At the exit, we found a petting zoo; Rosa was fascinated with the miniature horses. She knelt down to pet one.

"Hi there guy," she said to the horse. "Don't you think he's cute, Jay?"

"He sure is," I said, rubbing his back, "but not as cute as you."

"Awwww," she said with a sigh, giggling and then kissing me on the cheek. "You're such a sweetheart."

"And you are my Spanishheart," I said, putting my arm around her while we walked out of the petting zoo. "What do you want to do now? Whatever my girl desires—well, almost anything."

"Let's do bumper cars," she answered.

After we rode around in circles hitting each other, hunger pains pulled us to the hot dog stand. Dessert followed with churros, those tasty cinnamon Mexican pastries. We did some more rides and played the carnival games for another couple of hours.

"Hey, the sun is setting and I wonder what time it is?" Rosa asked.

There was a dark purplish, midnight blue tinge to the sky; with a few stars that sprang up. The lights on the rides and in the booths started to turn on. Peering down at my watch proved that the evening was slowly winding down.

I regrettably told her. "I can't believe it's that late. I guess we have an hour before we meet your dad."

"Oh darn, and I was having such a good time with you," Rosa said. "Actually, I'm having a great time. I didn't even feel like we had to look over our shoulders."

"Yeah, I know what you mean, but let's not worry about that," I said.

"Hey! Do you know what I want to do?" Rosa asked.

"I have an idea, but why don't you just show me," I replied.

Minutes later, we climbed on the Ferris wheel as the attendant secured the car. The both of us were pretty excited, my heart and mind ran a mile a minute. I remember in the old movies the Ferris wheel was always the romantic part.

"How did I know you wanted to do this?" I asked.

"I didn't know, you must have read my mind," she said giggling.

"I heard that," I said.

"What was I thinking?"

"That you wanted me to hold you tight," I said, wrapping her in my arms. "—'F*or meaning'*—Rosa, Rosa, Rosa, I Love You."

"I love to tell you, I love you too," she said, resting her cute head on my shoulder. "You know what Jay? Even though we have been together, well, three months, I feel like this is our first date. Not that being with you at the park this summer wasn't wonderful…it was."

"I think so too," I said. "It doesn't matter as long as I am with you—'For meaning.'"

Tenderly, I kissed her on top of the Ferris wheel, for the short moment it stopped. What a cliché that was?

"Oh, I almost forgot," she said, reaching in her pocket. "I wrote you a poem."

I read it:

<u>'For Meaning'</u>

Our love is 'For meaning'
And at times, I feel like I am dreaming
All my affections signify a purpose,
Which fondly grows and goes and goes
We just don't kiss and huggly
Or hold hands snuggly
Because it oh, feels so good
Only its love reminders understood.

Before we knew it the Ferris wheel completed its circuit and we exited the car arm-in-arm. A deep voice made us pause—then we quickly let go. "Jay, Rosa!"—*Caught–Manny!* Many horrible things flashed through my mind. *What would we say to him? No, you can't be with my daughter. You kids are too young for dating.* For a moment those were my first thoughts. They echoed in my mind.

My eyes focused on Rosa's dad, but it wasn't him; I smiled with a big sigh of relief.

"This is a surprise!" De'von announced, his Adam's apple bobbing up and down.

"We didn't know you guys were going out!" Zoey exclaimed. She lit up like a light bulb when she looked at me and then at Rosa.

Looking to their right, my heart sunk to my stomach. There was little Kaylee with wide eyes and her mouth hanging open. She stood there, just feet from us, like an ice sculpture. Her first movement was tears welling up in her blue eyes. Crushed was the look on her face. A knot jumped to my throat. I didn't know what was worse, being caught by Kaylee or Manny. Each carried different emotions for me, but I didn't have time to think about it. I wanted to give Kaylee an explanation. Words formed on my lips, but no sound came out. Kaylee bolted from the group running behind De'von and Zoey. Instinctively, I ran after her.

"Kaylee wait!" I called out when I caught up to her. She stumbled a bit and I grabbed her arm before she fell. "Kaylee wait! I know seeing Rosa and I like that together was weird."

"Weirdly! Leave me alone," she said, trying to squirm away from me.

I turned around and saw Rosa standing between me, De'von, and Zoey. That's when I let go of Kaylee. Rosa walked up to me.

"I don't know why I ran after her," I said. "You're not mad at me, are you?"

"No, why should I be," Rosa replied. "She is your friend and mine too. We will both talk to her."

"What was that all about?" De'von asked, walking up to us.

"I think Kaylee was upset," Zoey said, then whispered something to him.

"Oh," De'von said.

"Tell you later," Rosa said. "So you found out that me and Jay are together."

"I knew it!" Zoey said. "I was just talking to De'von the other day about my suspicions."

My ears warmed up as they talked about Rosa and me being a couple.

"What makes you think that?" Rosa said, giggling.

"Gee, I don't know," De'von countered.

"Shoot!" I said, laughing with them. "I guess now we can't keep it from you guys. Look guys, it's getting late and we have to meet up with Rosa's dad."

The next day Kaylee wasn't at Sunday school or morning service. Rosa and I wondered about her as we walked home from church.

"I had such a wonderful time last night," Rosa said.

"Yeah, me too," I said.

"I just love going to church with you," Rosa said. "I just love going to church—praise Jesus!"

"Praise Jesus!" I said. "He sure knows what we need. He has His reasons for everything."

"Yeah, He brought me to you," Rosa said, squeezing my hand.

Before the first period bell rang on Monday, I talked with Rosa. Her locker was near mine in the same wing, just a couple lockers away. Amber, Billie's girlfriend saw us and began to socialize.

"I hear you guys are going out," Amber said, after a minute or two.

Oh no! I thought and then said out loud, "Did Billie tell you?"

"No, he hasn't mentioned it," she replied. "Actually, Nikki told me…saw you at the fair…"

"I was the first to know about Jay and Rosa—last summer I think it was," Billie said. "I saw them being quite affectionate." He left for a moment to get some books from his locker, which was all the way at the end of the hall. Billie hurried back so excited about playing on our varsity football team. *RING*—saved by the bell.

"So much for people not knowing," Rosa said, before we parted for our classes. "See you in English."

By the end of the week the whole freshman class, it seemed, knew we were an item. At first I hated the idea that most of the school knew about us, but soon I felt pretty good with the notion. I just hoped it didn't get back to Mom or Manny. *What could we do if it did?* I thought.

I haven't seen Kaylee in a week, I wondered the last period on Friday—would she tell them because she's mad? We tried to call her a couple of times but she was never available; the answering machine sometimes picked up. When Manny drove us home and parked in front of his house, there was Kaylee sitting on the front step.

"Hi Kaylee, how's school?" Manny asked, walking up the sidewalk.

"Fine," she answered.

"You can come on in," Manny said, unlocking the door.

"Hey Kaylee," Rosa and I greeted.

"You're probably wondering what happened to me," Kaylee began. "I was kinda upset with you guys for not telling me—just shocked seeing you like that, that's all. I was going to tell you at church, but my grandma was in the hospital.

"What happened? How's she doing?" I asked.

"She's okay, fell down and broke her leg," Kaylee said.

"That's not good," Rosa said.

"But she's home now," Kaylee added. "Also, you can see I got braces, so you can say I've been busy—I probably look silly."

"Nah, not at all," I said.

"If you say so...Well, gotta go home and do homework," Kaylee said.

"Why don't you come in and do homework with us?" Rosa suggested.

"Okay," she replied, without much expression on her face.

As we hung out in Rosa's room, I noticed Kaylee wasn't comfortable being there. We tried the best we could to make her feel part of the group. She seemed to settle in though. If she was torn up inside, it didn't show.

The 2004 high school football season began and was in full swing. Our team, the Deer Park Stags, played Division 1A football in the Great Northern League with seven other teams including our rival the Riverside Rams just up the road.

We would be playing our first game against the Jenkins High School Cougars in Chewelah. Billie was really excited for his first game; even though he wouldn't be starting. The team bus already left on Friday afternoon headed to Chewelah, thirty-five miles north. Rosa and I grabbed a ride from Billie's parents, Henry, Gale, and Kaylee. We arrived early to watch the teams warm up and stretch. Billie trotted up in full uniform, a blue jersey with gold lettering. Henry had his camcorder out pointing it at Billie, giving commentary.

"Here comes thirty-three, running back, Billie Knight, my son who I am so proud of," Henry announced, as Billie ran up to the fence.

"Yeah, watch out linebackers," Billie warned.

"Hi everyone," Amber said in her cheerleading outfit.

"Hopefully, you'll get to play," Henry said.

"I better get going," Billie said.

Henry got us all refreshments while we sat down on the grandstands. The crowd was slowly trickling in.

"I have some good news," Rosa said with excitement. "My mom is coming out to spend a week with Dad and me before Christmas."

"That's great," I said.

During halftime, Rosa and I excused ourselves to walk around a bit, just to be alone and talk.

"I sort of asked my Dad about me dating," Rosa said, then saw the look on my face, "but I didn't tell him about us."

"What did he say?" I asked.

"He said not until after my Quinceañera—he's so excited," she replied. "I forgot he told me about that when I was like nine or ten."

"What's a Quinceañera?"

"It's a coming out party when a girl in Mexico turns fifteen," she explained. "Sort of like Sweet Sixteen."

The next day, I went out to Rich's property, across the highway in the country. I helped him in the garage, being his gopher, handing tools and parts. He was working on his latest car project. It was a 1974 model American muscle car, which he bought from a little old lady who had it in her barn for years. Rich had the engine block sitting on a stand and its parts were laid out neatly on the garage floor like an assembly line.

"How was the game?" Rich asked, shining a socket wrench.

"Deer Park won 21 to 14," I answered, as he handed me a socket.

"Could you hand me that three quarter inch?" Rich asked. "Did Billie play?"

"He was in for one play when the starting running back needed a breather," I said.

"How's everything going with you and Rosa?"

"We're doing fine," I replied. "Her mom is coming this Christmas."

"That's exciting," Rich said.

In November, I was ready to be tested for my black belt. Because of the secrecy with the ceremony, it was best for me not to describe what happened. It was an enormous challenge to say the least. I was tested mentally and physically. Soon I was graded and then found out I passed. With much honor, I was presented my black belt.

Chapter Sixteen

PASTOR DAVID Stapp was born on September 24, 1954 in Liberia, West Africa. His father was the head doctor on the Firestone Rubber Plantation. Five-year-young David and his family returned back to the United States settling in Crowell, Texas in 1959.

David's earliest memory of church was when he was asleep in the front pew at FBC Crowell next to his mom who also played the organ. His dad sat in row four, being an on-call doctor, occasionally having to leave in the middle of the service.

After going forward to an alter call several years before, somewhere around the fourth grade, David realized he was spiritually lost and while lying on his bed scared, he wondered, if he died tonight, was he going to Hell. This made him feel stupid since he knew he could do something about it. Getting immediately down to his knees, he asked Jesus to save him. David was nineteen when he was baptized.

He graduated from Baylor University in December 1976 with a Bachelor of Music Education degree and Southwestern Baptist Seminary in May 1988 with a Master of Divinity degree.

In August 1978, he met his future wife, Tana, at the Avoca Baptist Church in Avoca, Texas. A few months later they were engaged and were married February '79. Their first child of ten was born in '81.

1982-84 David accepted a part-time position as Ministry of Music Southside Baptist Church in Wichita Falls (also band director of Archer City High School). Still in Texas, he pastored 1985-91 FBC in Strawn; and 1991-97, at Woodrow Baptist Church in Silsbee. 1997-2002 Minister of Music FBC in Crowell, while also the band director of Crowell High School. In Nederland, Texas, he was Associate Pastor at Seventh Street Baptist Church from 2002-2004 with responsibilities of preaching, music, and education.

Winter 2004

The Pastor Search Committee is pleased to recommend David Stapp for pastor of the Deer Park First Baptist Church. Signed, December 1, 2004.

David officially began preaching January 1, 2005 at FBC of Deer Park. His first impression of FBC Deer Park was the thorough organization of Diana and the pulpit committee. He remembered Terry's jovial laughter and the positive nature of the congregation. Also, the rural town setting and location near, but not too close to a larger city, appealed to him and his family.

THE FIRST semester ended and we were on Christmas break with a couple weeks of freedom. In about a week, Rosa's mom, Ella, would be arriving from Seattle, landing in Spokane.

Following Thanksgiving, I began my Christmas shopping and already found gifts for Gramma, Mom, and Rich. (Since I was ten I earned money, along with my allowance by mowing lawns during the summer, raking leaves during fall, and shoveling snowy driveways during winter) I even found something for Kaylee and Manny. I'm not a big spender, but always look for something just right. Rich took me to the mall so I could finish with the rest of my shopping.

"Who are we shopping for?" Rich asked, as we pulled into the mall parking garage. The place was packed so I wasn't the only one waiting until the last minute.

"Oh, something for Rosa, but I don't know what to get her," I replied.

Rosa was the last person on my list. I thought I would get her mom something too. All month I wracked my brain thinking what to get Rosa. I didn't know what it was, but buying something for your girlfriend was harder than getting a gift for someone in your family or a good friend like Rich. Rosa should get something extra special I thought.

"I don't know, what does she like?" Rich asked, scratching his head as he hunted for an open parking spot.

"Something pretty I guess," I said.

"Well...you can get her some jewelry, like a necklace," he suggested, watching my concern. "I guess everyone doesn't know yet, do they? Sooner or later you'll have to tell your mom. We can talk about it if you want...Think about it...Let's head into the store and maybe you'll see something."

But what? I thought when we entered one of the large department stores. I started off walking around the store in the tool section where Rich was glued.

"Are you going to buy Rosa a chainsaw?" Rich asked teasingly.

"No, I thought about maybe a weed-wacker," I said. "What do you think, gas or electric?"

"Well, depends what she would do with it," Rich said. "We better get out of here or I'll be here all day—let's go into the women's section…you know they like clothes."

I cringed when we approached the women's department. Just hoped no one would see us. Delicately, I stepped into the unknown, where many guys dare not to go. I held my breath browsing the nearest rack.

"Oh, hi guys," came a little voice. I ignored it, hoping it was for someone else, but of course the way things happen to me, it wasn't.

"Hi Jay, hi Rich," Dora, Rosa's cousin greeted, with her older sister Miranda.

"It was my day off and I promised Dora I would take her Christmas shopping," Miranda explained.

"So Jay, who are you shopping for?" Dora asked. "Did you get something for Rosa yet?"

"Not yet," I replied, wishing I would wake up from this nightmare.

"Hey, Rosa would just love this sweater," Dora said, pulling it off the rack and holding it up to herself.

"I see you kids are busy," Rich said. "Jay, how about I meet you in the food court later?"

I couldn't think of any reason to keep Rich there and I certainly didn't want to be there, so I said, "Sure," with no way out under my breath.

"What do you think Jay? Wouldn't Rosa look good in this?" Dora asked.

I poked my finger at the sweater wondering how to get out of this mess the fastest way I could, but patient enough not to settle on just anything.

"I think she would," I said, still unsure.

I followed them as they showed me a few other items of clothing. Dora piled a half-dozen sweaters and shirts into my arms. I then started putting things back. During all of this, Miranda and Dora talked about fashion, then guys and silly gossip.

"I think I will take these two things," I said without hesitation.

"That was fast," Miranda said. "We were just getting started. Don't you want to check out other stores? I know this one store that has cool stuff."

"No thanks, I found what I wanted," I replied, carrying the sweater and slacks to the cashier.

"Hey, these are nice, why don't you get these too?" Dora asked, handing me a pair of socks with a rose theme.

Following fashion frenzy, I got Rosa's gifts wrapped at one of those places that do it for you. Gramma's courtesy nagged at my brain as we started up to the food court.

"I wanted to thank you guys for helping me out," I said, turning toward them.

"You're welcome, Jay," Miranda said. "Rosa will love what you got her."

I ran into my house with my gift bags and greeted Mom, passing her on my way to hide the gifts in my room. Coming back downstairs, I told her I was going over to Rosa's house with my Bible tucked under my arm.

"Jay, slow down, I want to talk to you," Mom said from the couch.

"Sure," I said, turning on my heels and sitting down next to her.

"You know, I see the way you look at Rosa and the way she looks at you," she began. "Well, I have been noticing this for quite some time. I think there's something going on between you two—I don't want you to think I'm putting my nose in your business... Son, I just want to let you know that it is okay with me for you guys to be dating—you know your dad and I started dating at fourteen and I know how it is."

"I'll use good judgment," I said, after some silence. "I want to act how God wants me to."

"That's great Jay. It sounds like you really think things through," she said, looking somewhat relieved. "You may run along, don't let me keep you."

I sighed when I closed the front door and just stood there. In not so many words, and without coming right out and saying Rosa was my girlfriend, Mom finally knew. Actually, it relieved a lot of pressure from me knowing Mom knew.

When I went over to Rosa's house, I told her about my encounter with Mom. We sat in the living room with our Bibles open on the coffee table. Manny, I saw briefly as he was lifting weights in the garage.

"I wish we could just tell him," Rosa said. "But I don't want to disappoint my dad—he is looking forward to my Quinceañera."

"Your birthday is just a couple months away," I said.

"Yeah, I guess it can wait till then," Rosa decided and I agreed.

A week passed and Rosa and I were building a snowman in her front yard. She told me her mom landed in Spokane late the night before and slept in a hotel. Her mom said she would be coming to Deer Park sometime in the morning. Mom suggested I give them some space when she comes. Soon a car pulled into the drive, parking in front of Manny's truck. When a woman climbed out, Rosa raced to her.

"Mommy, Mommy!" Rosa hollered.

"Surprise!" Ella greeted, hugging her daughter. "There is my little Rosy, not so little any more. Since visiting last spring, you sure have grown to be a fine young lady."

"Hi, Mrs. Ella," I said when they approached me.

"Oh, hi Jay," Ella said. "Good to see you again. It's okay; you can give me a hug. The way Manny and Rosa talk about you and how much I have gotten to know you over the years, I feel you are part of the family. How are you?"

"I'm doing most wonderful," I replied, receiving her embrace.

"Rosy tells me you earned your brown belt," Ella said, pulling away.

"Actually, I am a black belt now," I said.

"That's awesome, wow congratulations!" she said amazed. "On that note why don't I take you guys to lunch and we can celebrate?"

"Actually, I have to shovel driveways right now," I replied. "Could we do it tomorrow? It would have to be after church though."

"Sure, we can do that," Ella replied. "I can take you guys to lunch and then ice skating. How does that sound?"

"That sounds great!" Rosa and I answered enthusiastically.

"I thought I heard somebody out here," Manny announced, stepping outside. "Hi Ella, come on in."

"Hi, Manny," she said. "I was gonna take you and Rosa to lunch."

"I guess, I'll see you later," I said, backing off from the house.

While her parents were engrossed in conversation, Rosa turned into my direction, stopping me briefly and giving me a quick kiss on the cheek.

Sunday, the next day, the church bell rang outside in the garden and Sunday school was over. Gramma, Mom, Rosa, and Manny sat down in our usual pew.

Ella planned on joining us for the morning service after she finished her last minute Christmas shopping. A few minutes after the church bell rang, she entered the Worship Center. She exchanged greetings with us and then sat next to Rosa.

"Sure glad I didn't miss anything. Nice church you have here. The people are friendly," Ella observed. "I haven't been to church in ages, so this is good for me."

It was a cool feeling to see Rosa, Manny, and Ella together as a family. I could get used to seeing the three of them together under one roof.

I was surprised to see Ella sing when we sang from the hymnal. She had a nice voice. Right away, I could tell where Rosa got her talent for singing.

After church, as planned, Manny would drive Ella, Rosa, and I to lunch, followed by ice skating, but he suddenly felt under the weather. So, we piled in Ella's car on our way to Spokane. She turned on the Oldies, one of my favorite radio stations, and started singing.

"So, how do you guys like high school?" Ella asked, turning to Rosa and looking at me through the rear-view mirror. "I bet you're having a blast—soon you'll be dating—of course, Rosa has to wait until after her Quinceañera. I'm sure Rosa has mentioned this before."

"Yes ma'am," I said.

"Anyway, I asked Rosa if she was interested in any guys," Ella continued. "She said 'she wasn't,' rolling her eyes like she is doing now. I'm sure the guys are falling all over themselves—How about you, Jay?"

"Watch the road!" I yelled.

Abruptly, a truck with braking red lights slowed almost to a stop. It caused Ella to slam on the brakes because she was too busy talking with us.

"Is everyone okay? Sorry about that," Ella said.

"I'm fine," I replied, catching my breath and also relieved that the incident came when it did because I really didn't want to answer Ella's question about dating.

"Me too," Rosa said.

"Good. I'm glad to hear everyone is alright," Ella said. "That was too close—all this excitement has made me hungry and I wasn't before."

We decided to eat at a Mexican fast food restaurant and then found ourselves entering the skating rink. Rosa and I had ice-skated there before at least a half-dozen times during the year and a couple times the winter before. We were both pretty good roller-bladers and it wasn't much different from ice-skating. Instead of four wheels in a straight line, it was one blade.

We sat down on the bench and changed into our ice skates. I was surprised when Ella pulled out a pair of her own.

"Do you skate Miss Ella?" I asked.

"Yeah, Manny and I used to skate a lot when we were kids," she said and I started laughing. "It's true."

"I can't picture Manny on the ice," I said, chuckling.

"Well, I told him if he wanted to date me, he had better learn how to ice-skate," Ella replied.

"Praise the Lord that he did," I said, pulling Ella up from the bench then helping Rosa. "Then I—we wouldn't have Rosa."—*oops, what did I just say.*

I turned and at the same time thought how to explain my statement, but Ella was halfway to the rink. We started to follow her, walking like a couple of penguins.

"I can't believe you said that with my mom standing right there," Rosa said, giggling.

"Do you think she heard me?"

She just shrugged her shoulders and then reached down to pull off the rubber guard from her blade. "That was so nice what you said about me, you're cute," Rosa said smiling, then hurrying onto the ice.

It was a little awkward on the ice at first from not skating for a while. I guess we were pretty good for amateurs. Last time, I learned how to skate backwards just like the figure skaters do on TV. There were a dozen skaters, mostly kids; one little boy fell on his butt. Voices echoed from the rink. I found Rosa and her mom somewhere in the center and I watched them for a bit before going up to them. Racing upon them, I braked late and stumbled toward Ella who luckily caught me.

"Whoa there speedster!" Ella hollered.

It took me by surprise. "I'm a little rusty, just need to get use to this."

We skated around for a while and then decided to take a rest, holding ourselves against the side wall. We watched this one girl who did a couple jumps in the air. She was really good.

"I'd sure like to try that this year," I said. "I wonder how they do that."

Rosa's mom excused herself, saying she had to use the restroom and would be right back. After the coast was clear, I came up behind Rosa and put my arm around her.

"Oh Rosy, you look so lovely in your little outfit," I said, spinning her around. "You're my ice princess."

She giggled and smiled at me with a twinkle in her soft brown eyes. We skated around hand-in-hand; it felt like we were the only couple on the ice. As we followed the other skaters, I caught Ella out of the corner of my eye, so I let go of Rosa's hand hoping I was quick enough.

"There you guys are," Ella said. "I saw you guys ice dancing out there and thought you looked pretty cute together, *very* together... now, you can't deny it, but I get a feeling you and Rosa are more than just friends."

"Okay, I guess we could tell you," Rosa began. "Yes, Jay and I hooked up. You're not going to tell dad, are you?"

"Nah, don't worry, I won't," Ella said. "Besides, there's a time and a place for everything—you two make a cute couple." She skated between us and placed a hand on each of our shoulders. Then turning to look me straight in the eyes, she asked, "What do you think about this daughter of mine?"

For some reason, I felt really comfortable talking with Ella about Rosa and I being together. So I smiled from mother to daughter and then was lost for a moment, taking Rosa's hand.

"Well, she's wonderful," I finally replied, grinning. "She's my rose blossom, mi muchacha hermosa."

"Jay, you are one unique fourteen year old...romantic too," Ella said, circling us. "Be careful... falling is a long way."

Soon we were on our way home. This time Rosa and I sat in the backseat, just sitting close enough to ease anyone's mind. Every now and then I peeked at Ella's eyes in the mirror and she winked at me. Rosa fell asleep from the afternoon's activities, resting her head on my shoulder. Ella smiled back at me as I played with a few of Rosa's stray hairs. Reality set in as we pulled into Deer Park. Rosa woke from her nap.

"I guess it wasn't a dream," Rosa said. "Thank you for taking us, Mom."

"Yeah, thank you Ella," I said.

"No problem," she answered. "You know what? Your dad would be okay with it. He knows his little girl is growing up."

"I was gonna tell him on my birthday," Rosa said and I nodded.

"Yeah, he is a traditionalist in some ways; it's a good idea to tell him then. He really looks forward to your Quinceañera."

Following our day with Rosa's mom, we went bowling and another time or two at the ice-skating rink. Occasionally, my mom joined us during our outings and we really got to know Ella much better.

I haven't said much about Christmas up to this point, but it was my most favorite time of year. Celebrating our Lord's birth was a precious, spiritual moment that gave me joy. Mom and Gramma taught me the true meaning of Christmas. It's not about how many presents you get, reindeer, elves, or the chubby guy coming down the chimney. It's about God's gracious gift being the miraculous virgin birth of Jesus, the gift that keeps on giving even when the holiday passes into the New Year.

A couple of Sundays before Christmas, our church put on a Christmas play—the kids reenacted Jesus' miraculous birth and a couple tots dressed up in angel costumes. Also, our choir sang their annual Christmas Cantata.

Gramma Naomi had her own tradition for Christmas which started with a hearty dinner on the eve. The menu changed each year. For the past few years, Rich and his sister, Joan joined us. Following dinner, we visited while drinking coffee or hot cider and eating chocolate drop cookies. Then some of us went with people from church to a nursing home to sing carols. At midnight we prayed together, worshipping Jesus' special day.

Anxiously, I went to bed anticipating Christmas morning. I looked forward to giving Rosa her present. This Christmas was extra special with Rosa in my life. I thanked the Lord for bringing her to me. I hoped nobody thought anything different of the nice outfit and rose socks. Before I knew it, I was asleep.

I slept in a little on Christmas morning, waking up with a smile. Donning my robe and slippers, I cleaned up and met Mom and Gramma in the living room. The angel decorated Christmas tree glowed heartily with a few new presents.

"Merry Christmas," they greeted me with a hug.

I peered out the front window wondering if it was snowing. Actually, I really wanted to look over at Rosa's house. It was still. There was the snowman Rosa and I had made, which filled me with a wonderful feeling.

"We don't have a white Christmas yet—well, falling fresh snow anyway," Mom commented.

Gramma's tradition on Christmas morning began with the family gathered in the living room. Again Rich and his sister came over and we all held hands in front of the tree for prayer. Following that, Gramma brought in a tray of hot chocolate with clouds of whip cream and sprinkled cinnamon. We each selected a candy cane from the tree, placing them in our mugs.

The candy cane had a special significance in years' past when a candy-maker wanted to do something for Jesus. As it hung from the tree, the candy cane was shaped like a shepherd's stick, our Lord being the Good Shepherd. When you turned it around it changed to the letter "J," signifying the name of Jesus. The cane started out white, symbolizing the pure sinless nature of the virgin birth. It was also like solid rock, as Jesus is our rock, the solid foundation. Three small stripes were painted to show the sacrificial stripes Jesus endured for us. The large red stripe was the blood our Lord shed for us so we could have eternal life with the Holy Father.

After we drank hot chocolate and ate breakfast, we exchanged gifts. I got a nice green sweater from Mom, which I put on before we went over to the Manny's house. I ran up to my room to grab Rosa's present, including the ones I got for Ella and Manny.

"Feliz navidad," Manny greeted, as he answered the door.

"Hi everyone, Feliz navidad," Rosa said, giving everyone a hug and squeezing the life out of me. Then she saw the gift. "Is that for me? Wow!"

"Sure, it has your name on it," I said, as she grabbed the wrapped box excitedly.

"I got you guys a little something," Ella said, holding up a decorative basket, "just a few goodies, jellies, and cheeses."

"I wonder what it is?" Rosa said, curiously shaking her present. "Dad, can I open Jay's gift?"

"First, show everyone what your mom and I gave you," Manny said.

"Okay," Rosa said, blushing while heading off to her room. She came back quickly with a lilac dress in plastic. There were happy noises, especially from the ladies. "It's my Quinceañera dress—I knew I was going to get it."

"Jay mentioned what it was," Mom said. "A huge party at a girl's fifteenth birthday—kinda like sweet sixteen—maybe someone can explain it further."

"Sure," Manny began. "Like you said, it's a huge party…"

"Here we go again," Rosa said, rolling her eyes.

"Rosa, I know has probably heard me talk about it one million times," Manny said. "Come, I will tell you in the kitchen, then we'll open the gifts."

"Jay, I want you to open my present first," Rosa said, a few minutes later. I sat next to her in front of the couch where Mom and Gramma sat.

"Okay," I said, carefully taking off the wrapper exposing the white box. I looked over at Rosa full of smiles.

"What is it Jay?" Mom asked.

"It's a journal. It's really cool…It says 'Jay's Journal' with next year 2005," I said, handing it to Mom who looked it over. That's when I noticed something else in the box. "Wait a minute there's another one 2006." I exchanged glances with Ella who I knew had something to do with the gift as she winked at me.

"I know you write in your journal every night," Rosa added.

"Thank you so much," I said briefly, giving her a hug.

"I also got you," Rosa said excitedly, pulling out a box from behind, "a pen and pencil set with your name on them."

"Now it's Rosa's turn," Ella said who knows too much.

Unlike me, Rosa ripped through the paper. All my worrying on what to get her, how she would react, and what everyone would think was over in an instant. Happily, she showed off her sweater and I knew she really liked it.

"Jay, thank you so much. It's beautiful," Rosa said.

The women thought the rose socks were the most precious things they ever had seen. Mom gave me the look that says how did you think of all this? It wasn't something a fourteen-year-old boy usually came up with. Of course, Ella was winking at me. Manny didn't have much of a reaction who then started talking to Rich about a tool he got.

As soon as all the gifts were unwrapped, Rosa and I excused ourselves to play in the snow. When we stepped out into her backyard, the snow began to fall. We threw snowballs at each other. Waldo joined in for a while, and then left us after finding an old scent. We purposely moved out of view from the sliding glass door.

"Let's go somewhere so we're not bothered," Rosa suggested, looking carefully around. "Just want to be alone with you for a few minutes."

"I know why," I teased, as she pulled me where she wanted to go.

We rounded the corner to the other side of the house and sheltered ourselves somewhat under the eaves.

"I'm not tired of saying 'for meaning,'" Rosa said, kissing me. "I wish I could have done that right after I opened it. Thank you so much again for the gifts—I really love them!"

"I really love you," I said. "I'll love you forever."

"Jay, I love you so much too. I have something else for you," she said, reaching in her pocket. "Here, I want to give you a bracelet and I have the matching one. It's to express my love to you and when we wear these bracelets, well you know, to remind us that we'll stay pure together until ah..."

"Yep, I know what you mean to stay pure—to save ourselves," I said, tying the bracelet around her wrist. Then she did the same to mine.

"I didn't know how to express this to you or how you feel about it," she said. "I don't want you to think I'm silly to be thinking about stuff like that right now."

"No, I don't think you're being silly," I said. "We want what God wants. I think the bracelets are a wonderful idea, something special between us."

"Let's go before they wonder where we're at," Rosa said, giggling.

When we stepped back into the house, Rosa's Aunt Juanita and Uncle Peter arrived with her cousins Dora and Miranda. We all greeted one another with hugs of yuletide cheer. The Sanchez family exchanged gifts and we exchanged Christmas cards. Mom, Gramma, Ella, and Juanita gravitated toward the kitchen in conversation. The men gathered in the corner and we kids hung out in the living room.

We visited for a while and later had lunch. The women prepared Christmas quesadillas, which were made with red, green, and white tortillas. Salsa, guacamole, and sour cream completed the meal.

"I have an announcement," Ella said, after we finished our meal. "Well, Manny and I have been discussing it. You know I have been away for a while and it has taken a toll on Manny, Rosa, and me. I have accomplished much success in my time associated with *Fuller & Chan Law Firm.* I have come to a crossroads in my life, realizing the need to refocus my priorities with my family." She paused to put her one hand on Rosa's shoulder and the other patting Manny's knee. "I'm getting disillusioned with Seattle. I have stepped down from my current position in the office there. One of the Senior Execs left *Fuller & Chan* a couple years ago to start her own law practice here in Spokane. She finally talked me into becoming a partner, so just recently I accepted her offer."

"Mom, you're coming to live with us!" Rosa said, jumping up to hug her. "When are you moving?"

"One step at a time, sweetheart," Ella replied. "I already decided to move into an apartment in Spokane near my new office, just for now."

"Now we can visit you more often," Rosa said with excitement.

"Congratulations, Ella," Mom said.

During this week, our new pastor, David and his family visited Deer Park. They stayed with a couple of the church families. On Wednesday, David and three of his middle children came to our home to introduce themselves. They were Caleb, Bethany, and Miriam, who were the closest to my age. David was a friendly fellow, around fifty years young with dark hair, glasses, and carried a distinct southern Texas accent. We visited a bit and sang a couple of Christmas songs. Pastor David prayed with us and then they went on their way.

Toward the end of the week there was a welcoming reception for David and his family at the new elementary school. He introduced himself and we got to know a little bit about his children who all played various instruments. We had deli plates and then members of our church asked David questions regarding his preaching, background, and whatever else. The evening closed with a couple of hymns and prayer.

David flew up to Deer Park the end of February 2005 to look for a potential house for him and his large family.

His first few sermons were on the *Ten Commandments.* He presented the Word with much inspiration and glory for Jesus Christ. He was a real blessing for our church and the church family, which he then started calling us "The First Family."

There was a fresh change to the bulletin, newsletter, and music. To go along with the traditional hymns, modern songs were added. We now have a band with the additions of the Stapp kids. Other youngsters had also joined the band. The choir even had more depth.

Nine members of David's family came to Deer Park the middle of March. David said in the church bulletin, *"The Simple* family has been as gracious as anyone can be. They had invited the rest of the family to also stay at their home, but other families also offered to house some of the children which seemed to lessen the burden."*

It wasn't long before a couple, Tina and Mark, who would soon be having an empty nest, offered their home. With much prayer David and his family moved in.

* Names changed

Chapter Seventeen

Dora C. Dillion
&
Rosa E. Sanchez
Invite you to their Quinceañera,
Fifteenth Birthday Party
On February Twelfth, Two-Thousand five
2 p.m. till 9 p.m.
At the Touch of Class Hall
5820 East 4th
Spokane, Washington
Food and Live Band Provided
Black tie, RSVP

There was a decorative card inserted in the invitation, it read:

Jay Asher
Rosa has chosen you
To be her
Dance partner for her Quinceañera

THE NIGHT before I was on pins and needles anticipating this big event. Not only because it involved Rosa, but because I made special plans for the day.

Rich had taken me shopping for Rosa's birthday present. This time her cousins didn't help me in my selection. I took the wrapped gift out of its hiding place and shook it in examination. I said a prayer to our good Lord, thanking Him for His provisions.

The next morning, I was full of energy bouncing off the walls like a rubber pinball. I flew past Gramma in the kitchen and tried briefly to exchange good mornings, but she stopped me.

"Slow down Jaybird, have some breakfast," she said before I could run out.

Hastily turning on my heels, I grabbed a bowl of cereal and sat down next to Gramma at the kitchen table.

"Are you in hurry or something?" Gramma asked.

"No, not particularly," I replied with my mouth full.

"Where are your manners?" Gramma asked. "Sit up straight."

"Sorry, ma'am," I said.

"I know why he's full of vinegar," Mom announced from behind. "He's probably excited about Rosa's birthday."

A short time later, I settled down for my daily morning routine. Before I knew it, the time slipped by and it was time to get ready.

Now, I never wore a tuxedo before. After putting it on and looking in the mirror, I thought I looked like a penguin. When I got to the bow tie, it was a struggle as I made it into something resembling a tangled knot. I untied my mess, deciding to go downstairs so Mom could help.

The door to her room was closed so I knocked.

"Come in," she said from within.

"Mom, will you help me with this thing?" I asked, entering her room.

"Sure," she said, talking to me from the vanity mirror. "Give me a sec to put these earrings on." Finished, she turned back to me. "Don't you look handsome?"

"I guess," I said.

"Rosa won't be able to keep her eyes off you," she said, looking me over. She grabbed the bow tie and stepped behind me. "Let me help you with that. You know, I had to help your father a couple of times."

"Mom, do you think we will ever find him?" I asked.

"I hope so some day," she replied, tying the knot. "There, what do you think?"

"Looks like a bow tie," I said, unsure with the question I put to her about Dad. "I've been praying about him."

"That's all we can do, God will do the rest in His time," Mom said. "We'd better be going soon. Gramma wants to get there early. Make sure you brush your teeth."

"There you are Jay," Gramma said, as I entered the kitchen a few minutes later. "Could you carry this warming pan out to the van please?"

Gramma offered to cook some food for the party. She made two enchilada recipes, which she had perfected, as she would say; one was meat, and the other vegetarian.

A short time later, I climbed in the minivan and Mom asked if I had Rosa's present. I smiled taking it out of my pocket.

"You know some of the nicest gifts come in little boxes," Mom pointed out.

Twenty minutes later, we pulled into a parking lot of a large stucco building. A dozen cars were already there. I recognized Ella's car up in the front. When I stepped out of the van, I took in the whole moment, drawing a picture in my mind. I knew the day would be special and I wanted to remember every minute.

With my shoes on the pavement, I squinted at the sun and the winter blue sky. It was a crisp day and I could see my breath. Behind me was light traffic. I turned back to the van as Gramma handed me the food, then we headed toward the Nice Touch Hall, our feet clip-clapped across the parking lot. Upon entering the lobby, we saw Ella sitting at a small table.

"Hello, Rachel, Naomi, and Jay," she greeted, standing to help me with the pan. "Here, let me take that so you guys can sign both of the girls' guest books."

I waited after Mom and Gramma signed their names and disappeared into the dance hall before taking my turn. Choosing Rosa's book first, I carefully scanned the names of who was already there. The most precious name, of course, was Rosa E. Sanchez; a little heart I drew next to it. After a sigh, I penned my name, then went on to Dora's.

Inside the hall there was soft music and the first thing I saw was a huge sign that said, "*Feliz Quinceañera Dora and Rosa!*" Then there were purple and white streamers, banners, and balloons. I heard girls laughing as my attention turned to them across the hall. Rosa's voice tickled my ears. Mom stepped in front of me taking pictures.

"Mom, may I have the camera?" I asked.

"Sure, I forgot you probably would want to take some pictures, getting your own perspective," she answered, handing me the camera. Then I saw her stroll off to the buffet table where Gramma was peeking in at the other food.

Screech—pierced the room—I jerked to my left on the stage where a man said into a microphone, "Sorry… testing, testing. I think it works." I didn't recognize him, but he appeared to be one of Rosa's relatives—Manny's brother, I thought. Manny was also on the stage tuning his guitar. The sweet voices of laughter made me turn on my heels.

I peered into the camera viewfinder and zoomed in on Rosa, taking a few shots. Placing the camera in my pocket, I viewed her with my own eyes admiring her from a distance. I took a few steps noting her lilac dress and a lighter lilac chiffon shawl draped gently over her slightly brown shoulders and arms. White gloves and the thing on her head completed my first impressions. I listened to Ella, Mom, and Juanita talking about Rosa's dress on Christmas. I caught some of the fashion terms and the name of fabrics and such.

"Rosa, Jay is coming," Dora announced, giggling with girls I didn't know; I figured they were Dora's friends.

Rosa's face brightened up as my eyes met hers. Approaching her, I got ready for "plan one," which I practiced the day before.

"Rosa, miras muy bien," I said. "Tu eres mi princesa."

There were several comments and teasing from the girls coming our way, but we didn't care because we were caught up in the moment.

"Amor, amor, amor," Dora sang. A chorus of laughter erupted.

"Don't tease him, he's sweet," Rosa said to her girl friends, then turning back to me with a big smile. "Gracias Jay."—I finally remembered what the thing on her head was—

"Your hair looks nice with the tiara," I complimented.

"Thank you, I thought it looked silly," she said, standing up while her lilac satin dress rested on the floor.

"No, not at all…well, it's you," I said.

"You think so?" Rosa asked, putting up her hand to feel the head piece.

Her tiara was a semi-circular band of white fabric and lace, decorated with two bands of beads and rhinestone. To the sides of it, two fabric flowers with ribbons descended from each flower. When Rosa turned around, I saw a satiny bow and draping down from the hairpiece were two strings of beads with soft netting covering the back of the tiara.

The back of the dress was covered with satin and lace work from her waist which met wide straps crossing the shoulder blades at the neck. The straps conservatively showed a little shoulder and formed a slight v-neck in the front that was all satin with a floral design beadwork.

"Whoa, is all I can say," I replied.

"You look great too," Rosa said, twirling around.

"You better watch it Jay," Billie said, hitting my shoulder from behind. "It sure looks like a wedding to me—run and hide!"

"Don't you know anything Billie," Rosa returned. "Today's party theme is Quinceañera, which means fifteen, duh."

"Don't mind Billie," Amber said, "always kidding around. I love your dress Rosa."

I turned around toward the stage and saw Rosa's Aunt Juanita motioning for the birthday girls to come up front.

"May I have everyone's attention," Juanita announced. "Everyone is accounted for and we're ready to begin."

Let the production begin, I thought, as the crowd slowly stopped what they were doing and moved toward the stage.

"My name is Juanita Dillon. This is my daughter Dora's and my niece Rosa's Quinceañera—fifteenth birthday celebration. Now they won't be turning fifteen 'til next week, but we wanted to combine their birthdays being so close together. Before we continue, I asked Pastor Williams from North Spokane Baptist Church, the church that we attend, to lead us in prayer. I would like everyone to gather near the stage in a circle and hold hands."

Pastor Williams, wearing a microphone on his lapel, stepped from the side. He was middle aged with graying hair. Rosa and Dora joined his hands on both sides. Then their dads took the girls' hands. Together, other family members and close friends started locking hands. Some old men from the far corner of the hall came from their seats slowly.

"Come on Jay," Ella said, from out of nowhere and without asking, she grabbed my hand, pulling me to the front. She placed my hand on top of Rosa and the pastor's.

I saw Mom smiling and waving at me down toward the line. Billie was making kissy faces at me so Kaylee slugged him in the arm. Then I turned to Rosa, her starry eyes smiling. We closed our eyes as the pastor began.

"We celebrate Dora and Rosa's fifteenth birthday and we ask our Holy Father to bless these girls as they continue on into their tender years toward womanhood. Father, we ask you to guide them, nurture them with Your knowledge and wisdom, and just be with them...in Your Son's, Jesus' name. Amen."

"Thank you Pastor Williams," Juanita said, taking the microphone again after everyone dispersed. "Now I will let my brother, Manny Sanchez, tell you more about the Quinceañera ceremony."

Manny was up on stage strumming his guitar in a constant rhythm. He stood and spoke in a storyteller's voice.

"A little history," Manny said. "When our ancestors arrived in the United States from Mexico, we kept many of our traditions from the homeland, including the Quinceañera. The word, for those who are not familiar with the Quinceañera, means fifteen. This ceremony spans many generations of Mexicans and Hispanics around the world. Now the meaning of the ceremony has changed over the years and many of the traditions shadow the modern form of the Quinceañera. In a sense, when a girl turns fifteen, she is entering young adulthood. Nowadays the Quinceañera signifies that a girl can start dating. I'll be watching you all—Rosa will always be my baby. Anyway, all our family members who are near and our closest friends, as you could figure are invited. There's food, games, and dancing. Music is important in all occasions in our culture. Many family members who can play an instrument or sing will perform at Quinceañeras. Now, the Sanchez family is a talented bunch of musicians. See that man on the keyboard? He is my cousin Jorge, and I will let him introduce the band."

"Hola everyone, I hope you're enjoy this evening," Jorge greeted. "The name of our group is 'The Mexican Pride Band.' On the fiddle is my wife Sylvia."

"It's great to be here," Sylvia said, after bowing.

Jorge then introduced the other family members in the band including a drummer, a bass and acoustic guitarist, and a trumpet player. Meanwhile, I thought about plan two.

"And finally, also here today," Jorge finished, "is one of Manny's other brother's Roberto, who plays both sax and trumpet, my cousin Juanita who sings, and of course Manny playing the guitar."

"Yeah," Manny added, "the three of us played in the family band years ago, but not as much, just here and there now. Well, have a good time and we will now show you what we can do."

Jorge leaned over his keyboard toward the members of the band and played a couple quick chords while he said, "Ono, dos, trace."

Manny's hands picked quickly across the guitar strings, Roberto's trumpet blared, Sylvia was animated on her fiddle as the rest of the band followed. They started playing in a fast Latin beat without lyrics and then Juanita sang.

Some of the people in the hall were tapping their feet to the music. A couple of kids got on the dance floor. It wasn't the type of music for Rosa, Dora, or any other girls who wore fancy puffy dresses to dance to, so they just bobbed their heads and moved their arms. I remembered watching people on TV doing the salsa or whatever that was, but I did not dare imitate their moves. The couple, I remembered, swung their hips and the guy was twirling the girl. For a moment, I pictured Rosa and I doing that, then I chuckled. The band played for another five minutes and while they wound down, Juanita picked up the microphone again.

"Thank you everyone in the band," Juanita said. "The next thing for the Quinceañera will be solo dances for Dora, Rosa, and their dance partners. Traditionally, the waltz is one of the dances performed at the Quinceañera, in which our kids have been practicing for a couple of weeks. Jorge and Sylvia will play a waltz duet.

"Since Dora, my daughter, is a few days older than Rosa, she'll have her solo dance with her partner, Vince first. Both attend Mead High School."

Vince came from the crowd as the music began. Just like we practiced, he approached Dora in the middle of the dance floor. Gracefully, he bowed with two out stretched hands placing one on her shoulder and the other in her free hand, while she placed her other hand behind his waist.

I'm glad they went first, because it gave me a chance to observe, and also time to think about my plan two. As I went over this in my head, I began to have doubts of even going through with it. I was extremely nervous, my hands sweating. I went back and forth changing my mind. *Was this the time Lord?* I prayed. I watched Vince and Dora spin around. Then I realized that it was no big deal, Mom already knew about Rosa and me. The proverb "Open rebuke is better than secret love," came back to me. Perhaps the Holy Spirit spoke to me because I felt God guiding me and giving me courage.

Thank you Lord, I'm going to do it, I thought, as the music seemed to be finishing. The audience applauded as Vince and Dora left the dance floor. Juanita picked up the microphone. I started to feel nervous, but I told myself, *Be Cool Jay*.

"That was my daughter, Dora and her partner, Vince," Juanita said. "Now my niece Rosa and her partner, Jay will dance. They attend Deer Park High School."

Rosa hovered across the floor almost like she was on air, due to the fact that her dress reached just above the floor. She stood there holding her gloved hands in front of her. The music began and I slowly walked up to her in awe. Rosa's eyes sparkled and she smiled just for me.

"Rosa, you're such a dream," I said, in front of her, then bowing.

She kinda giggled as we probably thought this whole thing was corny. I placed one hand on her shoulder and met her other hand off to the side. One, two, three, step to the left.

"It's a little different with this dress," she said.

I looked at her tiara and then lowered my eyes to hers, tender and brown. My heart sighed and skipped a beat. If I had a piece of paper, she would be a poem to write about.

"Tu eres mi princesa bonita," I said to her, one of the phrases I practiced for my plan.

"Gracias, mi príncipe," she said. "You make me feel very special Jay, talking in Spanish."

"I can't believe how lovely you are," I said—kissing her on the cheek, altering my plan.

I wanted to give her a long kiss, but decided this was not the place or time. Such a foolish idea it was in the first place I concluded afterwards.

As the waltz wound down, I decided to give her one more kiss on the cheek, but I missed and caught her on the lips. Pulling back a little bit, the room spun even more as we waltzed around. Everything seemed fuzzy from my eyes, like it was a dream. Whatever it was, I shook it off and refocused, turning my attention back toward Rosa. I worried about how she reacted, after kissing her. She just smiled at me as before, which relieved my tension. From the corner of my eye, I wondered if anyone saw that. Of course, they did. I heard chatter from Dora and others.

The music ended and we stood there together. As everyone applauded, we watched the crowd's reaction. The adults didn't change, but a few of the kids, especially Billie, took notice. For now, I avoided Billie and the peanut gallery. I yielded to where Manny was standing—I'm sure he wanted to know about the kisses, but he just smiled and clapped.

My whole plan centered on introducing Rosa and I, indeed being an attached complementary couple. I didn't think it eased much at all, just complicated matters, something I had not considered. Perhaps some thought it was just a spur of the moment reaction.

"You guys look so cute out there," Mom said, as I walked up to her. "Both of you danced so eloquently."

"It was nothing, just comes natural," I said, getting something to drink.

"Way to go Jay! I bet you could have really shown everyone," Billy said, meeting me at the punch bowl. "Hey Vince, where's your kiss? Wasn't it part of the dance?"

"Dora's not my girlfriend, she just invited me," Vince replied.

"You should ask her out," Billie suggested. "Fess up."

"Billie, leave him alone," I said.

"Okay, but you know I'm right," Billie replied, walking off to talk with Amber.

"Sorry about that," I said, turning to Vince. "Don't mind Billie, he just likes to joke around."

"That's cool," Vince said.

We constantly watched Rosa and the girls from across the room. They giggled and whispered secrets with their cupped hands. No one else approached me after my dance with Rosa.

"Not too many people know Rosa and I were together," I said. "Dora knew—she's cool. How do you know her?"

"She's in my algebra class," Vince answered. "Actually, I really like Dora. Do you think that's why she invited me?"

"I don't know," I said.

"I would be embarrassed to tell her," Vince said, his face turning red.

"When I felt about Rosa that way, I thought it was a big deal too, but as it turned out, it really wasn't," I commented.

"How did you tell her?" Vince asked.

"Well, I finally just came out and told her my true feelings," I replied.

"Hmm—I don't know, maybe next week I'll tell her," he said.

"That's what I did, put off telling Rosa—believe me, you would feel much better if you just told her," I suggested.

"Maybe you're right," Vince said, squirming. "But I wouldn't know what to say."

"Well, first go over to her, thank her for inviting you, and tell her how much you enjoyed this evening," I suggested. "Then say you really enjoyed her company and end it with maybe you guys can hang out together."

"Will you go with me?" Vince asked.

"Okay, let's go," I said, as we started toward Dora and Rosa.

"Cool," Vince said, with anticipation on his face.

We eased our way to Rosa and the giggling peanut gallery. There was some teasing, but I ignored it.

"Hi Vince, Jay," Dora greeted.

"Ah, hi Dora," Vince said.

"I'm glad you came," Dora said.

"Thanks, for inviting me—hope to talk to you later," Vince said. I just knew he was going to walk away, so I gently stopped him, putting my hand on his shoulder.

"Vince and I were just talking about how much we really enjoyed ourselves," I said, giving Vince another encouraging tap on the shoulder.

"Yeah," began Vince. "I really enjoyed your company tonight, Dora, thank you for the invitation."

"Me too," Dora said. "Hey Vince, we should hang out, like away from school."

"Sure that would be cool," Vince replied, looking up smiling. With that, my job was done.

Rosa stepped up to my side and cupped her hand to my ear. "I made you miss," she whispered, referring to the kiss on the dance floor.

"Maybe I didn't miss," I said, kissing her gloved hand as "The Mexican Pride Band" was back from their break. "Let's dance."

Juanita sang a song and so did Jorge's wife. We were having such a good time and before we knew, it was dinnertime. I sat next to Rosa of course. Mom suggested I offer to get Rosa's plate. Vince and Dora seemed to hit it off wonderfully.

Following dinner, there was more dance music and games including hitting the piñata. Without warning, as the cake was wheeled in from nowhere, the band struck up the birthday song as we sang. The cake was white and trimmed with lavender frosting. It was aflame with fifteen tiny torches for each of the girls. Rosa and Dora had the usual embarrassed "Please stop singing" comments. Some of us ended the song with "God Bless You" and finished the rest of the lyrics. Of course, Billie jested, "You look like a monkey too."—"Make-a-wish!" someone hollered.

"Rosa, Dora, do you have any wishes?"

"Not really, I think I have everything I need," Rosa replied, looking toward Heaven and then directly at me.

Soon everyone gathered in front of the table filled with a kaleidoscope of presents. When everyone in the hall visited, I snuck behind the table, found my present to give to Rosa, and hid it behind my back. The girls took turns opening the gifts. Gramma made Rosa a quilt and Mom got her perfume. One of the last things she received was a red leather jacket and boots from her parents, which soon became her trademark during high school.

"Is that all the gifts?" Ella asked.

"No," I said, stepping in front of Rosa, handing her the little box from behind my back. "You didn't think I would forget you?"

"You never do," Rosa replied.

"Go ahead and open it," Dora encouraged with a few others.

"Hold on, give me a minute," Rosa said. "Some things can't be rushed."

She delicately untied the ribbon, took the wrapping off carefully and folded it up neatly. There was the white box that everyone knew was a container for jewelry. At this point I was on pins and needles. The room was quiet. Rosa slowly took the lid off and peered in.

"What is it?" Dora impatiently asked.

"It's a..." Rosa began, pulling something out attached to a gold chain. "It's a heart locket with a rose on it...Wow..."

"Is there a picture inside?" Ella asked.

"Let me see," Rosa answered. I already saw how she was truly touched. "There is a picture of me...and...Jay."

She said the last part in a whisper while staring up at me. I just expected tears in her eyes, but they suddenly turned to a fountain of golden river-lets. Springing up with the necklace in her hand, and while caught up in the moment, she hugged me and kissed my face.

"Jay, it's wonderful," Rosa said, squeezing me tightly. "I'm just, I'm just—can't believe—I'm so surprised! Thank you—thank you—thank you!"—Then whispering, "I love you."

"She must have really liked it," Manny said, chuckling and walking toward us. "Rosa, can I see it?"

Rosa handed it to him. He examined it and then peered at his daughter. After he handed it back, he looked at me and said, "This is very nice, Jay. You must have put a lot of thought into it."

For a brief moment, Manny gave us a curious stare that may have implied, "I'll keep a close watch on you two." The next thing I knew, Manny ruffled my hair, quickly giving me some reassurance.

The band fired up and for the rest of the evening a few of us danced. We had a great time the remainder of the evening visiting, laughing, eating, and other things relating to a party. Half the guests left before nine o'clock including Rosa's grandparents. Rosa and Dora's Quinceañera came to a satisfying close. Giving Rosa the locket pretty much was the last spices to the enchilada.

The morning after, I officially told Mom that Rosa was my girlfriend. Neither Mom nor anyone else asked how long we were together.

Chapter Eighteen

A FEW days later, Rosa's real birthday came around. She celebrated with a little party at their house and ordered pizzas; Gramma brought over cupcakes. Kaylee, De'von, and Zoey joined us. I was more than excited, like it was my own birthday because Rosa told her dad about us going on a date. We discussed our official first date.

Rosa visited with the girls in her room and I found myself alone in the kitchen with Manny. We made some small talk for a while and then he shifted the conversation to where I cared not go, but I knew it had to be done.

"Rosa tells me you guys want to go on a date," Manny said, as we stepped onto the back porch.

"Uh huh," I croaked out, being somewhat nervous.

"It's fine by me," Manny began. "Let me know where you guys are going so I can drop you off and pick you up."

"Well, we are going to the Mexican place, here in Deer Park," I offered. "How about six o'clock?"

"That will be fine," he answered. "Since you guys are now dating, here are my ground rules which Rosa understands. During the week, when I'm at work, you two can walk to your house and/or go to one of your friends' houses just as long as I know a responsible adult is there. With regards to after school activities including karate class and the like, the same rule applies. I'm usually home by five o'clock. If I'm working overtime, Rosa is to go to your house until I get home. I expect responsibility and good behavior. Now weekends, you may stay up until ten o'clock on Friday and Saturday nights, but Rosa has to spend time with her mom and me on Sunday evenings. If I see something lacking in either of your parts, I will tighten the rules. Especially with schoolwork, I stress. I will confirm these rules with your mom and grandma. Do you understand?"

"Yes, sir," I replied.

"Good," Manny said, patting me on the shoulder. "You're a decent young man, Jay. There is you and then there are other guys."

Rosa and I went on our first date the following weekend. Manny would drive us to the Mexican restaurant in Deer Park, which was just on Main Street. I walked to their house and visited with Manny, as Rosa was not quite ready. Of course, I had my camera.

"How is school?" Manny asked. "Rosa says your Spanish is becoming more and more fluent."

"It is," I replied. "I really enjoy it."

"Glad you do. It's good being bilingual," Manny said. "Sure helps when visiting Mexico—would like to go back one day. Ella and I want to take Rosa one of these years."

"That would be cool," I said, trying to think of some conversation. "Maybe I can go with you guys—Mom and Gramma too."

"Yeah, you guys would love it there," Manny agreed.

"It sure would be a wonderful experience of a life time," I said.

"Speaking of, time sure flies," Manny reminisced. "I told Ella, it seems like just yesterday we walked Rosa to kindergarten."

I was distracted for a moment so I didn't hear Rosa enter the room.

"I heard you two talking about me," Rosa said.

"Yeah, all nice things," I said, and then spoke Spanish, "Te ves asombroso."

Rosa sure was a lovely sight. She wore a deep purple conservative dress just below the knees. Her hair was tightly woven in a French braid, which always suited her very nicely.

"Gracias, you look nice too," she said.

"Gracias, recepcion," I replied.

"Are we ready mi ninos?" Manny asked, and then we were off to the truck.

We pulled in the parking lot in front of a pink stucco building. The Mexican restaurant was called Rancho Allegre. It was a small establishment chain that preferred small towns like Deer Park.

"I'll be back here in the parking lot at seven," Manny said, after taking our picture.

We entered the sidewalk entrance and waited until the waitress finished seating another couple. Wonderful sounds and smells came from the kitchen. Mexican music found its way to our ears.

"This is so exciting Jay, our first official date," Rosa said.

"Yeah, I'm dreaming," I said, as the waitress welcomed us.

"Table for two?" a Mexican waitress asked.

"Si una mesa para dos," I said, indicating an empty space in the back.

"Ven por este lado," she said, leading us to a booth and handing us menus. After telling her what we wanted to drink, she left.

"I'm already having so much fun," Rosa commented and giggled.

"Me too," I agreed. "We have waited for this occasion for so long…"

"And now it's here," Rosa said, reaching for my hand.

"At last," I added while placing my other hand on top of hers.

The waitress came back with a small bowl of salsa and a basket of freshly baked tortilla chips. Moments later, she came with our drinks.

We munched on salsa and chips after ordering from the menu. I chose two enchiladas and Rosa ordered a quesadilla—both with chicken.

The Mexican music had fast singers and I couldn't make out the words, so Rosa translated for me. We talked about our friends and karate class. We laughed and joked about silly things. We shared our flavorful meals, just enjoying ourselves every second. Our first date went just the way we imagined it.

The following week we were definitely high school sweethearts. For the most part, we obeyed the rules and looked forward to our walks home everyday. It was the only time we could be truly alone. No parents looking over our shoulders.

April came along and I noticed three new guys in the karate school's men's dressing room. There were two boys about eleven or twelve and a guy about my age. They were all new beginners with stiff white belts and crisp uniforms right out of the plastic.

The two boys were having trouble with their belts, so after I tightened my belt, I walked over to them.

"Hello, my name is Jay. Let me help you with that," I said, bending forward. Then I demonstrated tying a knot with them. "Open your belt full length, place it around the front of your waist, then take the two ends behind your back and crisscross it to the left hip since you're a guy."

"Thanks Jay," one boy said. Their names were Mel and Roy.

The other new guy approached me. "Name's Morry," he said. "My sister, Molly, and I signed up—she's my twin sister—so you're a black belt, that's cool."

"Yep, since last fall," I replied, as we headed out. "You'll like it here. Sensei Lance is a very good martial artist—respectful and fair teacher."

"Hey, there is my sister, you can meet her," Morry said, as we walked up to her. "Hey Molls, this is Jay—he's a black belt."

"Hey," Molly said. "I already like it here; Rosa and Patty are showing me around."

Molly had blonde hair, pulled back and fixed in a bun. They both seemed nice and friendly.

"Nice meeting you," I said to Molly. "We better get going."

Rosa and I showed the newcomers around the school and acquainted them with the everyday routines. Not many females signed up for the Kenpo hard style of karate, but soon the number did grow; males still made up the majority of the class. Besides Rosa and Patty, there were two other girls under eighteen in our class. Rosa and the other girls made Molly feel comfortable.

I led the newcomers to the training room entrance where I had them wait. "Please be quiet and respect the class in session," I explained. "Follow me to the back mat perimeter."

"Those who are white and yellow belts will be lined up in the last row," Rosa whispered on the way.

"When this class is over, Sensei Lance will say line up," I said quietly to the new students at the perimeter.

"Today, we have some new students with us," Lance announced, after we lined up. "Give them a good Kenpo welcome."

We proceeded with our stretches and warm-ups. Lance followed by going over some basic Kenpo wisdom and techniques, including stances mainly for the new students. I went in front to demonstrate. The rest of us were reinforced with the basics.

"Let's break up into groups," Lance said. "Howard will be working with the orange, purple, and blue belts. Jay will work with white and yellow. Let's have a satisfying workout. Remember focus and pay attention to your instructor."

I gathered Morry, Molly, the other two boys, and Jacob the lone yellow belt into a group. First, I had them meditate and practice some stances.

Morry and Molly were eager students with good attitudes. Of course, there were always students to discipline especially with the boys Mel and Roy. Previously, I helped with others one-on-one who already knew many skills, making it easier to teach them.

After teaching my group for a few days, Morry approached me following a recent workout. "Jay, Molly and I were wondering if you would do private lessons? Perhaps here after class or just on the weekend since we are all in school."

"Sure, that will be fine with me, but let me check with Sensei Lance first," I said.

Manny and Ella renewed their wedding vows the last weekend in April. It was a nice small ceremony at our church. They had a little reception down in the Fellowship Hall.

Ella happily moved back in with Manny and Rosa and became a family again. Everything seemed to be running smoothly now that Manny and Ella were back together. Recently, Ella had rededicated herself to our Lord and became a member of our church.

Chapter Nineteen

May 2005

ROSA AND I, along with our friends and classmates, came upon our mid-teens, a most delicate time for all. We were vulnerable to temptations of many sorts and colors. At our age, the twenty-first century was filled with a variety of means to lose oneself. Our bodies and minds were being challenged as we matured into the individuals we would become later on. For some, physical growth matured faster than our minds could keep up and vice versa.

I guess for myself, I was an average teenager. My faith in the Holy Trinity was strong and I kept God's commandments close to my heart, but that's not to say I was perfect. We all knew as Christians the one person who was perfect, this being Jesus Christ and I strived to be just like Him.

There were a series of moments in my life where I just lost total sense of reality. Everything that I learned from God and His Holy Bible were somehow forgotten for a brief time. Rosa and I never realized it, but we would set ourselves up for a fall. As humans we were sinful creatures. At the time, things started off innocent and they seemed right.

It all began a couple months after our first date. The third semester of our freshman year came to a close. We didn't think much about our report cards when we received them, nor did we think it could affect our close relationship.

The last period bell rang and I met Rosa at her locker.

"What did you get on your report card Jay?" Rosa asked, grabbing some books.

"Not as well as I hoped, but I did okay," I replied. "Let's see, I got one A, a couple B's, and the rest are C's—I could have concentrated on algebra more."

"You did better than I did," she said, viewing my card and handing me hers. "I got one A in choir, B in algebra—my dad is going to kill me, the rest are C's and one D—Jay, I'm scared."

"It will be alright. Just tell him we will study harder," I said, hugging her shoulders. Manny's words came to me—*if I see something lacking on either of your parts then I will tighten the rules.*

"Maybe you're right," Rosa said, as we stepped outside into the sun. The last of the buses were leaving and parents were picking up their kids.

"It's not like I'm failing—just a dumb D—isn't C average anyway?" she said.

"Right," I replied.

So we walked home on a nice Friday, May, spring day. We just enjoyed each other and tried not to think about our report cards, but there was worry in our voices. The subject changed often to lead us away from the anticipation of the adults' reactions—most particularly, Manny.

By the time we were halfway to my house, our report cards found their way back into the conversation. We tried to reason our grade problems away.

"You know, you got a D plus—which is almost like a C," I said.

"Yeah, you're right, it is," Rosa said, finally smiling again. "Thanks Jay, you always make me feel better."

With that we felt more at ease about our situation, entering our street and walking into my house. Gramma was busy in the sewing room and Mom was off doing laundry or something, so I didn't have to present my report card right away. We sat on the living room floor in front of the coffee table, laying out our books.

"Let's start this new semester right," Rosa said. "I want to concentrate harder on my studies. Where do we start?"

"Hi guys," Mom announced, popping her head in sometime later. "How was school?"

"Well, you know, just school," I replied.

"Yeah, same old, same thing, school," Rosa said.

"Life as a ninth grader—homework is harder and you would rather be somewhere else," Mom said, gathering misplaced items. "Don't mind me, just need to straighten the room up. Hey, did you guys get your report cards today? I can see you're busy so you can show me later."

Diligently, we worked into the afternoon on our homework, finishing most of it. We tried not to get too distracted with each other much and kept our attention more on the school assignments.

"I forgot to do some chores for my dad yesterday," Rosa suddenly said, starting to pack up. "I guess I should go home right now before he gets home."

"Yeah, I probably have some chores too and need to work on my karate form," I agreed. "I'll come over after dinner. I'll be thinking about you."

"But then again, I have five minutes," Rosa said with a sneaky smile on her face, pulling me down on the couch next to her. Five minutes turned into ten then fifteen. "Oh, I hate to leave....but I suppose..."

"Yeah, I don't want you to get into trouble," I said. "I'll walk you out."

We stepped out on my front porch, holding hands and smiling, while looking into each other's eyes. Following a little kiss, we tried to say good-bye like it was the last time we would be together. I decided to walk her home.

An hour later, I finished dinner and was about to head out the door to Rosa's house, when the phone rang. It was one of those unexpected rings where you just knew who it was followed by dreaded bad news you didn't want to hear.

"I'll get it!" I hollered, holding my breath and reaching for the cordless phone.

My first feeling was right when I picked up the phone and saw the word 'SANCHEZ' on the caller ID. Before I could say hello, there was Rosa on the other end.

"Oh Jay, oh Jay, what are we going to do?" she cried desperately. "He can't do that to me...not fair!" My heart jumped to my feet, my head spun.

"What happened?" I asked, knowing instantly what it was, but hoped it was something else—maybe this was where I woke up.

"I gave my dad my report card, then he grounded me right there," she replied. "I tried to tell him I would study harder and get my grades up, but he wouldn't listen—I'm grounded for six weeks—can you believe that?"

"No, that stinks," I replied.

"He said I couldn't have friends over or go anywhere—no phone, he took away my cell phone and my stereo in my room. I especially can't see you until report cards come out again—I can't go for that long without seeing you—Oh Jay, I just don't know what to do."

"Well, at least we can see each other at school, but still," I said.

"I wish you could be with me—I know, maybe you could convince my dad," she suggested.

"What can I say?" I said. "I really don't think he will listen to me, I'm part of the problem."—In my ear I heard bang-bang-bang—

"Dad, I'm telling Jay he can't come over, okay," she said away from the receiver, then to me, "I guess I better go. I don't want him to be any angrier." She lowered her voice to a whisper. "Love you Jay…I'll see you at church."

"Love you too Rosa, you know where to reach me," I said.

I stood there after hanging up, just staring at the phone. Rosa grounded for six weeks. That seemed like a long time and I couldn't comprehend being away from Rosa either. What went wrong? I thought we studied reasonably well.

"Mom, here's my report card," I said sometime later. "By the way, Rosa's grounded for six weeks."

"Oh honey, what happened?"

"Manny didn't like her report card," I said, dropping to the couch. "I thought she did okay, but her dad won't listen—just doesn't seem fair." I leaned on my elbows and rested my chin in my hands.

"I see that you could have done better too," Mom pointed out. "I know you'll improve, but I'm not going to ground you."

"At least you understand."

"I trust you to prioritize your schoolwork, karate, your friends, and especially your girlfriend."

"I know, but still," I began. "I just don't get it—maybe you could talk to Manny."

"I don't think it would do any good. You know Manny, once he makes up his mind there's no convincing," she said. "Besides Jay, it's only six weeks. It will be over before you guys know it. You'll see her at school."

"I guess you're right," I said, giving in, but wanting to fight it. "Oh well, I'll be in my room doing my homework."

The afternoon and evening dragged on and on. I imagined Rosa tucked in her bed, staring glumly up at the ceiling. Six weeks still seemed like an awfully long time, so I stopped looking at the clock. It helped for about half an hour then I was back counting the minutes.

Gramma made my favorite meal, her "Most Excellent Pot Roast," which I came to call it and it stuck with everyone. I could see Gramma and Mom trying to make me feel better. They did ease my mind a little. I sure was famished, but after eating a few bites, I was lost in my thoughts and began to play with my food. I figured Manny finally convinced Rosa to come out of her room to eat. He would make her laugh seeing her so blue.

Bedtime made it worse. Perhaps the Lord had some reason for all of this so I prayed asking for His guidance.

"Dear Lord, I feel lost—I know it is just six weeks—I know I haven't been focused on you. Actually, I can handle it and I pray for patience. Maybe You know I need some time for myself…"

I drifted off to sleep sometime later and started having a mixture of dreams. They were weird and startling at first yet one seemed real. My cell phone rang in my dream and I was talking to Rosa.

"Jay, are you awake?" she asked in the dream.

"No, I was supposed to be asleep," I heard myself say.

"Sorry, maybe it is a bad idea for me to see you now," she said somberly.

"What?!" I asked, suddenly realizing it wasn't a dream. I was actually talking to her, the cell phone in my hand with its face glowing blue at me. I looked at my alarm clock, but couldn't focus on the red numbers as sleep sand bothered me—"What time is it?"

"1:45 in the morning," Rosa answered. "I just wanted to hear your voice…probably should let you sleep…see you tomorrow at school—Oh, I guess we can't, tomorrow is Saturday."

I rubbed my eyes and it was indeed fifteen to two. "Rosa don't hang up, I'm awake now. What were you saying when I was half asleep? About coming over now?"

"Maybe, it was a silly idea," she said. "I know it's my fault that we can't see each other—I know I'll see you at school, but…I just want to see you one time alone, you know just to talk—probably think I'm a dummy…"

"It's not your fault. Your dad's just being unfair," I said. "Rosa, you're not a dummy. You're my smart girl, my beautiful smart girl."

"You're just saying that because I'm your girlfriend," she said.

"No I'm not—you're the math whiz," I said. "You just got one measly D in history and soon I know it will be history."

"But you got a C."

"Doesn't make me any better. I did get a C minus, it's almost like a D," I said. "You know it's only Friday night and we can sleep in tomorrow. Since we're both awake anyway, why don't you just come over—"

"Oh good, I'll meet you in your backyard!" she said, hanging up before I could say anything else.

Not wasting any time, I threw my robe over my pajamas and slowly came out of my room. I tried to be as quiet as possible while approaching the top of the stairs. When I came upon the staircase, I became wary and paused, peering down into the darkness below. I stood there listening to the familiar creaks and groans of the house. Just heard the normal noises, so I stepped down a couple of steps and listened. I repeated this until I reached the second to the last step which was noisy, so I slipped over it. Stopping on the last step, I peered at Gramma's bedroom in front of me. Her door was closed as usual which meant she was sleeping and not in the kitchen when she couldn't sleep. Next I looked around the corner to Mom's bedroom. This was not the time for me to make a noise because her door was open. If I was caught, I hoped it would be then because I would have an excuse that I couldn't sleep. It wouldn't help Rosa though. The longer I waited, the more chance I would be caught.

I briefly visited the bathroom, quickly sprayed that mint stuff in my mouth, and turned on the sink faucet carefully to splash my face. As I looked in the mirror, it hit me—*what are you doing Jay?* I suddenly thought. *Sneaking around like this in the middle of the night with your GIRLFRIEND! What was wrong with me?* I knew better, and if someone caught us we would be in even more trouble. We could even be grounded for the rest of the summer, or worse!

I imagined Rosa already there in my backyard waiting for me. Spring nights were pretty chilly and there was always a chance of a couple more frosts before summer. I didn't want her to wait too much longer in the cold. It would just be one night, we would talk for a while then that would be that. *Okay here we go.*

I ventured into the dark hall keeping my senses alert. Feeling my way around the dining room table, I made my way around to the French doors. I thought of something when I went to unlock the door.

I backtracked and looked down the hall. If Mom was awakened she may have followed me. No one was there. I felt my way around again and carefully unlocked the door. Slipping out to the back porch, it was a cool and clear night, just as I expected. I wondered where Rosa was; I didn't see her yet. Stepping off the porch I was startled.

"Boo!" Rosa hollered, grabbing me from the side.

"You scared the crap out of me," I said. "You could have woken the whole neighborhood."

"Sorry, I wasn't trying to scare you, just wanted to surprise you," she said, embracing me. "I know this must be crazy coming out here, I just couldn't sleep."

"It's not crazy—whatever makes you happy," I said, having doubts but pushing them away. "I can't help it, but you smell good."

"Thanks," she said, holding me tighter. "I could stay like this forever."

We sat on the back steps talking and enjoying each other's company, while listening to the nightly neighborhood noises. Rosa had her head on my shoulder. Soon we were outside for almost an hour. I started to become drowsy and about to fall asleep when I suddenly jerked awake. I heard Rosa snoring, which must have been what woke me.

"Rosa, wake up," I said, shaking her.

"Oh Dad, not yet, I was having a wonderful dream," she mumbled.

"Rosa, it's not a dream. Remember, you called me."

"No, it's still a dream," Rosa said. "Did I fall asleep?"

"Yeah, maybe we should say goodnight," I said, as we stood stretching and rubbing our eyes.

"Oh Jay, wish we didn't have to go," Rosa said, grasping my hands as a small kiss ensued. "Oh, goodnight Jay, I love you. I feel much better."

"I am glad you suggested doing this," I said. "I love you too, goodnight."

I snuck back in and everything seemed just like it was before I snuck out. The kitchen was still dark, Gramma's door was still shut, and it appeared Mom hadn't moved. I hit the pillow at four in the morning.

The next moment I was awakened with a start. Someone knocked on my bedroom door. I sat straight up and saw that it was 9:30 in the morning. Man, I could have slept another couple hours.

"Come in," I said.

Gramma crept in. "We were wondering if you were going to wake up soon," she said. "And thought you would like to sleep in, but then I checked the fridge calendar. Did you know you had a—"

"Oh, I totally spaced that out," I said, remembering. "I was supposed to do a workout with Morry and Molly at their house. Thanks for waking me."

Once a week I agreed to do private karate lessons at their home. Morry and Molly wanted to thank me for helping them with the extra lessons, so they invited Gramma, Mom, and me to a barbeque afterwards.

The next day I looked forward to Sunday school because I knew Rosa would be attending. I convinced Mom that I needed to get to church fifteen minutes early. Perhaps Rosa was thinking the same thing, but she came in exactly on time. All we could do was exchange smiles, easing our moods a little.

Rosa and I raced outside to the parking lot following the service. This gave us a couple minutes to be together to at least say hello while Manny and the others were busy visiting with the people from church.

Monday came around and Manny drove Rosa to school while Gramma took me. Rosa was dropped off minutes before first bell sounded as I waited for her. She ran to me and threw her arms around me.

"Oh Jay, it's only been three days and I'm going to die without you," she said, desperately squeezing me tight.

"I know, I can't stand it without you either," I said. "Cheer up mi muchacha hermosa."

The following Monday, at the end of school, we were both gloomy getting ready to leave each other for the day. I tried my best to make Rosa feel better. She did manage a smile that was probably for my benefit.

"Rosa, I don't want to see you like this. You're always so cheerful," I said.

"Sorry, I wish this was all over," she said. "I'm trying harder. Maybe, if I do extra chores…oh well."

"Oh, I know what would make you feel better," I began.

"What is it? Don't keep me in suspense," she said with curiosity and excitement.

"Come over tonight like we did the other night," I said.

"Really?!" she said.

"Sure, it's no big deal," I said. "Your dad sleeps like a freight train and I am pretty quiet."

"Oh Jay, that would be wonderful!" she said, springing so jubilantly up to hug me.

"But just this one more night," I added.

So we planned on meeting in my backyard about 1:30 in the morning. I said goodnight to Mom and Gramma about nine that night. I waited until the time approached, keeping busy. I did nothing for a couple hours just watched the clock. Of course, Rosa was like a butterfly flittering in my mind, which inspired me to write a poem. Being so excited, I left a half hour early. Rosa must have thought the same thing because she was standing right there. She embraced me warmly.

"There's my Honeybee," she said.

"Here's my Butterfly," I responded. "You smell like strawberries in the fresh rain."

"Oh Jay, I always love the way you talk to me," Rosa returned.

"I'm so glad you are in good spirits," I said. We stood just holding each other tight. All of our worries disappeared into the good night…"Let's not sit on those cold hard steps. I thought of something better."

"More surprises," she said.

"Step right this way," I said, leading her inside the garage where I usually did my karate workout.

"I like your idea already," Rosa said. "I can't see anything."

"Hang on for one second," I said, fumbling in the dark, then snap!

"Cool, you put Christmas twinkle lights up!" Rosa exclaimed, with eyes gleaming delightfully. She saw me reach into a plastic bag. "Now what are you doing?"

"Well, we might as well be comfortable on our last sneak-around-night," I explained, taking out a rolled up sleeping bag and spreading it out on the bench. "Here we go—a nice place to sit."

"Jay, you're spoiling me," Rosa said, giggling as we sat. "This is real cozy."

"And for the cool night, a blanket for my girl," I said.

I placed it around her shoulders and hugged her. "Wow Jay, when did you plan all this?"

"This afternoon," I whispered. "There's even an old alarm clock already in here. I knew it would have new uses."

"This is great, our own little sanctuary," Rosa commented, returning the whisper. "Hey, Jay, I don't want to be a blanket hog—let's share." She lifted up the blanket and I snuggled beside her.

"Now, you're spoiling me," I said, in the soft light.

"You make me so happy!" Rosa said, squeezing the air out of me. "So thoughtful and romantic, not to mention poetic."

"Speaking of…I wrote you a poem," I said.

<u>Kisses from My Butterfly</u>

You are a butterfly fluttering in my mind,
Making my head dizzy all the time
Then soon drifting into my sweet dreams
Spinning lovely fumes remain so it seems
Hoping, I happily visit the garden with glee
Awaiting silky kisses from my butterfly, can't you see!

Our secret rendezvous didn't stop there as they continued to take place the next three nights. It was wonderful, enjoying our two hours or so those nights together. Somewhere in the back of my mind I knew it was wrong, but I just hated to see Rosa blue during her grounding. It felt good to make her smile and laugh. We were careful, weren't we? Who would find out? No one would catch us. Those statements were foolishly thrown around in the garage.

Everyone was excited when Friday came along because summer break was on the horizon. So when Rosa and I met at our routine time, we were extra frisky. She jumped in my arms all giggly with happy eyes.

"Shh, we don't want to ruin this," I said, but she laughed some more.

"Who is going—" she started to yell out, but I kissed her before she could say anything else, leading her into the garage.

"Oh Jay, we're kissing in the dark," she said, pulling away as I turned on the Christmas lights.

"I sure feel hyper, must have been all those sodas after school," I commented, feeling the caffeine buzzing through me.

"Me too," she said, fidgeting. "I could stay up all night with you." She giggled some more.

"Now don't get too greedy," I said, laughing along with her.

"So what if I'm greedy. What would you do?" she teased, advancing toward me and we were kissing again. I pulled away.

"Oh Rosa, I so love you," I said, playing with her hair and gazing into her brown eyes. "There will be no one else." She circled around me singing a little tune.

"You know Jay, I think we truly are high school sweethearts," Rosa said, softly putting her arms around my neck. "Then you know, like what your folks did…duh, dah, dah, duh…you know… after graduation."

"You mean…Oh, us together forever," I said, with a serious smile.

"Till death do us part," she added. "I know you would, won't you Jay? What if I said maybe or no?"

"It depends on what I would ask," I teased.

"What else would it be?" she said. "I dare you to ask me now—this very moment."

"I know I would ask you what you wanted to hear, but then it wouldn't be a surprise would it?" I questioned, as we sat on the bench.

Now, the next moment, we were just sitting there enjoying our closeness, when Rosa suddenly grabbed the collar of my pajamas. She brought me to the mat without letting go and we headed out of control, far from reality. During this we were kissing crazily.

Two things happened which scared us to death, not to mention God looking down on us. I don't know how it happened, but between the bench and us rolling around Rosa's shirt opened up in the front to something I shouldn't be seeing. For a brief period of time, I was transfixed with wonder, my mind racing in different directions. Rosa finally realized what had happened. Frozen, we could not move. That was the first thing. The other was I noticed my position toward her. Quickly, her bracelet caught my eye and she also saw mine. Startled, I backed off suddenly sitting next to her.

"Oh my, what are we doing?" I said, out of breath.

"Oh no!" Rosa exclaimed, pulling her shirt closed, then hugging herself. "This is embarrassing. I'm so sorry. I don't know how this all happened."

"Me either, sure didn't expect that…"

"I guess we almost failed," Rosa said, getting up to put on her robe.

"Yep."

"Jay, I don't want you to think that these bracelets mean nothing to me…I still mean…I will save myself for you…" Her mood changed suddenly and she was crying.

"What is it sweetheart?"

"I can't tell you—you would think I'm a horrible person," she replied, sobbing.

"No, I wouldn't."

"Promise you won't break up with me?"

"I promise, but it never crossed my mind," I said, now becoming worried. "Rosa, please tell me."

"I wanted to pretend, you know—oh, Jay, I'm so horrible to think that," she said, turning away. I gave her my shoulder to cry on. "I'm a horrible person…I'm lost…I liked the way it felt…"

"Rosa, you're not a bad person…" I said.

"Yes, I am," she said, pulling away. "If I hadn't called you this would never have happened…all my fault, leading us to do wrong."

"It is not all your fault, I freely participated too," I said.

"But…"

"But we have Jesus," I said, comforting her head. "Maybe it was all those soda pops we drank—we were sure wired."

"Maybe you're right," Rosa said, finally chuckling. "Oh, Jay, you're such a wonderful boyfriend and I love you so much."

"I love you, too, sweetheart," I returned.

"Walk me home," she said relieved.

That was the final night of our secret meetings. We sure learned a lot from that intimate moment. Something deep inside woke me up and I know God was looking down on us. It was real hard fighting those fleshy temptations. I never imagined putting myself into that predicament. We knew it was wrong meeting in the middle of the night, in our sleepwear, sneaking, knowing we could get caught and be grounded for the rest of the summer. We threw out what was right and did whatever we felt like doing. It just snuck up on us like a surprise birthday party. Of course, it's never planned.

Chapter Twenty

WHEN THE following Thursday came around, there were four weeks left on Rosa's grounding. Rosa hinted that her dad might let me see her real soon. So that afternoon, when I came home from school I was extra excited and looked forward to spending some daylight time with her. Gramma was busy at a quilting bee with her friends so it was just Mom and me.

While sitting on the couch doing my homework, I heard some commotion across the street. Walking up to the window, I saw Manny and Rosa getting into his truck. *Maybe her dad wants to get her out of the house,* I thought.

A half hour later, came rap, rap, rap of the front door. *Rosa!* I thought. *Maybe they just drove around to talk as they sometimes did.* Quickly, I put down my pen, rushing to open the door.

"Molly?" I began, my hopes vanishing. At first I didn't recognize her because she had her blonde hair down. She usually wore it up during karate class. "Hi, Molly, how are you? Were we supposed to do some karate today? Where's Morry?"

"No," Molly replied. "I just dropped by and thought you might like some company. I brought my homework. I was feeling bored at home. Parents are having some get together. I hope it's alright—if you're busy I can leave."

"Where's your ride?"

"Jeff dropped me off," Molly answered, turning toward the street for a moment and pointing. "He was headed out here anyway to do some golfing, so here I am."

"Sure, you can come in, I was just working on my homework," I said, feeling some what odd. I turned back taking a few steps toward the couch. "Have a seat, you can sit anywhere. Would you like something to drink?"

"Water would be fine," she replied.

I grabbed a glass of water out of the kitchen. As I was headed toward the living room, I glanced over at Molly who was sitting on the couch. I started feeling uncomfortable with the visit for some reason. Perhaps it was still the fact she came alone. I laughed to myself and thought, *who am I kidding?* Delusional.

Molly's visit was not out of the ordinary, her and Morry hung out on occasion. She was a friend; I have a lot of girls that are my friends. There's Kaylee, Zoey, and the twins who were in our poetry group. I imagined nothing. There was a reason for everything. Maybe I could help her with homework or something with karate.

"Here you go," I said, handing her the glass.

"Thanks," she said, looking up briefly to take the glass. There was nothing in her eyes to indicate anything more than a friendly visit.

Now a crew cut t-shirt and shorts were not much to fuss over because that's what many girls wore in the summer.

Also, this could be an opportunity to spread the Lord's Good News to somebody who may or may not have given themselves totally to Jesus. The Lord said we are supposed to minister to our family and friends. Molly and Morry mentioned a time or two they attended church occasionally and they believed in God.

"Morry told me to tell you 'hi'," she began, as I sat down wondering how I was going to bring up God. "He's doing something with his nerd friends."

Some people were leery about others talking about religion or God so I liked to ease into it.

"Tell him 'hi' for me," I said. "Hey, have you and Morry ever been to Bible camp?"

"No, the only camp we went to was when we were in sixth grade," she replied.

"Well, it's great! I think you would enjoy it," I said. "I went last year and had a great time."

"What do you do there, just read the Bible? Or is it just like other camps?"

"Yeah, we do other things, hiking, swimming, all kinds of stuff," I replied.

"Are you going? I probably wouldn't know anybody," she said.

"I'm going. It happens in July—I could give you some info if you're interested," I offered.

"Sure, sounds like fun and I may even learn something from the Bible—I know I haven't been loyal to God, not attending church. Don't know the last time I opened a Bible up—I bet you could teach me a thing or two—what's your favorite verse? I kinda like the one that sorta goes like 'The Lord is my shepherd; I shall not want. He maketh me to lie down in green pastures: he leadeth me beside the still waters'—don't know the rest."

"'He restoreth my soul: he leadeth me in the paths of righteousness for his name's sake...'" I finished it for her. "Psalm 23, that's a good one."

"Hey Jay, I'm going to have to go to the store, forgot something for dinner," Mom said entering. "Oh hi, Molly didn't know we had company."

"Hi, Jay's mom," Molly said delightfully.

"Well, I was going to ask Jay if he wanted to go with me, but I see you guys are busy with homework. Jay do you need anything from the store?" Mom asked.

"No, nothing I can think of," I said.

"Well, I'll let you get back to your brainwork," Mom said, then left.

"So, what were we talking about?" I asked Molly who looked interested and excited about the Bible discussion. "Oh yeah, I guess I was going to tell you my favorite verse. It's in the Book of Proverbs chapter 3 verses 5 and 6: 'Trust in the Lord with all thine heart; and lean not unto thine own understanding. In all thy ways acknowledge him, and he shall direct thy paths.'"

We proceeded to do our homework, which I noticed Molly had barely any. It took me ten minutes to finish my work so we sat there talking. The conversation went on to karate and school. Whatever delusions I had earlier were gone. There was a pause in our conversation.

"So, what should we talk about now?" I asked, fishing for interesting topics. I wanted to direct her back to God.

"I don't know," Molly said in thought. "What are you doing for the summer?"

"Let's see. Well, I like to go to Rich's cabin, do some fishing," I replied.

"I love to go to the lake, go swimming, water skiing, and get a tan for these white legs," she said, placing her feet on the coffee table.

For some reason I watched her massage her thigh, but did not think I was staring—my heart jumped when Molly turned her attention from her legs to my eyes. It was too late, I was caught, and she followed where my eyes had been. She smiled at me and I gave her an embarrassing smile. I began to have those delusions again.

Uncomfortably, I shifted in my seat and felt sweat form on the palms of my hands. I leaned to rest my elbow on the arm of the couch while my fist supported my cheek. Innocently, I looked around pretending nothing happened. *Calm down Jay, take a breath. This can't be happening.*

"You who, Jay?" she said.

I turned to her avoiding eye contact and cleared my throat. "Sorry, where were we?" I asked. "Oh yeah, so which lake do you guys go to? You know what, I have never water skied before—couldn't be any different than snow skiing."

She pulled her legs onto the couch, hugging them. "They're different, but I like to be warm. Every year mom and dad and some of our friends get together for boating and camping on Lake Roosevelt."

"Sounds like fun," I said.

"Hey, why don't you join us this summer?" Molly suggested. "You know what? I never have fished before. All these years on the lake and I never fished. But I am willing to try. How about I take you water skiing and you can teach me to fish?"

I shrugged my shoulders and gave her a half sure. Looking down, I twiddled my thumbs and felt the couch sink. From the corner of my eye I saw Molly adjust her legs beneath her.

"So, when is Jeff coming to pick you up?"

"In an hour or so… why?"

"No reason, just wondered," I replied, feeling time slowly moving and hoping Mom would be back real soon.

"Jay, loosen up!" Molly said, turning sideways and resting her elbow on the back of the couch, facing me.

At this time I was dying, in my mind all I could see was her legs. She smiled at me like she knew what I was thinking. There was something devious about her smile.

"I'm fine," I said.

"You look anxious. Did I do something wrong?" she said, moving slightly toward me.

"Oh, nothing." I mumbled looking away—

Before I knew, Molly wrapped her arms around my neck and I was stunned when she kissed me hard. I couldn't move, frozen in her grasp. For some reason I didn't push her away. Now the only girl who kissed me that way was Rosa. *Rosa!* I was suddenly worried about Rosa and what was happening, but at the same time Molly's kiss intrigued me. It was different, and I was more curious. I didn't know if she was going to pull away, but I instantly placed my hand behind her head and kissed her back. Suddenly, I felt guilty and began to come out of the embrace. At the same time, I heard someone coming from the kitchen—what will Mom think? Then I heard a girl's voice.

"Jay, Jay!" Rosa said with a big smile that soon vanished from her face.

"Rosa wait!" I yelled out, as she darted out the kitchen door.

I ran after her stumbling around the dining room table and tripping out the door. There was a flash down the street and I saw Rosa move quickly. Anxiety flowed through me trying to catch up. We were on a dead sprint. I saw her turn the corner and was not making any ground on her. Soon we headed down the street toward Main. At this time Rosa stopped before crossing Main Street. She was hunched over probably out of breath. I did the same thing, a block in-between us.

"Rosa, will you wait up?" I hollered, between panting. "It's not what you think! She means nothing to me! Let me just explain."

"I have seen enough," Rosa yelled back. "How could you Jay? And Molly, for goodness sake, I saw you all over her!"

"I made a mistake, please believe me," I said. "I don't know what came over me. I'm sorry. I didn't mean to hurt you."

"I don't want to see you again—stay away from me!" Rosa cried, tears streaming down her face as she took off again.

This can't be happening, this can't be happening, I thought, feeling tears behind my eyes. Rosa crossed the street and then I saw her turn on Short Road that went out to the countryside. Most likely she was headed toward Zoey's ranch. I pursued her, but had to stop for the traffic. I lost precious time.

When I finally ran onto Short Road, Rosa was nowhere in sight. I slowed to a jog, deciding it was no use. Zoey lived five or six miles away. So I just walked. It gave me a chance to think. I just really wanted to make up. Many questions entered my mind. What did Rosa see? How long was she there? What did she hear? Why did I have to be such an idiot? I knew better than to kiss Molly back.

By the time I reached the edge of Zoey's ranch, I had somewhat of an idea the things I would say to Rosa. They were probably conspiring against me. Halfway down the dirt drive, I saw a group of girls across the way in front of the house. It wasn't long before they saw me. Zoey stopped me from going any further. I was close enough to hear the girls talking.

"Haven't you caused enough trouble?" Zoey asked with fire in her eyes and her arms crossed tightly.

"I'm not here to fight, just want to talk to Rosa," I replied, looking over Zoey's shoulder.

"She doesn't want to talk to you," she returned, blocking my view. "Why don't you just leave?"

"Not until I talk to Rosa!" I said so everyone could hear me. "Rosa I'm sorry. Please let me explain."

"Don't you get it, Jay? She doesn't want to *talk* to you, or *see* you," Zoey pointed out.

"Just let me say my peace then I will be gone, but I don't want to yell across the yard," I said, not waiting for an invitation.

"Get away cheater!" the twins said.

Kaylee and De'von were there, but they didn't really take any side that I could see. Rosa sat on a picnic table with her back turned from me. Zoey was behind me kicking dirt and gravel. I walked to the other side of the table so I could see Rosa's face, but she turned away.

"Rosa, I'm really, really, really sorry," I began. "I don't know if you will ever forgive me and I can't blame you for hating me. I admit my mistake, it will never happen again. I will get on my knees to show you and beg you to forgive me." At this time, I came around to where she looked away. I kneeled in front of the picnic bench grabbing for her hand. "Please forgive me, please…you mean everything to me. You know I Love You."

She got up before I could say any more and then said, "You *love* me! You didn't show it back there—kissing her."

"I lost my mind, it won't happen again," I said, walking on my knees.

"Yeah, you lost your mind and you lost me," she scowled at me, taking out her necklace that I gave her for her birthday. "Oh yeah, you were thinking of me when you were kissing that wench. It's over Jay."

Rosa got a hold of the necklace, ripping it off and throwing it at me. She stomped off inside Zoey's house. The other girls followed like a magnet with Kaylee and De'von lagging behind. De'von offered a hand, but I refused, getting up on my own with the necklace. I considered going up there to plead my case some more, but didn't want to make things worse. Stepping a few feet from the house, I looked away and studied the heart locket. If Rosa and my relationship were a piece of fabric, it was slowly tearing. Mending the fabric was my only concern.

I felt so lost walking home. There was a tin can and I started kicking it, being so mad at myself. It was those girls putting ideas in Rosa's head—that's it. What do they know about us?

Stopping for a moment, I held the necklace close to my eyes and began talking to it.

"What have I done?" I asked. "Just a kiss…didn't mean–that stupid Molly, why did she do that?—Molly!"

I started kicking the can harder down the road. Anger shot through me. *I'll give her a piece of my mind!*

When I stomped off Short Road, taking the same route, I realized Mom would be furious, taking off and coming home with just Molly there. Suddenly, I heard movement up in the tree, a black magpie cackled. He joined his friend in another tree. As they exchanged greetings, it sounded like they were saying, "You cheater, you cheater," or "Jerk, jerk!"

"Like you know!" I said, picking up a rock and throwing it at the magpies. They left laughing at me. Even the birds were picking on me. Everything felt like it was out to get me.

I kicked the can all the way to my house and stomped on it in the driveway. I sure was in for it, but all I thought about was finding Molly. Nothing else crossed my mind as I stormed through the kitchen door.

"Where is she?!" I demanded, finding Mom in the living room. I was a mad man looking out the window and opening the front door.

"Oh there you are, glad you came home—what's going on?" Mom sternly said. "Where are you going? Molly left, if that's who you're looking for." She followed me into the dining room as I looked out the French doors.

"Crap!" I said, going pass Mom and pacing in front of the coffee table.

"You know Jay, I was just gone half an hour and everything was okay when I left—what am I to think when I come home and you're not here and now you're so upset—Molly said that you and Rosa had a fight."

"That little…" I started, mumbling the rest of it, my teeth clenched.

"Jay, calm down and tell me what happened."

"I can't calm down," I said, sitting quickly on the couch and laying down. "I can't talk right now…oh I've got a headache."

"I don't like seeing you like this, Jay," she said. "What can I do for you?"

"Oh nothing," I replied, jerking up and placing my feet on the floor with my hands in my face. "Just rewind the day or wake me up… this can't be happening…Oh Mom, I lost her."

"Who have you lost, Rosa?"

"She doesn't want to see me anymore," I replied, holding up the necklace. I mumbled, "I'm such an idiot—I should have seen it coming with *that* girl coming on—just gave in—"

"I don't understand, you guys seemed fine, what happened?"

"When did Molly leave and what did she say? You probably believe her."

"Jay, I'm on your side and I haven't even heard your story," Mom said, sitting next to me. "Take a deep breath and start from the beginning."

"Molly kissed me and Rosa happened to see it," I explained, rubbing my temples. "I went over to Zoey's house and tried to apologize for what happened. Rosa would hear nothing of it—now everyone hates me—now my life is over."

"Son, you're talking nonsense," Mom said, trying to comfort me. "I'm sure Rosa will forgive you—you guys will make up, give it some time."

"I don't know," I replied, walking away. "I'll be in my room."

Finally calming down, I sat on my bed with my head spinning in chaos. The heart necklace was still in my hand. I played everything back in my head trying to make some sense of it all. After a while, I heard a noise outside my window and saw Manny walk out of his house. Maybe Rosa will be home soon and I could talk to her. I hurried downstairs.

"Jay, your dinner is on the stove when you're ready to eat," Mom said, standing at the table.

"I'm not hungry," I said, opening the front door.

"What are you doing?" Mom asked from behind me.

"Waiting for Rosa."

"Jay, just close the door, give her twenty-four hours and she might think differently tomorrow," Mom suggested, closing the door and leading me away.

Later, after Mom finished dinner, I went up to her giving her a big hug. "Sorry about the way I acted, I shouldn't let it get to me," I apologized.

"Son, it's understandable. A teenager's life is rough, especially now-a-days," she said, massaging my head. "But it really wasn't that different when I went to school—same peer pressure. Some things we have no control over. The only person you can control is yourself, but sometimes your emotions get out of control. You just have to learn to re-direct them."

"I know, but it's all my fault," I said. "Rosa will never forgive me. I saw it in her eyes."

"Things just happen. People see things differently and it's especially tough because you and Rosa were so close. I know you Jay. You wouldn't do something on purpose just to hurt somebody. Rosa probably thought she saw something that wasn't really what she thought she saw."

"Thanks Mom, I guess I feel a little better, and you're right, tomorrow is another day," I said just so she wouldn't worry. It was still tearing me up inside.

Without warning, I jumped when the phone rang. I heard Gramma answer it. Nervously, I walked toward her, my heart pounding.

"He's right here," Gramma said into the receiver. *Could it be Rosa?* I thought with excitement. "Phones for you Jay, it's…"

I grabbed it before she finished. "I'm glad you called R-R-Ro—oh, hi Kaylee," I answered, trying not to sound disappointed.

"Sorry, I shouldn't have called, you probably expected Rosa… I'll call you tom…" Kaylee said.

"Why did you call, to get on my case like everyone else?" I snapped but caught myself. "Sorry, it's been a long day." I stepped into the den and closed the door, just something I did when Rosa would call. "I guess everyone hates me."

"I don't hate you, Jay, I feel for you—so how are you doing?"

"Okay. So, what happened after I left?"

"Nothing much."

"I bet they were talking bad things about me."

"Yeah, you were the topic of the day."

"So, was Rosa really upset? How is she?"

"Well, she was hurt."

"I feel so bad—it happened so fast—I didn't mean it," I said. "Why am I telling you these things?"

"Jay, I just wanted to see how you were doing and to tell you that I'm still your friend…I guess I'll talk to you later," Kaylee said.

"Thanks for calling, bye," I said, hanging up.

It felt nice knowing that I still had a friend.

I was pretty worn out by the time I went to bed. The whole day nagged at me. I just couldn't shake the look in Rosa's eyes. My one little action spiraled into so much trouble. Why couldn't Rosa forgive me? Perhaps Mom was right that tomorrow was bound to be better. I would talk to Rosa and we would make up. We would soon be laughing about it. Then Molly entered my mind as I played it back in my head, again and again. How could I kiss Molly back? What was I thinking? Now I have no girlfriend and I have alienated my friends.

I tried to put it out of my mind and go to sleep—it was 9:30—but I tossed and turned. Ten minutes went by and I faced away from the clock. I laid there for a long time, staring in the dark. When I turned back to the clock, it had only been five minutes. I placed the pillow over my face and don't remember what happened after that, but I was angry with myself, that much I knew.

The next thing I knew, I was in the garage furiously hitting the punching bag. Every time my fist landed I called out, "Stupid!" I guess I wanted to get it out of my system. My hands became real sore and I was nearing exhaustion. I could not hit anymore, my muscles cramped, so I hugged the bag. Tears began to run down my face and I felt sorrow in my heart. Getting to my knees I cried out to God. I realized I wasn't doing the right things again. I kept telling myself that I was doing things wrong, but what did I go ahead and do anyway? The night Rosa and I almost went too far… Kissing Molly back…Getting angry…Doing what I desired without thinking or going to the Lord!

"Lord, if only I prayed to you!" I cried. "Please forgive me, I let satan tempt me…punish me if you have too—I learned my lesson." That was my last memory of that night.

Chapter Twenty-one

WAKING UP the next morning, I sensed I was still in a dream, but out of place. It was dark and cold. For some reason there was the smell of grease. My bed was not very soft beneath me. Suddenly, I realized it wasn't a dream; I was awake inside the garage. Garage! How did I get here? This was where I sat up, shaking out the cobwebs while orienting myself. Looking around, I began to have a sense of urgency—*what day is it? Friday! School? Rosa!—it wasn't a dream.* My heart was heavy, knowing that I had to try and mend the fabric that was slowly tearing.

The clock read a quarter after six—*a quarter after six! Only forty-five minutes until the first bell.* Jumping up, I noticed the blanket on the mat and I briefly reminisced those nights sneaking out with Rosa. Then I rushed out the door and into the kitchen. There Gramma sat with Mom entering from the dining room.

"Where did you come from Jaybird?" both women commented nearly at the same time.

"I thought you were getting ready for school upstairs," Mom wondered.

"Got up early, couldn't sleep," I lied—"Actually, I slept in the garage…I would love to talk, but I don't want to be late."

Grabbing a banana, I hurried to the bathroom. I contemplated what I would say to Rosa as I placed my head under a steamy shower. Hopefully, she had a restful night's sleep when I approached her, and just maybe, she would be more understanding. After a quick prayer, I exited and finished getting ready.

I flew into the kitchen with my backpack around my shoulder and reached in the cabinet for one of those cereal breakfast bars.

The two-minute drive over to the high school was agonizing to say the least. I couldn't imagine life without Rosa. There was nothing earth shattering I could think of to tell her how sorry I was.

"You have been quiet," Gramma said, a few blocks from our house.

"Just thinking," I replied, looking out my window, wondering if I would see Manny's truck.

"Cheer up Jaybird," Gramma said, patting my arm. "Sometimes people get over things—one minute the sun is out and the birds are singing, then there are dark clouds and we get soaked. But then everything dries out and there are rainbows, so look forward to rainbows."

She dropped me off in front of the school. I felt somewhat better with Gramma's words of wisdom rattling in my head. Rosa wasn't around, but I heard someone call my name. I turned and saw De'von waving at me.

"Hey Jay," he greeted. "I felt bad for you yesterday, hope it works out for you."

"Thanks, yeah, me too," I replied, as we entered the building.

We went to our lockers and I expected to see Rosa at hers. She wasn't there. Nor did I see her down the halls.

First period dragged on slowly. There was just a week and a half of school left. Everyone was excited for the summer; some were antsy in their seats, while others were more talkative. I was not in the mood to think what I was going to do for the summer, just thoughts of making up with Rosa. Maybe everyone was right, it was a new day, and God was in control.

Rosa attended my next class, so I knew this would be my chance to set things straight. When the bell rang, I was the first one out into the hall. I turned the corner and saw Rosa walking to the classroom. I made my way quickly following the same path she had taken. The teacher stepped out to watch the students switching classes.

Sitting at her desk, Rosa didn't indicate that she noticed my entrance, nor when I walked up to her. She just stared off into space.

"You're probably still mad at me and I can't blame you," I began. "I feel awful about what I did to you and I am truly sorry to have hurt you. I admit that what I did was wrong and I hope you can give me a second chance. However long it takes, I want to make it up to you. If it takes the whole summer, I'm willing to wait. I won't bother you again. I will cherish all the good times we've shared. I hope you know I still love you...guess that's all for now."

The only movement Rosa made was tears welling up in her eyes. She quickly wiped them away. Students began to file in as I sat down at my desk behind Rosa.

Second period went easier, after finally talking to Rosa. I don't know if I got through to her, but I felt better that I tried. An unexpected thing occurred following the bell. As I came out into the hall, someone pushed through me from behind—it was Rosa like she didn't see me. When she passed me she said something.

"I'm breaking up with you. I'll never forgive you," she said abruptly.

Running up to her, I grabbed her arm briefly. "Just like that? You want to breakup?" I said.

"Yes, I've already made up my mind," she said. "*You—and that girl —ewww—just sickens me—leave me alone!*"

I watched her stomp off and disappear into the crowd. The little rip in the fabric I had so desired to mend, severed into two pieces. Rosa was suddenly disconnected from my life. Sure, I could give it more time, but in my heart, I just knew it was over.

"Are you satisfied now, Jay?" Zoey sneered. "I thought you were different, but I guess you are like all the other jerky guys. That girl loved you and look how you treated her."

At this point, the crowd around me laughed, made jokes, and whispered to each other. I ran to my next class ignoring everyone in my path. The following periods were fuzzy and up until lunch, I was lost in my thoughts. I spoke to no one; the teachers could have been speaking Greek if I paid any attention to them.

Lunch came and I managed to avoid contact with everyone. I picked a tree in the shade furthest away from the students, especially Zoey. I'm sure Rosa would lose her appetite if I were in view. There weren't too many people behind the school, so that's where I ended up. I didn't feel like eating, but took my sack lunch and picked at it. Company was not on the menu.

I closed my eyes in meditation, just enjoying the peace and quiet. Soon I heard foot steps in the grass near me and I prayed it would go away. It wasn't to be true. The sun behind my closed eyelids went from light to dark. A presence was upon me.

"There you are," De'von said. "Would you mind if I ate lunch with you?"

"Sure, help yourself to the lawn," I replied, feeling sarcastic. "Wait a minute, are you sure? I don't want to cause you problems being seen with me. I don't want Zoey mad at you; it would be my fault if you guys breakup."

"Doesn't matter, she's already mad at me, but I don't think for long," he said.

"I wish that were true with Rosa," I began. "No matter how many times I said I was sorry, she just wouldn't listen. I don't want to talk about it because I'm getting a headache."

Setting my lunch aside, I leaned back in the grass, covering my eyes. My stomach grumbled hungrily, but my head pounded, so I decided not to eat.

"That's okay, we don't have to talk about it," De'von said. "So do you have anything planned for summer?"

"Oh, I can't think about that right now. With all the trouble I caused and Rosa not wanting to see my face again, I will probably hide in my room all summer long."

"You know what, my folks are going camping, maybe you want to tag along," De'von suggested.

"Oh, I don't know. All I know is it will be a long summer," I said.

"Jay, don't let her get to you—girls, who can understand them," De'von said.

"Yeah, not me," I chuckled weakly, stuffing my backpack under my head. "Let me know when it's ten minutes before the bell. Help yourself to my lunch."

"Time to go," De'von announced not too long.

"I don't feel too well—kind of dizzy, my head's pounding," I said, staggering to stand.

"Are you okay? You look pale, man."

The world spun around me. "I think I am okay now—just got up too quick."

The last bell was a relief, the final period of the day. I was about the first person out of the building. My headache was nearly gone, but I started to feel weird, sluggish. Of course, I was not quick enough to avoid people.

"Hey Jay, wait up," De'von said.

"Just wondering, did you see, what's her face? Is Zoey still irritated with you?" I asked.

"Yeah, you could say," he said.

"Was Rosa with her?"

"Yeah, she was and they gave me a dirty look," he said, looking back. "Speaking of…"

"Oh, I had such a wonderful day," I groaned. "It just gets better and better—let's get out of here."

So we ran until they were out of sight and I was out of breath. We took our time getting to my house. De'von couldn't stay because he had chores to do on his folks' ranch.

The couch was a welcome sight as I dragged my feet into the house. A nap would feel so good I thought.

"So how was your day?" Mom asked, coming into the room.

"The second worst day of my life—" I replied, falling back.

"What happened? Want to talk about it?"

"What didn't happen?" I replied, holding my head in my hands.

"Did you talk to Rosa?"

"Yeah, she broke up with me."

"Oh honey, sorry to hear that."

"On top of that, I don't feel too good," I groaned, "headache, stomachache."

"Here, let me take your shoes off and get you comfortable."

I laid there for a while, then fell asleep. If a train went through our house, I wouldn't have heard it. Mom let me sleep through dinner.

"How are you feeling Jay?" she asked, as I sat up.

"I feel queasy—better head to the bathroom," I said, running down the hall. I felt sick.

Waking the next day before noon, I bounced out of bed feeling great. I found Mom sitting at the kitchen table and I hugged her.

"So how do you feel?" she asked.

"I feel much better, like my normal self. My stomach doesn't ache and I'm starving," I replied.

"Did you have a temp last night? Any chills?" she asked. I shook my head twice. "I think you may have had food poisoning. Make sure you drink extra liquids today."

"Okay, I will," I said, finding a piece of bread.

"Oh, before I forget," Mom said, as I sat down with my toast. "Kaylee stopped by yesterday and asked how you were doing. She said she may come over today."

"I think I may cancel karate class today," I said after a bite. Also, I wasn't ready to face Molly, still ticked at her. "Do you know if Rich is doing anything?"

"I think he was finishing up something at the shop," she replied.

"Maybe I will visit him later."

That afternoon, Kaylee came over. I considered her one of my best friends next to Rosa. Well, now she was my best friend. When she sat down next to me on the couch, I flashed back briefly to the other day with Molly.

"Thank you for coming by yesterday—well, today too," I said. "Felt like crap, but better today."

"Sorry to hear about you and Rosa," Kaylee said. "I know you guys were really close. I surely wouldn't have thought nothing like this would tear you apart."

"Yeah, I know," I said lost in thought. "Oh well…I deserve it…I sure did it now. Anyway…"

"Yeah anyway," she said, beginning to stand, "you probably don't want company, just wanted to see how you were."

"You don't have to go away, unless you have some—"

"No, I don't have anything planned besides dance class later. I just thought you wanted some time alone."

"Actually, I could use some company—if I think about what happened, I'll just go crazy," I said.

"Yeah, makes sense," she said with a laugh.

"So let's talk about something else," I said.

"Sure, hmmm let's see," she began. "For some reason I can't think of anything."

"Me either—I guess we could listen to some music," I said, walking over to the stereo and turning on the contemporary Christian rock station.

"I like that song," Kaylee commented, as I sat back down. "Jesus is a perfect miracle."

"I thought I heard some talking," Mom said, entering the room. "Hi, Kaylee."

"Hi," Kaylee said, getting up to hug Mom, which she did from time to time. "How are you doing?"

"Doing just great, praise the Lord," Mom answered.

"Praise the Lord," Kaylee said.

"Would you like something to drink?" Mom asked.

When Mom said that, I imagined asking Molly if she wanted something to drink. Then I started laughing, slapping my knees. "Just don't ask for water."

"What's so funny? Did I miss something?" Mom asked, looking for something that made me laugh.

"Oh nothing, just reminded me about something," I replied laughing some more. "Okay, I'm done."

"My son the laughing hyena," Mom said and we all were laughing, being silly.

"That's too much," I said, holding my stomach as I stood. "Would you like something to drink?" I started belly laughing again.

"Nah, I'm fine," Kaylee answered.

"We have grape sodas—I know they're your favorite," I said to Kaylee.

"Okay, I guess I'm a little thirsty then," Kaylee said.

"I knew you wouldn't refuse a grape soda, who would? They are so good," I said. "…Want one Mom?"

"Sure sounds good," Mom answered.

"Be right back," I said, and then moments later I walked back into the room.

"So how do you feel about going to high school next year?" Mom asked Kaylee.

"Oh, I'm really, really excited," Kaylee answered.

"Boy, you guys grow up so fast," Mom reminisced. "Kaylee I can remember this shy little girl—well, look at you now, more out going, so ladylike."

"Mom you're embarrassing her," I said, approaching them. "One grape soda for Kaylee, and one for Mom."

"What about you Jay?" Kaylee wondered.

"I guess there's none left," I said glumly, and then came out with the other hand behind my back. "Where did this come from? Thank the Lord he sure provideth." They both thanked me.

"Are you going to get into the band this coming year?" Mom asked.

"Yeah, since I have my braces off, I can take up the flute again," Kaylee replied.

"It's cool that you will be going to school with us again, like old times," I said.

"Yeah, we can hang out at lunch—maybe be in some classes," Kaylee said.

"You have always been a math whiz, weren't you taking algebra this year?" I asked.

"Yep, should be taking geometry in the fall," Kaylee replied.

"Most likely, we might be in the same class, since I'm taking geometry too," I said. "Math, as you know, is not my strongest subject. Ros…ah, usually helped me with that—"

"I'll help you, Jay," Kaylee offered.

"That would be wonderful, thanks Kaylee," I said.

Mom yawned. "Didn't sleep very well last night, it's catching up with me. Nice chatting with you all."

"Let's go outside, get some fresh air," I said after Mom left. I peered out the front window to see Rosa playing with Waldo. "Let's go to the side yard."

Gramma stood there, watering flowers. "Hi, Mrs. Asher, your pansies are looking nice," Kaylee commented.

"Thank you, nothing much to them," Gramma replied. "Keep them watered and they're happy."

"You know what?" I began, after hearing Rosa and Waldo at play. "Let's get out of here and go to the park or something."

We walked to the park near Kaylee's house to hang out for a while. It was a nice change of pace for an hour or so; then we parted. Kaylee went home to eat and to get ready for her dance class. I left and visited Rich at the auto shop.

Rich was closing up when I got there. He usually quit early on Saturday when work was slow. Sometimes Manny stayed longer, wanting to finish the job if he was almost done. It suddenly hit me that Manny could be around. I hadn't seen him at all since the official breakup. His truck was not in its usual spot so I breathed easier. Not quite ready to face him yet.

"Good, there you are Jay," Rich said, closing the garage door and locking it. "I was just headed to your house to see if you wanted to see the progress I've made on my car."

"Thanks, I need something to keep myself occupied because Rosa and I broke up," I said.

"Wow that comes as a surprise!" Rich exclaimed.

I told him on the way across the highway to his property. We worked on his car and talked a while before he took me back home.

Some time later, as I comfortably read a book on the couch, there was a knock at the door. It was almost eight and I could not figure who it would be.

"Oh, hi Manny," I said, catching my breath. "What's up?"

I thought I would die in front of the door. Manny stood there with a box.

"Well, let me make this fast. Rosa wanted me to give you some stuff," he said calmly.

"Uh," I uttered, opening the door. A horrible feeling ran down my spine. I received the box without a word.

"I hear you and Rosa broke up," he said. "She was really upset with whatever happened, but she wouldn't tell me. I'll support her in anyway I can, but I won't get involved with what happens from here on out. That's between you two, unless there's a reason to."

"I understand sir," I finally spoke.

"Good, I know we are on the same page," Manny said, leaving.

I didn't have the heart to really look in the box as I was mentally and emotionally exhausted. Sitting down, I rummaged briefly through the mementos I had given Rosa over the past three years or so, then leaned back with Manny's words still echoing in my mind. I placed the box inside the closet of my former playroom.

Chapter Twenty-Two

ON SUNDAY, the last one of May, Rosa wasn't at church yet and I wondered if she would be in attendance. Manny's truck was not in the parking lot. *Perhaps they were running late*, I thought. Moseying downstairs to our class, Kaylee, De'von, and the other regulars were there, but not Rosa as of yet. Jeff, our Sunday school teacher, was out in the hall talking with a member of the church.

"I doubt if she'll come," I said, watching the clock strike 9:30.

Jeff walked in and sat, taking attendance. "Is Rosa not here?" he asked, knowing she rarely missed a class. "I hope she isn't ill." We just shook our shoulders.

An hour later, with much anticipation on my part, Sunday school adjourned. Quickly, I went upstairs and outside. Still no truck!

"Man, what have I done!" I said, throwing my hands up.

"Jay, don't blame yourself," Kaylee said. "If I know Manny, he always makes the service whether or not he goes to Sunday school."

"Maybe you're right," I said.

Hoping beyond hope, I hoped Rosa would still come to church because I worried about her faith.

Throughout the morning there was an air of excitement at church. The former pastor, Charles Hargrove, came back to visit with his wife, Joyce. Also in attendance was Rick and Julie Taylor who you remember came to help out at the church in the beginning. Gramma said it was almost like a church reunion. Sure was a special day. This occasion helped me a little bit to keep my mind off the breakup.

Mom and Gramma already headed for our pew. The usher, Mel greeted me with his cheery face. I sat down trying to concentrate my thoughts on God. *I pray Lord that Rosa comes.*

Kaylee Knight sat with her folks behind me. I wished Billie would come more often. At least once a month he and his girlfriend, Amber made an appearance during the morning service. I would have to see how he was doing.

Surprisingly, right before Rory read the bulletin announcements, Manny and Rosa came through the doors. *Thank you Lord.* As I expected they passed our pew, finding a different place. Well, at least she came. I felt a little better, but it was empty next to me where they usually sat. I sighed with relief, deciding to relax and enjoy the reunion.

It was interesting and humbling at the same time to see Charles, Joyce, Rick, and Julie. I never met them and only heard about them through Gramma and other church members.

"I guess that's all for announcements," Rory said. "You may greet one another, then go back to your seats when the music starts."

I walked around the room, said "Hi," and shook hands. Rosa stayed where she was across the room, exchanging words with a lady. Manny worked his way over to Gramma and Mom, talked briefly with them, and then came to me.

"Hey, Jay, it's good to see you," Manny began. "It must have been awkward the other day. Don't mind Rosa, she's stubborn like her mom."

"It was my fault—" I said.

"You don't have to explain, it's a teen thing," Manny said, as Richard began singing.

I looked over at Rosa. She didn't hold a hymnal, but Manny appeared to encourage her with his. I don't think she had any desire to be here and to sing especially. Joyce played the piano during a portion of this.

The reunion really began with Rick Taylor's heart-warming speech. He reminisced about him and his wife's stay and servitude at Deer Park First Baptist. At one point, he had tears in his eyes and so did many of the congregation.

Charles followed with his memories of the church before preaching for us. He became emotional when he talked about Lloyd, our former pastor, who was no longer with us. It was a wonderful sight to see Charles up on the podium presenting the message on the subject "Grace." We were all really moved by the end of the service. Afterwards, we all met for a potluck.

June 2005

Soon there were just four days of school left and I was glad it was almost over for the year. Rosa treated me like a stranger—someone invisible. If I were in her path she would look straight ahead or go in a different direction. She ignored me when we both were at our lockers. Zoey still gave me dirty looks, which died down before the last day of school. The rumors and the whispers were still apparent, but I just ignored them—they could think what they wanted to think.

One day before English class, I saw something on the seat of my desk. It was *The Stag,* the Deer Park High School newspaper. I had seen them at the student store many times, but had never thought to pick one up and read it. After the first couple pages, I became engrossed with it, but didn't have time to read as class began.

I took it home and read it from cover-to-cover. It was just like a real newspaper with the layout, black and white photographs, and advertising from the stores and businesses in Deer Park. There was even a page where students' artwork and poetry was posted. I enjoyed the editorials and featured articles. I thought it was the neatest thing. The articles were interesting, which made me want to read more. I knew Mr. Stevens always had one at his desk and extra school papers too. Suddenly, I was struck with the idea that I could write for *The Stag.*

So the next day, as my English teacher, Mr. Stevens, was rummaging on his desk, I approached him about it.

"Ah, Mr. Stevens, do you have a moment?" I asked.

"Sure, what's on your mind Jay?" he asked.

"About *The Stag*, I think I'd like to write for that," I replied. "Looks like fun—interesting–Do I see the counselor or something? Maybe I'm not a good enough writer."

"I meant to talk to you about that," Mr. Stevens said. "I was going to ask you about taking journalism next year. But that's evident, I see. You are one of my best students and you have a knack for writing."

"Do you think so, sir?" I asked.

"I think you have the potential for journalism—I know the advisor, Ms. Perry and she is looking for students like you," he said. "To answer your question, those who want to take journalism just go to the journalism room and pick up an application."

"Thank you Mr. Stevens," I said about to turn around. "One more thing, do you have any back issues I can borrow?"

"Which one?"

"Well, all of them."

"You sure are enthusiastic," Mr. Stevens laughed, unlocking a file cabinet.

Joyfully, I headed back to my desk with thoughts of writing for the school newspaper. I pictured myself taking photographs for it. Photography was right up there with karate and fishing for me. Mom and some others told me I had a good eye.

When I came home, I was truly excited about writing for the paper.

"You seem to be in good spirits today," Mom said curiously.

"I think I want to take journalism next year," I said, littering the coffee table with copies of *The Stag*.

"That's wonderful Jay," she said excitedly.

"Yeah, I want to be more involved with school," I said. "Maybe this is what the Lord wants me to do."

During lunch the next day, I headed over to the journalism room. I was leery stepping up to the door, not knowing whether I should just enter or knock first, so I knocked. Nobody answered, so I waited a few moments before I knocked again harder. Still nothing. I shrugged my shoulders and about to leave, when the door opened. A girl stuck her head out.

"I guess someone was knocking," she said.

"I hope I wasn't interrupting anything—maybe you're busy—"

"Nope, we're just having lunch," the girl said. "Are you looking for Ms. Perry?"

"Oh, oh yes, I was, I guess," I replied. "I wanted to get an application for next year."

"Sure, come on in."

There were rows of tables and the floor was littered with papers. Recent issues of *The Stag* were pinned up on the bulletin boards. On the far wall were half dozen computers. I imagined it being busy like the pressrooms in the old movies I watched, of course, on a smaller scale.

The girl who opened the door, stood in front of a huge counter with drawers where two other girls sat chatting with their lunch. Ms. Perry was at her desk in the front of the classroom.

"Can I help you?" Ms. Perry asked.

"Yeah, I would like an application for journalism please," I replied.

"Okay," she said, standing and reaching into a file cabinet, then handing me a couple forms. "One you fill out and you'll need two teacher references. One has to be your English teacher and the other any teacher of your choice. When completed, turn them all in to me with a sample of your writing. Any questions?"

"No, thanks," I replied.

Before the end of the day, I gave Mr. Stevens the reference form and the other I gave to my history teacher. I went home to fill out *The Stag* staff application. There was a place for my current grade point averages, etc. I responded "yes" to questions like: are you willing to work after school to meet deadlines? Would you accept a leadership role? Do you enjoy interviewing or writing? Help with fund raising and advertising?

The last two questions were about my keyboarding and computer experience, which I was both quite familiar with. Then I described a personal strength that would make me an asset to the staff. I wrote: I'm a hard worker, good listener, I don't judge people and circumstances, and I work well with others.

Next, I checked the areas that appealed to me: News writing, Feature writing, Editorial/Commentary, and Sports.

I had no previous journalism experience, so I left that blank with not applicable—mom suggested that.

The last thing on the application was: why I want to be a member of *The Stag* staff? I basically wrote down I wanted to be involved with the school and report truthfully.

My freshman year came to an emotional ending. I was exhausted with the whole Rosa breakup and the pressures of teenage life. My love for Rosa was still there somewhat as the summer was in sequence. Soon I pushed thoughts of Rosa to the back of my mind. I had better things to do than beat myself up. What's done happened and that was that. As Christians, we don't worry about the past because that distracts us from moving on to do the Lord's will.

Arriving home, I just sat there on the couch; my first action was a deep relieved exhale. Quietly, I was in deep thought, wondering about my summer break and where it was headed. Closing my eyes, I prayed to the Lord.

"Dear Lord, thank you for getting me through the school year. I don't know why things went wrong with Rosa, but I know you had a reason—a reason for everything. Maybe it was a lesson of sorts for me and I think You were telling me to wake up—my soul hurting, I yearn for You—I know I was perhaps headed toward destruction. Lord, show me what You want me to do this summer; lead me in

righteousness. I don't just want to do things for myself and be selfish. Humble my heart and I pray through the Holy Spirit, asking for guidance and Your gracious wisdom and knowledge. Whatever You want Your servant to do, I'll respond. I let myself get lost in worldly things, not focused on Your kingdom..."

The next moment, somebody shook me awake. I realized I had been sleeping and rose with energy, stretching my arms over my head. As my eyes came into focus, I saw Rich standing right there.

"What time is it?" I asked, finding the clock.

"About 5:30 in the evening," Rich replied.

"I can't believe I slept two hours," I began and wondered. "How long have you been here?"

"Not long," he said. "How would you like to get away right now for a few days? How about a little camping and fishing to begin the summer? For starters, we'll go night fishing at Chapman Lake. Then we'll go from there anywhere your heart desires."

"Sounds wonderful—most wonderful," I said, getting up joyfully. "Cool, let's go!"

Some hours later, we launched Rich's canoe with a small horse powered prop into Chapman Lake. It was just an hour before twilight and many people were headed back from a day of fishing. We found a little cove and cast our lines to test the water for hungry bass. Bass were usually not very active in early summer, but we got a few nibbles at the end of our lines. We were just enjoying ourselves visiting and relaxing in the fresh air. While baiting our hooks with crank bait, the first stars specked the sky.

"Thanks for taking me away—great idea," I said. "I needed this to get away from the city and from all that..."

"No problem, I needed a day off too," Rich agreed.

"You know what? I'm tired of girls right now," I said. "I just don't get them. One minute they're all over you, then the next they despise you...not like I have to follow the rest of the sheep."

"Yep and vice-versa," he said. "It's a timing thing with God, especially. You're right, we don't have to let the world dictate our lives—oops...I think I got something!"

He excitedly reeled in the line, ready for a fight. I had a net ready. We both were disappointed as he pulled in weeds.

"I just want to focus on the Lord and His Word. If only I would have listened to my conscience—but that's all behind me." I said.

"Yep, I've learned that also," Rich said.

"Next time I will do it right—no more kissing, gets me in trouble," I said. "I was going to ask you why you didn't warn me about this, but I figured you'd want me to figure it out for myself, right?"

"That's right young man, have to learn on your own," Rich said smiling. "God gives us the manual for life, called the Bible, giving us the basic principles, but we have to be the ones willing to make the right choices and obey. Whether or not I told you that making out is wrong or not, it's fruitless for me to believe you would listen. Our spirits, as you know, constantly fight the rebelling sinful flesh."

"Especially during puberty," I said. "If I told myself three years ago that I would be making out with a girl, I would've said, *no* way! I want to stay pure until my wedding night."

"One thing to add about that, and I think I may have mentioned, the girl or girls you may be dating could very possibly be your future wife or some other guys," Rich said.

"Oh, for some reason, I forgot about that," I said surprisingly.

Rich and I had our own little service outside our tent on Sunday morning. We arrived home that afternoon. As we neared Deer Park, I remembered needing to get in touch with Billie. I hadn't talked to him since the breakup. He was a regular of our church up to high school, but he slacked over time. Sports and his girlfriend, Amber were always his famous excuses. I thought back when Billie accepted the Lord. He was about nine and couldn't stop talking about how excited he felt about Jesus.

After I unwound from my little camping trip, I called up the Knight's residence. Kaylee answered. "Hello," she said into my ear.

"Hi, Kaylee," I said.

"Oh, hi, Jay, how was the camping trip?"

"We had a wonderful time, didn't catch much—just some silvers."

"Glad you had a nice time."

"But it's always nice to be home," I commented. "So how was church today?"

"Heavenly, of course," she answered, giggling.

"Of course," I chuckled.

"Pastor David had another good sermon," Kaylee said.

"Yah, I like the way he preaches too," I said.

"Rosa was at the morning service."

"That's good," I said. "Makes me feel better to know she is going."

"Yep, me too," she said. "So, what are you going to do today?"

"I don't know, thought about visiting Billie—of course, my best friend Kaylee too."

"I never thought you considered me your best friend—makes my day, Jay to hear that."

"Really, I figured you to be my best friend—truest friend."

"That's nice to hear," Kaylee said. "Hey, we talked about going to play miniature golf. Even Billie and Amber are going; if you are not doing anything."

"Let me check my schedule—nope, nothing planned except Thursday and Saturday karate class."

"We'll go Friday. De'von's dad is taking us," she said.

"Count me in," I said. "So, is Billie there?"

"He's out back hanging with Amber," Kaylee replied.

"Good, tell him not to run away," I said, then we hung up.

Gathering some things in my backpack, I grabbed my camera, and headed down the street on my bike. It was a nice day, not too hot, just right. There were a few clouds and a nice breeze in my face. Mr. Magpie sent his greetings as he hackled away. I crossed busy Crawford and turned onto shady 'A' Street where Kaylee lived.

About this time, the Knight's completed their remodeling to the house. Facing the street, beneath a new green roof, were wooden shake shingles surrounding the master bedroom's eyebrow window with a flower planter. This was the attic, being the second floor, which used to be Billie and Kaylee's bedroom/playroom. Now it's the master bedroom, with Billie's room in the back. The shakes went down to the top of the first floor, where it turned into a cream-colored vinyl siding. A few stairs went up to the front porch that was inverted or cut into the house; a lone colonial column and cap supported the structure. The house style could be called "Country Living."

Mr. and Mrs. Knight's cars were not there as they were at work. One of Kaylee's cats, the grey one, Bubbles, prowled across the front lawn. Kaylee was on the front porch swing reading a book and petting her other cat, a calico named Paddy. Paddy was more of an indoor cat and friendlier than Bubbles. I thought it would make a good candid shot as I didn't think she had seen me yet. Quickly, I flipped on the camera and took several pictures. I think she sensed something so I put away the camera.

"Oh, hi, Jay, I didn't hear you come up," Kaylee said, descending the stairs.

I rode my bike up the sidewalk. "Hey, Kaylee, what have you been doing there?" I asked.

"Oh nothin', just reading," she replied. "Billie and Amber are still in back. They didn't know you were coming—hey, let's sneak up on them and you can get their picture."

"Okay, but it's your idea," I chuckled.

We quietly walked around the house to the back gate. I set my bike against the tree and left my backpack. While I readied the camera, Kaylee giggled undoing the latch.

"Shhh, you're making me laugh," I said, trying to be serious. "I'm ready, where are they?"

"Just near the patio," she said, as we opened the gate and stepped behind it.

We tiptoed along the wall of the house and I looked around the corner. Billie was on the lounge chair with Amber sitting beside him and running her fingers through his hair. They were listening to music, which helped our entrance. There was a shrub near the patio and Kaylee followed me to it. She just couldn't stop giggling as she covered her mouth. So I took a few shots and then Kaylee unexpectedly yelled out to them.

"Come on smooch—!" Kaylee burst out.

"What are you guys doing over there?" Billie snarled, throwing his shoe at us.

"Got you," Kaylee said, going toward them as I followed her taking more pictures.

"Jay, I know she put you up to this," Billie said. "I wouldn't let her."

"Well," I said, shrugging and letting the camera straps hang on my neck.

"Hey, Jay, sorry to hear about you and Rosa," Amber said. "Oh, maybe I shouldn't say anything."

"That's okay, no matter," I said, pulling up a lawn chair.

"Yeah Jay, that bites—" Billie said. "I was shocked—never thought."

"Yeah, I really messed up," I said. "I tried to apologize, but she won't have anything to do with me. Nothing I can do about it... Anyway, just stopped by, wondered what you guys were up to."

"I know what they are doing—kissy, kisssy..." Kaylee teased.

"Mind your own beeswax—" Billie said glaring. "Not much. I thought about shooting some hoops, maybe a game. You can come."

"Sure, not doing anything else," I said.

While Billie and Amber walked, Kaylee and I rode our bikes slowly. I told Billie about my outing with Rich. Billie talked about the upcoming football season.

"If things go well in camp, coach says I will be starting this year," he said.

"That's cool," I said, changing the subject. "You know, we miss you two at church. I know you have enjoyed it."

"Yeah, I feel bad, not very obedient. I'll try to make it," Billie said.

"I'll make sure he gets there," Amber said.

"You're right Jay, we'll start going again," he said.

We walked around the pool, which was empty, then passed picnic tables and the jungle gym, making our way to the basketball courts. Halfway through the park, I paused and looked over at the skateboard park. I knew I was not imagining things. There was Rosa over there hanging out with some skater guys and a couple of girls from the same crowd.

These kids listened to heavy metal rock, had different lingo, and T-shirts that said, "What's Up!" Now, there wasn't anything wrong hanging with skaters, but I just had nothing much in common with them. Actually, I had quite a few things in common with them. We attended the same school, were all teenagers, had the same peer pressures, and similar problems with relationships.

"Shoot Jay! I didn't know she would be here," Billie exclaimed.

"Can't be helped—let's play some ball," I said, dying inside.

De'von was there at the courts waiting for us. He practiced a lay-up and passed the ball to Billie. Three other guys, who were on the varsity squad, joined us for a three-on-three-game. I left the shooting up to Billie and De'von while I just passed. I didn't last long because I wasn't wearing the right clothes. Walking off the court to where Kaylee sat, I saw Rosa leave with her friends.

Thursday evening came along, I felt uncomfortable knowing Molly might be at karate class. She never said she was sorry or explained her actions. I thought about getting there early to talk to her in the parking lot, but when I saw her, suddenly not in the right mood. During class time was out of the question to mix personal matters. I put my game face on upon approaching the building. Immediately inside, I saw Molly walking out of the dressing room.

"Jay, you're back! I know you're still mad at me, but I want to explain—" Molly began.

"Let's focus on where we left off, or have you moved onto another technique?" I cut her off.

"Can't I just explain?"

"Never say 'can't' in karate class, do ten push-ups," I said quietly.

Molly got down and started to do push-ups and paused to look at me. "I didn't mean to come on to you like that," she said.

"Do those three techniques," I said, walking away. There was no more discussion about anything.

"Jay, I'm sorry about the way I acted in class today, I lost myself," Molly said later when she called me. "I know I'm not supposed to be talking about personal things during class."

"That's right," I said, "I understand you wanting to explain what happened last week, but we all need to stay focused on class. I know I was coming off hard on you, but it is important to use your time wisely."

"I understand," she said.

"Good, now you can explain to me what happened the other day," I said.

"I never really planned on that happening and I'm really sorry for it," she began. "I don't know what came over me—hope you forgive me someday."

"I am a forgiving person and I don't carry grudges for long, so I forgive you," I said.

"Okay, well…I feel better that I got it off my chest…later, I guess," Molly said.

"Yeah, bye," I said, hanging up with an exhale of relief.

Mr. Collins, De'von's dad, took Billie, Amber, Kaylee, and me to Excite Land Miniature Golf on the edge of Spokane. I had been there for many birthdays and a couple times with just mom.

"Have fun everybody," Mr. Collins said with a newspaper under his arm. "I'll be over here at the bench if you guys need anything."

"Thanks Mr. C.," Kaylee said.

"Who wants to play video games?" Billie asked. "De'von, how about that air hockey re-match?"

"You're on," De'von said, turning to Kaylee and me. "What are you guys going to do?"

"I thought we were going to do something together Billie," Amber said in the background.

"Just a couple games with De'von, babe," Billie said.

"Amber, you can play miniature golf with me," Kaylee suggested.

"Okay Billie, do what you want," Amber said, walking toward Kaylee.

"I think I'll go with them," I said.

I went over to the counter where Amber and Kaylee were renting the golf clubs. It was interesting to see Billie and Amber in disagreement—kind of humorous. Funny in the sense, I never really saw them argue.

"Hey guys, wait up!" I hollered at Kaylee and Amber after getting my club.

"Jay, you're not going with the guys?" Amber asked.

"Nah, I'd rather do this," I said. "Air hockey and video games just don't appeal to me."

Chapter Twenty-Three

TURNING FIFTEEN just days later, I had my birthday party at the bowling alley. It was nothing magical like Rosa's Quinceañera, which seemed like a long time ago. I didn't want anything elaborate for my birthday, just something simple. Cupcakes suited me just fine. I invited De'von, Kaylee, Billie, and Amber. That was my group for the first part of the summer.

Zoey showed signs of tolerance toward me because of De'von and my friendship. It was interesting to know that Zoey's group didn't question Kaylee being my friend. Nonetheless, Kaylee remained in their group. This was a good thing because Kaylee became a spy for me, as Rosa was often there. Kaylee told me Rosa just ignores her.

Back to my birthday: we had a wonderful time at the bowling alley. I was elated because I finally beat my high score of 183 and made it to 220, thanks to two strikes in the last frames.

Summer 2005

Rosa attended Deer Park First Baptist Church for the rest of June. Then she just quit coming. Mom talked to Manny about it. He said Rosa wanted to check out other churches in town. Everyone probably figured the reason was because of me. Later, found out she started going to the Nazarene Church nearby. At least it seemed like her faith in God wasn't faltering, even though it was in a different congregation. Three weeks into July, she dropped from the church scene altogether.

When Rosa wasn't at Zoey's house, she was at the skateboard park or elsewhere with her new friends. Occasionally, I saw her on the streets with her rollerblades. Soon she left Zoey and the gang, focusing on other people. Rosa's appearance drastically changed. Her clothing of choice seemed to be raggedy and immodest, sometimes too much skin showing. She cut her hair just above her shoulders and dyed a strip bright green.

At this time, I had a real weird encounter with Rosa. It was an extremely hot summer day when I came out of the house to turn off the hose in the front yard. Rosa sat outside her house like she was waiting for someone. She wore tiny shorts and a halter-top, a beach towel nearby. *Going to the lake,* I thought. I went about my own business, but when I looked over I noticed she had gotten up to stand on the edge of her grass. She met my eyes on purpose, gesturing for me to get a good look. I just stared in awe. Her actions became tasteless and out of character. I wanted nothing to do with her little show. I could've just walked back into the house, but it was the first time after a month that she acknowledged my existence. Just keeping my eyes locked with hers while ignoring whatever dance it was she was doing. Throwing my hands up and slapping my legs in frustration, I turned around and headed back to the house. Soon a convertible screeched to a halt in front of the Sanchez house and Rosa hopped into the car laughing with the occupants.

Back to the fun parts of summer break 2005. It was much better than I expected with everything going on, but I knew it would be. I wasn't going to let one girl or any circumstance ruin my summer.

Our church had many activities going on during the next couple of months. It all started the third Saturday in July after Vacation Bible School, which lead up to a planned parade and Block Party for all the people from Deer Park and surrounding communities. Those who signed up to be in the parade gathered that afternoon at the junior high parking lot. There was an assortment of vehicles like old fire trucks, an Army Hum-V carrying military veterans from our church, four wheelers, and kids riding their decorated bikes for a contest, which Kimarie won. Oh! We can't forget some of the animals and other characters. There was a big brown horse, cute little ponies, an odd llama, a tiny dog, and Deacon Bob's 160-pound Rottweiler pulling a cart with Joshua, the pastor's son, riding along. Diana was dressed up as a sleepy clown and Rory was some type of urban cowboy.

A large tent was erected behind the church for the block party. There were free hamburgers, chips, popcorn, snow cones, and cotton candy. There were many games for the kids and they got to win prizes. Contemporary Christian music was played and in the evening we had live bands. The first was a Gospel bluegrass group, which was made up of former Pastor Danny's daughter and her musician friends. They were really good.

There was something for everyone to enjoy. We had a good turnout from the people we invited. All in all, it was a most wonderful event. I would do it again. Thanks to Post Falls First Baptist for letting us borrow the tent and for all the helpers from both churches.

Between my karate class and Kaylee's dance and flute lessons, we spent a lot of time at the Collins' ranch hanging out with De'von. Sometimes we helped him in the barn so we would have more time together. Now and then they invited us to a barbeque.

Mr. Collins, being the Deer Park High School baseball coach, recently cut a baseball diamond behind their house. The infield dimensions were regulation with real bases at nine feet apart and the mound to home plate six feet-six inches. Often guys from the team came over and worked out. Even Billie showed up a couple times, until he went off to prepare for the high school football camp. De'von had always been a center fielder ever since we played Kids League and he earned his spot on the team.

Kaylee and I just watched from under a nearby apple tree. She wrote in a notebook, while I read a novel. We also read the Bible out loud and discussed the Lord.

One day Mr. C. came over to me during some throwing drills. "Hey Jay, Ron didn't show up and we're short a player, would you like to fill-in?" he asked.

"Sure," I replied.

Greg, the team's regular right fielder, was my throwing partner and began throwing me balls. It was fun and I became more involved with the team. I also made some new friends. There was Jeb, the best player on the team and Chad, a pretty good athlete, who also played football.

When the team wasn't doing anything on the ranch, De'von and I tossed the ball around. He taught me how to play pepper, which Mr. C. frowned upon because it tore up the ground. Mr. C. watched us often as he passed to work in the barn.

One evening, De'von and I were messing around, pretending we played in the World Series. I noticed Mr. C. stuck around to watch De'von hit me ground balls.

"A grounder, hit to Asher," I announced after De'von threw the ball up and slugged it with his bat my way. "Looks like a base hit to shallow right…wait a sec…he dives for the ball and makes a marvelous play! Seattle wins the seventh game of the World Series!"

"Who were you playing?" Mr. C. asked.

"Denver, I think," De'von replied.

"Looks like you're having fun out there guys," Mr. C. said. "Hey, I'm going to be the first baseman. Jay, go out there where you were and I'll have De'von hit you a sharp grounder to the right."

Clink, the ball came off the bat like before, bounced twice in the dirt toward me. Diving for the ball, it must have hit a rock so I missed it.

"Let's try it again," Mr. C. suggested. "This time, Jay, catch it before the second hop."

So we repeated the play. I ran up to the ball as it hit the ground once and into my glove. Quickly, I threw it to first base where Mr. C. received it.

"Jay, you have good reflexes, good job," Mr. C. stated. "What do you think De'von?"

"Pretty good," De'von said.

"Jay, what are you doing this summer? I know you are really involved in karate," Mr. C. wondered.

"Nothing really—karate class twice a week—why?" I asked.

"Well, I've been watching you play and I'm impressed with what I see, soft hands and average arm," Mr. C. answered.

"Really?" I asked.

"Sure, I think you should tryout for the team next season," Mr. C. advised.

"Nah, I'm not that good of a hitter."

"I could always use a good fielder on my bench and I could help you with your batting," Mr. C. said.

"Oh, I don't know," I said.

"Come on Jay, you would have a blast," De'von said.

"Maybe, I still—how long is it?" I asked.

"Just eight games, two months," Mr. C. replied.

"Well," I began, considering all this. "You're not just saying that because I'm De'von's friend?"

"No, no, I'm talking to you as a coach. I have to consider my team," Mr. C. commented. "Honestly Jay, you have good composure out there. Defense is half the game and you don't have to be a homerun hitter. Like in karate, you need a good defense before offense. Of course, with anything, it takes practice, practice, practice."

"Well, okay, I will come over and you can help me with my batting," I said. "And who knows, Lord willing, I may want to go tryout. Thanks Mr. C."

"You're welcome, Jay."

Mr. C. then helped me two days a week with my baseball skills. Karate and baseball were similar in that they both used mental concentration and flexibility.

Chapter Twenty-Four

Fall 2005

SO WE advanced to my sophomore year of high school. Classes became harder, especially since I took geometry. A challenge was good for a young mind, right? I really looked forward to my first journalism class though.

My love for Rosa slowly vanished, the past fluttering images of someone else's life. I deserved the treatment she gave me for what I had done, but didn't understand the way she acted. I still cared a little about how she took care of her health, spiritually and physically. Prayer was the only thing I could do to help her.

I moved on and decided to forget the whole high school dating scene for now. If there were a romantic relationship in my future, I trusted it to the Lord's will. Only He knew when I would be ready.

De'von and I helped Kaylee get acquainted with Deer Park High. We met as her dad dropped her off. Quite a few new freshmen arrived early.

"Hey, you're new here," I said to Kaylee. "You sure look familiar, do we know you?"

"Yes, she sure does," De'von said. "Isn't your name Katie, Kelly."

"Very funny guys," Kaylee said with a laugh.

"We'll show you to your locker, what's the number?" I asked.

She told us as we walked her to the main building, directing her to the locker. On the way, the twins and Zoey greeted us. De'von went off to talk to them.

"Here you go," I said, touching Kaylee's locker. She instantly opened it.

"I already memorized the combination," Kaylee said, then wondered, "where's yours, Jay?"

"Just right down here," I said, as she followed, turning back toward where we just were. "Actually, I'm across from your locker."

One moment Kaylee and I joked and then the next we weren't, pausing to see Rosa coming down the hall. She was hand-in-hand with Jack, one of the skater guys, who I guess by the end of the summer started going out with her. Jack was a tall guy, reserved, and always seemed to show up for class. They passed us without even looking our way. I put it out of my mind and shrugged my shoulders as Kaylee did the same.

Journalism was my last class for the day. I was thrilled with excitement. The way it worked was we journalists sit around what was called the "Round Table" and threw around, in discussion, story ideas for the next month's edition. We mainly wrote about school issues, social issues, and anything that revolved around Deer Park High School.

We tried to cover and be open-minded to many different subjects, including controversial ones, by staying objective and writing the stories fair and responsibly.

The way the class worked, if I wrote a piece, another student would take pictures and vice-versa. Sometimes we had to leave class to do interviews with students or faculty. After a month, I had a blast, fitting right in with journalism, and feeling an important part of the student body. God sure knew what He was doing by directing me to my new spiritual gift.

Rosa dumped skater boy Jack after a month. Then I saw her at one of our football games in October talking with one of the jocks. Reed was a senior and a smooth talker. Rosa laughed throwing her head up and I could tell she was flirting with him. I watched them from afar. It wasn't long before Reed had Rosa under his spell. Soon they were an item and she went to all his games. Reed picked Rosa up at her house in his super charged truck with roses, being their first date. Some nights I would just hear this rumble and know they were going out. Rosa's skirts were shrinking and her blouses didn't leave much to the imagination. I tried not to think what they did on their dates and continued praying for her to be more responsible.

March-Spring 2006

Rosa turned sixteen and I heard they had the party over at Dora, her cousin's house. Soon after, Rosa received her driver's license and her parents got her a nice used car.

In March, I found myself at the beginning of baseball tryouts. For two weeks after school, Coach Collins met us on the baseball field at the sports complex, which was across the street from the high school. At the end of tryouts, Coach C. picked me for one of the reserve spots on the team. He told me that I would start on the bench, but be prepared to pinch-hit or to take the place of an injured player. Actually, I'd admit, with a lot of practice, hard work, and commitment, plus help from Coach C. during the previous summer, fall, and winter; I felt I was chosen by my athleticism. I spent a good deal of time in batting cages and also using other methods to improve my swing.

With tryouts finished and the team assembled, we practiced twice a week for two hours after school until April and our first game.

Our home uniforms were white with blue trim, and our away uniforms were black with blue and gold trim. The helmets and caps had a big white "D."

We played our first game at home against Medical Lake. It was a crisp afternoon at the sports complex. I found myself cheering for my team from the bench. I kept myself loose and ready in case the coach needed me.

Medical Lake was up first to bat. On the first play, a routine grounder was hit to Jeb and as he moved to get the ball, he stepped the wrong way twisting his ankle, going down in much pain. The runner was safe and time called as the coaches ran to his aid. Jeb was helped off the field, his face in agony. We all knew this meant bad news—an Achilles tendon injury we found out later. I heard this was the most painful injury you could get. The spectators groaned watching in horror. Not only was Jeb the best player on our team, but the team captain.

"Jay, you're in there at second," Coach C. said. "Billie's going to short."

Hearing this, I popped out of the dugout sprinting back and forth warming up, then stretched before heading out to second base. I practiced briefly taking grounders with the infielders.

The next guy was announced and I was ready if the ball was hit to me. I hoped this wouldn't happen, but it did. *Clank!* went the aluminum bat. Of course, it came right to me. I went for it like we did at practice hundreds of times—*oops*—I bent down to catch the grounder, the ball never made it to my mitt. It scooted between my legs and into the outfield. The right fielder quickly retrieved the ball, throwing it to the infield. Not the way I imagined my first play. Error on the scorecard, some boos.

"It's okay Jay, you'll get the next one!" Coach C. hollered.

With no one out and runners on first and third, Coach C. maneuvered the infielders to double play depth. It was a good call from coach as the next batter hit the ball to short stop and I took the throw at second base—good, I caught it, but when I threw it to first base it sailed over his head. The next outs were in the outfield and it was our turn up to bat. I batted seventh, so I had to wait.

It wasn't until third inning when I finally came up to bat with the score, Deer Park 0, Medical Lake 4.

Strike one, strike two, strike three, and I went out swinging. I had a horrible game when it was all said and done. Two more strike outs, no more errors, thank the Lord. We lost 6-2 and most importantly we lost Jeb to injury. We had reason to doubt the rest of the season.

"It's okay Jay, sometimes we have bad games," Chad said, as we came off the bench to shake hands with the other team.

"Yeah, I know," I said.

The next two games were on the road. Lost the first and won the second. I played better at second base and even got my first hit. When we were at home, Jeb with his ankle wrapped up, cheered us on from the bench.

I happened to notice the anniversary of my big breakup with Rosa soon was just around the corner. Not like it was really something on my mind. Rosa, I saw, was really happy with Reed and it was confirmed they were "*in love.*" I hoped Rosa was smart enough to look out for herself. Gossip was everywhere at school, as they were the hot topic. I tried not to listen to it, but there was no avoiding hearing about it. Just gave me the willies with all those rumors and such.

Spring was in fresh bloom and with the snow gone from the streets there was a sense of new beginnings. New romance was in the school halls and talks about who's going out with whom. I was an observer watching this unfold and there was a pang in my heart, something missing that would not go away. I wanted those same feelings I had with Rosa. Perhaps God would lead me in the right direction; I prayed often about this. The conversation with Rich was still fresh in my mind. It sure made sense knowing somebody's potential future spouse might be out there waiting to be discovered in our Lord's time.

One day after I finished writing an article for journalism, I sat at the table relaxing in meditation. When there was a break in the action, I would just talk to the Lord. I found sanctuary conversing with Him. So, I told Him if it were His will for a girl to be in my future or not, I would accept this. *If You do lead me in this direction, I want to do things right next time. I want to be more respectful if I do get into a relationship. Maybe Lord, you could give me a hint or a sign of what to do with all my feelings. In Jesus' name. Amen.*

Suddenly, the door opened like it was *the* sign. As my ears perked up, I tried not to jump to conclusions. There was a small form in the door with long hair, my mind spinning in anticipation. I took a double take as the girl stepped into the room. I was surprised and stunned at the same time. *Kaylee!*

I almost fell out of the seat as Kaylee walked over to the teacher. Jerking up into my chair, I awkwardly settled down, wanting to make sense of this event. For some reason she looked different. She transformed before me like a butterfly climbing out of its cocoon. *What's happening?* I thought. *She's my friend, but now arrows struck me?* Now my mind was going at mach fifteen. I couldn't believe I had these lovely feelings for my best friend. Words echoed in my mind: *there was a reason for everything. Calm down now Jay*, I told myself. *Get a hold of yourself.*

As she peered over at me, her face blossomed into a smile, her hair like golden sunshine—my angel. I thought I was caught and she could read my thoughts. How could she read my thoughts when I could hardly read them? *What did I say?* I tried ignoring whatever it was that seemed to stir within me, but there was no denying my attraction toward her. What did this mean? All I knew, she became this beautiful young lady. I'm not talking about her outside appearance; she was a beautiful young lady to my eyes, but it was her heart that attracted me most. Her true friendship, compassion, faithfulness—her whole person hit me like Mount Raineer. Such a sigh came to my bones, my inner most being. God whispered, *this could possibly be your wife.*

Hopefully, she didn't discern the way my feelings came forth. I nonchalantly smiled back with an acknowledging wave of my hand. Man, I could have died inside. She left unexpectedly taking my heart with her. I already missed her, sighing and melting into my chair.

Now what? I thought back to my prayer just minutes ago about wanting to do it right. *Patience, Jay. So, I discovered these new feelings for Kaylee, but I have to let God tell me that she is the one.* I shouldn't jump right into asking her out. Maybe the door opening was just one sign from the Heavenly Father.

At this time, I noticed the last bell would ring at any moment—school out—Kaylee and I usually walked home! I would be out of my mind knowing she was next to my side in reach. There was no time to think about it as the bell sounded.

My heart beat a mile a minute as I rounded the corner to my locker. Kaylee's locker was right there across the hall. I candidly caught a glimpse of her putting books into her denim backpack with the embroidered rainbow on the pocket. I was so distracted that I fidgeted with my lock and could hardly open it. Finally, I was successful and then started jamming things into my backpack. By then I felt her presence.

"Are you in a hurry?" Kaylee asked. "Do you have an important date?"

"Who, me? *Nah*," I replied. "Do I look like I'm in a hurry?"

"Kinda—I guess, it's Friday," she said, looking around at other kids rushing to get out.

I stole a quick glance noting her pretty face. I wanted to be lost in those blue eyes, but remembered where I was, my face feeling warm.

"Now that I think about it, I just want to get out of here," I said, trying to act normal with my new feelings for Kaylee.

We walked out of the school and into the sun as the last of the buses left.

"I wonder where De'von is?" I asked. "He probably hurried home—maybe we'll catch him later—or maybe Kaylee you would rather do something else. Do you have dance class or anything?"

"Oh, I need to practice for my piano recital, but we could hang out at my house for a little bit," she replied, as we turned onto the bike lane.

"Yeah, sure," I said, not knowing how to deal with myself as she walked beside me.

Kaylee's golden hair streamed in the wind and I was mesmerized. I saw her push her hair away from her eyes as I quickly turned away so she wouldn't notice.

"How is journalism going for you?" she asked.

"I really enjoy it," I replied, "just finished a piece on one of the seniors."

"That's neat," she said. "I thought about signing up next year."

"You would love it," I said. "I'll take you there during lunch on Monday so you can get an application."

"Thanks Jay, that would be great," she said.

Five minutes later we turned down 'A' Street toward the Knight's residence. At this time I hadn't said much about the inside of their house. There was a living room as you entered, with a partial wall open to the hall on the left. A small dining room was adjacent to the kitchen, which was down the hall in back of the house. On the right side down the hall, was a computer room where a spiral staircase led up to Billie's room and the master bedroom.

I followed Kaylee to her room next to the stairs. A rainbow and clouds were painted across the peach walls. The main feature was her canopy bed with a few favorite stuffed creatures.

Suddenly, something came over me as I approached the threshold of Kaylee's sleeping quarters. I never spent very long in her room at any given time, maybe a few minutes here and there. At first, when I was ten, I would never go in there because she had a crush on me and I didn't want Billie teasing me. Going in her room right then was not in my plans. Not that I couldn't or it was against the house rules, but yes, I did spend time in Rosa's room. It was because of my new found feelings toward her that I decided to browse in the computer room briefly as Kaylee put away her school things.

"So, what do you want to do?" Kaylee asked from behind.

"I don't know, listen to some music or something," I said, feeling antsy to get out of there.

"I know, we could listen to my new CD," Kaylee suggested, while waltzing into her room.

I felt more at ease as we entered the living room where I found Paddy roaming about. She saw me and wagged her tail like a dog, following me over to the couch where I stroked her back. Kaylee worked the stereo and as soon as the music began she danced to the beats.

"Come on Jay, you can dance," she said.

"No way! I'm out classed," I said, concentrating on Paddy.

"Hey, you're not that bad," she said.

"Okay, I give," I said, joining her while keeping a safe distance.

Soon, we settled on the couch with the cat making itself a barrier between us. We talked about school stuff and God. There was a pause in conversation and we just enjoyed the music and Paddy. For a while, I forgot my inner feelings for Kaylee, but they mingled back into my thoughts, imagine that. A few times, I wanted to just reach over, hold her hand, and tell her how I felt. Then, I wondered if she still had that crush on me. Our friendship continued to blossom and I didn't want to ruin it in any way. I thought back again to my prayer in journalism about being patient and waiting for God to lead me. I continued these same thoughts after I left. Kaylee was on my mind all the way home and I couldn't wait to rummage for any picture of her.

Chapter Twenty-Five

<u>Rainbow Knight</u>

Oh Rainbow, my Rainbow Knight
I dreamed of you since first sight
Being in your presence makes me true
And you bring me up when I am blue

Oh Rainbow, my Rainbow Knight
You seem out of my reach in the sun's light
So many other clouds have come between us
But I never lost my longing expresses

Oh Rainbow, my Rainbow Knight
Your faith in God is tight
Bringing always my heart gladness
For I too, love His graciousness

Oh Rainbow, my Rainbow Knight
That you just might, just might...
I will always notice your colorful attire
Alas, alas, no other created Arch I desire

THIS WAS what I unexpectedly came across on Monday while reading the final year's installment of *The Stag* school newspaper. Just a half hour before, I brought Kaylee to get her application like I said I would. Then we had our lunch in the journalism room. My heart started racing as I read halfway through Kaylee's poem. There was no doubt that she wrote it for me. I was overjoyed with emotion and could not wait to see her after school. God whispered the word "patience" as it entered my thoughts. So at this point, I figured Kaylee still had feelings for me. I still wanted to wait for God's guidance. Setting the paper down, I leaned back in the chair and closed my eyes to meditate.

Before I knew it, the last period bell rang. I felt more relaxed after talking with the Lord again. Working my way to my locker, I walked with ease and focused. Kaylee was there at her locker like I had seen on so many occasions and felt a smile come to my face. I wondered if anybody approached Kaylee about her poem.

So I composed the very words I specially created for her, which swirled vibrantly in my mind.

I finished at my locker and joined Kaylee as she turned away from hers. We exchanged greetings. Her gaze was cheerful, but had an edge of uncertainty. Maybe I acted different. There then seemed to be an air of uneasiness between us.

Silently, we walked outside, so I thought some conversation would help. "Man, it sure has been a cruddy day," I commented, looking at the overcast sky.

It rained as Mom drove me to school. If I was going to spill my heart, the weather sure didn't inspire the mood. Though a little rain shower would create a romantic setting, as I pictured sharing my umbrella with Kaylee. No fresh drops.

"Yeah, that it is," Kaylee said. "Makes you want to have hot chocolate."

"That sounds good," I said.

For a few minutes we didn't speak. A couple of times we started to say something but nothing seemed to come out. Finally, Kaylee spoke as we rounded the corner seeing the elementary school up ahead.

"So, I guess you're finished with *The Stag* this year?" she asked.

I felt she fished for whether I had read it. "Yep, I will miss it." I said. "Speaking of…the poem you wrote was wonderful."

"Really?" she said. "Just something I wrote."

"Truly, Kaylee, it was most wonderful, one of your best," I said.

"Thanks Jay, I know you're not just saying that," she said.

"Nope, I have always loved your poetry," I pointed out. "You have a way with words—so colored with emotion—you even inspire me to write more polished poems."

"Stop, you are flattering me," Kaylee said.

"Sorry, when I really like something I tell it the way I see it," I said.

Again, we didn't talk for several minutes while crossing the street and passing the hospital. I could have told her almost anywhere, but the Holy Spirit held me back. The Deer Park Public Library came and went from view. Suddenly, the sky opened up with the sun poking its head out and soon everything was made clear to me. I was surprised because I guess Kaylee didn't see it. I held her hand to stop, pointing up ahead a block or so to where I was looking.

"Look Kaylee, above that church!" I said excitedly. What more of a sign from God?

"Wow a rainbow!" she exclaimed, her face blossoming. "Now my day is complete."

"Not just yet, I have something to tell you," I said, but I don't know if she heard me. She was still in awe with God's miracle.

"Sorry, what did you want to tell me?" Kaylee asked.

"First, let me ask you," I said, with her hand in mine, facing her. "Am I your Rainbow Knight?"

Kaylee blushed, turning her head away from me. "Uhh…" she began, nervously running her free hand in her hair, but didn't pull away from my grasp.

"It's okay Kaylee," I said, placing my hand and turning her head toward me. "I would be honored to be your Rainbow Knight."

"For real?" she asked, looking up at me.

"As real as God who sent that rainbow," I said, taking both her hands in mine. "Ever since last Friday, I discovered deep feelings for you and I can't deny them."

"So, that's why you acted odd when we walked home," she said. "You could have told me then."

"I wanted to so bad, just wasn't God's will at that time," I said, squeezing her hands. "I waited a whole week to hold your hand, touch your hair, and gaze into your eyes."

She sighed, and then giggled.

"Please, will you go out on a date with me, Kaylee?"

"Of course, I will," she said, wrapping her arms around me. "Well, it's about time Jay Matthew Asher."

"Hey Kaylee, how about we go bowling this Friday?" I asked, as we started off again to her house.

"That sounds wonderful," Kaylee replied.

"What would your mom and dad think about me taking you out?" I asked.

"They would be cool about it," she said. "On my birthday, they said I could go out now that I was fifteen. But they said they wanted an adult nearby. Actually, I guess it's okay. I wouldn't mind being alone with you on our first date, but parents in general get weird.

Let's see, who could take us? Be kinda weird to have any of our parents tag along."

"Hmmm, let's see," I said, thinking. "Hey, I know! I think everyone would feel better if my Gramma took us—maybe she'll sit in the car."

"Yeah Jay, she would be a better choice," she said.

Let me say one thing before I continue. God answered my prayer for the desires of my heart as the Psalm says. Usually there isn't a sign for answered prayers or the will of God, but most of the time it is some kind of feeling deep within your soul. When you discover God's will, it hits you right where it hurts, your yearning spirit. The flesh blushes while the soul illuminates.

Arriving home, I told Mom and Gramma about me going on a date with Kaylee. They agreed Gramma would go with us to the Deer Park Bowling Lanes. The plan was relayed to Kaylee's parents. They had no problem even with me driving and Gramma sitting in the backseat. Billie teased us a little bit, but seemed to be a protective brother. It felt good not keeping Kaylee a secret, so we could just be ourselves.

Kaylee and I were excited when Friday arrived. We visited at her house after school, then I went home to get ready for our date. I dressed in my nice slacks and shirt. Before heading over to Kaylee's house I took a short trip over to the flower shop.

I parked in front of the Knight's cars at the side of the house. As I approached the front door, Gramma followed me a few steps behind ready with the camera. Ringing the bell, I saw some movement, then Mr. Knight opened the door.

"Good evening, Jay," he greeted, then peered over my shoulder. "Hi Naomi, how are you guys this evening?"

"Really good," I said.

"Just splendid," Gramma said.

"I will see if Kaylee is ready," Mr. Knight said, closing the screen door.

We heard some conversation from within and I distinctively recognized Kaylee's voice. Soon she came out, her hair glowing under the porch light. She greeted me with a bright smile. She wore purple jeans and a white blouse.

"Kaylee, you look very lovely this evening, like a rainbow princess," I said.

"Why thank you, my Rainbow Knight," Kaylee returned. "You look dashing."

"Here, this is for you," I said, handing her a cluster of flowers. "These are lily of the valley, which Gramma says means sweetness and return to happiness."

"Thank you, that is so thoughtful," she said, taking them.

Gramma entered the bowling alley with us and took more pictures. She seemed to stick around, following us to the shoe rental counter. We got ours and then Gramma rented a pair.

"I think I will play one game with you guys," Gramma said, coming toward us.

"I didn't know you bowled Naomi," Kaylee said.

"Didn't Jay tell you?" Gramma questioned. "His Granddad, Rich, and I were in a bowling league."

"Nope, he didn't," Kaylee said.

So we found an open lane and put on our shoes. I didn't do very well in my first frame, only knocking down four pins. Kaylee faired better taking out nine pins. Gramma hit nine in one shot and finished with a spare.

I had to say my Gramma was still a good bowler. Kaylee and I were dumbfounded as she beat us both by fifty points.

"Well, that was fun, and I'm pooped," Gramma said, sitting down. "I'm sure you two had enough of me. How long do you think you're going to be?"

"About an hour or so," I replied.

"Okay, I'll wait for you at the grocery store," Gramma said.

"Sure, that would be fine," I said.

Finally we were alone and it actually began to feel like a real date. We played one game and Kaylee won. There was a little time left so we talked a while.

"Jay, I sure had a wonderful time," Kaylee remarked.

"Yeah, I definitely did too," I said. "Even with Gramma."

"Yep, she is surprising," she said.

"Kaylee, sweet Kaylee," I said, taking her hand. "You sure were always there for me all these months—all these years, weren't you? I know I've even probably hurt you, but here you are."

"Yeah, here I am," Kaylee stated. "You don't need to explain yourself, I believe in you. Yeah, I was hoping that it was me with you instead of Rosa. But I was happy for you."

"Same here. You returned my happiness," I said, squeezing her hands. "I came up with a special saying when involving our affection toward each other. So, any time we hold hands or give a hug it is 'For Meaning,' not just because it feels good—"

Kaylee hugged me and said, "Like this? This is 'For Meaning,' Jay."

"Yep, 'For Meaning,' Kaylee," I said, noticing the time. "Well, I suppose we don't want to keep Gramma waiting."

"Yep, I guess we should be going, but I wish this could go on forever," she said, as I pulled her to her feet.

"There will be many more dates, that's for sure," I said.

"Where are we going next?" she asked.

"Where ever my Rainbow Princess wants to go," I replied.

On our second date we went to see a matinee movie at the mall. Billie and Amber were also there. I drove again and this time Henry Knight rode with us. He probably wanted to observe my driving skills. It made me nervous, but as soon as we were down the highway I settled.

Chapter Twenty-Six

June 2006

THE FOLLOWING week I turned sixteen. Over the last few years, I've observed girls my age talking about turning the magical age of sixteen. Some girls made a big production out of this. Now for me, I was excited because soon I would get my driver's license. Like most of my last several birthdays, I just wanted a simple celebration. Miniature golf and go-carting with my friends was enough for me.

On an important occasion, like one's birthday, some people liked to sleep in and take a day off, not me, just another day getting closer to the Lord's second coming. Sometimes I slept in, but it was not very often. I liked to wake up early when everyone else was asleep, so I could be totally at peace with myself, preparing for the day.

After my daily routine, Gramma made a huge breakfast for me. Rich and his sister, Joan would join us. I thought it was them, hearing a little knock on my front door. Kaylee greeted me with her precious sunshine.

"This is a surprise," I said, smiling.

"Happy birthday, Jay," Kaylee announced.

She walked in giving me a peck on the cheek and warmly found her way into my arms. Just that little piece of affection was electrifying for me. I was content with these expressions of hers.

"This is the only way to start off my birthday," I said, "my Rainbow Princess at my door."

"I knew my Rainbow Knight would like to see me," she said, breaking away and reaching into her pocket. "And I couldn't wait to give you one of your birthday presents—open it now!"

"Okay, if you insist," I said, taking a small box from her and shaking it. "Hmm, wonder what it is?"

"I saw it and thought it was the neatest thing," she commented, as I held the gift.

"Well, here goes," I said, unwrapping it. Then the item was revealed upon flipping the lid. "I should have known you would pick something with a rainbow in mind."

"Do you know what it is?" Kaylee asked.

"Looks like a rainbow charm on a chain," I replied, carefully examining it. "Thank you Kaylee, it's really nice—I love it—very unique."

"There's one more tidbit to add to it," she said, pulling out the exact same charm from around her neck. "See you put the rainbows together like a puzzle—two rainbows connecting into one heart. You have one part, I have the other."

"Oh, how cool," I said, hugging her. "I will treasure it always. Thank you so much."

"You're welcome," she said.

"Jay, how would you like your egg?" Mom asked, walking into the room and paused, "Oh, good morning Kaylee, didn't know you were here."

"Morning Rachel," Kaylee said, hugging Mom.

"Did you have breakfast?" Mom asked.

"Just some toast," Kaylee replied.

"If you're still hungry we have plenty," Mom offered.

"Nah, that's okay."

"Please Kaylee, we have strawberries," I said.

"In that case, I think I will," Kaylee said.

Soon we sat down for the traditional gigantic Asher birthday breakfast. This meal began with my Grampa Gus' Grandmother and it used to be a bigger deal than Thanksgiving. In the past, I was told a dozen or so family members and close friends would attend. You were required to stuff yourself to the gills.

An hour later, after breakfast, we met De'von, Billie, and my other friends at the Miniature Golf Excite Land. We stayed there until mid-afternoon playing golf, video games, and racing go-carts. My birthday shifted over to my house for cake and ice cream where I opened gifts from everyone. As usual, Billie gave me gag gifts, but also did find something more practical. I received a wallet from Kaylee that had a rainbow border and the cover had scripture from Genesis 9:13: "I do set my bow in the cloud, and it shall be for a token of a covenant between me and the earth."

My birthday party came to a close upon dinnertime. All my friends left except Kaylee. Mom and I visited with her, but soon she had to go babysitting.

"Well, I guess I had better go," Kaylee announced.

"I'll get Gramma's keys," I said, as I would drive her home.

Mom went with us, as I still could not drive by myself. When we walked out the kitchen door to Gramma's sedan, a car pulled in behind it. Rich waved from the driver's seat. At first I did not recognize his 1974 muscle car, which I had helped him restore over the last three years, because of the new red paint. Not just any red, but cherry red. Rich let me pick out the color. The car recently was painted at the shop and this was the first time I saw the final product. Rich stepped out with a beaming smile like it was his birthday.

"She sure looks beautiful, all shiny and looking fast," Rich said. "Don sure did a fabulous job on the paint, didn't he?"

"Yeah, like brand new," I said.

"Very nice, Rich and Jay," Mom said, touching the hood.

"Jay, since it's your birthday, I'll let you take my car for a spin," Rich said.

"We were going to take Kaylee home anyways," I said.

Mom and Rich slipped into the backseat while Kaylee and I sat in the front. I placed my hands on the red steering wheel and worked the doorknobs. The dash was bi-color, charcoal on top with a red face around the dials. Charcoal flowed through the bench seats, carpet, and door panels.

"Is everyone ready?" I asked.

"Go ahead buddy start her up," Rich urged.

I turned the key already in the ignition and the car came alive. The floor under my feet vibrated. Checking the rear-view mirror, I put her in reverse without mishap, backing into the street. There was not much traffic and I wanted to be extra careful.

"She runs really smooth," Rich pointed out.

"Nice comfortable ride," Mom said.

"I decided to leave in the original 250," Rich said. "Not as much power as the 350, but still cruises quite nicely."

When we came to Crawford Street, I was a little nervous watching the busier vehicles. It was clear both ways so I wasted no time crossing the intersection and turning on 'A' Street next to the post office. A few blocks later, I parked in front of Kaylee's house.

"Thanks for the ride," Kaylee said, unbuckling. "Like your car Rich."

"Soon it will be Jay's car," Rich said, surprisingly handing me a key ring with Jay on it. "Happy birthday, buddy!"

"No way," I said twisting toward him. "You're joking."

"No, she is yours, after you pass your driving test of course," Rich replied.

"Cool Jay!" Kaylee exclaimed.

"Wow, Jay, your own car!" Mom remarked happily. "That was awfully generous of Rich."

"I don't know, it's awfully nice, but you haven't enjoyed it yet," I said looking around. "I would feel guilty if I dented it."

"Don't worry Jay, you're a good driver," Rich said. "This is a great first car and besides, I didn't want you to have just any old car."

"Thanks! Thank you a whole lot," I said.

"I can't wait Jay," Kaylee said. "Now you can drive me around."

"Of course," I said.

"I better get going," Kaylee said, starting to open the door, but Mom stopped her.

"Don't go yet Kaylee," Mom said excitedly. "I have an announcement. I was going to tell Jay first, but I just can't wait."

"What is it?" I wondered, turning to face her in the backseat.

"Let's get out of the car first, then I will tell you some good news," Mom said, who then explained, "Well, for a couple weeks I have been feeling different. I had some tests done and got the results today. Dr. Halbur first examined me just like she always does and when she saw the x-rays she noticed the lesions, which have been causing the MS, have vanished. She commented that my motor skills are back to their normal limits. It was like I never had MS!"

"It's a miracle!" Kaylee rejoiced, giving mom a big hug.

"I must be dreaming," I said, scratching my head. "What you're saying is you don't have MS—like you're cured?"

"You're not dreaming, it truly is a miracle, I'll prove it," Mom said, as she walked without a limp, then jogged around the car.

"Thank the Lord," I said, rushing to give her a hug. "This is the best birthday present ever!"

Rich taught me how to drive ever since I was ten years old. When restoring his old cars, he would let me drive them around the yard before working on them, especially if they were really in bad shape. This gave me great experience, so when I went to take my driver's test, I passed on the first try. Everyone always complained that their driver's license photo was not a good shot. Now, I could see why. Mine looked like a mug shot too!

I kept thanking Rich for the car over and over again. Many people my age envied me and thought I was the luckiest guy in town. Some had to buy their own cars and sometimes parents bought them a car at graduation. Kaylee and my friends enjoyed riding in my car. We didn't have to rely on others to take us places, which gave us more freedom. I earned the reputation for being a safe driver from many of my friends' parents and people around town. I tried not to be alone in the car with Kaylee very often if it could be helped.

Lance offered me a job at the karate school working two to three times a week helping with the classes. Once in a while, I cleaned the bathroom and wiped down mirrors in the training room.

I still did yard work and other odd jobs to help pay for things us teenagers needed. Of course, I humbly tithed my ten percent to the Lord every week. Sometimes, I even helped pay for the groceries, which helped Mom and Gramma.

Chapter Twenty-Seven

July 2006

ONE HIGHLIGHT of that summer was our church's Fourth of July concert. We performed for the community of Deer Park and the outlining areas. Pastor David, being patriotic, wanted to do something special. After weeks of prayer and thought, he decided on a concert which he titled "God, Country, and Apple Pie." Along with the concert, the public was treated to free apple pie and vanilla ice cream. The United States Army Reserves were also there passing out free fresh water.

The band already consisted of the pastor's wife and eight of their children who played various instruments, plus Arlene on the keyboard and our very own drummer. Other musicians from our Deer Park area were also invited to partake in the band.

The concert was set up on that afternoon on the west-side of the Deer Park Civic Center. The scorching sun beat down on the stage of singers and the band right below. It all began with three kids dressed in 1770's Colonial American Revolutionary uniforms marching while playing the drums, piccolo, and bearing the flag.

David invited a guy named Luke, who was a professional musician and composer of some of the songs that were sung at our concert, along with other famous familiar patriotic tunes.

The one hour performance was well appreciated by our community and the Deer Park Council. It was even put on the front page of our local newspaper.

Following the concert was the annual fireworks display and it was spectacular as usual.

KAYLEE AND I had been dating for six weeks come mid-July. We were crazy about each other and no doubt, I knew love was in our hearts. Those special three words did not have to fall from our lips. At times, both of us wanted to say it, but we were not in a hurry. Perhaps she wanted me to tell her first. Soon, I was ready. As for kissing and holding her close, it did cross my mind; nonetheless, I was determined to remain a gentleman.

One afternoon, I drove Kaylee into Spokane to spend a day at Riverfront Park. Taking a look at a postcard of downtown Spokane, you would notice its familiar landmarks. They were the pavilion, gondola ride spanning the Spokane Falls, and a huge clock tower, which was saved from the old railroad stations. All were remnants of the 1974 World's Fair.

It could have not been a nicer day. At the Pavilion we saw one of those movies on a three-story tall, huge screen and then had ice-cream cones afterwards. We just enjoyed walking through the park, riding on the carousel horses, being together, holding hands, and talking. It was great.

With the clock tower looming right behind us, we sat there visiting on the steps. The sun made us hot so we moved nearby, standing beneath the underpass that crossed the Spokane River. Concrete and a rod iron fence was the river's bank. A few mallard ducks floated on by a sculpture strutting out of the water.

"Oh, Jay, I'm having such a wonderful time," Kaylee said.

"Yeah, me too," I said. "Speaking of, I wonder what time it is. But I don't want to leave. Oh darn, we should go in an hour or so—dinner probably."

"Yeah, I suppose," she said.

"Kaylee, we have the whole summer to be together," I said.

We rested a while on a bench and then it was time to go. Something occurred spontaneously while helping Kaylee stand. I pulled her up gently, meeting her blue eyes. She was surprised when I stepped in closely pausing to push away the hair from her eyes.

"God has blessed me with you," I said. "Kaylee, I love you more than anything on this earth. I was struck by your heart-felt arrows."

"Oh Jay, you love me, like I love you," Kaylee said, happily embracing me. "If I'm dreaming, I never, never, never want to wake up—just want to hold you forever and not let go. The Lord wanted us to be together, I just know it."

"I have been praying about us being together and I was sure in my heart that I had fallen for you, but I wanted God to guide me," I said.

"Yeah, me too," she said. "We can't do anything without Him."

"Let me see you," I said, pulling a tad back from her. "Your face will be etched in my memory…my girl."

Kaylee sighed. "Wow, Jay, your words spin my world…so charming…romantic," she said.

"Now my mind is spinning," I said, so tempted to kiss her.

"This is usually where the guy kisses the girl. I know I want you to kiss me, but I don't want to disappoint you," she said, turning away from me.

"No, no, you won't ever disappoint me," I said, bringing her face toward me. "I think I know where you're coming from."

"I don't think you do know where I'm coming from—you may think it's unusual."

"You want to save that kind of kiss for your future husband, as I have learned to save myself for my future wife, Lord willing, of course," I said.

"Oh Jay, that makes me so happy to know we share those same thoughts," she said, hugging me tight.

"Yep, I have been looking at the Lord's big picture and figured my future wife would be disappointed," I said.

"Yeah, Lord willing, it could be you, but who knows what Jesus' plan is?" Kaylee pointed out. "That kiss would be all the more priceless just the way I imagined it—gentle, memorable."

"Yeah, very memorable," I said, "'For meaning.'"

"Oh Jay, I love you, I love you," Kaylee said, then holding me tight. "Yes, 'For meaning.'"

"I love you too Kaylee, very much," I said and kissed her forehead. "Hey, let's get a picture."

"You think of everything," Kaylee said.

"If you think about it, just seems we have been together for more than six weeks," I said, as we headed back to the car hand-in-hand.

"It sure does," Kaylee agreed, "like God prepared us to be together."

That day at Riverfront Park was much more special telling each other to save that certain kind of kiss for our future spouses, rather than if we were locked in a long kiss. One would ask themselves, well isn't kissing a part of dating? In my opinion, as a Christian I would say 'no.' The world says there was nothing wrong with kissing and making out (going all the way would be added to the world's way of thinking), but that's the world. I felt it's much more genuine and respectable when you save yourself for that future spouse. Once you commit yourself to making out, what's next?

I loved Kaylee with all of my heart. She was no longer the little girl with a simple childhood crush on me, but a young woman whose crush matured into real love. Sure, there was a physical attraction between us that could not be helped because of our human nature. Kaylee was very affectionate and caring toward me. Little kisses on the cheek and forehead and hugging seemed like enough for her. We developed a mutual respect for each other.

During the summer, I enjoyed doing different activities with Kaylee involving our friends, De'von, Zoey, and the twins to name a few. We even put the poetry group back together.

In the journalism class, we did write about religion. I wrote an article on prayer, but I couldn't expound much on it, so I decided to create my own newspaper online. There really wasn't much to it, just three pages, articles from Kaylee and me, plus a couple poems. At first, it was something fun for Kaylee and I to do, but then other kids at our school became involved including a couple from the journalism class. Mainly, in the beginning, it centered on God and church. Then the topics expanded to anything about teens' lives. Of course, I was the editor and for the most part, I was non-judgmental with materials others submitted.

Fall 2006

My junior year was quite busy with the regular high school schedule. I also signed up for this accelerated program where juniors and seniors take courses at the community colleges in Spokane. The classes I attended at the college counted on my high school records and credits toward college. I elected to take my courses in the morning and then head back to high school for journalism.

Three evenings a week I worked at the karate school. Lance was flexible, so he let me pick out my own days. If he was in a bind, I helped out. I still trained hard six mornings a week maintaining my black belt rank. A second-degree black belt was in my near future, but that didn't distract me from what I needed to do. When the test eventually came, I would be ready.

I wanted to leave Friday nights open so I could do things with Kaylee. We both enjoyed going to the home football games. Whether *The Stag* needed pictures or not I always had my camera at the games. I also used some of the images for my website. We lost about half the team when last year's seniors graduated. Billie continued his running back starting position.

Last year, our backup quarterback, Chad Fortay, assumed starting quarterback position. He was over six-feet tall and very talented. Chad also had a younger brother who was a backup receiver, named Tadd. Both brothers had blond hair and blue eyes. If I were a girl, I would consider them handsome.

During a blowout last season, the coach used a couple players on the bench to finish the game. He sent Chad and Tadd onto the field. After leading the team in the huddle, Chad brought the offense up to the twenty-yard line.

Unexpectedly, there was a bad snap from the center lineman and Chad missed the ball, which bounced off his shoulder pads. He then chased and recovered the ball on the ten-yard line. Our team usually fought to the end, but with the ball way back there and only fifty-seconds left on the clock, the coach usually ran the ball, using up the rest of the time.

Chad brought the team up to the ten-yard line. We held our breath, when the ball snapped (we could just see a fumble coming and the other team recovering it for a touchdown) and to our surprise, Chad faked the hand-off to Billie. Then Chad while stepping back, looked to the right and left, pumped his arm back once, and threw the ball up the field. I thought it was headed to De'von fifteen yards up the field, but the football sailed passed him. Overthrown, I figured. Cheering erupted from the stands when we saw that it was not a busted play. There was Tadd uncovered by the defense sprinting passed the fifty-yard line. He looked back catching the ball over his shoulder. TOUCHDOWN! We didn't win the game, but it was a victory nonetheless.

I got to know Chad quite a bit better while playing with him on the baseball team. We were friends at school, but never really hung out together. One day, in the middle of October, Chad approached me about asking Rosa out on a date. I think he was trying to question me for some reason on whether or not he could date her and if it would affect our friendship. I told him it wouldn't because she was part of my past. After Rosa broke up with that Reed Davis character, I didn't think she had been with anyone else until I saw her with Chad.

I thought Chad was a much better choice for Rosa because he wasn't a jerk and would treat her right. He had some good qualities that I admired to go along with his God given athletic talents. Chad was decent toward everyone and did not have a huge ego. No one had anything bad to say about him. He was very social and talked to pretty much anybody. In the classroom, Chad wasn't a student who slacked; he was serious about his schoolwork. As for girls, I didn't remember him having a girlfriend before Rosa. Maybe he was immersed into football. Whatever the reason, Chad hooked up with Rosa and soon she wore his letterman's jacket.

March 2007

Kaylee's sixteenth birthday came upon us and I was already prepared with her special gift. She wanted her party to be at my house because it had more room. "Irish" was the theme she chose, so the house was decked with green ribbons, balloons, and even the cake. Some of the other food was also dyed green including the punch and ice-cream, which was mint flavored. Of course, being Kaylee, there was a rainbow decoration in a pot where you would find the gold. In her case, that was where we set the gifts. There was also Irish/Celtic music playing in the background.

De'von, myself, and two other guys were in the midst of a dozen giggly girls—they included Zoey, the twins, Kaylee's closest cousins, and several girls from our church. In the beginning, there were games, food and snacks before and after the party.

Brother Billie surprised his sister dressed up as a Leporcon, I think. Anyway, he dowsed her with green silly string from the can—two guys in gorilla outfits held her down. It was a zoo, to say the least, as everyone joined in to help Kaylee from the attack. We all laughed about it at the dining room table while a blazing birthday cake arrived. About one hour later all the gifts but one was opened.

"Here Kaylee," I said, handing her a small box.

"Thank you Jay, I love it already," Kaylee said.

"You haven't even opened it!" I exclaimed, taking a picture.

"Well, it's from you, my boyfriend. Isn't it supposed to be nice?"

"Okay, okay, just open it," I said excitedly.

"Alright, here it goes," she said, taking off the paper and opening the box.

"What is it?" a couple girls asked with wonder.

There was a slight frown after she peered inside. "There's nothing in here?" Kaylee said, with a curious smile from the box to me.

"Whose boyfriend would give their girlfriend an empty box?" Zoey asked.

"No gift could express how much I really love you," I said, then whispered, "'For Meaning.'"

"'For Meaning,' Jay," she said, hugging me with joyful tears in her eyes.

"Wait a minute, there's one thing for you," I said, quickly running into a room.

Hurrying back with a balloon, I gave her the string to hold. There was a hush coming over the room with an air of anticipation, knowing I had something else up my sleeve.

I quickly popped the balloon with a needle. People jumped back and someone screamed. Kaylee's eyes went wide as she placed her hand by her heart, it was probably beating fast.

"Look Kaylee! There's something on the end of the string!" Lana exclaimed.

"Oh my goodness, there sure is," Kaylee said. "Oh my goodness! It's an aquamarine ring, my birthstone, I love it, Jay." She gave me a kiss on the cheek along with a hug.

"For you Dollheart, 'For Meaning,'" I whispered in her ear.

One Saturday night, during March, after my prayers, I heard this distinct noise. *Where was it coming from?* I wondered. I thought it was my clock radio because the noise sounded like music, but it was off. Whatever it was, it stopped. I slipped under the covers and turned off the light.

Half asleep, the same noise entered my brain again. The first time I heard it, I ignored it easily, but the second time it was getting on my nerves. *Oh what could it be!* I sat up listening from all around in the dark. The noise seemed to be coming from my desk very faintly, so I ventured over there to further investigate. Nothing on top of the desk could have made that distinct noise. It sounded muffled, like it was in something. The drawers didn't have any clues. I sat in the chair scratching my head and that's when I realized it was coming from my backpack hanging on the chair.

Oh, my cell phone, I thought, quickly unzipping my backpack. *Who in the world is calling?* The ring wasn't the usual tone. When Kaylee called the cell phone rang differently than when mom called. This ring tone I didn't remember, but yet it was so familiar.

I flipped the phone open and had to do a double take at the number on the caller ID. Nope, I read the number right. If I were asleep, I'm awake now. Rosa! I almost dropped the phone, fumbling to answer it.

"Hello," I answered, holding my breath.

She didn't answer right away, but I heard her breathing and there were added half sobs. Before I could say anything, she hung up. I began dialing her number, but was startled when it rang. Rosa spoke this time.

"I wanted to let you know Waldo died," she said.

"I'm sorry to hear about that," was the only thing I could say.

"He died just an hour ago," she explained.

"He was a good dog," I said, trying to console her.

"You probably wonder why I called you, since we haven't been on good terms."

"Yes, I did wonder," I replied. "You probably needed to talk to someone—you probably already talked to your boyfriend."

"Well, I knew you really liked Waldo, so I wanted to let you know," she said.

"Thanks, I appreciate you calling me," I said, and then there was silence for a few moments. I thought there was more to the story than just Waldo.

"My dad arranged to have Waldo cremated," Rosa said. "And we're having a little ceremony at the house over the weekend. You're welcome to come."

"Sure, I'll stop by," I said. "Well, I guess I'll see you then."

"Sure, okay," she said.

Following church a week later, I started across the street toward the Sanchez's house. For some reason, I paused in the middle of the street. I reached out toward their house thinking there was some force field, which had always kept me from Rosa. I couldn't even visit Manny, who sometimes invited me to their house. No force field awaited me this time, just a cool spring breeze.

It was a gloomy day and it pretty much described the mood when I stepped into the backyard; there was quiet conversation. Rosa and Chad had their backs facing me. Rosa's mom, Ella, was the first to see me as she came through the sliding glass door.

"Hi Jay," Ella said.

"Hi Mrs. Sanchez," I said, as Rosa and Chad turned to face me.

"Hey Jay," Rosa said.

"Howdy Jay," Chad said.

Very quickly it became quiet, not even the birds chirped. I had visions of Waldo running around the corner with his slobbery green tennis ball. Manny opened the door bringing me from my memories.

"Jay, I didn't know you were here," Manny said. "I guess we can get started. Rosa would like each of us to say a little about Waldo, a favorite memory, and then spread his ashes around the yard. I'll start."

Manny picked up a tin, which I guess was Waldo, and all eyes were on him as he stepped into the middle of the yard.

"I can remember the first time I brought Waldo home," Manny began. "The expression on Rosa's face was pure joy. It was almost like they were meant to be together."

Manny sprinkled some ashes over the lawn. He handed the can over to Ella, who said something, then it was Chad's turn and he wished he'd known Waldo better. I guess I was next and thought for a while about what I would say.

"Since I really never had a dog," I began, "I guess Waldo would have been the closest thing to having one. Rosa and I had some really good times going camping and fishing with Waldo."

"Waldo, you were such a good friend," Rosa said. "When I felt down, you were there to nudge me forward. You were the best dog a girl could ever have."

After Waldo's ceremony, we had finger sandwiches inside. It felt odd being in Rosa's house. Everything looked the same except for the new carpet. I listened to their conversations, but I felt awkward not knowing how to join in. I was just out of place, so I excused myself.

"I better go, some things to do at the house," I announced to the party, then to Rosa, "Thanks, for inviting me Rosa."

"Glad you could come," Rosa said.

"Nice talking with you, Jay," Chad said.

"Same here," I said, then leaving.

The afternoon wore on and it passed dinnertime when we got a knock on the door. Surprisingly, Rosa stood on our front porch. No one else was present outside.

"Hey Rosa, what's up?" I asked, curiously.

"Just wanted to say something quickly, then I'll leave," she said.

"No, please come in," I said, opening the door.

She stepped in as I closed the door. I turned to her and noticed she was nervous, rubbing her hands together.

"Chad is a nice guy," I said.

"Yeah, I like him a lot," Rosa said. "Listen Jay, I know we've had our problems, but I'm growing out of being so childish. I treated you like dirt—"

"And I deserved it," I said.

"But I understand it more clearly now with everything that has happened between us," she continued. "I don't know how you feel, but I would like us to be friends again."

"Sure, that would be okay," I replied.

"Well, okay then, I guess I'll talk to you later, have to finish doing my homework," she said, going out the door.

I didn't know what to think about Rosa being my friend again. It seemed weird hanging out with your old girlfriend, especially with a new boyfriend in the picture. I wondered what Kaylee would think. I could easily talk to her about anything, but it felt strange talking to her about Rosa. It didn't seem to bother her much when I told her Rosa invited me to Waldo's funeral, so perhaps I made too much of the issue.

Not long after, Rosa mentioned to me that Chad accepted the fact that I was her friend. The following week at my locker, he approached me about the issue. "Yo, Jay, what's up?" he greeted. "Say, the other day when you came over to Rosa's place—you know, for Waldo, you probably felt awkward with her and all."

"Nah, not too much, just surprised," I said.

"I just wanted to tell you that it's cool with me that you and Rosa are friends," Chad said, not batting an eye. "You can hang out with us anytime."

The four of us even double dated a few times and over the next two months, we all became good friends.

Chad and I had a few things in common like fishing, camping, and sports of course. He was a decent fellow, as I mentioned before.

Two weeks later, Kaylee and I went out with Chad and Rosa. We met them at the Miniature Golf Excite Land. Kaylee and I wondered about Chad's religious background and where Rosa was in her spiritual journey. During all this, I knew the Lord had some reason for Rosa coming back into my life. Hanging around Chad gave us an opportunity to witness and/or help out in some way. I knew the two of them were not close to the Lord. So maybe I was to lead them in the right direction. Kaylee and I prayed daily for the two of them.

Toward the end of the afternoon, there was the opportunity for spiritual discussion. We had just exited the park and were talking by our cars, when Rosa asked how the Deer Park Baptist Church Youth Group was doing.

"They are doing well. We have some new members that have joined recently." I answered. "Rory—along with Caleb, who is becoming an outstanding leader—we're fortunate to have them both."

"My folks took me and my brother to your church when we were little," Chad said. "We were bounced around from different churches in Spokane and Deer Park. Now we go to the Methodist Church in Deer Park. I believe in God, but don't read as much of the Bible as you probably do, Jay."

Chapter Twenty-Eight

May 2007

THE FIRST Saturday was the Deer Park High School's junior/senior prom. I didn't know if I even wanted to attend. Just wasn't a big deal to me. A certain female persuasion, you guessed it, changed my mind. It only happened once I guess.

So, it was planned for me to meet Kaylee, Billie, and Amber at the Knight's home. Mr. Knight wanted me to be there thirty minutes early so he could take our pictures. Then he was to drive us to the prom.

I rented a tuxedo earlier to beat the rush because last time I had to settle with pants that were too short. I mastered the bow tie, so Mom didn't have to help me. Picking up my camera, I headed downstairs.

"There's my handsome son," Mom announced. "You must be excited. Let me get your picture."

"Well, I guess I'm ready," I said after the picture was taken.

"Enjoy yourself," Mom stated.

"I will Mom," I said, starting toward the door. Mom hollered to stop me.

"Jay, you forgot your corsage!" Mom reminded.

"Thanks Mom," I said, taking the corsage out of the refrigerator. "Now, I'm ready."

A few minutes later, I walked up to the Knight's front door and Mrs. Knight greeted me with a warm smile. She led me into the front room where Billie and Amber were getting their pictures taken. Mr. Knight had created a backdrop behind them. I watched them finish up, anxiously awaiting the appearance of Kaylee. Soon Kaylee entered the room looking absolutely—

"Kaylee, you look stunning—angelic," I said, "my earth angel."

Kaylee wore a full-length light pink, floral gown. It had a bone bodice with beaded flower shoulder straps resembling the leis you wear around your neck in Hawaii. A complimentary shawl accompanied the gown, completing her striking silhouette. Her natural curly, blonde hair streamed down her back. It was adorned with a single rhinestone hairpiece and baby's breath. Just a dusting of make-up to bring out her features was worn.

"Thank you Jay," Kaylee said, letting go and giggling. "Jay, you look great too."

"Here, let me put on your corsage," I said, tying it to her right wrist.

Our high school usually rented the Masonic Temple in Spokane on the South Hill for the proms. So that's where Mr. Knight dropped us off about an hour later. Some students rented limos as groups and others drove themselves or were chaperoned. I didn't mind Mr. Knight being ours.

As we entered the lobby, there were couples getting their pictures taken by a professional photographer. Other couples waited in a short line.

"I can't believe I'm going to the junior prom," Kaylee said, her arm wrapped in mine.

"Does this mean I have to go to yours?" I asked.

"Only if you want to still be my boyfriend," Kaylee teased.

"Whatever my girl wants," I said, squeezing her hand.

We strolled into the main hall to country music booming from the stage. A disc jockey was busy preparing music. There weren't many people dancing, just a lot of socializing. Well, I don't really dance to rap and some of the other fast music, but there was something for everybody.

The theme at this year's junior/senior prom was "Snowflakes in Spring." The junior class was designated to decorate and prepare the temple every year. So, the juniors had cut up hundreds of paper snowflakes a week before. Snowflakes, along with blue and yellow streamers, hung from the walls and the ceiling.

We ran into De'von and Zoey and a few others. Rosa and Chad had not arrived yet. Kaylee went off with Zoey and some of the other girls. I hung out with Billie and De'von while taking pictures.

When a slow song began playing, I went looking for Kaylee. I saw her across the dance floor mingling with friends. I decided to surprise her, so I snuck up behind her with romantic words on my lips.

"How about I dance with the only earth angel here?" I asked.

"Maybe," Kaylee said.

"Please?" I begged. "Pretty please?"

"As long as you say please, I think it could be arranged—how about later," she said, walking off, but came back toward me. "Any later then I'd miss my chance. Of course, I would love to dance with you, Jay."

"Kaylee, you will never miss my dance," I said.

"Oh, Jay, you're too much—you always make me feel special," she said, resting her head on my shoulder.

We danced for another fifteen minutes, followed by some refreshments. As we hung out with our friends, it dawned on me that something was missing or one certain couple was not in attendance.

"I wonder where Rosa and Chad are," I said.

"I don't know," Billie said. "They never miss any school dances."

"I know they're coming because I helped Rosa pick out her dress," Zoey pointed out.

It wasn't long before we saw them coming through the doors. All eyes were on them like a spotlight. We knew something was wrong as soon as they entered. First, Rosa came in with crossed arms and smeared mascara. Then, Chad made his appearance just seconds later.

"Rosa, I said I was sorry," we heard Chad say, with slurred words. They walked toward us.

"It's over Chad," Rosa said, getting something to drink and you knew where it would end up.

"You don't mean that," Chad said. "I'm very, very sorry, can we talk about it?"

"I don't know if I'll ever talk to you again," Rosa said.

"Please baby, I'll make it up to you, just give me a chance," Chad said, hugging her arm.

"Just get away from me," Rosa said, jerking out of Chad's grasp, running back toward the rear entrance.

At first, I wanted to run after and rescue her, but I held myself back. I did not want to give the wrong impressions, especially with her boyfriend and my girlfriend, Kaylee standing right there. Yes, Rosa was my friend and I had every intention of comforting her as a friend. Chad was also one of my good friends and he needed my help too, so I decided to check up on him first, since he was on the way. Turning and walking into that direction, Chad slipped to the floor. He began struggling to his feet, so I gave him a hand.

"I got to get to her," Chad demanded, tugging my hand.

"Jay, I have it from here," Billie said from behind.

"Are you sure?"

"Yep, we can handle him," Billie replied, as one of Chad's teammates joined.

Slowly, I strolled back to where Rosa and the girls were. Behind me, Billie and another friend of Chad's held Chad back.

I walked through the rear entrance to a hall that connected to the stage. The girls stood against the wall and listened while Rosa explained what happened. Approaching them carefully, I too just listened.

"Why couldn't he have waited until after the prom to party with his buddies?" Rosa wondered. "He knew how important this evening was to me. I just hoped things would go smoothly—But *oh no*! He just couldn't leave the drinking alone for this one night, our prom night." She began to cry.

"Here you go," Kaylee offered, handing her a tissue.

"Yeah, I would be upset also," Zoey said.

"I'm sorry for all this everyone," Rosa said.

"It's not your fault," Zoey said.

"I know, but still," Rosa said.

"Don't worry about us," Kaylee said, "the prom could wait."

"I will be fine," Rosa said. "Why don't you two go without me?"

"No, why don't you come out with us and make the best of it," Zoey suggested.

"Yeah, don't let it ruin your whole night," Kaylee said. "It's pretty much out of your control."

"Maybe you guys are right," Rosa said, sniffling. "No, you're right, I should still have fun. I didn't buy this dress for nothing."

"So, we'll meet you out there?" Zoey questioned.

"I'll be there," Rosa said. "Give me a few minutes and then I'll join you all."

"Okay, are you sure?" Kaylee asked.

"I'm sure, go ahead and have a good time. I will be with you shortly," Rosa answered.

We went back out to join our friends on the dance floor, but Chad and Billie were not there. Billie was probably cooling off Chad. Amber said they were in the lobby. I saw Billie enter from there, so I approached him.

"Chad feels bad about the way this evening started with Rosa," Billie began, straightening his bow tie. "He's ticked with himself and is outside right now cooling his jets, thinking about it."

"I don't think Rosa wants to see Chad right now," I said. "Is he coming back in here?"

"I believe so," Billie replied.

I saw Kaylee and the others across the room mingling. "Thanks Billie," I said. "There still is some prom left, so let's not worry about Chad and Rosa right now."

"Sounds good to me," Billie said.

"Shall we dance?" I asked Kaylee, offering her my hand.

"I would be happy to," she replied, taking my hand.

Billie and Amber joined us for the next song on the dance floor. Rosa came out of the ladies' room, deciding to really have a good time. Sometime toward the end of the hour, Chad lingered in and just watched, leaning against the wall.

When it was over, I had a fun time. I found out it was not about whom you were with, but how to enjoy yourself with your closest friends.

While the girls were busy refreshing themselves in the ladies' room, I was just standing there minding my own thoughts, when Chad came up to me and spoke.

"You must think I'm a big jerk," Chad said.

"No, Chad, I just think you messed up," I replied.

"I know, I sure did," Chad said somberly.

"Chad, don't beat yourself up, we all make mistakes," I pointed out. "Been there and done that with Rosa."

"That you have," Chad said and we laughed. He became serious again. "Oh Jay, what can I do to make it up to her?"

"Well, for now, I think you should give her some space," I suggested.

"For how long?" Chad asked.

"As long as it takes," I said. "It's not the end of the world, these things take time."

He thought about it for a few moments then said, "You're right Jay, I don't want to put pressure on her. Thanks for setting me straight. I hope this has not affected our friendship."

"Not at all," I replied, patting him on the shoulder. "Friends are there for each other regardless."

"Boy am I glad to hear that! I did not need to lose two friends tonight."

"Trust God that He knows what is best and praying helps."

"I will do that," Chad said, locking eyes with Rosa for a moment as she stood a few feet away. "Hey, Jay, I know you will be talking to her soon. Will you tell her something for me? Let her know that I love her and have her best interest in mind."

"Will do."

Billie decided to drive Chad home. Rosa went with us in Mr. Knight's van. He dropped Rosa and me off in front of her house. We hadn't talked much during the prom and I felt like I should say something, but I didn't want to interfere too much.

"If you need someone to talk to, just give me a ring—or Kaylee," I said.

"Thanks, I will," Rosa said. "I saw you and Chad talking, how is he?"

"Okay, I guess, he feels sorry for the way he acted and how he hurt you," I answered. "You guys are my friends and I hate to see you both hurting like this. I'm saying you should consider forgiving him. He just wasn't thinking due to the alcohol. I told Chad to give you some space, he understands."

"Thank you for letting me know that he's okay and I will think about what you said," Rosa replied, turning toward her house.

"Rosa, one more thing," I said. "Chad wanted me to tell you he cares for you, loves you with all his heart, and would never do anything to harm you intentionally."

"Tell him, I wish I could say the same thing, but I can't right now," she said, then going inside her house.

Chad called me the next day with guilt in his voice. "I still feel real bad about the way things went at the prom and beforehand," he said. "On the way home Billie said some things that made me think some more. He's right. I'm letting down a lot of my friends and teammates. I was supposed to be the leader. Instead, my selfishness and self-centeredness got me in a lot of trouble. After thinking about all this and the way I hurt Rosa, it scared me and made me realize that I needed some help. I decided to get some counseling because I realized I do have a problem."

A week or two later, Rosa had still not forgiven Chad for what happened at the prom. I hung out with both of them separately. At first I was their mediator. Sometime after, I told them I wasn't going to relay anymore messages and that they should be talking to each other instead.

I remembered Chad and Rosa being together. They were a young couple in love and I had a feeling their relationship wasn't solely on looks. Kaylee and I prayed for them faithfully. We felt that, God willing, they would be back together again someday.

What a funny thing time did for people. One day, they were happy and everything was satisfying. Then the next day, there was crying, yelling, and hurt feelings. Through a space of time, but not all the time, they were back to being happy.

As for Chad and Rosa, the hand of God would finally decide their destinies. One day, while Kaylee and I were at my locker, Rosa came up to us all bubbly and full of spirit.

"You're looking chipper these days," I commented.

"Yeah," Kaylee said, touching Rosa's arm. "Where's Rosa? Is this the same person we saw yesterday?"

"I don't know Kaylee, she seems a fraud to me," I replied.

"It's me you guys!" Rosa gleamed. "I just happen to have found the Lord again!"

"Wow! This is good news," Kaylee said.

"Sure is Rosa, when did this happen?" I asked.

"Just last night," Rosa replied. "I realized I needed God's help in my life. I seemed to be making poor decisions lately for myself. I got down on my disobedient knees and asked for His forgiveness. I felt a change in me and decided to make God first in my life now. I'm going to, with God's help, rid myself of all distractions keeping me away from what He wants for me. I have decided to stop dating for now—"

"So, you and Chad are finished?" Kaylee asked.

"Well, I don't know the answer to that right now, that's up to the Lord," Rosa replied. "I told Chad that I need more time and thought we should take another step back. He is in agreement. We're on friendly terms though."

"That's good to hear," Kaylee said and I nodded.

"I wanted to concentrate more on the rest of my junior and senior years," Rosa explained further, "so I could get into a good college.

Therefore, I must buckle down on my studies more seriously and get better grades. That's what we are here for, isn't it?"

"Yes, that is right," I agreed.

"Yep, education is very important for the future," Kaylee said. "Minimum wage doesn't offer security."

"Right on! I don't know what I want to do yet when I graduate so I'm preparing myself for my future," Rosa said. "You know what? I've missed you two—our friendship, going to church, and being involved with the youth group. These were most important to me. I want that part of us again."

"Really! That is awesome Rosa," Kaylee said, hugging her with joy. "We have missed you too. We're excited having you back."

"Praise God," I said, touching her hand lightly.

"Our prayers were answered," Kaylee praised.

"That is the other thing," Rosa began. "Thanks for praying for me, I needed a lot of that! You two are the truest friends a person could ever have and I love the both of you dearly—my sister and brother in Christ."

Since then, Kaylee, Rosa, and me became the best of friends again.

"Glad to have you back," Mom greeted, hugging Rosa at her first church service in a long time.

Rosa's face was bright with joy. It was great having her singing from the hymnal book again. Her voice, I noticed, had changed for the better. It was more mature than I remembered. After Diana sang the "Special Music" and before Pastor David preached the sermon, Rosa walked to the front.

"I remember a few years ago when a girl my age came up here to speak," Rosa began. "Like her, I want to tell you that I have found the Lord again. I had been away from the Lord Jesus for too long, doing my own thing. Teenage life is too short to throw yourself away. Any wrong choice can have bad consequences for the rest of one's life. I'm not proud of the way I acted and the many liberal fashion statements I chose in my rebellion. I can't blame anyone but myself—but that's the past and I asked for God's forgiveness...He gave me a gift for singing—and I haven't been using it for His benefit, so from now on I want to use it for His glory."

Chapter Twenty-Nine

Summer 2007

WE DIDN'T see much of Chad, only in class and passing him in the halls. My junior year ended smoothly without anything significant to note. I turned seventeen as summer break began for us. At least once a week I hung out with Rosa and Kaylee, as teenage life was pretty busy. Summer jobs kept us occupied for the most part. Kaylee worked at the Espresso Shack in the mornings and in the afternoons continued her classes in the accelerated program. Rosa worked at the Pizza Parlor. I still worked at the karate school two nights a week and at the gas station in Deer Park as a cashier.

Early one morning at the gas station, I had a surprise visitor. I was at the register finishing up with a man customer, when I saw Chad next in line, but he didn't recognize me right away. The man handed me two bills for his gas and coffee.

"Here is your change, sir," I said to the man, handing him a few coins. "Thanks, come back again."

"Hope you have a good day," the man said.

The next customer placed a container of worms onto the counter.

"I heard if you fry them for a few seconds with a little garlic, they're mighty tasty," I said to Chad.

"Well, if I'm really hungry, I might try that," Chad said, laughing. "Yo, Jay, my gas man! Didn't see you back there. How is it?"

"Doing well," I replied. "How are things with you? I haven't seen you in a while."

"Not too bad," Chad answered. "I'm working for the forestry."

"Will that be all?" I asked.

"Let's see," he said, browsing through the snacks.

"Where are you fishing?"

"Dad is taking me and my brother over there to Long Lake," Chad answered. "Hey, Jay, remember we were talking about doing some fishing together."

"Sure, sounds like fun," I replied. "Let's go up to Rich's cabin like we talked about."

"I'll have these corn nuts," Chad said, as a few more people were getting in line. "Sounds like a blast."

Chad and I got together on our days off. He picked me up at my house one day in his truck and we headed out to Rich's property on Deer Lake. After we unpacked and prepared the cabin for the evening, we clambered into Rich's already docked aluminum boat. We tried some day fishing as we ate our lunch. Exchanging fishing and camping stories, we enjoyed the quiet and the company for a few hours. Not once was Rosa mentioned. At times Chad was talkative about his truck and football, the next he was reserved taking in the scenery. A light breeze skimmed the water and dragonflies sputtered on by. When the summer sun began beating down on us uncomfortably, we decided to go back to the dock for some swimming. Following that, we headed back on the lake to fish again.

"We're just not getting any bites," Chad commented, reeling in somebody's sock. "I'm bored—hey, let's swim over there to the platform, looks like they have a diving board."

"You mean from here? Isn't it too far?" I asked, as Chad began to take his shirt off.

"Where is your sense of adventure? It's not too far," Chad debated.

"I don't know," I said, measuring the distance in my mind. I could always float on my back if I get tired. "Okay, okay, I'm game."

"See, I told you it wasn't too far," Chad said, looking down on me from the platform while I pulled myself up the ladder.

"But I give you the gold medal."

"We should do this more often—you really know how to kick it."

"Cool, let's jump off the high dive," I said, racing to the ladder.

We stayed there for a little bit diving and then went back to the boat because we were hungry. Evening came upon us and we were back fishing.

A couple of hours later, we headed back to the cabin. As we strolled up the dock, Chad said he had some good news.

"Remember I told you I was seeking counseling? Well, I have been going to Alateen these past two months," Chad said.

"That's wonderful news," I said.

"I've been sober for those two months and I'm learning how to redirect my life without the abuse. I'm feeling much better about myself."

"Rosa will be happy for you too."

"Please keep this between us. I don't want Rosa to know yet because this is just the beginning of my changing. I have a ways to go," Chad said.

"Will do," I said.

"When she's ready, she'll get a hold of me. That will give me the opportunity to tell her the good news," Chad said.

"My lips are sealed," I said, as we walked off the dock.

"Thanks, Jay, I knew you wouldn't," Chad said.

"I pray that you keep up the good work."

"That's another thing," Chad explained. "In Alateen, one of the twelve-steps helps us to depend on God and not the substance. I realized I can't do it without Him."

"That's right!" I praised. "We cannot do anything without God in our lives as He has a plan for each of us. I'm so glad to hear of these positive changes coming from you."

"Well, I am not totally convinced of this right now," Chad said. "It is a trust issue and I don't trust a lot of anything these days. I'm open-minded though; maybe you can share some of your faith with me, but go slow."

"Sure, I would be glad to," I said, offering Chad a glass of pop. Together we had a simple Bible study.

Now another really confusing time came into my life. I don't know how it happened because no particular incident triggered my feelings. It crept upon me very gradually, catching me by surprise. I thought I was falling in love with Rosa all over again. Perhaps I imagined it. During the summer, I really got to know Rosa better. It was her faith, her outreach to people, and the peacefulness from within, that showed me her great qualities. What about Kaylee? I already had all this with her. Well, that's the thing. I'm in love with her too! There was a decision I had to make. I asked the Lord to guide me in this matter and then I prayed. It would be foolish of me to break up with Kaylee because of my newly discovered feelings for my old girlfriend, Rosa. Maybe God was redirecting me back to her and I couldn't ignore His will. Like with anything, time played a factor in our lives. I left everything up to God and sat back awaiting His outcome. In a perfect world we tended to let our guards down and revert back to the secular views. I sometimes daydreamed about Rosa merely because of her beauty, wanting to touch her hair. Now this was not wrong in our Lord's eyes, but if I continued, my thoughts would get the best of me.

Fall 2007

Going into my senior year, I continued taking courses at the community college in Spokane, and then upon graduation, I would be ahead of the game. I became senior editor of *The Stag* school newspaper. It was my new passion, in which I found journalism very intriguing. I felt I could make a career out of written and/or photo journalism.

Journalism and the Gospel of the New Testament were similar in the way news was spread. As Christians, we shared Jesus and His truth with people. So, a journalist would want to report the truth. Well, a good reporter with integrity anyway.

June 2008

A hot, cloudless, afternoon was the setting for our graduation. I had just turned eighteen. One-hundred-thirty-two students from my senior class were on hand to receive their diplomas. The ceremony took place at the football field. I met my friends there and we discussed our futures.

"De'von, I didn't know you signed up for the Navy," Rosa commented.

"Yeah the bum," Zoey said, giving him a playful shove. "I'll miss him."

"Let's see who is staying in the area," I said. "Billie is getting a football scholarship to Cheney and Amber will be going with him–"

"I heard my name, are you talking about me?" Amber asked.

"Only good things sweetheart," Billie said, hugging her with a kiss on the cheek. He whispered something in her ear. They went back and forth throughout the conversation.

"Do you know what you want to do Amber, I mean with classes?" Rosa asked.

"Oh, I don't know yet, finish taking my prerequisites, then I'll see," Amber replied.

"So they're staying," I said. "Don't know when I'll start or which Spokane community college I want to attend yet, but I think I'm going to take some time off."

"You take a rest Jay, doesn't sound like you," Billie teased.

"Well, I want to clear my mind and get closer to God, maybe do some exploring," I said.

"Like go on a mission?" De'von asked.

"Sounds like a road trip, eh?"

"Perhaps if the Lord wills it," I said.

"I feel the Lord has willed me to go to Kirkland Christian College near Seattle," Rosa said.

Maybe, with Rosa leaving for Seattle and me staying was God's way of telling me Rosa wasn't the woman I would end up with. Or with her away that would give me time to get in touch with my inner feelings. I wanted to go camping by myself without any distractions.

"I don't know what I want to do," Zoey said. "Something to do with horses."

"Do you want me to tell them now?" Billie blurted to Amber.

"What are you two blabbing about?" someone asked.

"We want to tell you guys we're planning on getting married after graduation," Billie announced.

We all shouted out congratulations!

"No way!" De'von spoke up.

"Are you sure about this?" I asked. "You have my blessing."

"Thank you, Jay, guys," Billie and Amber said.

"Hey everyone!" Chad announced. "There are two things I have decided. First, over the spring, I made the decision to accept Jesus and let Him run my life. Second, I chose to go to one of the universities in California."

We all hugged him.

"I think it looks like they're starting to line us up," I said.

So there we were, all lined up alphabetically two-by-two, sweating in our blue caps and gowns awaiting the familiar march music to begin. I stood with another gal, Cameryn Acres, in the front row. Cameryn was our Class President and Valedictorian.

Finally, the brass section began and we started down the aisle. I saw Kaylee in front of the band with her flute shining. She smiled at me after we were all seated and the music finished. I loved Kaylee and didn't know why Rosa was even a consideration. Whatever decision, it was still left in the Lord's hands. Kaylee was my girlfriend and I decided to really concentrate on her.

Cameryn presented a wonderful and thoughtful valedictorian speech. Then the scholarships were handed out. Finally, each one of us was called up to receive our diploma and one silk white rose.

"I proudly give you Deer Park High School's Class of 2008!" the principal announced.

Graduation hats went flying into the air. I guess you could say our lives were pretty much up in the air—the sky's now the limit. Cheers and much applause came from the grandstands. Kaylee came running and I opened my arms to receive her.

"Congratulations Jay!" she said with tears of joy.

"Thank you Kaylee," I said, handing her the rose. "For you—'for meaning.'"

"'For meaning' always," Kaylee returned.

"Oh, Kaylee my Dollheart, I so love you dearly," I said.

Most of us went over to De'von's parent's ranch for a celebration potluck. It was almost or pretty close to the last time many of us would be together. We made the very best of it, enjoying each other's company.

After this, Rosa was far from my mind. She was my past and Kaylee was my present and maybe, Lord willing, my future. I gave Kaylee my total attention and devotion. I sure spoiled her with my all. She enjoyed it when I visited her at work unexpectedly with surprises of flowers or a simple balloon saying "I Love You."

Kaylee was the first mortal person on my mind when I woke up and the last one on my mind before I fell asleep that night. Well, God came first, then family, then my job, my friends, and finally me.

"Kaylee, De'von, and I will be going on a trip here soon," I told her one July afternoon. "Something I intended to do for myself."

"Oh! Where are you guys going?" Kaylee asked with uncertainly.

"We decided to go camping and fishing in central Idaho. De'von also wants to go horseback riding," I replied. "Rich is going with us kinda. Since it is our first trip, he'll be right behind us by fifteen minutes."

"I understand you need to take this time. I will miss you every day you are gone," she said, squeezing my hand.

"I will miss you too, Dollheart," I said, kissing her hand. "I should not be gone more than two weeks. I'll call you every night."

"After the year you had, you do deserve a break," she said. "Absence is a good thing for the both of us."

"Come and you may help me pack," I said, leading her into my house.

A couple days later, De'von picked me up in his off-road truck and we set out on a trip of reflection. For a moment or two we sat in the middle of the street idling to discuss whether or not we forgot anything, which there wasn't. Then, he put it in gear and we drove through downtown Deer Park.

Soon we were on the highway heading north. Fifteen minutes later, we passed Loon Lake on my left. We came to Colville an hour later, taking a junction, which headed east to the small town of Tiger about forty miles away, near the Washington/Idaho border.

It was nearing lunchtime when we arrived in Sandpoint, Idaho. We stopped at a quaint park to eat one of the sandwiches Kaylee had made us. Someone was walking a miniature dachshund when we stepped out of the car. We found a place in the grass and enjoyed our lunch. I wrote in my journal.

Back on the road again, we headed south to Coeur d'Alene. When we stopped at the first gas station, I called Mom with my calling card and then Kaylee, who answered somberly until she heard my voice.

"Hi Dollheart," I said with joy.

"Jay! So happy you called," Kaylee said with excitement. "I miss you. Where are you calling from?"

I told her. "Thank you so much for the food you packed us. I ate one of your sandwiches earlier and it was most wonderful," I said.

"So glad you liked it," she said. "Where are you going next?"

"We're heading south. We're looking for a place to camp for the night," I answered.

A few hours later, we found a place to pitch our tent. The next day, we drove another three hours nearing the Sawtooth National Forest. Rich had recommended the Pioneer Trail, which began on a dirt road in Ketchum, Idaho. We found it easily, quickly discovering it was a twenty-mile trek down a bumpy dirt road. To be out in the woods exploring Kane Lake and appreciating God's beautiful creation was very refreshing to the both of us. Sometimes we were off by ourselves and other times we enjoyed the male bonding.

We got back way too soon because we were invited to Rosa's cousin, Miranda's wedding. Mom said I went to a couple of weddings when I was younger, but I didn't remember them. They were not very exciting for me especially since I did not know the couples. I kinda looked forward to Billie and Amber's wedding though. Rory and Diana's union at our church gave me a whole new perspective on the ceremony. At least Rosa would be there and I could talk with her. So I piled in the van with Mom and Gramma on an August afternoon heading to a church in Spokane.

The organ was playing as we entered the church lobby. Manny came over and greeted us. He told us Rosa and her mom were with Miranda and the other moms. Strangers came over and introduced themselves and of course, I would only remember a few names.

It seemed like it took forever before the wedding got started. A man in a tenor voice went up to the front and belted out a couple of ballads. I almost fell asleep, slumping in the pew. A freight train could've rolled down the aisle and I wouldn't even have known. His first song was lively. Now the second was lovely, but soon became slow and boring after a while.

I woke up suddenly. Mom was lightly shoving my shoulder and that's when I realized the singing voice had changed. There stood Rosa singing in all her glory. Right then, she rushed into my heart again. Maybe I imagined it, but she sang the song directly to me. Shaking my head, I thought maybe it was a delusional moment. I decided to take my mind off Rosa and shift my thoughts toward Kaylee.

I sighed when Rosa finished and the ceremony continued with a prelude from the organ. Heads turned as flower girls, looking like miniature brides, came down the aisle spreading rose petals. Then the bridesmaids and groom's ushers strutted up to the front. Well, the rest speaks for itself. Miranda, the bride, looked very nice and so did the groom. They sure seemed to be a good match.

It was an interesting experience going to a wedding and later the reception.

Soon we were throwing birdseed at the newly married couple as they ran to the limo. Mom told me of an old wives' tale where the guests stopped throwing rice because they thought when the birds ate the rice they would explode. Not true. Who would have thought?

We drove over to where the reception was held. To my surprise, it was the same place Rosa had her Quinceañera. Anyway, I was starving by the time we entered the hall and I went right to the buffet table without another thought. I always took advantage of free food! With a full plate, I strolled around stuffing my face. It was hard to avoid Rosa, not that I was, but right away she saw me.

"What are those things?" Rosa asked, pointing to something on my plate.

"I don't know, but they're darn good!" I replied, taking another bite.

"How long are you guys staying?" she asked.

"Depends," I answered. "Mom is pretty talkative and once she gets started you know…"

"I know how that is," Rosa said with a chuckle. "Kinda like me."

"Yep, you sure have been known to talk my ear off," I said.

Rosa led me off to greet Miranda where I introduced myself to the groom. I congratulated them as it was about time to watch the bride dance with her pa. A song played that said something about daddy's little girl.

Following that, some of the guests got on the dance floor. I sat with Rosa, Dora, and her date. We visited halfway through the first dance number, when Dora and her date went off dancing. I thought, *please don't go!* I will be stuck here with Rosa and my feelings for her. Maybe it was time for me to get some things off my chest. At least get a feel for whether or not she felt the same way. How would I do that? My mind was spinning and no ideas came to the front.

"So?" I began, turning toward her while trying not to indicate my discomfort or whatever it was.

"Yep, so," Rosa said with a hint of uneasiness.

"I guess soon you will be going over to Seattle," I brought forth, hoping conversation would help.

"Yep, a week from Tuesday and then I pack up and leave," she answered somberly. "Of course, I will miss you—everybody."

"You sure will be missed," I said, as something came over me. "Hey, how about a dance? I feel like a bump-on-a-log."

"Oh, I don't know," Rosa replied.

"Come on Rosa, one last dance before you go—between two good ol' friends," I began to beg, and then suddenly I pulled her to the dance floor, not waiting for an answer.

"This sure brings back good memories," Rosa commented, as we waltzed swiftly.

"Sure does," I answered. "Seems like ages ago."

"Actually, I was hoping you would ask me to dance," Rosa said with honesty in her eyes.

"I'm very glad I did," I said.

Before we knew it, we were slow dancing to the next song. With Rosa in my arms I was content. No words were exchanged and I didn't have to ask if she still had feelings for me. It was when she rested her head on my shoulder and held me tighter that I knew it was mutual. Naturally, I returned the gesture, holding her close to me.

Suddenly, the music halted as we heard cling, cling, cling. Rosa jerked from my grasp ending a nice moment. She looked up at me confused.

"Sorry Jay..." Rosa started, and then ran off.

The father of the bride was then making a toast, but I was lost in my thoughts and didn't know what was said.

What happened moments ago with Rosa showed me that there were still feelings between us. After all those talks I had with myself, I realized I was still in love with Rosa. Now what?

Too many people were in my way and I couldn't see where she went. I walked over to Mom's table when the crowd cleared.

"Son, do you want to talk about it?" Mom asked.

"I don't know what I want to do, just all mixed up," I answered. "I'm going out to get some fresh air if anyone is looking for me."

Outside, I ran my fingers through my hair in frustration. *Why do things have to be so complicated? God please help me figure this out.* Even though Rosa was going to college in Seattle, I'd still have these feelings for her. What am I to do? *Please God, help me!*

"Hey," came a little voice behind me. "Your mom said you were out here."

"I think there is something we need to discuss," I said, not wanting to, but I knew we should.

"I understand you have a girlfriend and I don't want to mess it up. You were just being nice comforting me," Rosa said.

"I wasn't just being nice, Rosa," I said, facing her, taking her hand. I could tell that she had been crying. "I can't deny it anymore; I'm still in love with you."

"What about Kaylee?"

"I-I, really don't know," I answered. "We have dated, but I haven't ever gotten over you."

"Oh, Jay, I haven't either," she said with streams of tears. "I forgave you a long time ago—I feel the same way Jay, I love you."

I took her in my arms and looked deeply into her brown eyes. "All I know is I want you back!"

And we kissed.

"Jay, Jay—Hey anybody home?" Rosa asked.

Just then I realized I had been daydreaming, but we were dancing. NONE of it happened! Rosa NEVER rested her head on my shoulder, no mutual feelings and no scene outside. I made it up.

"Hmmm?" I asked, shaking my head from the daydream. "Sorry, what did you say?"

"The toast is over silly. What do you want to do, dance or go back to the table?"

Indeed the toast had finished and the music resumed.

"Sure, how about one more dance?" I asked, hoping my daydream would come true.

One thing was true I had feeling of love resurfacing for Rosa Sanchez.

I thought it was time for me to tell her my true feelings or I would end up going crazy. Playing it cool as the evening continued, I just waited for the right opportunity to tell her. Nothing came about and I procrastinated the rest of the night. I believe the Holy Spirit held me back like it was not the appropriate time or place. Patience was what was needed and I had to trust the Lord in this matter.

Chapter Thirty

August 2008

ROSA PACKED her car on the eve before departing for Kirkland, Washington. Up to this point, as one would figure, I was twisted in knots of confusion. The whole week, I fought with myself like a rubber band. On one end, I wanted to express my love toward Rosa, and the other with my mind solely on Kaylee.

Rosa planned a party that evening to say good-bye to everyone. Ella wasn't going to be there because she was attending a Christian Women's Conference in Seattle. Manny would drive Rosa to college and Ella would drive him back home.

Going over to the party, I didn't know what my feelings would be for Rosa; I just went on with the flow. Kaylee was there and I felt guilty even thinking those thoughts of Rosa. I should have left when Kaylee and most of the other folks did, but I wore out my welcome.

It just so happened Rosa and I were alone talking on her back porch. We reminisced over the eight years briefly, but our little romance and breakup was avoided.

"Did I ever tell you about when you guys first moved here I thought you were a boy?" I asked.

"Really!" Rosa said.

"True story," I said.

"Easy mistake wearing a baseball cap," she said.

"Then you turned thirteen," I commented purposely.

Rosa raised an eyebrow and started to smile, turning away. "Yep, where has the time gone?"

"We sure have changed since we..." I began, but Manny came out for some fresh air.

"Jay, are you still here?" Manny asked.

"Yeah, and I suppose I should let you guys get some rest," I said, getting up from the lawn chair.

"Yep, long day tomorrow," Rosa said with a yawn. "I guess this is good-bye, Jay."

"No, not yet," I said. "I'll see you guys off tomorrow morning."

Here I was at six in the morning on the last Tuesday in August, up by the crack of dawn, trying to decide what to say to Rosa. "You know Rosa," I began, standing on the passenger's side, "this isn't good-bye, just see you later."

"Yeah, see you later, Jay," Rosa said while we hugged for a moment. "Of course, we'll stay in touch and all that."

"Most definitely," I replied. "I may even stop in for a visit."

"I would look forward to it," she said.

"You two have a safe journey," I began, really wanting to tell her my true feelings, but Manny stepped behind the wheel.

"Thanks Jay," she said.

"I'll pray for you over there," I said.

"Same here—well, here instead of there," Rosa joked and we laughed.

Perhaps it was good-bye as I watched her and Manny drive away.

I went back home doubting myself that I should have told her. Proverb 29:11 came to mind and it all made sense not to contemplate matters: "A fool uttereth all his mind; but a wise man keepeth it in until afterwards."

Rich mentioned you would always remember your first love. So true was that. In many different ways, I knew I would be satisfied with either Rosa or Kaylee. I hid in my room for an hour or so in a funk, when Mom knocked on my door. At first I told her to go away, but my ears perked up when I heard the words "phone call" and "Rosa" mentioned. All I could think of was that she wanted to tell me her feelings for me. Excitedly, I rushed to open the door with my heart pounding, but I sensed something happened when I looked at my mom's face.

"Manny had an accident—" she started, as every possibility flashed through my mind that something horrible was wrong—"maybe I should just start over—silly me—Rosa's car broke down and Manny had a freak accident—broke his leg. Rich was on the phone and he wants you to ride with him to see what's wrong with Rosa's car."

"Where are they?" I asked.

"Somewhere on the South Hill is where they left Rosa's car—they took Manny to the emergency room."

One hour later, we walked into the emergency room and were directed to the back where Manny was laying. Rosa was at his side. The doctors had not gotten to him yet.

"What happened?" we asked quite concerned.

Manny laughed. "Oh, what hasn't? We were a couple of blocks from the on-ramp when the car suddenly died. I immediately pulled off on the shoulder of the road. As soon as I got out, I twisted my foot and fell hard on the road." He was out of breath for a moment and then Rosa continued.

"I tried to help him into the car," Rosa said, then turned toward Manny. "But you are just too heavy," she told him, playfully poking her dad in his shoulder.

"Yeah, he is a lug," I agreed.

"Anyway," Rosa continued, "someone driving by stopped and offered to help dad get to the hospital."

"I never had the chance to check out the car, but I suspect it's the water pump," Manny said.

"Now I don't know what we're going to do," Rosa said. "I called Mom and she said she would be here in about five hours."

"Obviously, I can't drive and somebody needs to drive her over there," Manny said.

"I can go by myself in Dad's truck," Rosa said confidently.

"No! I kept telling her, she needs someone with her," Manny said.

"I guess he's right," Rosa agreed reluctantly. "I already called my aunt and uncle, but they are busy—everyone else I called is busy too."

"I'll do it," I said without a thought, but no one heard me, so I spoke up. "I'll take Rosa! I'm really not doing anything."

"Sounds good to me," Manny agreed.

Rosa stayed at the hospital while I went home to pack a few things. By this time, Kaylee was off work and came over. I told her about Rosa's situation and she was fine with my decision.

"Well, I think that's about it," I said, looking around my room.

Kaylee followed me outside to the car and we said our good-byes.

"I won't be gone longer than two days," I said, hugging her and when I pulled back I could tell there was something on her mind.

"Been wanting to ask you Jay," Kaylee began, searching for the right words. "Oh never mind, silly of me."

"What is it, you can tell me?"

"Okay, it just seems like you have been distant to me lately."

"How do you mean? Am I acting differently?"

"Maybe it was nothing—well, let me get to the point," she said, turning away from me. "Are you falling for Rosa again? Maybe I'm imagining it."

"I-I really don't know," I said.

"Sounds like a *maybe* to me, like you're considering," she said.

"Honestly, yes, I'm having feelings for Rosa, but I love you too," I said, looking into her eyes.

"I was afraid of this," she said, as her eyes flooded with tears.

"Perhaps I'm imagining I love Rosa," I said.

"So, which is it? Are you having feelings for Rosa or are you just imagining it? If you're imagining, she's been on your mind."

"She may not even feel the same about me—so confused—"

"What if she does want you? What are you going to do?"

"I don't know," was all I could say.

"Well, until you do," Kaylee said, struggling with the ring I gave her.

"Kaylee, don't," I pleaded.

Jittery, she shoved the ring to me—"Maybe this will help you make a decision—no hurry. If it's not the way you've imagined it, I may not suddenly offer my open arms—just go run to Rosa's rescue."

Then she ran off. I wanted to run after and call out to her, but I choked air, my legs felt like rubber, not moving.

I stood there for a time frozen in my emotions. A lot of things floated in my mind. Nothing I could do about Kaylee. What was said was said and what was done was done.

Slowly, I found my way behind the wheel heading back to Spokane to pick up Rosa at the hospital. At first I was raring to go on this trip, but now it was more of a burden. I didn't feel like going inside, so I had Rosa meet me out front.

Rosa was there in the hospital loading zone with her two suitcases and a box. I parked when there was an opening and got out trying to pretend nothing was wrong.

"Your taxi is here," I greeted with the best fake smile.

"So, what's the going rate?" she returned.

"Well, for you, it will cost a lot if we are going with today's rates, but I have a special for today, just a pizza dinner on the other end."

"That's a fair deal," Rosa answered with a laugh.

"So, how is your dad?" I asked after popping the trunk.

"Stubborn as usual, trying to be a hero, don't you know?" she answered with the box in her hands.

"You can put that in the backseat," I said, placing the suitcases in the trunk. "Sounds like Manny. I can picture him walking without crutches."

"He's doing well, a couple of pins in his leg and a cast up to his thigh," she said.

"Yikes, that doesn't sound like a lot of fun," I said with a grimace face, then turned to see a large van pull up behind me. "Well, we'd better be going, somebody wants this spot." We got in and clicked the seatbelts. "Are you ready?"

"Yep, I think so," Rosa said, giving me the thumbs up. "Thanks for doing this for me, Jay. I'm sure you have better things to do."

"No problemo," I said, as we drove onto the main road. "Actually, I had no other plans."

"I bet Kaylee will miss you," she said, pausing when she saw the smile leave my face.

"We had a disagreement when I left. I think she's mad at me."

"I'm sure it won't last long."

"Do you need to stop for something to drink before we get on the highway?" I asked, eyeing the on-ramp up ahead.

"No, I'm fine," she replied with uneasiness, when I changed the subject.

We rode in silence for a while until we were out of the city limits. I decided not to worry about what happened with Kaylee, it would have to wait until I get back.

"You must be getting excited about studying over there," I said.

"I'm really looking forward to it," she answered with bright eyes. "I hear they have a pretty good choir."

"I'm sure you'll fit in quite nicely," I said, then asked, "So, are you going to have a roommate when you get there?"

"Yeah, they assigned me to an upper classman—a girl in my case, to room with and show me around," she answered.

"Sounds like a neat system," I said.

Rosa told me about the college the whole way to Ritzville which was an hour away from Spokane. We were hungry for lunch by that time, so we opted to stop at a sit-down restaurant.

"I think Kaylee may have broken up with me," I said after we ordered. I don't know why I said it right then.

"Oh no! What happened hon—Jay—you said you think, but did she actually say breakup?"

"Well, she gave me back her sweet sixteen birthday ring, I gave her," I replied.

"I'm sure she'll forgive you—every couple has their fights—look at me and Chad."

"Yeah, you're right, it will be different after we have a good night's sleep," I said and then we ate lunch.

I avoided the reason for the breakup and Rosa didn't push because I think she knew why.

Soon after, we were back on the road. I was exchanging some small talk with Rosa, when I had to concentrate on a slow moving eighteen-wheeler. Turning back to say something, I noticed Rosa had fallen asleep. There was silence and I had some time to think. Part of me wished it were over for Kaylee and me. I pondered this for a while, but I still couldn't decide. *There's no hurry*, I thought.

About two and a half hours later, I had driven through Snoqualmie Pass, which cut through the Cascades, a mountain range on the west side. It was quite a workout maneuvering the pass with its many twists and turns. Occasionally, I caught a glimpse of Rosa in slumber. She looked so cozy and precious to me. Sleeping beauty, as some would say. When I pulled over to the first rest stop, Rosa awoke.

"What time is it?" Rosa asked, stretching and yawning in her seat.

"It is almost 4:30," I answered, looking for a place to park.

"I can't believe I slept that long!"

"Yeah, nothing would have awakened you," I commented. I anxiously parked in front of the restrooms.

A few minutes later, while we enjoyed a snack at a picnic table we contemplated the map. There was a nice cool breeze, much more refreshing than my hot car with no air conditioning. By the time we reached Seattle, we would be right in the middle of rush hour, not my idea of fun! Instead, we opted to stop in Bellevue, a suburb of Seattle, for a bite to eat.

We had a great time at the pizza joint, laughing and joking. There was a little time to kill so we played air hockey. I really enjoyed hanging out with Rosa that evening. It loosened all the stress built up in me.

Rosa gave me directions to Kirkland Christian College. An hour or so later, we were back on the highway. City lights of Seattle began to fill the streets. We passed the baseball and football stadiums on our right. On the left side there was Seattle Harbor and Elliot Bay where ferries moved like giant turtles. Soon we saw a sign: "Welcome to the City of Kirkland." Nothing indicated that we entered a different city, as Seattle and Kirkland seemed to meld together.

The college was found quite easily as directions were a big help. First, we parked at the main entrance and Rosa checked in at administrations where she collected the key for her dorm room. A girl of African decent with dark, mid-length hair met us at the entrance of the dorm.

"Hi, you must be Rosa," the girl said.

"That's me," Rosa said.

"I'm Pam, your roommate," the girl introduced and they shook hands. "They said you were here."

"This is my friend, Jay," Rosa said.

"Nice to meet you, Jay," Pam said while I set down the suitcases to shake her hand.

"How far have you guys come?" she asked.

"From Deer Park," Rosa replied.

"I'm assuming that's on the other side of Washington, near Spokane?" Pam asked.

"You would be right," I answered.

"Come inside, it's starting to rain and I have no shoes," Pam said, wiggling her toes.

We followed Pam up a flight of stairs and into a quaint dormitory. There were two single beds and two desks.

"What church do you attend?" I asked, setting the suitcases down.

"I go to the chapel on campus," Pam replied.

"I saw on the college website that students and faculty are encouraged to attend services three times a week," Rosa said.

"The chapel is non-denominational," Pam said. "Jay, you're welcome to attend Wednesday night if you're around—you'll love Pastor Vern, he's a people person, very into the Lord."

"Thank you, I'll consider it," I answered. "I thought of staying around for a few days and hanging with Rosa, maybe catch a baseball game or something while I'm here, too."

"That'll be fun," Rosa said.

"Well, I guess I'll be going, saw some hotels on the way near the school," I said.

At my hotel, Wednesday, the following morning, I was very anxious to call Kaylee and try to make things better with her. I was about to dial when I realized I never made my decision. I said a prayer and asked the Holy Spirit to guide me.

After a continental breakfast, I met Rosa and Pam in front of their dorm. Pam showed us around the campus followed by lunch at the cafeteria. A tour of Kirkland with Pam as our guide was next. There were some nice parks with hiking trails.

That afternoon Pam had some important errands to run, so I finally had some time alone to spend with Rosa without a third wheel. Rosa and I went exploring in Seattle. We visited the famous Pike's Street Market and then strolled along Pioneer Square. The evening ended with a Chinese dinner before we headed to the on-campus chapel.

On the edge of the college was the On-Campus Kirkland Community Chapel. It was a large octagonal building with a bell tower strutting into the evening sky. Members of the chapel greeted us at the door. It was quite spacious inside the main hall and there was even an upper deck. I imagined it could easily hold one thousand people. We found the nearest pew and sat down, but it wasn't long until Pam spotted us.

"Hi guys, so glad you came," Pam greeted.

"Thanks for the invite," I said.

"Welcome," Pam said, standing. "I have to say hello to someone, be right back."

An oriental man in a three-piece suit approached us. "You two are new here. I'm Pastor Vern Ling," he said.

We told him who we were and then he disappeared in the crowd, greeting people along the way. Minutes later, someone else made the announcements and a couple of hymns were sung. Soon Pastor Vern stepped up to the altar and joyfully welcomed the service.

"Joining us this evening are some new guests," Pastor Vern said. "Rosa who will be attending Kirkland Christian College this year and her friend, Jay, both from the Eastern Washington area..." Then he pointed out some others in the congregation.

The congregation was made up of mostly students and faculty of the college. Anyone else could also attend. I enjoyed church with Rosa.

Pastor Vern was alive for Jesus! He presented a wonderful sermon that struck my heart. "A lot of people, including Christians, look down on the poor with ignorance," Vern began. "We're supposed to contribute to the poor and at the same time minister to them. Jesus said in Matthew 5:3: 'Blessed are the poor in spirit: for theirs is the kingdom of heaven.'"

He preached on the familiar passage "For I was an hungered, and ye gave me meat: I was thirsty, and ye gave me drink: I was a stranger, and ye took me in:" ~Matthew 25:35.

He gave some statistics on the Seattle, Kirkland, and King County homeless. There were some tent cities of homeless in the area, which he also mentioned. Right then, I decided to stay for a few more days to do some volunteer work.

An older man of African heritage came over to introduce himself to all of us following the service. "The name is Isaiah Watkins, nice to have you here Rosa and Jay," the man said.

"Pleased to meet you," Rosa said.

"Same here," I said, shaking his hand.

"My wife, Tanika," Isaiah began, pointing to a lady across the way, "is the staff accountant here at the college. I'm a taxi driver."

"Cool!" we said.

"I'll pray that you have a nice time here Rosa," Isaiah said, then to me. "Are you attending college Jay? Or going out into the work force?"

"I'll be going or taking courses online, most likely at one of the Spokane community colleges," I answered.

"You guys know what you want to major in?" Isaiah asked.

"Yes, journalism is something I'd like to take," I replied.

"Singing and music are my passions," Rosa stated.

We chatted while walking into the lobby where Pastor Vern was greeting people on the way out. He seemed knowledgeable about the homeless and such.

"Pastor Vern, that was an awesome sermon—it has inspired me," I said, shaking his hand.

"Thank you, Jay," Pastor Vern said.

"Sir, I was wondering, if you would please steer me in the right direction because I would like to volunteer with one of the tent cities," I said.

"Sure, be glad to help," Pastor Vern began. "Actually, the chapel helps out at a nearby tent city—Isaiah would be the one to contact. Where is he?"

"Right behind you," Isaiah said. "I heard you talking about volunteering. We could really use your help."

"Isaiah is pretty much an expert and can tell you anything about the homeless in our area," Vern said.

"I don't know about that, but I do know a lot," Isaiah said, "just one of my callings, which I feel strongly about."

"Well Jay, it looks like you are in good hands," Vern said to me as he patted Isaiah on the shoulder, "Isaiah is a godly man."

"Thank you, Pastor Vern," I said.

"Not a problem," Vern returned.

I then turned to Isaiah. "When do you need me? Where do I go?" I asked.

"Can you be in the chapel basement tomorrow morning at seven o'clock?" Isaiah asked.

"Sure, I'm not doing anything," I said.

"I would like to join you guys. I don't start classes until Monday," Rosa said.

"Well great! Then it's all set," Isaiah said. "I'm taking a couple student volunteers with me to help out at one of the tent cities."

Chapter Thirty-One

THURSDAY THE next day, I met Rosa, Pam, Isaiah, and a couple others in the basement kitchen. Isaiah told us that we would be taking prepared breakfasts to the tent city residents. A couple students were stirring hot cereal in crock-pots and someone poured coffee in thermoses.

"Mornin' Jay," Isaiah greeted, wearing an apron.

"Morning. What would you like me to help you with?" I asked.

"You may help Ned load the coolers into the van," Isaiah replied.

Soon we all clamored inside the chapel van with Isaiah at the wheel, always in good spirits. Along with Pam, a guy named Ned joined our group.

"Jay and Rosa, there are two tent cities in Kirkland," Isaiah explained on the way. "One is set up downtown across the street from City Hall, in a church parking lot. We're going to the other one on the East side. There are about two hundred homeless at this site, about a third are couples and families."

"There are limited shelters that cater to couples who want to stay together for the night—same with families," Ned said.

"Many women feel safer in the tent city," Pam said. "It's a tight knit community that doesn't tolerate the abusers of battered women or anybody who is harmful."

"That's what is nice about the tent cities," Isaiah said. "It's a place of refuge. Everyone participates in the well being of the camp. The organizers have a few rules—no drugs, alcohol, weapons, and violence both physical and/or verbal."

"How do the neighborhoods tolerate the tent cities? I imagine people complain," I asked, starting to feel like a journalist.

"Most of the time, the area around the tent city is not affected, but there are always those who complain," Isaiah answered. "We're always willing to solve a problem with the community. If the camp can't work it out then we just leave."

"Where would you go?" Rosa asked.

"That's the tricky part," Isaiah said. "Usually someone else will donate their land for use, but that could take weeks or months."

"So with full shelters, I guess they're back on the street," I said.

"Yep, with almost nowhere to go, and it's illegal to stay in the park, I might add," Pam said.

"The homeless used to be able to ride the bus all night, which was better than sleeping under the bridge," Ned said.

"Getting back to the camp's impact on the communities," Isaiah said. "For people who want to stay, all they have to do is follow the rules, participate with maintaining the camp, and governing it. Plus we require the residents go out into the neighborhood and clean up trash."

"How much does it cost to run a tent city?" I asked.

"Depends on the size of the camp," Isaiah replied. "With the one we are going to, it costs between four and five thousand dollars for four to six months."

"Most of it is for renting porta-potties, trash pick-up, laundry services, and transportation," Ned added.

"Don't the tent cities hamper the efforts to build indoor shelters?" I asked.

"On the contrary, every time we develop a tent city there's a burst of new shelters and affordable housing," Isaiah said.

"Here we are, Eastside Village is what we call this tent city," Pam announced.

"One advantage of the tent cities is the ventilation being outdoors," Isaiah said, while parking the van.

We had driven behind a supermarket to what once looked like an old parking lot. Here was a tall covered chain-linked fence. Beyond, a couple blocks away stood a park and a neighborhood.

"How long can the people stay here?" I asked.

"As long as they want to, the average usually sixty to ninety days," Ned answered, as I helped him unpack the coolers. "We give them enough time to find a job and decent housing."

"That's cool," I said, as we entered a good size opening in the middle of the chain-linked fence. Inside the entrance to the Eastside Village was a separate area.

"As you can see," Ned began, as we carried the cooler, "we have tents marked 'Red Cross' and 'counseling.' And over here we have an outdoor kitchen." That's where I helped Ned set down the cooler. "We call this place the neutral zone," Ned added.

Further inside, about a dozen feet or so, was another fence dividing the neutral zone part of the camp to where the resident tents were located. I saw a large generator safely enclosed a few feet from the camp.

People were lined up for coffee and a hot breakfast that we passed out. It was all well organized. Everyone was friendly and helped each other out. Isaiah knew the residents by name and greeted them warmly like they were all his family.

"Hi Mrs. Johnson," Isaiah said to a woman in her mid-thirties. "How's the job hunting?"

"I guess you could say it's coming along, filled out a half dozen applications," Mrs. Johnson answered.

"Most of the people here lost their jobs from downsizing companies," Isaiah explained to me. "They're not all substance abusers and mentally ill people, which a lot of people might picture when you think of homeless. Most are just down on the times and a lot are just a paycheck from being on the street. Housing is pretty expensive. Six hundred dollars just to rent a decent place to live, that's over half of the average paycheck. Not much left for food and utilities."

"You would think in our country that we would never have any homeless," I said.

"One would think," Isaiah said. "We would rather give our money to strangers in third world countries than think of us first. As a Christian nation we should help everyone out, but I just don't see much of that happening here. I think we could do both if we all worked together to defeat homelessness."

"I'm glad I'm doing this, helping out and it feels good," I said.

"Been doing this for fifteen years and I never get bored," Isaiah said, and then turning to a couple of men, "Hey, Gabe and Joel, how's your morning?"

Both men were Caucasian wearing blue jeans, flannel shirts, and hefty boots. Gabe was skinny and in his late thirties. He was bald with a red mustache turning white. Joel sported a plain olive green cap, dark hair going over his ears, and a short beard. Most likely he was in his mid-to-late forties, and just about six feet tall.

"Not too bad," Gabe said, as he took a bowl of oatmeal.

"Doing well," Joel said, doing the same.

"Hey Joel, we can use our lawn cut before you leave town," Isaiah said.

"Be glad to Isaiah, be there this afternoon," Joel said warmly.

"Those two guys are what we call coastal drifters—no moss collected under their feet," Isaiah explained after they left. "Actually, Joel is a classic coastal drifter. During the summer, he's up here until sometime in September, and then he moves onto Portland, San Fran., and southern Cal. for the winter. Then he works his way back up here."

"Why doesn't he stay in one spot?" I asked.

"Oh, it's hard to say, everyone has their reasons," Isaiah replied.

"Does he have family that he's running from?" I asked.

"One thing I honor is confidentiality. People confide in me and I keep it to myself. It is a trust factor," Isaiah said.

"Yeah, I understand kinda like doctor to patient," I said.

"That's right," he agreed. "But you are eager to help. Joel and Gabe, they're all lost souls. Joel is a good guy. I could tell you everything I know about him, but that wouldn't do you any good—get to know him. It will give you more experience with life, journalism, and at the same time help these people. Be patient and find some common ground. Gain their trust."

"Sure, I can do that," I said, starting toward the residents.

"Just remember some of these people's lives are delicate," Isaiah advised.

I had in mind, when I crossed into Joel's world, that a little small talk would be a good start. First, I had to find the guy among hundreds of tents varying in size and colors. I saw Pam and the other volunteers talking with the homeless. Rosa must have come in with them, but I didn't see her right away. She was singing to a small crowd and looked to be having a good time. My feelings for Rosa were still present. Gabe, the other drifter, stood outside an open tent conversing with another resident. Joel most likely was nearby, so I decided to peek inside the tent. There he was sitting inside on a cot intently reading a book. I didn't know how one was supposed to greet a tent dweller.

"You are new here," Gabe said, startling me.

"Yup," I said in hesitation after jerking my head outside the tent. "I'm Jay and I'm here to visit you guys."

"Good to have you around."

"This is a nice place they have set up here."

"Sure is, no one bothers you here."

"Must be a relief not being bothered."

"Sure is, this is like me and Joel's rest stop before moving on down south," Gabe said.

"What's down south?" I asked.

"Nothin' particular," Gabe said.

After a while, Gabe really did not have much to say that interested me. I tried my best to find something in common with the guy but couldn't. Soon he excused himself and I was relieved.

Joel was still there in the same position when I turned to look inside the tent again. I didn't want to bother him as he was so engrossed in his book. Suddenly, he began to speak.

"'Make hay while the sun shines,'" he began with his eyes fixed on the book. "'Making the beginning is one third of the work.' 'Though wisdom is good at the beginning it is better at the end.'" Joel looked up closing the book and asked me, "Don't you just love a wise proverb? Those Irish sure have some good ones."

"'Happy is the man that findeth wisdom, and the man that getteth understanding,'" I said. "'Boast not thyself of to morrow; for thou knowest not what a day may bring forth.'"

"Oh thy youth with wisdom is a virtue to us all," Joel said. "I've heard that said in many ways, so true. Old English Proverbs?"

"Proverbs of Solomon," I replied.

"Ah, the Bible, good for some, but sometimes for others questionable," Joel said. "I should've known, you're one of Isaiah's new recruits, but you may have already heard my name—Joel Smart—Smart is my name, smart is my game."

"Nice to meet you, I'm Jay," I said with a firm handshake.

"Are you a native, a traveler, or just visiting?" Joel asked.

"You could say a little of each, depending on your perspective," I answered. "My friend needed a ride so I brought her over to college."

"Well, I should do as I say, 'Make hay,'" Joel said, placing a backpack over his shoulder and pointing to the sky, "'while the sun shines.' Grass is better cut dry. Hopefully, we'll talk again before I leave. If not, good travels to you."

For those few hours at the tent city, I was glad I volunteered. I enjoyed myself and found it very rewarding. All those people really needed, was a chance and some encouragement along with kindness and love. They didn't need to be ridiculed, belittled, or shoved aside like the stuff seen in the gutters. Jesus' purpose was to come heal the sick, help the poor, and bring sinners to salvation. So this gave me a whole new perspective on God's ministry.

It was noon when Isaiah drove us back to the chapel. The evening was already set with Isaiah inviting Rosa and me to his home for dinner. So we had the rest of the day to ourselves. We thought about grabbing a deli sandwich from the college cafeteria and explore some hiking trails, so we did. Pam directed us to a cool trail. Again, Rosa and I had a great time spending the day together. We exchanged stories about volunteering that morning.

Half past five that evening, we pulled up to Isaiah's house, just minutes away from Eastside Village. Isaiah led us into the house, which smelled like home. I would've pictured Gramma coming out of the kitchen with her apron snuggly around her waist. Mom would be carrying out plates and reminding me to go wash my hands.

Isaiah left us in the living room. A large tropical fish tank was the first thing we noticed.

"Cool, you have angel fish!" Rosa exclaimed, going up to take a look.

"Thanks for inviting us," I said.

"No, thank you two for coming," Isaiah said, gesturing to the couch. "Please have a seat. Anyway, we don't eat very many home cooked meals during the week, always doing something."

"So it's a good thing we came," I said.

"That's right!" Isaiah laughed and then heard cooking noises coming from the kitchen. "Here, let me get my wife and introduce her—by the way, Joel will be joining us for dinner."

It wasn't long after Isaiah went to the kitchen, when Joel came in from somewhere. He looked different from when I first met him. I remembered he cut Isaiah's grass, so he must have showered.

"Hey, Joel," I greeted. "This is my friend Rosa, the friend I told you about."

"Hello," Joel responded. "I heard you're going to college here—Isaiah showed me one day, nice campus."

"Yes, it is," Rosa agreed. "I can't wait until classes start."

"How long have you guys known each other?" Joel asked.

"Oh, about seven years," I said.

"Here we all are," Isaiah said, followed by his wife, Tanika.

"You may call me Tani," she said, shaking our hands. "Dinner is just about ready, waiting on the biscuits."

"Smells as good as always, Tani," Joel commented.

"Why don't we head to the dining room?" Isaiah asked, as we followed him. "What would everyone like to drink? I know that Joel wants water."

"That's fine with me," I replied.

Soon we sat down to chicken, stuffing, and mashed taters. I wondered how Joel reacted with Isaiah blessing the meal. A quick peek and I saw his eyes open. He caught me and shrugged his shoulders.

"Rosa, are your parents going to make the Friday banquet?" Tani asked.

"I hope they can, but my dad broke his leg," Rosa answered.

"God bless his soul!" Tani and Isaiah said.

"For real! What happened?" Joel asked with concern.

Rosa briefly explained the incident.

"That was nice of you, Jay, to drive her over," Tani said.

"It was nothing—we do things for a friend in need," I said.

"You can count on Jay," Rosa said, throwing a big smile at me, one that could melt butter.

I hoped nobody noticed me blushing. One person did as Joel winked.

"Yeah, you could say I'm reliable," I said, changing the subject. "Tani, the dinner is most excellent. I bet that is one of the reasons why Isaiah married you."

"Such a nice thing to say," Tani said.

"Yep, she sure knows how to hook a man," Isaiah said, chuckling.

"Ooh, stop!" Tani said, pushing him.

Our conversation continued into the living room.

"Jay, are you and Rosa doing anything this evening?" Joel asked.

"We thought about seeing the Space Needle," I said, feeling like it was a date.

"Should be a very nice clear night," Tani said.

"Just to do something while Jay's here—then we will all be busy," Rosa said.

"I will probably visit or she will come home to visit her folks," I said. "Seattle is a nice place to visit, but I don't care for all the traffic. Actually, my girlfriend is back home."

"Oh?" questioned Joel.

"Yep, Kaylee. I sure miss her," I said.

Her face suddenly entered my mind and a sorrowful lump developed in my throat, hitting me straight in the heart. No doubt, I sure missed Kaylee. I started to wonder, but somebody left, bringing me back to the table.

"Where are you staying, Jay?" Isaiah asked.

"At the Circle Inn, just down the street from the college," I replied.

"You're welcome to stay at our house," Isaiah said.

"No, that's okay, I don't want to impose," I said.

"No problem, we would be glad to have you," Tani said. "We have plenty of room ever since our son left for college."

"Be nice to have a young man stay with us," Isaiah said.

"Okay, the both of you have talked me into it, but first I have to take Rosa back to her dorm and check out of my hotel," I said.

We didn't get far down the highway on our way to downtown Seattle, bumper-to-bumper traffic. The traffic guy on the radio said there was an accident. He said there would be delays for the next hour until they cleared up the scene.

"We could go through the side streets, but I would get lost," I suggested.

"Naah, that's okay, maybe another time," Rosa said.

"Yeah, I don't know how long the Space Needle stays open," I said. "What do you want to do? I should have had another option for us...let's get out of this and go back to Kirkland."

"Hmm...don't know what I feel like doing," Rosa said.

"It's about eight o'clock," I said, inching my way to the off ramp.

Finally we were off the highway and our entertainment stared us smack in the face. "How about bowling?" I asked.

"Why not?" Rosa agreed.

After bowling, dropping off Rosa, checking out of the hotel room, and arriving back at Isaiah's house, it was just before midnight. Isaiah gave me a key to the backdoor and he already showed me the guestroom. Surprisingly, Rosa was not on my mind as I got ready for bed. Perhaps I have made a decision, when I said at dinner, that I missed Kaylee; the Holy Spirit was talking to me. Kaylee was the one I loved. I had a nice prayer before slipping off to la-la-land.

I awoke at six o'clock in the morning and put on my sweat suit, then made my way to the back door. Isaiah was sitting at the kitchen table with the newspaper and a cup of coffee. A small plate showed remnants of toast.

"You're up early," Isaiah said, his eyes scanning the paper he held out.

"I workout early every morning to practice karate," I replied.

"Did you know Joel practices martial arts too?" Isaiah asked. "He's out back right now."

"No, I had no idea," I said, now remembering, find common ground.

I was a little excited and curious, stepping outside the back door. Joel was in the middle of the yard and I watched him for a moment. He wore a sweat suit and across his forehead was a white bandana with black Oriental characters written across.

"You have good form," I commented.

"You must be a martial artist," Joel said.

"What style do you use?" I asked.

"Kungfu," he answered. "A little Chinese guy, Mr. Chan taught me the fundamentals. A strange hermit I stayed with for a while—long story."

"Kenpo Karate is the style I use, pretty similar to Kungfu," I said, walking down the steps to level ground.

"Been doing it for ten years," Joel said.

"I guess I have been doing it just as long. My friend Billie and I started when we were eight or nine," I said.

"It's a good thing to take up," he said.

"Yeah, I really enjoy it, Sensei Lance is a good teacher," I said, running in place.

"So, what's Kaylee like?" Joel asked, out of the blue.

"Well," I began, wondering after talking about martial arts. "Kaylee is Billie's sister. Anyway, she's great—beautiful and smart—golden curly blonde hair and the prettiest blue eyes. She's little and short, has a ton of spirit, and loves the Lord like I do."

"She sounds nice, you should be with her," Joel said. "How long has it been since you've seen her?"

"Since Tuesday, but I could explain," I answered, knowing where he was going.

"You don't have to explain anything to me. It's your business, just asked a simple rhetorical question," Joel said.

"I know, but maybe I just want to talk about it." I said.

"I'm all ears," Joel said.

"You are probably wondering why I stuck around," I said. "Once upon a time Rosa was my first girlfriend in junior high—just two immature fourteen year olds who broke up."

"And Kaylee was your rebound?" Joel asked.

"You would be correct," I replied. "While Rosa gave me the silent act, Kaylee was there when I needed a friend. We became pretty close. Then Rosa grew up and we became friends again. She had a boyfriend, which then blew up in her face. I guess somewhere after that, I discovered I still had feelings for Rosa and Kaylee saw it coming so she broke up with me. I couldn't make a decision between Kaylee and Rosa. I realized last night I was a fool thinking about having feelings for Rosa again. I'll probably be leaving tomorrow and hopefully make up with Kaylee."

"The way you described her, and I think I know you well enough, that I know she'll forgive you," Joel commented.

"I get the same impressions that you have been there, done that," I began, then teased, "Come on you can tell me. You were once in love—come on I told you some personal things, now it's your turn."

"That's not the way it works Jay," Joel said, sternly walking passed me.

"I'm sorry, come back we can talk about something else," I pleaded.

"Okay, if you really want to know," Joel said, coming to face me. "I had a wife and a kid who died in a fire, about a dozen years ago—there, now you know."

"I didn't mean for you to tell me, I was out of line," I said.

"Actually, for some reason, I do want to talk about it," Joel said. "For years I had it bottled up inside me and now I need to get it off my chest. Don't know why I'm telling an eighteen year old." He peered up into the clouds. "I told Isaiah once about my family and thought he would leave me alone, but he just kept pushing." At this point, he turned toward me. "I know he was just trying to help. I don't know if I believe in a higher power or not. But if there is this God, why do bad things happen to good people?"

"There's so much we don't understand on why things happen and He has His reasons," I began. "His ways are beyond our understanding and you have to remember there's another force at work here, too. Satan is the prince of darkness ruling the world. Why doesn't God just take care of him and make the world a better place? Because He gave all His creations choices, even the angels. Satan is the deceiver, who would stop at nothing to make God look bad. Another thing is, God tests us and wants us to succeed. If He makes it easy and spoon feeds us, we can't learn and grow."

"Makes sense to me, but I don't know yet," Joel said.

"Right now, I could step out onto the street and get hit by a car and become paralyzed. A) I could be mad at God and blame Him for the rest of my life, but where would that get me? Or B) I could say to God, 'Okay God, I don't know Your reasons, but I'm willing to be Your example, and so in my condition I could make something good from this.'—Joel I believe that things happen for a reason. God has a plan for you. If you go on like this, satan wins your soul—maybe too much for you, sorry I just get excited about sharing the Word."

"Thanks Jay, I...think I understand a little better, I'll give it some thought," Joel said. "Isaiah and I discussed this, but I wouldn't listen—I was too angry to listen. Ignorance is bliss."

"Glad to be of help," I said.

"Well, I'll let you get to your workout," Joel said, going up the steps and into the house.

When I was through with my workout, Isaiah and his wife had already left for work. I contemplated during my shower what I was going to do for the day. There was no reason to stick around, but I felt obligated to at least attend Rosa's college banquet. Tani had offered to wash my clothes and they were waiting for me, nicely folded on the bed, when I arrived. I decided to at least pack up a few things I wouldn't need. I lounged around for a bit, fired up my laptop, and uploaded pictures off my camera, making room for the day. I didn't quite decide yet what I was going to do.

A lawnmower, I heard from my window. Joel was across the street mowing someone else's grass. Isaiah told me Joel did a lot of odd jobs for people in the neighborhood, especially older folks. Mrs. Lazlo, a seventy-five year old, lived across the street. Her yard must have been small to cut because it wasn't long before I saw Joel walking back this way. The front door opened and closed. I heard him moving throughout the house. His guest room was downstairs in the basement; I guess his-own little apartment.

I got to browse through some of the pictures on my laptop when Rosa called. She probably wanted to discuss what we were going to do today.

"Guess what?" she asked, with her voice all excited. "My mom and dad made it!"

"That's good news, how are they?" I asked.

"They are pretty tired. Dad sat uncomfortably across the backseat of the car," she replied.

"Wait a minute, what's this?" I asked, looking at the screen.

"What's that Jay?" Rosa asked.

"Oh, I'm talking to myself," I replied, preoccupied by what I was doing.

"Hopefully, you don't talk back," she said, as we chuckled.

"So, do you guys have plans?" I asked.

"We're trying to decide, probably not much as Dad is not very mobile," she replied.

"I need to check on something," I said. "How about I call you back and maybe we'll all do lunch?"

"Yep, maybe, talk to you then," Rosa said, hanging up.

I walked out of the room with my laptop and knocked on the basement door. Movement from within was followed by the door swinging wide open. Joel stood at the threshold drying his face with a towel. When he was done with the towel, he threw it into the room. That was when I noticed his beard and head were shaved.

"Hi Jay, didn't know anyone was here," Joel said. "Oh, this is what I do before I head south…something wrong?"

"I want to show you something," I said, turning to my laptop so he could see the pictures. "Maybe, I'm making this up, but isn't that you? That one looks just like you…your real name isn't Joel Smart is it? Your real name is Leonard Steven Asher—I know I'm right! I'm your son!"

"That's not me, are you insane kid?" Joel said, storming back into his room. He threw on his flannel shirt with haste, and then began to stuff things into his backpack. "Is this some sick joke? I have no son, he's dead."

"By your reaction, I must be right, you are my dad!" I remarked, following him around.

"I'm hurrying because you're a lunatic," he said.

"If I'm a lunatic then I'm a threat, so why aren't you defending yourself?"

"I don't beat up kids!"

"Especially your son," I commented.

"Will you quit saying that? I'm nobody's father," he said. "Go back to Deer Park Jay Matthew Asher!"

"How did you know my middle name's Matthew?" I asked, following him up the steps to the first level.

"Lucky guess!" he said with me right behind.

"I don't buy it," I said.

"You can believe what you want to believe!" he said, as we headed for the front door.

It suddenly hit me, "Part of your real name, Leo, which is spelled backwards, is in your fake name Joel."

"I can see I'm not getting anywhere with you," he said, turning to me. "Okay boy detective, you've caught me—so now what? I go home with you and live happily ever after?"

"It could happen that way, Mom has never stopped loving you—even after all these years," I said.

"I've changed," Leo said, walking away from me. "I'm not the same person. It was seventeen years ago."

"We have all changed," I said, as I chased him onto the front lawn. "I'm not expecting sunshine and rainbows right away."

"Son, this is my life, as the saying goes 'talk is cheap'—I'm sure you will tell your mom that you found me—I-I-I couldn't face her," Leo said, turning down the sidewalk.

"Go ahead Dad, leave us again, you seem good at that!" I hollered to his back. "One thing you don't know, if it means anything to you, Mom's MS has been in remission for three years now! Her doctor says there's no trace of it, she's good as new!"

My dad didn't change his pace, just kept on walking without looking back. I was torn between running after him or just letting him go. I watched him go to the corner and cross the street, but unexpectedly he stopped in the middle. I thought he would turn around because he had a change of heart. Not the case as he avoided a bicyclist nearly running him over and then continued across the street. I watched my dad continue walking at a steady pace, just hoping and praying he would change his mind. Soon he crossed another street, disappearing at the next corner.

Somberly, I stood there in the same spot, looking down the street. What could I do? What did I expect? *Does it end here, Lord?* I prayed. Sitting on Isaiah's front porch, I felt totally lost. For more than a half hour, I sat with my chin in my hands, when my cell phone rang.

"Jay, here," I answered.

"Hey, Jay," Rosa said. "Just wanted to let you know we have decided to do brunch at the campus cafeteria. Does that sound good....let's say about ten? Jay, are you there?"

"Oh...yes, I'm here," I replied, turning inside the house.

"Good, I thought we lost the connection," she commented.

"Sorry, there's something on my mind," I said. "Anyway, did you say brunch at ten?"

"Yes, at the cafeteria," she answered.

"Great, sounds wonderful!" I exclaimed. "I'll be there—that gives me time to pack up for my trip back home."

"Oh...are you leaving after brunch?" Rosa asked.

"I don't know yet, haven't decided," I replied.

"Well, I should let you go so you can pack," she said.

"Yeah, I'll see you guys at ten."

"Yep, see ya."

"Later," I said, flipping the phone off.

After packing my car, which didn't take me very long, I made a decision to leave following brunch with the Sanchez's. I called Isaiah's cell phone to tell him I wouldn't need his key. He told me to give it to Tani at the campus since I was headed there anyway.

While driving to the campus, I kept wondering if I would see my dad. I tried to get him to understand, but you can't lead a cat to water and make him swim.

So I was a couple blocks from the campus when, without warning, I heard a huge explosion—my heart skipped a beat. *What in the world?* I thought, looking through my car windows to see what made the noise. The car started to vibrate and the steering became difficult. *Oh, I must have a flat tire!*

The campus was just up ahead, so I eased the car the rest of the way. Finding the nearest place to park, I got out and examined my tires. It was the left front. I could change it with the spare, but I couldn't risk going over the pass with it. My only option, switch to the spare and go somewhere to buy a new tire. That could wait until after we had brunch. The administrations' building was in the same parking lot where Tani worked in accounting, so I might as well give her the key then.

Ten minutes later, I entered the cafeteria and instantly saw Manny in a wheelchair with his big cast sticking out. Rosa discovered me first, waving me over to their table.

"Hola, buenos dias," I greeted, squeezing Manny's shoulder and giving the girls a quick hug.

"It's about time, Jay," Manny announced, giving me a hard time. "I am starved. Snacks just don't do it for me—I need something hearty."

"Yeah, I worked up an appetite too," I said, taking a seat, then explained, "I would have been here sooner, but I got a flat tire on the way."

"That's a pain," Ella said.

"What are you going to do now?" Rosa asked with concern.

I briefly told them. "So, I guess I'm stuck here for a little bit longer."

"We're glad that you're safe," Rosa said.

"Thank God it didn't happen on the freeway," Ella commented.

"Yeah, I know," I said.

"Let's eat," Manny spoke. "I'm having the Rancho Steak Omelet."

"Hm, what do I feel like," I began, opening the menu.

"Jay, looks like they have a wonderful selection at the buffet line," Ella suggested.

"That's what I'm doing," Rosa pointed out. "I need to watch my figure."

"Yeah, right and I'm the new dean of the college," I said, closing the menu. "I'll do the buffet also."

"I will be back, my love," Ella said to Manny, while standing, then bending down to kiss him.

Rosa and I moseyed behind Ella on our way to the buffet.

"So I guess you're going back home," Rosa said.

"Yep, hopefully Kaylee will forgive me..." I answered.

"Jay, can I ask you something?" she asked, as we both grabbed a tray and plate.

"Sure, what's on your mind?" I replied, eyeing fixings to make myself an egg salad sandwich.

"I have to know," she began, then asked with much hesitation, "am I the reason Kaylee broke up with you?"

"Honestly, yes," I replied.

"I was afraid of that," she said, placing a banana and apple on her plate.

"It's not your fault," I said, "something I did."

"I knew I shouldn't let you take me up here—I could've found someone else."

"No, no, Kaylee was fine with that until ..."

"You don't need to explain."

"Perhaps you are right," I said naturally, putting my hand upon hers and peering into her eyes. "Lord willing, someday a wonderful guy will sweep you off your feet."

"I know," she said unsure, "if it were any different..."

"Don't finish," I suggested.

"That's some good advice," she remarked, then laughing.

After everyone sat down for their meal, I told them I had some interesting news. "It came to me by surprise this morning," I started. "I ran into my dad."

"You're kidding!" Rosa yelped, nearly losing the apple in her hand.

"Really!" Ella exclaimed.

"True story," I said, then summarized my encounter with Joel/Leo.

"Oh, Jay, you probably feel shot down," Rosa said.

"Well, there's not much I can do," I answered.

"Is there anything we can do for you?" Ella asked.

"No, I'll be fine, thanks for the offer," I replied when my cell phone rang. "Jay, here–oh, hi Isaiah—my dad is in your cab! Okay. Okay, I'll be right there. " I hung up and told everyone, "My dad wants to meet me in the courtyard."

"That's great news," Rosa said.

I burst from the table with hope and anticipation. Sprinting out the cafeteria door, the courtyard was just outside. I slowed down when I saw my dad standing next to a bench, facing away.

"Uhh, Dad?" I asked.

He turned around without much emotion. For a few long moments, we just stared at each other.

"Hi Jay....my son," Dad greeted, removing his baseball cap and sunglasses.

"I thought you left town," I said.

"Well, I had second thoughts," he explained.

"Hey, let's talk over here on the bench," I suggested.

He backed up with no answer and sat on the bench, continuing where he left off. "When I left you this morning I walked and walked, thinking things over about what you said—oh, this is hard for me."

"Take your time," I said.

"I hurt your mother really bad and I feel ashamed even facing her," Dad said.

"Don't be," I said. "She'll be happy to see you, I know she will."

"I hope you're right," he said.

"So it wouldn't be easy, just give it a chance."

"My Rachel—your mother is indeed all cured?"

"As God is my witness," I said, standing while raising my hand toward heaven. "It was a miracle, like she never had it."

"I am really not so sure," he began, and then there was a glimmer of new life in his eyes. Suddenly he stood confidently, putting on his cap and uttered, "I'll give it a shot—show me the way home!"

"Not so fast," I said, "my car needs a new tire, but first let me introduce you to my friends—actually, they are more like family." As I started to head back to the cafeteria, Dad surprised me with a hug.

"You're alright, Jay," he commented.

"Hey, there's Isaiah and Tani across the courtyard," I said. "Let's go talk to them."

"Isaiah, thanks for everything," Dad said, shaking his hand, then taking Tani's hand. "You both have been kind."

"Yeah, thank you for letting us stay at your home," I said.

"Are you guys leaving?" Tani asked.

"No, not yet," Dad replied. "Jay needs a tire and I need to gather my things."

"If you need any assistance, let us know," Isaiah offered.

"Jay, Joel—I mean Leo—I can't believe all of this—finding each other," Tani said. "Praise the Lord!"

"Yeah, I had specific reasons why I came to Kirkland," I said. "But God had other plans for me."

"That He did," Isaiah agreed.

"One of His miracles," Tani said.

"Speaking of," I began. "My mom had a miracle happen to her. She had multiple sclerosis for quite some time and it recently vanished, a real miracle—" I heard some commotion behind me and saw the Sanchez clan headed this way.

"Jay, there you are," Rosa greeted.

We were all introduced.

"Well, we have to be going," I said. "Dad and I have to get to a reunion."

Chapter Thirty-Two

FOLLOWING THE courtyard scene, Dad helped me change my tire. Even though we became dirty and greasy, we had a wonderful time being together. Dad didn't say much, just exchanged small talk.

After I bought my new tire and had it put on, I drove dad back to Isaiah's house. I had to give my dad a shove in the right direction as he took his time to pack. The shove was a large plastic bag, which I brought to his room and started cramming things into it. Dad saw my eagerness to get home so he joined me.

Upon leaving Seattle, I had a million questions, but held them back, knowing we had a lot of time, Lord willing, to catch up. Dad didn't seem very talkative anyway, deep in thought. I could only imagine what was running through his mind. Just having him sit in the passenger seat next to me was an answered prayer. Tears of joy welled up my eyes.

From Isaiah's house, through the pass, it poured down sheets of rain. On the other end were crystal clear blue skies with cheery smiling sunshine.

We arrived in Spokane about 5:30 Friday evening. Even though it seemed like we wanted to hurry home, we decided to be fresh and well rested for the reunions. Saturday morning sounded more logical. It also gave us time to think about the words and how we wanted to present them.

We went shopping that evening to buy new clothes. It was odd seeing Dad in a new outfit. At first I convinced him to throw away his old clothes, and he did mostly, but he just couldn't give up his favorite flannel shirt.

I bought a digital camcorder to be able to remember yesterday.

Dad was already awake when I woke the next morning. The bathroom light was on and I heard water running. I smelled coffee brewing in the room and I was excited about the day. Soon we would leave and head home to Deer Park. The bathroom door clicked open.

"Mornin' sleepy head. Thought you would sleep the day away," Dad teased. He wore the khaki slacks and blue shirt that we bought the day before.

"Are you sure you are ready for this?" I asked.

"I don't know—excited and scared," he replied. "I thought about the words I would say to your mom all the way here, but I still don't know."

"I think you being home, says enough," I remarked.

"I think you're right," Dad said.

"So great to have you back," I said, hugging him. "After I shower, we'll discuss the day during breakfast."

We looked over the room service menu. Dad ordered our food while I had a refreshing shower. I wondered how Dad's reunion would unfold, thinking it should be a memorable day.

Dad was busy at the small table arranging our plates. He was unsure when we sat down to pray. I could feel God's Holy presence shining down.

"You said last night you had a plan," Dad said.

"Well, I want it to be a special homecoming for you," I replied. "So, my plan is for us to see Kaylee first and then go home for Mom's reunion."

"Sounds fair. I'll follow your lead," Dad said.

"I began writing a poem for Kaylee, just need to finish it before we go."

"That sounds good to me," Dad agreed.

Forty-minutes later, we entered Deer Park. On the way, I told Dad my plan of action. It was a perfect summer day. There was a nice breeze and it was not very hot.

We drove down the road to the florist and I hurried inside. A few minutes later, I climbed back in and had Dad hold the flowers.

"Next stop, we'll see if Kaylee is home. She doesn't work at the Coffee Shack on the weekend," I said.

I drove through the alley behind Kaylee's house. With Dad carrying the camcorder, I followed him around to the front door. I was behind him when he rang the bell. We waited. It felt like an eternity. Finally, the door swung open, my heart racing faster.

"Excuse me, may I help you?" Kaylee's mom asked. I half expected the scenario.

“Is your daughter, Kaylee, here?” Dad questioned.

“She’s not here. May I ask what this is about?” Mrs. Knight asked.

“Sorry, Mrs. Knight,” I said, stepping from behind.

“Jay, you’re back! Kaylee said you were on a trip,” she began with questioning looks.

“Yup, I was. Hey, I’d love to chat, but we need to get going—” I said, then realizing, “Forgive me Mrs. Knight, this is my dad.”

“Nice to meet you,” she said, knowing the story. “I’m at a loss for words.”

“We’ll tell you everything later, but we have to go now,” I said.

“Well of course, I sure understand—I guess you wanted to know where Kaylee is—let’s see…this is unexpected. She’s at Mix Park with her poetry group, I think.”

“I know a good place we can park—so she won’t know we’re coming,” I said minutes later.

We pulled onto a gravel road that led to what used to be the Deer Park Motel apartments. They were individual bright green cabins. Dad got the camera ready while I memorized my lines I would say to Kaylee.

We got out and moseyed through the cabins, passing the office, and crossing another gravel road to the park’s side entrance. Following Dad from behind, I caught a glimpse of a group of kids from afar. Kaylee was there as I saw her long curly blonde hair across the way, and my heart sang. They looked pretty absorbed with themselves, we weren’t even noticed. So, just like we did at her home, Dad walked up to her, pretending to be a tourist. With the poem in my hand, I walked in front of him toward Kaylee. She looked up at me with surprise as I read it to her.

I Am A High-Flying Kite

I am a high-flying kite
Soaring, soaring, left and right
Many hands held my string
First young love that sings
A storm of sorts soon brewed
One error caused the blues
Spinning, spinning, out of control

Hitting the ground with a blow
A fault I truly admit
Forgiveness would not permit
Broken I was, hearts smashed
A friend picked me up from the trash
A new favorite she became
A perfect bond still remains

"Kaylee, I would still like to be your kite. I had a moment of insanity leaving you the other day," I said, offering her something behind my back. "A purple hyacinth signifies that I am sorry and ask your forgiveness. Please accept my apology."

She took it from me, tears pooling from her blue eyes making them a sea of happiness. Sorrow and joy crossed her face. Hesitate; she did not as she spoke.

"Sure Jay, my kite, you have my forgiveness, but don't expect a hug yet because you know I'm still mad at you," she said, and then I continued.

"And of course, a red rose 'for meaning' 'I Love You,'" I said, as she stood to receive it. "Kaylee, I love you!"

"Ooh Jay, I just can't help it, my love for you has always been unconditional," Kaylee said, running to my outstretched arms, hugging me. "*So* glad you're home!"

"Kaylee, when I'm with you, I'm home," I said, then remembered, "Your ring, back where it shall stay."

"Everything 'for meaning,'" she said.

"Yes, 'for meaning,'" I said, as she pulled away.

"Okay, I know who you are Jay, but who is that?" Kaylee asked.

"Kaylee, this is my dad," I said.

"Your dad!!" she screamed with celebration.

"Nice to finally meet you, Kaylee. I've heard a lot of lovely things about you," Dad commented.

"Wow, this is too much! How...?"

"I'll tell you all about it later, over dinner," I said. "Come with us and enjoy the reunion."

Well, that's my story so far and Lord willing for years to come. There are more journals to fill and I hope to give you something worth reading. The reunion with Mom and Gramma I will share with you another time.

Some people had the misconception that Christians are perfect, but as you see with me, that's not the case. There's only one person on earth who was perfect, and He was the Lord, Jesus Christ who died and rose again for our sins.

If you are a Christian, take it from someone who has been there, no matter what you have done in God's eyes, He will forgive you if you ask Jesus our mediator to plead your case. Had I done anything wrong—really wrong? I know I had, by sneaking around with Rosa and all that went with it. We had forgotten the whole 'For Meaning' of it all. On the surface our actions, not all the time appeared pretty, but on the inside it was really ugly.

Anyway, I learned the bottom line was, that it's not all about *me* or *my* will, but *God's* will. If we put all our faith and trust in Him to run our lives, He will give us all the desires of our hearts. Our aim was to be just like God as best we can, but we fall far short. We will stumble and fall many times because of our sin nature, then with a merciful and loving Father; He'll bring us back up through His son, Jesus, our mediator.

Perhaps you haven't decided to make Jesus Lord and Savoir of your life and then I would suggest you truly consider this. I don't know how I could live without Him.

"Everything happens for a reason, everything we do is done 'For Meaning' through Jesus Christ, the son of the living God—the God of Abraham, Isaac, & Jacob. Amen." ~ Jay Matthew Asher.